LET THE DEAD SPEAK

Also by Jane Casey

JANE CASEY

Let the Dead Speak

HarperCollins*Publishers*

HarperCollins*Publishers*
1 London Bridge Street
London
SE1 9GF

www.harpercollins.co.uk

Published by HarperCollins*Publishers* 2017
1

A catalogue record for this book is available from the British Library

ISBN: 978-0-00-814898-0

This novel is entirely a work of fiction.
The names, characters and incidents portrayed in it are
the work of the author's imagination. Any resemblance to

Typeset in S   Stirlingshire

Print   s plc

Al   ɔe
re   d,
ir   ,
ph   or

www.fsc.org   FSC C007454

FSC™ is a non-profit international organisation established to promote
the responsible management of the world's forests. Products carrying the
FSC label are independently certified to assure consumers that they come
from forests that are managed to meet the social, economic and
ecological needs of present and future generations,
and other controlled sources.

Find out more about HarperCollins and the environment at
www.harpercollins.co.uk/green

For Ariella Feiner, with love and thanks.

For the good that I would I do not: but the evil which
I would not, that I do.

Romans 7:19

1

It had been raining for fifty-six hours when Chloe Emery came home. The forecast had said to expect a heatwave; it wasn't supposed to be raining.

And Chloe wasn't supposed to be home.

She came out of the station and stopped, shifting her big black bag from one shoulder to the other. The rain poured off the awning, splashing onto the pavement in front of her. It coursed into the gutters where filthy water was already swirling, dark and gritty, freighted with rubbish and twigs and dead leaves. Chloe's T-shirt clung to her back and her stomach. She twitched the material away from her skin, self-conscious about the swell of her breasts. She hadn't ever really thought about them until her stepmother had mentioned them.

'Big girl like you, you need a better bra. Better support. You can't blame men for looking, you know.' A thin, spiteful smile. 'You might as well enjoy it, though. They'll be down to your knees in no time and no one will care then.'

It had taken Chloe a long time to understand what she meant, which had annoyed Belinda. She still didn't know why Belinda was angry with her about her body, or people looking at her. A wave of unease passed over Chloe, remembering –

the familiar nausea of not knowing things that other people took for granted. It wasn't her fault; she did try.

There was no point in waiting for the rain to stop. Chloe bent her head and trudged away from the station. Her clothes and hair were saturated within a couple of minutes, her jeans cold and heavy, dragging against her skin. Every raindrop felt like a finger tapping on her head, her shoulders, her back. Her shoulder was burning where the bag strap rubbed it. There were no other pedestrians, except for a mother pushing a buggy on the opposite pavement, striding fast, the hood on her sensible anorak pulled down low over her face. Who would be out for a walk on a wet Sunday afternoon if they didn't have to be? Not Chloe, not feeling the way she did, sick and tired and still a bit sore. But there was no one to meet her at the station. No one knew she was there.

A car engine hummed on the street behind her and she didn't think anything of it, even when it got louder and closer. It wasn't until the car pulled in ahead of her with a jerk of the brakes that she noticed it in any detail. The driver was leaning forward to peer into the rear-view mirror, adjusting it so she could see his eyes staring into hers. The fear came first, a thud that shook her chest as if someone had kicked her. Then recognition: it wasn't a stranger watching her walk towards him. It was a neighbour. More than a neighbour: it was Mr Norris, who lived across the road from her, who always smiled and asked her how she was, who had very bright eyes and white teeth and was Bethany's father. Bethany was younger than Chloe but she knew so much more about everything.

Chloe went over to the car, peering in through the window he'd lowered on the passenger side.

'Where are you off to? Going home? Jump in, I'll give you a lift.'

Mr Norris never waited for an answer. She'd noticed that before. She didn't know if it was because she was so slow or if he was like that with everyone.

2

'I don't need a lift.'

'Course you do. You've got that heavy bag.' He was smiling at her, his eyes fixed on hers. She stared at the bridge of his nose, unaware that it made her look slightly cross-eyed. 'How come your mum didn't pick you up?'

'I can manage.' It wasn't a proper answer, and Chloe's palms were wet from the fear he'd ask again, but there were good things about being thick and not having to answer questions properly was one of them.

'Now you don't have to manage. Stick your bag in the back and jump in.'

There was no point in arguing, Chloe knew. She trailed to the other end of the car and put her hand on the latch for the boot. It clicked and she tried to lift it. Nothing happened. She returned to the window.

'It's locked.'

'Not the boot. Put it on the back seat, I meant.' He bit off the ends of the words, obviously annoyed. And he hadn't said the boot, Chloe thought, mortified. He'd said the back and she'd assumed he meant the boot. She'd got it wrong, as usual.

She fumbled one of the doors open and dumped her bag on the seat, then opened the passenger door and hesitated.

'Get in. What are you waiting for?' He was checking his mirrors, scanning the pavements. Getting ready to drive off, Chloe thought, remembering that and not much more from the three humiliating lessons that were the sum total of her driving experience.

She got into the car, scrambling to close the door and get her seatbelt on before he got annoyed again. He helped her with the seatbelt, smoothing it out carefully across her lap before he slid the metal tongue into the lock. The belt flattened the thin, sodden material of her T-shirt against her body and she thought he was staring at her chest for a second, but he wasn't, probably. That was just her stepmother and what she'd said. He was a dad, after all. He was old.

'So where've you been? Away somewhere nice?'

'Dad's.'

'Oh yeah?' Mr Norris went quiet for a minute, concentrating on the road. It didn't occur to Chloe that he was choosing his words carefully. 'See much of him?'

'No.'

'I've never actually met him.'

Chloe stared out of the window, not thinking about her father and the last time she'd seen him, not thinking about how angry he would be now, now that he'd realised she was gone. Not thinking about that took up all of her mental energy. He might have phoned her mother, she thought with a sudden lurch of fear. She hadn't thought of that.

Mr Norris was talking, words filling the air in the car, telling Chloe about his weekend, about Bethany and what she was doing during the school holidays, about nothing that mattered to her. She stopped listening, drifting a little as the windscreen wipers sang across the glass, until something touched her knee – Mr Norris's hand was on her leg. She stared at it in mute panic until he moved it away.

'We're here.'

The car had stopped outside her house, she realised, the engine still running.

'You can get out here. I won't make you run across the road in this weather.'

'OK. Thanks.' She reached down to push the seatbelt's release button but he got there first. 'Thanks,' she said again.

'No problem.' He was frowning at her. 'Chloe, love, are you all right? You look a bit—'

'I'm fine.' She pulled on the door handle and it didn't open and her heart rate went spiralling up like a bird spinning through clear air but he reached across her and gave it a swift shove and it came open. His arm brushed against her chest as he drew it back, but that was just an accident, the contact brief.

'Needs a firm hand.'

'Oh,' Chloe whispered. Her ears were hot, her pulse thudding so hard that she could barely hear him, but he was still talking. She got out of the car without waiting for him to stop, slamming the door on him. She turned to scurry up the path, glancing up at the house to see Misty in the window of the front bedroom, her paws braced on the glass, miaowing with all her might. The horn blared behind Chloe twice, very loud. It made her jump but she didn't look back, her whole being focused on her need to go inside without saying anything else, or crying, one two three four five six seven at the front door eight nine ten eleven keys out twelve thirteen the right key in the lock and the door was opening and she almost fell through it into the narrow, long hallway but she got it shut behind her in the same moment and that was it, she was alone except for Misty, and she could collapse or scream or crawl into a corner and shake or chew her nails until they bled again or any of the things she'd been holding back for days now.

Misty hadn't come down the stairs yet, she registered, and as if in response a thunder of scratching – sharp-clawed paws on wood – echoed through the still, silent house. The cat was shut in, then. Mum had shut her in. Chloe put her keys on the hall table. She should let the cat out.

Unless the cat wasn't supposed to be out.

Chloe started towards the stairs.

Unless.

She stopped.

There was a mark on the wall. A big one. A smear, with four lines running through it like tracks. Chloe's eyes tracked from the smear to the ground, to the droplets that ran down the wall and trickled over the skirting board and puddled on the ground. It was dark, whatever it was. Dirty.

Mud.

Paint.

Something that would make her mother *furious*.

Maybe that was why the cat was shut in, Chloe thought.

5

Maybe that was it. Misty had made a mess. She started up the stairs, one hand resting lightly on the banisters, and it felt wrong, it was rough, as if something had dried on it, some more of the same dirt. Chloe looked down at it, at the stairs, and then at the hall below, and her legs were still carrying her up but her brain was working, trying to make sense of what she saw and what she felt and what she *smelled* and the carpet, the carpet was ruined in the hall upstairs, it was dirty and soaked and smeared and the pictures were all crooked.

Behind the closed door Misty set to work, digging her claws under the wood, splintering it as she scraped.

Let her out.

What had happened? The bathroom door was open but it was too dark in there, darker than it should have been. The whole house was dark. There was no reason to look, Chloe told herself.

She didn't want to look.

. . . *scratch scratch scratch* . . .

Let her out.

Because if not, she'd damage the door.

Damage.

Let her out.

What . . .

Let her out, or there'd be trouble.

Chloe reached the door, and hesitated. She put out her hand to the handle, touching it with her fingertips. Behind the door the cat howled, outraged. She scratched again and the vibrations hummed across Chloe's skin.

Let her out.

She turned the handle and pushed the door, and a grey paw slid through the gap, dragging at it to get it open, and Misty's face, distorted as she pushed it through, her ears flat, her eyes pulled back like an oriental dragon's as she forced her way to freedom. And then the door was open enough for her to rush through it to the hallway, and for the air inside the room to rush out along with her, dense with the smell of cat shit or something worse.

Before Chloe could investigate, the doorbell shrilled. It was loud, peremptory, and there was no question of ignoring it or hiding: she had to answer it. She hurried back down, narrowly avoiding the dark shape that was Misty crouching at the top of the stairs. There was a big smear up the door, she saw now, as she reached out to open it, a big brownish smudge that ended near the latch.

The bell rang again. Through the rippled glass she could see a shape, a man, his outline blurred and distorted. With a shudder, Chloe opened the door.

'You forgot your bag, love.' Mr Norris, with rain spangling his jacket, his tan very brown, his teeth very white. He held the bag out to her but she didn't take it. She didn't have time before his eyes tracked over her shoulder and took in the scene behind her and the genial smile faded. 'Jesus. Jesus Christ. Christ almighty. What the—'

Chloe turned to see what he was looking at, and she could see a lot more when the door was open. A lot more. At the top of the stairs, Misty was still squatting, her eyes glazed and wild, her mouth open. Even as Chloe watched, she bent her head and gently, tentatively, began to lick the floor.

Behind Chloe, Mr Norris retched.

'I don't understand,' Chloe said, and the panic spiralled again but she kept it down, held it back. 'I don't understand what's happened. Please, what's happened?'

Mr Norris was bent over, the back of his hand to his mouth. He shook his head and it could have been *I don't know* or it could have been *not now* or it could have been something else.

'Mr Norris?'

He had his eyes closed.

'Mr Norris,' Chloe said, very calmly, because the alternative was screaming. 'Where's Mum?'

2

I sat in the car, not moving. The rain danced across the empty street in front of me. It was unusual for it to be so quiet at a crime scene. Murder always attracted crowds, but the rain was better at dispersing them than any uniformed officer. The journalists were hanging back too, sitting in their cars like me, waiting for something to happen. Walking across the road would count as something happening, so I stayed where I was. The less attention I attracted, the happier I was.

The light wasn't good, the dark clouds overhead making it feel like a winter day. I checked. Not quite six o'clock. More than three hours to sunset. Two and a half hours since the 999 call had brought response officers to the address. Two hours and ten minutes since the response officers' inspector had turned up to get her own impression of what they'd found. Two hours since the inspector had called for a murder investigation team. Ninety minutes since my phone had rung with an address and a sketchy description of what was waiting for me there.

What I saw was a quiet residential street in Putney, not far from the river. Valerian Road was lined with identical red-brick Victorian townhouses with elaborate white plasterwork and black railings, their tiled paths glossy from the rain. The residents' cars were parked on both sides of the street, most of them newish, most of them expensive.

The exception: a stretch about ten houses long where blue-and-white tape made a cordon. Inside it, police vehicles clustered, and an ambulance, the back doors open, the para-medics packing up as they prepared to move off. And halfway along the cordoned-off bit of street, a hastily erected tent hiding the doorway of the house that was my crime scene.

A stocky figure emerged from the tent, yanked down a mask and pushed back the hood of her paper overalls. Una Burt. Detective Chief Inspector Una Burt, acting up as our superintendent. The guv'nor. Ma'am. My boss. Her hair was flattened against her head: rain or sweat, I guessed. My skin was clammy already, the shirt sticking to my back, and I hadn't done anything more energetic than drive across London on a wet Sunday afternoon. It was warm still, despite the rain.

Beside me, Georgia Shaw shifted in her seat. 'What are we waiting for?'

'Nothing.'

'So let's get going.' She had her hand on the door handle already.

'We are murder detectives. By the time we turn up at a crime scene, by definition, nothing can be done to save anyone. So what's the rush?'

She cleared her throat, because when you're a detective constable you don't say *bullshit* to a detective sergeant. Not unless you know them very well indeed. Even if the detective sergeant is so newly promoted she keeps forgetting about it herself.

'We're not going to find the murderer by sitting in the car, though, are we?'

'I once caught a murderer while I was sitting in a car,' I said idly, more interested in the crime scene in front of me than in talking to the newest member of the murder team.

9

'Who was that?' Georgia narrowed her eyes, trying to remember. She had read up on me, she told me on her first day, and made the mistake of saying it in front of most of the team. If we'd been alone, I might have been able to be nice about it. As it was, I had turned on my heel and walked away, too mortified to say anything. I didn't need to. I knew my colleagues would say plenty once I was out of earshot.

Some of what they said would even be true.

'It doesn't matter,' I said now. *Be nice.* 'Ancient history. The thing to remember is that it's not a waste of time to take your time.'

Georgia smiled, but in an irritable stop-telling-me-what-I-already-know way. She was strikingly self-possessed for someone who'd been a member of the team for two weeks. Maybe it was just that I expected everyone else to be as diffi-dent as I had been. Self-confidence had never really been my strong point but it was irrational to dislike Georgia simply because she was assertive.

It was a lot more rational to dislike her because she was absolutely useless. A graduate, she was on a fast-track scheme and had been moved to my team straight after her probation. She was young, she was pretty, she was articulate and confi-dent and ambitious and not all that interested in hard work, it seemed to me. She was a filled quota, a ticked box, and I didn't think she deserved to be on a murder investigation team.

Then again, that was exactly how the other members of the team had felt about me when I joined.

So I disliked her, but I sincerely tried not to.

Kev Cox emerged from the house, his face shiny red. He scraped back his hood and said something to Una Burt that made her smile.

'Who's that?'

'Kev Cox. Crime scene manager. The best in the business.'

Georgia nodded, making a note. I'd already noticed that

her closest attention was reserved for senior police officers – the sort of people who might be able to advance her career.

And a glance in my rear-view mirror told me that one of her prime targets had arrived, though the best thing she could do for her career was probably to stay far away from him. He inserted his car into a space I thought was slightly too small, edging it back and forth with limited patience and a scowl on his face. Not happy to be back from his holidays, I deduced. He had sunglasses on, despite the rain, and he was on his own, which meant he had no one to distract him.

And I suddenly had a reason to go inside. The last thing I wanted was a touching reunion with Detective Inspector Josh Derwent in front of Georgia. There was no way to know what he would say, or what he might do. He would have to behave himself at the crime scene.

At least, I hoped he would.

'Let's get going.' I grabbed my bag and slid out of the car in the same movement. It took Georgia a minute to catch up with me as I strode across the road and nodded to Una Burt.

'Ma'am.'

'Maeve.' Limited enthusiasm, but that was nothing new. I had been disappointing Una Burt for years now. Georgia got an actual smile. 'Get changed before you even think about going into the house. We need to preserve every inch of the forensics.'

As opposed to obliterating the evidence as I usually do.

'Of course,' I said politely.

'This is a strange one. Come on.' She led the way into the tiny tent where there were folded paper suits like the one she wore. It was second nature to me now to put them on, to snap on shoe covers, to tuck my hair under the close-fitting hood and work my hands into thin blue gloves and settle the mask over my face. There was a rhythm to it, a routine. Georgia wasn't quite as practised and I remembered finding it awkward when I was new. I slowed down, making it easier for her without showing her I'd noticed she was fumbling with her suit.

'What's strange about this one, guv?'

'You'll see.'

I looked down instead of rolling my eyes as I wanted to. *Just tell me . . .* But Una believed in the value of first impressions.

My first impression of 27 Valerian Road was that it was the kind of house I'd always wanted to own. It was a classic Victorian terraced house inside as well as out, long and dark and narrow, with coloured encaustic tiles on the hall floor and stained glass in the front door. I could have done without the blood streaks that skated down the hall, swirled on the walls, splotched the stairs and – I tilted my head back to look – dotted the ceiling. It was enough to take a hundred grand off the value of the property, but that still wouldn't bring it into my price range.

'Cast-off.' The words came from behind me, and I'd have known Derwent's voice anywhere, even if I hadn't been expecting him, but I still jumped. Georgia gave a stagey gasp.

'That's what I was thinking,' I said. *And hello to you too, DI Derwent.* 'Was it a knife, Kev?'

'Possibly. We're still looking for the weapon,' he called from his position at the back.

I could picture it: a knife swinging through the air, wet with blood after the first contact with the victim, shedding droplets as it carved through space and skin. And those droplets would tell us a multitude about the person who'd held the weapon: how they'd stood, where they'd stood, which hand they'd used, how tall they were – everything, in short, but their name.

So I understood why Una Burt was particularly determined to preserve the finer details of this crime scene, and if possible I walked a little more carefully as I moved through the hall, stepping from one mat to another to avoid touching the floor.

It wasn't a large space and there were five of us standing in it, rustling gently in our paper suits.

'Has this been photographed?' I asked.

'Every inch,' Kev said. 'And I've got someone filming it too. But the blood-spatter expert won't be here for an hour or so and I want her to map it before anything changes.'

I nodded, glancing into the room on the right: a grey-toned living room, to my eye untouched, although there was a SOCO rotating slowly in the middle of the room holding a video camera. Film was much better than still photographs for getting the atmosphere of a crime scene, for putting things in context. Juries liked watching films. I moved back, not wanting to appear on camera. 'Where's the body?'

'She always asks the right questions, doesn't she?' Kev nudged Una Burt happily. She didn't look noticeably thrilled behind her mask.

'Have a look upstairs.'

Derwent was closer to the bottom of the stairs and he went first. Georgia went next, followed by me. She put her hand out to take hold of the rail and I caught her wrist. 'Don't touch anything unless you have to.'

'Sorry.'

The lights were on in the hall and at the top of the stairs, and it was too bright for comfort. Blood flared off every surface, dried and dark but still vibrating with violence. I didn't know anything about the victim and I didn't know what had happened here, but fear hung in the air like smoke. *Don't think about it now.* The facts came first. The emotions could come later.

'What happened here?' Derwent had stopped at the top of the stairs, moving to one side to let the rest of us join him. A huge wavering bloodstain had soaked into the sisal carpet that covered the floor.

'We think this was possibly where the first major injury was inflicted. There's a lot of blood downstairs but in small quantities up to this point,' Una Burt said. 'Maybe defensive wounds. Maybe transferred from up here on the attacker's clothes and hands.'

'Or the victim's,' Kev said, and got a glare from Una Burt. *Interesting.*

The blood had settled into the weave, spreading out so it was hard to tell how much there was. Not enough to be an arterial injury. Survivable, potentially, I thought. 'This isn't a great surface for us, is it?'

'Nope.' Kev gestured at smudges on the woven surface. 'Those are footprints and kneeprints. No detail, no definition. Give me a nice tiled floor any day.'

'You've got the hall downstairs,' Derwent said.

'Except that we had people in and out with wet feet before I got here. The coppers had the sense to step carefully but the others . . . ' Kev raised his eyes to heaven. 'You'd almost think it was deliberate. If it hadn't been for the rain we'd have a lot more to go on.'

'Who was that?' I asked.

'One of the two residents – a female aged eighteen – and one of the neighbours,' Una Burt said. 'He gave her a lift back from the station. They came in and found this. You'll need to talk to both of them.'

I nodded and followed the trail to the small bathroom on the right, staying in the doorway because there was nowhere to stand that wasn't covered in brownish red residue. The shower curtain hung down, ripped off most of its rings, streaked and splattered like the walls, like the ceiling, like the cracked mirror where we were reflected like a gathering of particularly awkward aliens. There were partial handprints on the sink, which was chipped, and the toilet. The seat had come away from the hinges on one side, so I could see the blood ran down inside the bowl, where it had settled thickly under the water.

It had been a white room, once.

'Christ,' Derwent said. 'How many victims did you say there were?'

Una Burt ignored him. 'This is the main location for the attack. It's human nature to want to hide and there's a lock on the bathroom door but this was the worst possible place to run to. It's a small space with one exit and not much you could use to defend yourself. The attacker was able to stand in the doorway and cause maximum damage at his or her leisure.'

'His, surely,' Georgia said. Her eyes were round and very blue above the white mask, but her voice didn't tremble.

'Sexist,' Derwent observed under his breath and she turned to look at him.

'You can't assume it was a man,' I said. 'You can't assume anything.'

'Indeed not. Come on.' DCI Burt led us back towards the front of the house. 'Down the hall beyond the bathroom there's a further bedroom but it's not disturbed and the blood trail doesn't lead down there. It belongs to the daughter. This seems to have been used as a guest room.'

It was a large room with a bay window and a cast-iron fireplace on the wall opposite the door. The bed was rumpled. There was a chest of drawers in an alcove, but the bottles and brushes on top of it had been knocked askew. I couldn't see any blood, but something else was all too evident.

'What the fuck is that smell?' Derwent stepped backwards.

'Watch where you put your feet. The cat was shut in here,' Kev explained.

'For how long?'

'That's the interesting thing,' Una said. 'The daughter left here on Wednesday. It's Sunday now. It would appear the cat defecated on three separate occasions and it obviously urinated as well, quite copiously.'

'You'd think it would have run out of piss after a while.' Derwent was crouching down, peering under the bed at the carpet.

15

'Yes, but look at this.' Una pointed to the corner of the room where there was a half-full bowl of water. I went over for a better view and saw short, fine hairs suspended in the liquid. I nudged the bowl with a gloved knuckle to check the carpet underneath, and the single circular mark told me that it was a one-off arrangement.

'Someone locked the cat in here deliberately, but they didn't want it to suffer. They didn't bother with a litter tray but they left enough water that it could survive until the cavalry came. It could manage for three days without food but it couldn't have lived without water.'

'The girl was away from Wednesday,' Derwent said. 'Did anyone know she was coming back today?'

'I don't know. Maeve, you can ask her about that. I want you to interview her.'

I nodded as Derwent flashed me a look that said *Don't think I won't try to come along just because you're a detective sergeant now.* I ignored him. He was still getting used to the idea of me being a little more senior, with more responsibilities and, crucially, more independence from him.

To be honest, so was I.

'Who else lives here?' I asked Una.

'The girl's mother, Kate Emery, aged forty-two. Her bedroom is upstairs.'

I leaned back to check: no blood on the stairs. 'Was it disturbed?'

'Not as far as we can tell. Not during or immediately after the attack, anyway. No blood.'

'Is she the victim?' Derwent asked.

'We don't know.'

'Don't you have a photograph of her?' Georgia hesitated. 'Or – or is the body too badly damaged to be identifiable?'

Una Burt exchanged a look with Kev that seemed to amuse them both. 'Come downstairs and tell me what you make of it.'

It was strange how quickly you got used to the blood, all things considered. We picked our way down the stairs and already it was more like a puzzle than an outrage. That was how it would stay for the moment, and it was useful to have that detachment even if I knew it wouldn't last. I followed Una Burt down the hall, Derwent treading on my heels he was so keen to see what lay ahead. On the left, under the stairs, there was a small shower room. She threw open the door and stood back.

'Voila. What do you make of that?'

'Is this where the attacker cleaned up?' I scanned the walls, seeing faint brownish streaks on the tiles. 'I smell bleach.'

'And drain cleaner. Highly corrosive, designed to dissolve hair and dirt that blocks pipes. I found the bottle in the kitchen, in a cupboard. Homeowner's property.' Kev's eyes crinkled as his mask flexed: he was actually smiling. 'We know they were in here. We know they tidied up after themselves. What we don't know is whether we'll get anything useful from it.'

'Great,' I said, meaning the opposite. 'What else?'

'The blood trail goes into the kitchen and *through* the kitchen.' Kev guided us into a smart white kitchen, pristine apart from the dried blood that dragged across the wooden floor and marked the corner of the cabinets. It was smeared across the doorframe and the handle of the back door. 'And then it disappears. I'm not going to open the door because it opens outwards. It's still raining cats and dogs and I don't have a tent set up there yet. I don't want to lose any of the marks on the inside of the door, but I can tell you what I found – or didn't find. There's a patio out there and I can't currently locate a trace of blood, or a usable footprint, or anything that might tell us where our victim ended up. The rain has obliterated everything.'

'So no body,' I said.

'No body,' Una Burt confirmed. 'At this stage we can't even

be certain who we're looking for. We won't be sure of that until the DNA results come back. What we do know so far is that Kate Emery hasn't been seen since Wednesday night. We could run this as a missing person inquiry but I don't want to waste time. She's left her phone, her handbag, her wallet, her keys and a whole lot of blood behind. There's no way someone loses that much blood and walks away. We'll hope for a sighting of her alive and well, but what we're really looking for is a corpse.'

3

The girl's name was Chloe Emery. I checked it twice on my way across the road to the neighbour's house where she was waiting, 32 Valerian Road. The ambulance I'd seen earlier had been for Chloe, Una Burt explained as we stripped off our protective gear in the tent outside the front door.

'Went to pieces. Unsurprising, really. But she didn't want treatment and she wouldn't let them take her to hospital. They couldn't force her. The girl needs a gentle conversation about her weekend plans – in particular who knew about them. She was with her dad in Oxfordshire, as I understand it. The parents are divorced. Dad's remarried. Mum wasn't.'

'Seeing anyone?' Derwent asked.

'That's something we need to find out. Obviously, I also want to know if anyone had a reason to harm her mother or her. Or if her mother had a reason to harm anyone, I suppose. Can't rule that out.'

Derwent had patted me on the shoulder. 'I'll let you take the lead on that conversation, Kerrigan.'

'You will, because you won't be there. I want you to stay here,' Una Burt said crisply. 'You need to look after the crime scene for me.'

'But I want to go and talk to the daughter.'

19

'Kerrigan can take care of that on her own.' To me, she said, 'Take Georgia Shaw with you.'

Derwent frowned. 'Who the fuck is Georgia Shaw?'

'New DC,' I said.

'The blonde?'

I nodded.

'What's she like?'

'You'll have to decide that for yourself,' Georgia said, coming to stand beside me. I hadn't noticed her but of course she was within earshot. She smoothed her hair, which was already immaculate. I was all too aware that no amount of finger-combing was going to sort my own hair out. Heat and rain were a deadly combination.

'Georgia Shaw, Josh Derwent,' Una Burt said. 'He's my detective inspector.'

My detective inspector. I hid a smile. It was a nice way of reminding Derwent who was the boss, in case he'd forgotten about it during his two weeks off.

Georgia put out her hand and I thought for a brief moment he was going to ignore it but he shook it, without enthusiasm.

'We haven't met. You've been on holidays since I joined the team.'

'And now I'm not.' He turned back to Una Burt. '*Please* let me go and talk to the girl.'

'Don't wheedle,' she said. 'I don't like it and it won't work.' Her face softened very slightly. 'NPAS is going to be overhead shortly and they need someone on the ground to help coordinate the search for the body.' NPAS was the police helicopter; she was pulling out all the stops on this investigation. 'There'll be a dog unit and a search team. It's not just babysitting Kev Cox.'

'Great.' He stretched, frustrated. 'A search through a million gardens in the rain, looking for a missing body. What a welcome back.'

'Don't say I don't find interesting murders for you to investigate.' Una Burt nodded to me. 'Get on with it.'

Which left me trying not to mind that Georgia was walking right behind me, leaning to read the notes I'd scrawled on my clipboard.

'Are you going to ask her why she walked all over the footprints in the hall?'

'I don't expect to.'

'Why not?'

I stopped and faced her. 'Because I want to get to know her first. I want to get her to trust us. If I need to ask some hard questions, I will, but that's not why we're here. She's the one person who can tell us what happened in that house before she left it last Wednesday, but she'll only do that if she wants to help us.'

'What if she did it?'

'Did what? We don't even know what happened.' I turned away. 'If she doesn't want to help us find out where her mother is, that tells us something too. But I don't want to give her a reason not to talk to us. That's why DCI Burt found something else for DI Derwent to do.'

'He seems fairly aggressive.'

'Mm,' I said, and Georgia could make of it what she liked. Derwent would either piss Chloe Emery off until a day after the end of time or win her heart forever. Extreme reactions were his speciality, and too high-risk for this particular situation.

'Whose house is this?' Georgia had dropped her voice to a whisper now that we were right outside the address, which was already a lot more subtle than Derwent would have been.

'The neighbour who gave her a lift from the station and called 999.' I checked my notes again. 'Oliver Norris.'

'Shouldn't she have been kept away from him? Until we've spoken to them, I mean? In case they're getting their stories straight.'

I raised my eyebrows. 'Don't you trust anyone? Ring the bell.'

She did as I asked. 'But—'

'They were kept separate. There's an FLO with the girl. Burt said the officer was a dragon and she wouldn't let Norris near Chloe.' I grinned. 'Burt doesn't trust anyone either.'

The green-painted door swung open to reveal a slim woman with light brown hair and a worried expression, which was fair enough when there were two police detectives standing on her doorstep. She was wearing a long-sleeved white blouse buttoned up to the neck and an ankle-length skirt. I glanced down at her feet to see flat, round-toed shoes in soft blue leather, and buff-coloured tights. I was wearing my lightest trouser suit over a sleeveless top and I was melting. I would have collapsed from heat exhaustion after five minutes in that outfit.

'Mrs Norris?'

'Yes, I'm Eleanor Norris.'

'We're here to interview Chloe, Mrs Norris.'

'She's upstairs in my daughter's bedroom.' She looked back as if she was expecting to see the girl standing behind her. The house was a mirror image of the one I'd just visited and I studied it with interest, trying to imagine what the Emery house had been like before most of the contents of a human being had been emptied out all over it. It was hard to see through the clutter of family life – the coats slung over the end of the bannisters, the keys and post on the table by the door. The house I'd left behind me was immaculately tidy, apart from the blood. Here the wallpaper was dated and rubbed, the carpets old-fashioned, the house badly in need of a makeover.

'Have you spoken with Chloe?' I asked.

'No. I mean, I asked if she wanted anything to eat or drink.' Eleanor Norris squeezed her thin hands together as if they were cold. 'My husband told me about the house. About what they saw.'

'Very unpleasant,' I said blandly.

'Do you think you're going to be finished across the road

22

soon?' Eleanor's voice dropped so it was whispery low. 'Only, I think it would be good for Chloe to know when she can go home.'

'Not soon,' I said.

'Even if she wanted to,' Georgia added. 'I wouldn't want to, would you?'

'She can stay here for a few days, but . . .' Eleanor shrugged helplessly. *But I can't accommodate a neighbour in my house indefinitely.* Her cheeks were flushed.

'We'll know a lot more in the morning,' I said soothingly. It was true, but probably not relevant to Chloe's plans. Eleanor Norris didn't need to know that though. 'Has Chloe spoken to her father?'

'No. She won't call him.'

He'd been informed, I knew. Una Burt had asked Thames Valley Police to speak to him, to get the measure of the man at the same time as breaking the bad news. I hoped for his sake he'd reacted with the requisite shock and horror, and for our sake that he hadn't, that he had no alibi, that he had been nursing a grievance, that there was a murder weapon conveniently located in his car along with a few telling blood-stains . . . Ex-husbands made good suspects in murder investigations.

'Do they get on? Chloe was visiting him, wasn't she?'

'I don't know. I'm sorry.' Eleanor looked past us to where the police helicopter was hovering. It was shining its search-light into the garden behind number 27, the beam piercing the unnatural gloom. 'What are they looking for?'

'It's just part of the investigation,' I said quickly, before Georgia could say anything about the body, or rather the lack of one. 'When was the last time you saw Kate Emery, Mrs Norris?'

'Oh – I don't know.' She bit her lip. 'Wednesday night, I think. We were putting out the bins at the same time.'

I made a note. 'Did you speak?'

23

'No. I waved at her. I had no idea – I mean, I couldn't know.'

'Of course. Do you know her well?'

'Not really.' She hesitated, then added, 'My daughter is friendly with Chloe.' It came out in a rush, as if she didn't want to say anything about it but knew we'd find out anyway.

'What's your daughter's name?'

'Bethany.'

'How old is she?'

'She's fifteen. Just turned fifteen, actually.'

'Younger than Chloe,' I observed.

'Yes, but Bethany's very mature and Chloe—' she broke off and gave me an embarrassed smile. 'You'd probably like to speak to her.'

'Yes, please.'

'It's the door straight ahead of you at the top of the stairs.'

I was aware of her watching us as we went up. I didn't look back at her, even though I was wondering about a couple of things, like her choice of clothes and whether that was why she had sweated through our conversation, and why she had been so concerned about her daughter's relationship with Chloe. And yet people did behave weirdly around the police, especially on the periphery of a murder investigation, and parents did worry about protecting their children even if they had nothing to hide, and the shock of being close to a violent crime could send your body's thermostat out of whack. *Trust no one* . . . It was a reasonable enough approach, all things considered.

I knocked on the door at the end of the hall and a suspicious face appeared. 'Yes?'

I showed her my badge. 'Can we speak to Chloe?'

She was short and middle-aged with close-cropped hair and kind eyes, and I wouldn't have dared to try and persuade her to do anything against her orders. She peered at me, and then at Georgia behind me, before she nodded.

'Come in.'

'Has she said anything?' I asked in a whisper as I passed the officer, and got a shake of her head in response.

Chloe Emery was curled up on a chair, staring at the rain that was sluicing down the window. She didn't look round when we walked in. I took a moment to scan the room, more out of habit than anything else, noting amateurishly painted white walls, a crammed bookcase, a single bed, a bedside table with nothing on it but a lamp. Then I shifted my attention to Chloe. She was tall, with slender limbs and long dark hair.

'Chloe?'

She turned to look at me. Her face was beautiful but somehow blank, with heavy dark eyebrows over blue eyes. 'Yes?'

'I'm Maeve Kerrigan. I'm a detective sergeant with the Metropolitan Police. Do you mind if I ask you some questions?'

She shook her head but she drew her legs up to her chest. She looked nothing short of terrified.

I sat down on the bed opposite her. *Start with an easy question.* 'How old are you, Chloe?'

'Eighteen.'

She seemed younger to me, like a child. I couldn't shake the feeling that she needed an appropriate adult to be with her.

'I know you've had a difficult day, Chloe, and I don't want to take up too much of your time, but I need to ask you some questions. Is that OK?'

She nodded, but warily.

'Can you state your address for me?'

'Twenty-seven Valerian Road, Putney, SW15.'

'And that's where you live most of the time, is that right?'

'Yes.' Her voice was toneless and her eyes wandered around the room as she spoke. I felt she was working hard to stop herself from fidgeting.

'Who else lives there?'

'My mum.'

'And what's her name?'

She thought for a second. 'Kate.'

'Kate Emery.'

'Yes, Kate Emery.'

'Do you have the same last name, Chloe?'

'Yes.'

'Is that the same name as your father?'

'Yes.'

'But your parents are divorced.'

'Yes.' Her answers were getting softer. I felt I was wandering onto dangerous ground without knowing why.

'You were away for the weekend, is that right?'

Another nod.

'Where were you?'

'With my dad.'

'Were the two of you alone?'

'No.'

I waited but she didn't say anything else. 'Who else was there, Chloe?'

'My stepmother.' There was a pause and I was about to ask another question when she added, 'And Nathan. And N— his brother.'

'Who's Nathan?'

'My stepbrother.'

'And his brother,' I said. 'What's his name?'

She stared at the corner of the room, pressing her lips together. No answer. It wasn't a question that was designed to trip her up – quite the opposite. These were the easy, factual questions, the ones that gave people confidence, that settled them into an interview. But I was hitting a wall I hadn't even known I'd find.

'Do you have any other brothers and sisters?'

'No.'

'So you live with your mum. Does anyone else live in the house?'

'No.'

'Can you tell me when you left home for your weekend with your dad?'

'Wednesday. In the afternoon.'

'Did you see your mother before you left?'

A nod. 'She was at home.'

'Did she say anything unusual? Anything that concerned you?'

Another helpless shake of the girl's head. 'I don't remember anything.'

'Did she seem worried or preoccupied?'

'N-no.' She wasn't sure, though.

'What did she say, Chloe?'

'She was talking about work. She was busy with work and she – she wanted me to go. She was afraid I'd be late. She had lots of work to do, she said.'

'What work does she do?'

'She has her own business.'

'Do you know what kind of business?'

'It's something to do with babies.' Chloe shrugged helplessly. 'She doesn't really talk to me about it. She doesn't think I'll understand. She's probably right.'

'What time did you come back, Chloe?'

'I got off the train at three twenty-one.' It was an oddly precise answer, as if she'd made a special note of it.

'Were you expecting anyone to meet you off the train?'

'No. You see, no one knew I was coming back.'

'Oh?'

'I left my dad's house early.'

'When were you supposed to come back?'

'On Tuesday.' She gave a little gasp of a laugh. 'I thought Mum would be surprised.'

Surprised. Not missing.

'Was your mum planning to be away while you were away, Chloe, do you know?'

'No. She wouldn't have left Misty.'

'Misty?'

'The cat.' Chloe looked stricken. 'I don't know where she is.'

'Downstairs.' The FLO gave her a smile. 'She's down in the kitchen. I saw her when I went down to get you your cuppa, love.'

Chloe glanced down at the full mug on the floor beside her. It had a thick film on top of it. 'I didn't drink it.'

'That's all right. We can get you another,' the FLO said.

The girl looked nauseated. 'No. No, thank you.'

'So no one was expecting you to come home,' I said, dragging the interview back on track. 'Was there some reason you left early?'

She was bright red, instantly, and she locked her eyes on the floor in front of her. Her lips were pressed together, as if she didn't want to run the risk of letting as much as a word out. One for the dad to answer, I decided.

'OK. We're nearly done. You got a lift from the station, is that right?'

'Mr Norris saw me. He drove me back here.'

'Did he come into the house with you?'

A big, definite headshake. 'I was on my own.'

I looked up from my notes. 'But he rang 999.'

'I forgot my bag. I left it in his car. I'm always doing that kind of thing. I should have remembered because I had tried to put it in the boot and he shouted at me – well, he didn't shout but he told me not to open the boot.

It was in the back seat – my bag, I mean. And I forgot.' She shivered. 'I just wanted to go home.'

'So you went inside on your own. Did you notice anything strange?' Like the dried blood on most of the surfaces . . .

'Not at first. I mean, I did, but I didn't know what it was.

28

I don't really know what happened. I don't understand why Misty was shut in and the house was all dirty and Mum wasn't there.' Her voice was shaking. 'I don't understand anything except that I came home and it was all wrong. It was all wrong and bad, and I don't know anything except that I want it all to be right again.' She jumped up, suddenly agitated, and the FLO rushed past me to guide her back to her chair.

'It's all right, lovey. You sit down.'

'We'll come back and talk to you tomorrow,' I said. 'Try to get some rest, Chloe.'

'I don't want to rest. I want to go home. I need to go home. I need some stuff from home, and I need to go there, right now.'

'That won't be possible, not at the moment,' I said. 'But we can get things for you if you give us a list.'

She was shaking her head, tears starting into her eyes. 'I know where it is. I need to get it. I need it.'

'What is it?'

Chloe caught her lower lip between her teeth, stopping herself from answering. She shut her eyes for a long moment, then relaxed. 'Nothing. It's nothing.'

I exchanged a look with Georgia, who gave a tiny shrug.

'I can't help if I don't know what I'm looking for. What does it look like?'

'My medication. And . . . '

'And?' I prompted.

'An envelope. With my name on it.' She had gone back to looking out at the garden. The agitation had disappeared. She seemed detached.

Withdrawn.

I'd lost her.

'If I see it, I'll make sure you get it,' I tried, and got no response at all. With a nod to the FLO I left her alone.

'That didn't go very well,' Georgia observed, having shut the door behind us.

I whipped around. 'What makes you say that?'

'Well, she's upset.'

'That's normal when someone you love is missing.'

'And she didn't tell us much.'

'I thought she told us a lot. Much more than she knew.'

'Like what?'

'Think about it,' I said, and started down the stairs wondering if it was promotion that made people unpleasant, and if I'd be as nasty as Derwent by the time I was a detective inspector myself.

Assuming I made it that far.

4

The hall was empty when I came downstairs. I followed the sound of voices to the kitchen at the back of the house. It was narrower than the one on the other side of the road, and full of people. Eleanor Norris was standing by the sink twisting a tea towel in her hands. A teenage girl sat at the table leaning against a man with short dark hair and a golden tan, who was deep in conversation with a second, white-haired man. A third man sat on a chair he'd pushed away from the table, balancing on the two back legs. He glanced up as we came in.

'Look out, it's the filth.'

'Morgan,' the tanned man snapped. 'That's enough.'

'Just a joke.' He let the chair slam back onto the floor and stood up. 'Morgan Norris. I'm Oliver's brother.'

'For my sins. I'm Oliver.' The dark-haired man stood too, glaring at his brother. I'd have known they were related without being told. They had the same quick way of moving, the same tilt of the head, the same light eyes. Oliver was darker and handsome in a square-jawed, rugby-player way. Morgan was leaner, more like a runner. He was looking at me with frank curiosity which I ignored. I got a lot of that, one way or another. I didn't look like a murder detective, I'd been told. Too pretty, they said. Not tough enough. Too tall.

Such nonsense.

'I need to speak to you, Mr Norris. I need to ask you some questions about what you saw this afternoon. Is there somewhere we can talk?'

'Of course.' He started to detach himself from the teenage girl who clung on to his arm more tightly.

'No.'

'Bethany, I have to go.'

'Let go of him, Bethany.' The white-haired man stretched out his hand but didn't touch her. He didn't have to. She let go of her father instantly and dropped her hands into her lap.

'I'm sorry, I didn't catch your name,' I said to him.

'Gareth Selhurst.'

He said it as if I should recognise him, his voice resonant, his barrel chest inflating with pride. An actor? I didn't know and couldn't ask. I'd never seen him before.

'Are you a neighbour? Or family?'

'I live nearby.' He gave a vague flourish, not indicating any particular direction. 'And we are all family here, my dear. All part of God's family.'

'Amen.' Eleanor Norris had whispered it.

'Gareth is the lead elder of our church,' Oliver Norris said. 'He's here to support us.'

Not an actor: a preacher.

'I wanted to offer my help,' Selhurst said. 'In case there was anything I could do. Sometimes prayer is a great comfort.'

'Do you know Kate Emery and Chloe Emery?'

'Yes. Not well.' He smiled blandly. 'They don't worship with us, but the door is always open.'

Not worth interviewing, I thought, and immediately wondered if that was what I was supposed to think.

'I'll try not to take too long, Mr Norris.'

'I want to come with you. I want to hear what happened,' Bethany said. She sounded like a spoiled brat and looked like a child. Fifteen, her mother had said, but I'd have guessed

of the fitting in the ceiling and a large chip was missing from the plaster on the corner of the chimney breast.

'No. Not really.' A smile. 'But when the wife tells me to go and help out a neighbour, I go. Couldn't let her down.'

'So you help lots of the neighbours.'

'If they need help,' he said evenly. 'Kate was on her own.'

'Was?'

'Is. Was. I don't know. Did they find a body?'

'A body,' I repeated.

'I assume they're looking for a body. I didn't see one in the house.' He shifted in the chair. 'I didn't go looking for it.'

'You walked around quite a lot, I gather. The crime scene technicians found a few of your footprints in the hall.'

'I was in a bit of a panic. I didn't think. I saw all the blood . . .' He was back to looking green. 'I don't like blood. I'm not used to seeing things like that. I went in to see if I could help but I couldn't see Kate. Then I thought it was probably better to take Chloe out of the house and call you lot. And that's all I know.'

'Why were you there?'

'Chloe forgot her bag. Left it in my car. I didn't want her to worry about it so I carried it across the road for her. As soon as she opened the door I saw that something was wrong.'

'What did you see that made you think that?'

'You've been in the house,' he said with a flash of anger. 'What do you think I saw? Blood. A lot of it.'

'How did you know what it was?'

He shrugged. 'What else could it have been? Ketchup? It looked like an abattoir in there. And my stomach went, I can tell you. I was heaving. I couldn't even speak. It was like an instinct. I just knew.'

'So what did you do?'

He looked up at the ceiling, remembering. 'I went in. I made myself go in, even though I didn't want to. I didn't realise the blood was dry at first. I thought maybe Kate was injured and needed help.'

'Where did you go?'

'Into the hall and then on a bit further, to check. I looked into the sitting room. I looked through to the kitchen and saw blood there but no body.' He pulled at his lower lip, affecting to be shamefaced. 'I put my hand on the counter in the kitchen, I'm pretty sure. I might have touched a few other places too.'

'Did you go upstairs?'

'Yeah. I think so. It's all a bit of a blur. I mean, I've been upstairs in the house before, so if you find fingerprints of mine that doesn't mean anything.'

'Don't worry, Mr Norris.' I smiled at him, bland as cream. 'We have excellent technicians. They'll be able to tell if a fingerprint was made before, during or after the attack. So it'll be easy enough to tell if you're in the clear.'

He swallowed once, convulsively.

Not so confident now, are you?

'What were you looking for, Mr Norris?'

'A body. A killer.' He laughed. 'Glad I didn't find either, really. That's your job.'

'Whose body did you expect to find?'

'Kate's. Who else?' He looked at me as if I was stupid. 'Chloe was there. She was fine.'

So he didn't think of Kate as a possible aggressor. I didn't know enough about her to make that judgement.

'Go back a bit for me,' I said. 'When was the last time you saw Kate Emery?'

'I don't know. During the week some time.' He frowned. 'I saw her on Friday evening, I think.'

'Friday evening. Are you sure?'

'No. That's why I said I think it was Friday.' He wasn't bothering to try to charm me any more, which was a relief.

'What was she doing?'

36

'She was in her sitting room looking out of the window.'

'You're sure it was her.'

'Yeah. I was walking past on the other side of the road and I waved.'

'And you think this was Friday evening.'

'I'm fairly sure. I know I was looking forward to getting home from work and having a cold beer to start the weekend, if my thieving brother had left any in the fridge.'

'Your brother Morgan?'

He nodded. 'I only have one, thankfully.'

'Does he live here?' I asked.

'He's been staying with us for a while. Between jobs, apparently.' Norris snorted. 'No sign of him doing anything about getting one. He gave up a perfectly good job in an insurance company to go travelling for three years and got the shock of his life when he came home and no one wanted to employ him. Thank goodness he had us to fall back on.'

'You don't sound very happy about it,' Georgia commented.

'It's been months,' Norris said simply. 'Too long.'

'And you can't kick him out? I would.'

Norris flashed the teeth at her, instantly encouraged, trying to make friends again. 'It wouldn't be right. God has his reasons for sending him to live with us. Gareth says we have to pray for his soul, even if I'm sure it's a lost cause.'

'Gareth seems to be a big influence on you,' I commented.

'He's the leader of our church.'

'What church is that?'

'The Church of the Modern Apostles. It's an evangelical, charismatic church. Living Christianity. It's a growing move-ment, you know. Gareth planted the church here in Putney five years ago and the congregation is increasing all the time.'

'Including you and your family.'

'I'm actually an elder of the church. For the last two years, it's been my job.'

'You mean Gareth is your boss?'

He shook his head, smiling. 'God is. But he directs me in his purposes through Gareth a lot of the time. You know, you should come along to see us worship. Share in God's grace with us.'

I smiled politely and referred to my notes. 'So you think it was Friday when you saw Kate. What was she doing?'

'Just standing in the window. Looking out.'

'Waiting for someone?'

'It's a safe bet,' Norris said evenly.

'What does that mean?'

'Chloe spends one week in six with her dad. When she was there or otherwise engaged, Kate sometimes had . . . visitors.'

'What sort of visitors?'

'Men.'

I nodded as if I was unsurprised, as if I'd known about it already. And in fact I wasn't all that surprised. She was a single mother, after all, and forty-two according to Una Burt. She was entitled to a private life, whatever the neighbours thought. 'When you say men, did they visit her in groups or one at a time?'

'One at a time, as far as I could tell.' He gave a forced, awkward laugh. 'I don't think she was into anything as kinky as group sex, but you never know. It's outside my experience.'

No wonder you couldn't wait to go round and fix her dripping tap.

'Did you notice the same men visiting her more than once? The same cars?'

'I didn't notice.' He pulled a face. 'I didn't like it. Dating is one thing but that sort of activity in front of everyone, in her own home – it felt sordid.'

'Did you ever talk to her about it?'

'I tried. I invited her to come to our church. I thought she might find what she was looking for there.' He gave me a twitchy smile. 'It didn't go too well.'

I flipped over a page on my clipboard with a snap. 'Were you here all weekend, Mr Norris?'

'Yeah. I did a lot of gardening.' He held up his hands, which were scratched. 'Some of the bushes fought back. Morgan helped me, he can tell you about it.'

'What did you do with the clippings?'

He frowned. 'Took them to the dump. That's what I was doing when I came back and saw Chloe at the station.'

'I'm going to need your car keys and permission to search your car.'

'I don't see why. I mean, I don't think that's appropriate.'

I looked at him, eyebrows raised, and waited.

'You can look. I'm not trying to hide anything.' He laughed. 'I don't know why you'd want to, that's all.'

'Just routine,' I said. 'Did you notice anything unusual over the weekend? Any strange visitors to the street, any unexpected noises . . .' I trailed off. He was shaking his head.

'I mean, I've been racking my brains ever since I went over to Kate's house. Did I hear a scream? I really don't think so. Did I see anyone strange? Again, no. Did I have any concerns about anything? Not in the least.'

If he was going to interview himself, that was going to save me doing a lot of talking. I made a meaningless scrawl on the page in front of me. 'Is there anything you think I should know about Kate Emery or Chloe or anyone else?'

He blew out a lungful of air. 'Well. There is one thing. I feel a bit bad even mentioning it but I think I should. For everyone's sake. I know I'm not the only one to be thinking about it and if you don't hear about him from me, it'll be someone else who tells you sooner or later.'

I nodded, making my very understanding listening face. *Get on with it and stop justifying whatever it is you're about to say, you horrible man.*

'There's a lad. A young lad. He must be . . . oh, twenty. Twenty-one. Something like that. He lives down the road. Number six. His name's William Turner.'

I waited for him to go on.

'He was in trouble with the police a few years ago. Four years ago, it must have been, because it was shortly after we moved in. He was arrested for attempted murder.'

'Arrested? Was he charged?'

'No. I don't know why.'

'Who was the victim?'

'A friend of his.' Norris laughed. 'Some friend. He stabbed him.'

'What happened?' Georgia asked, her eyes wide.

'It was a fight after school one day.' Norris shook his head sorrowfully. 'Everyone knew he'd done it but they couldn't prove it.'

'Didn't the victim give evidence?' I asked, puzzled.

'He wouldn't talk. Wouldn't say a word. His family moved not long after. I don't blame them. We talked about it, but we couldn't afford to move twice in such a short space of time.' He shuddered. 'Not what you want to hear about, is it? Not when you've got an eleven-year-old and you're worried she'll be hanging around on street corners in a few years. But Bethany's not like that, thank God. We've been pretty strict with her. She knows the rules and she knows not to break them.'

'So, to be clear,' I said slowly, 'you think I should focus on William Turner because he was once involved in a stabbing.'

'Not just that. The kid is weird, let me tell you. He hangs around all the time. No job, obviously. It's no surprise. I wouldn't employ him. He has no education and no work ethic.' Norris leaned forward, dropping his voice, absolutely earnest. 'I've read about psychopaths and, if you ask me, he's a textbook case. It's one per cent of the population, you know. One in a hundred. That's a lot. There's more than a hundred people living in this street and I'm confident I've worked out who ours is.'

'OK,' I said. 'Thanks for letting me know.'

'He watches the girls.' Norris shook his head, disapproving. 'I've seen him. He sits on his garden wall and he watches them walking up and down the road. Talks to them, some-times. Calls out, you know. Gets them into conversation. I've warned Bethany to stay well away from him. Chloe too. She doesn't have the common sense to keep her distance. Not when he's a good-looking lad, which there's no denying he is. He knows it, too.'

'You seem to spend a lot of time thinking about Chloe,' I observed. 'You know her routine – you know when she's away and when she's here. You gave her a lift from the station. You carried her bag over to the house.'

His face went red. 'I don't know what you're implying, if you're implying anything. I worry about Chloe. I worry about all the girls round here. And the police don't do anything about Turner.' He remembered who he was talking to. 'At least, they don't seem to.'

'Looking and talking isn't against the law. We can't stop Mr Turner from socialising. Especially if – according to you – he wasn't convicted of anything.'

'Yes.' Norris narrowed his eyes. 'You don't think I'm right to be worried either. But you haven't met him. You haven't spoken to him. You haven't looked into his eyes. I have. And I know what I saw there.'

'What was that, Mr Norris?'

'He has no soul.' Norris leaned back in his chair, as if he'd struck a killer blow that ended the argument then and there. In a way, of course, he had. I certainly didn't want to prolong it.

'Thanks for your help, Mr Norris. If you think of anything else we might need to know, do get in touch. We'll probably need to speak to you again, to confirm the details of your statement. And we'll need to get your fingerprints and DNA, if you don't mind, for elimination purposes.'

'Right. Yes. Anything to help.' He was back to looking uneasy. 'Though I'm sure there's nothing that can't be easily explained if you do find some DNA of mine floating around.'

What exactly did you get up to when you went to fix the tap, Mr Norris?

I followed Georgia out to the hall and collected a set of keys for the Volvo that sat outside the house. As I was leaving, a thought struck me. 'Mr Norris.'

'Yes.' He was already closing the door, relief all over his face. He hadn't been anything like as relaxed as he'd pretended to be.

'What's your problem with the cat?'

'Oh – I don't like cats. I have a phobia of them, actually. The fur. The way they look at you. And if you'd seen what it was doing at the house—' He covered his mouth again and retched. Sweat stood out on his forehead. When he could speak again, he mumbled, 'Disgusting animal. A charity is coming to take it away. I'm not having it in my home. Why?'

'Just wondering,' I said, and followed Georgia down the path to the road.

'I don't get it,' she said once we were out of earshot. 'Why were you wondering?'

'Two reasons. Someone managed to lock the cat in that room, and they made sure it could survive being left alone for a few days. He wouldn't have wanted to go near it and he certainly wouldn't have cared if it had died from lack of water. Anyway, can you see him being able to stab someone to death? Even talking about the scene made him want to vomit.'

'You don't think he was faking.'

'I don't. But I could be wrong. I don't think I'm wrong about the cat.' As I spoke I glanced back at the house and saw a curtain twitch in an upstairs room: Chloe, I thought. And a second, smaller figure beside her, drawing her away. The light caught her glasses as she moved: Bethany Norris. They were gone before I could draw Georgia's attention to them.

'What do we do now? Go and see William Turner?' She was full of energy, straining at the lead like a dog with the scent of blood in her nostrils.

42

'The convenient local psychopath. I think it can wait – I'll get Liv to do some checks on his history before we call on him. I'd like to know more about what happened to Kate Emery and more about him before I speak to him.'

'So what? Go home?'

'Nope. Now we go and see another troublemaker.' I grinned. 'But this one is all ours.'

5

'Welcome back.' Derwent stood in the doorway of number 27, liberated from his paper suit, his shirtsleeves rolled up. He was still wearing shoe covers, and his standard mocking expression.

'Shouldn't I be saying welcome back to you?' I said.

'That would have been nice. I don't think I even got a hello, did I?'

'Hello.' I looked past him. 'What's going on?'

'Kev's blood lady is here. She says she'll be a couple of hours at least – she's got to draw a map of all the blood spatter. Easier to map the places that *aren't* covered in blood.'

'If Kev thinks she's good—'

'She must be good,' Derwent finished. 'But I've got the go-ahead to search the other areas of the house, as long as we don't get in her way, and as long as we're careful.'

'I always am.' I took a pair of shoe covers and handed another set to Georgia. 'Put them on.'

She did as she was told, but I was aware of her looking from me to Derwent and back again while she did it. I wondered what she'd been told about us. I wasn't sure what the current rumours were. I knew the truth, which was that there had never been anything romantic between me and Detective Inspector Josh Derwent. And with that in mind . . .

'How's Melissa?'

'Fine,' Derwent said shortly.

'How's Thomas? Does he like the new house?'

His face softened. 'Yeah. Loves it.'

'You spent your holiday moving house?' Georgia said.

'Some of it. Some of it in Portugal.'

'Whereabouts?'

Instead of answering, Derwent cleared his throat. I could tell that he didn't want to talk about his personal life any more. He was infinitely protective of the ready-made family that he'd acquired eight months earlier: his girlfriend Melissa Pell and her son Thomas, who was just four. Thomas was Derwent's greatest fan and the feeling was absolutely mutual. And I knew Derwent didn't even want to think about them in a house that stank of death, let alone say their names.

'I take it the helicopter didn't find a body for us.' I used my back-to-business tone of voice and caught the edge of a look from Georgia. Joyless was the kindest word she would use to describe me, I guessed. Then again, I wasn't sure how much fun she had expected in a murder investigation team.

'It didn't find anything,' Derwent said. 'We had a dog here for a bit, but even his handler said he was fucking useless. He found some fox shit, if you're interested in seeing that.'

'I can live without it.'

'What did you find out?'

'Not a huge amount. There's a perfect local suspect, though.'

He grunted. 'There always is.'

'He doesn't seem to fit the bill anyway.'

'Go on.' Derwent was listening closely as I told him about Oliver Norris and his suspicions about William Turner.

'I was more interested in what he said about Kate Emery.'

'Oh?'

'She had male visitors when her daughter was away. Mr Norris noticed.'

'What sort of male visitors?'

'Mr Norris thought they were misbehaving,' I said primly.

'Professional or amateur misbehaviour?'

'That I don't know. Yet.'

'If you want to join me in the lady's bedroom, we can have a look,' Derwent said with something approaching a leer.

'Can't wait,' I said briskly, knowing that Georgia was still trying – and doubtless failing – to get a read on our relationship. 'I should ask Oliver Norris if he saw anything suspicious when he came over to fix Kate's dripping tap.'

'Did you think Norris was watching Kate? Or Chloe?' Georgia asked. 'I thought you were implying that with some of your questions.'

'I don't know. Some people are nosy neighbours. Everyone likes to gossip. And Chloe is good friends with his daughter, after all.' I shrugged. 'It could be weird that he knows so much about the family's comings and goings, or it could be second nature to him to know what's going on in his neighbourhood. I don't know him well enough yet to say either way.'

'But you don't like him,' Derwent said.

'I didn't say that.'

He grinned at me and I knew I'd given it away, somehow, to him at any rate. But then, he knew me better than most.

'So you haven't managed to find us a body,' I said. It was always better to attack than defend, with Derwent.

'I tried.'

'We don't even know who we're looking for.'

'Kate Emery.' He handed me a photograph that he'd liberated from somewhere in the house: a close-up of a smiling woman with shortish fair hair. She was squinting into the sun, her eyes screwed up, her smile strained. It wasn't a picture I would have chosen to frame but she looked outdoorsy and cheerful. I knew better than to assume she was either, based on a single photograph. 'I still can't tell you if she's a suspect or a victim,' Derwent added. 'Kev says they'll hurry on the DNA.'

'As it stands,' Georgia said thoughtfully, 'we don't even know if it's a murder, do we?'

Derwent turned to look at her. 'Yeah. We definitely shouldn't leap to any conclusions. It could have been an accident. Chopping vegetables or something, nicked herself, dripped a bit of blood on the floor while she was looking for a plaster, as you do . . .'

'No, well, not that.' Georgia's cheeks were red.

'Maybe she tried to kill herself and just kept missing her wrists. After the tenth or eleventh time she got bored and went to find a tall building to jump off. Is that more likely?'

'It's possible,' I said mildly. 'Not the way you've described it, but it happens. When I was a response officer I turned up at a scene that looked like an attempted murder. The guy had awful injuries, but they were actually self-inflicted.'

'Spoilsport,' Derwent said. 'So we'll leave suicide as a possibility because – what did you say you were called?'

'Georgia. Georgia Shaw.'

'Because DC Shaw thinks it's feasible that someone did this to themselves. And then wandered off to dig their own grave, I suppose.'

I was lukewarm on Georgia Shaw but even so, I winced. I'd been on the receiving end of Derwent's sarcasm enough times to know that it stung. I'd also worked with Derwent for long enough to know that he had formed an opinion of Georgia already, and there was precious little she could do about it for now.

'Right,' I said. 'Here's what I think we should do. Georgia, I want you to get a SOCO to go over Norris's car, especially the boot. Make sure he wasn't moving a body around, not shifting garden rubbish. If you find anything suspicious, tell me, obviously. Don't give him the keys back yet, even if there isn't anything.'

'You want to make him sweat,' Derwent said.

'I don't mind if he's a bit on edge, put it that way.' I turned

47

back to Georgia. 'Then house-to-house. Find out if anyone else saw Kate Emery after Wednesday when Chloe left for her dad's house, or if Norris was the only one. Ask if they saw anything strange too. Find out if anyone else noticed men coming and going from this house – but don't suggest it, will you. Rumours become facts too easily, and everyone wants to help so they'll say they saw God Almighty visiting the house if they think that's what we want to hear.'

'I know.' She was still red, this time with anger, and it was directed at me. She knew very well that I was getting rid of her. She didn't know it was for her own good.

I checked the time. 'Half past eight. Don't spend too long on it. We've been here for long enough that anyone who has urgent information for us would have spoken to us already. The immediate neighbours have already been interviewed, so go a bit further down the street. But don't go as far as William Turner's house, and if you do see him, be careful what you tell him.'

'I thought you didn't see him as a credible suspect,' Georgia said.

'At the moment, everyone's a suspect. Off you go.' I waited while she stripped off the shoe covers again, very slowly, and gathered her things. Derwent was watching too, his hands in his pockets, whistling silently to himself. It was his habit when he was thinking, and a thinking Derwent was never good news.

As Georgia left I blew my hair out of my face. 'Hot in here, isn't it?'

'That's the warm glow you get from giving orders, DS Kerrigan. How do you like it?'

'Oh, shut up.'

He grinned. 'It suits you, I have to say. I always saw you as more the submissive type, but maybe I was wrong.'

I looked around, peering up the stairs. The lights were off and it was shadowy up there, the horrors half-hidden in the

48

dusk. The house was quiet. Waiting. 'Where do you want to start? Down here and work up?'

He dropped the mockery straight away. 'Fine by me.'

My skin was slick with sweat and my hair was sticking to my neck. The crime-scene tents at the front and now the back of the house meant that no air was circulating through it, and the temperature seemed to have gone up as the shadows lengthened. I took off my jacket.

'Did you iron that?'

I looked down at my top. 'Yes. Well, I didn't. I paid someone else to do it.'

'Why's that?'

'Because I find ironing boring and I have better things to do with my time. She cleans too.'

'Interesting.'

'Not really.'

'It is to me,' Derwent said simply. 'You usually look as if you've just rolled out of bed. Why the change of image?'

'I do not look scruffy usually. Anyway, what's wrong with wanting to look professional?' I was tying my hair up, scraping it back.

'All of a sudden. Because now you're a detective *sergeant.*' He stressed the last word, grinning at me.

'You can't get over it, can you?'

'I can believe you passed the sergeant's exam. I can't believe you managed to swing it so you got to stay on the team.'

I didn't say anything. He knew as well as I did that the detective sergeant's place had come up because Chief Superintendent Charles Godley had insisted on it, that he had personally intervened to make sure I stayed exactly where I was. He might be working elsewhere but he was still fully engaged with his team, much to Una Burt's disappointment. So he had insisted that we needed another detective sergeant on the team. And since we were a man down after one of our colleagues had died the previous year, he'd got his way.

Dead men's shoes. Opportunities carved out of tragedy. I'd found it difficult to celebrate, all in all. It was a death we'd all taken hard, but I'd taken it harder than most.

Then again, it was my fault.

As if Derwent knew what I was thinking, he dropped an arm around my shoulders. 'It's good to be back. Did you miss me?'

'Every day. It was so quiet and peaceful without you.'

'That's no fun.'

'None at all,' I agreed, and I actually meant it.

We split up on the ground floor. Derwent took the kitchen while I concentrated on the living room. They weren't readers but there was a big TV and a cupboard full of DVDs – film classics, cartoons, nothing edgy or unexpected. I met Derwent in the hall and we moved up to the next floor, to Chloe's bedroom where again I found no books, a small amount of make-up, a lot of clothes and a pile of junky jewellery in a drawer. Some of it was unworn, still labelled; one heavy necklace had a security tag on it. I stirred the collection with my finger. Shoplifted? Or was it my suspicious mind? I opened a drawer and found a stack of medicine: Ritalin and six months' supply of the pill. It shouldn't have surprised me that Chloe was sexually active but it did. Then again, maybe her mother had thought it was better to be safe than sorry. Preventing pregnancy was a lot better than dealing with an unwanted one. I gathered up all of the medicine to give to her.

Swearing, Derwent dealt with the guest room at the front of the house, without finding anything of interest. The cat-shit smell seemed to have got stronger instead of fading away, and I left him to it without the slightest twinge of conscience. There was a tiny box room at the front too, just big enough for a single bed. It was piled high with sealed boxes, all labelled Novo Gaudio Imports, shipped from China. I sliced one open with a key and found packages of pills. The contents matched the customs declaration on the side of the box though and I assumed it was all legal and above-board, even if I didn't know what the pills were.

Kate Emery's bedroom was right at the top of the house along with another bathroom and a study, and we went up there together. The blood trail ran out on the first floor, as we'd thought. Here it was the SOCOs who'd left their mark with traces of fingerprint dust that made the surfaces look grimy. Like the rest of the house it was extremely neat and very feminine – pale pink bedclothes, pink curtains, pink towels in the bathroom. The pillows were piled high on the bed, three on each side and one particularly ornate one in the middle.

'Melissa would love this,' Derwent said.

'Does she like the new house?'

Derwent slid open a drawer in the bedside table and started to work through the contents, setting everything he found on the bed. 'She keeps putting cushions everywhere. What is it about women and cushions?'

I picked up a picture that was on top of the bedside table: a much younger Chloe and Kate hugging one another, smiling, windswept on a beach. Happy memories. 'It wasn't a very girly place, your flat.'

'No, it was not.' He glanced at me. 'The house is better.'

'Nothing quite compares to the suburbs.'

'You should know. Sutton's not far from your mum and dad.'

'I wondered if you remembered they lived nearby. I have to say, I was surprised you chose to move there.' I'd left it behind without a flicker of regret.

'We needed to find a good school for the boy. And he needed a garden. Somewhere he can run around.' His face brightened. 'I want to get him a playhouse. They do one that looks like a command post.'

I hid a smile. Once a soldier, always a soldier. 'Sounds nice.'

'Yeah. Well. It's good.' I knew he'd be snappy for a couple of minutes, having given away more than he intended. The way Derwent behaved, you would think the worst thing in the world was to be liked.

Derwent, domesticated. It was strange, but it suited him. I'd never have thought that out of the two of us he would end up settling down first. But then I would never have thought my handsome, loving boyfriend, Rob, would sleep with someone else and leave me without so much as a goodbye, let alone an apology. It was more than a year since he'd disappeared and I still missed him more than I was willing to admit. I'd loved him enough to want to be with him for the rest of my life, and I'd lost him, and I couldn't help hoping against hope that I might get him back somehow.

I watched Derwent as he returned to the search, running his hand all the way around the back of the drawer and coming up with something that he inspected.

'What have you got there?'

'Two condoms. They must have been a pretty recent purchase, looking at the use-by stamp. But no sex toys. No handcuffs. No whips.'

'So, much less kinky than Oliver Norris was imagining it would be. What's that?' I picked up a leather holder and opened it to find a Kindle. 'Damn. I was hoping for a diary.'

'Make-up, moisturiser, eye cream . . .' Derwent shrugged. 'Usual female shit.'

I'd moved on to the chest of drawers, which was neatly arranged and completely full. 'I can't tell if there's anything missing, but I'd be surprised. She had good taste in underwear.'

'Let's see.'

'How did I know that would get your attention?' I held up a bra: Italian, lacy, insubstantial as cobwebs. 'That's not for wearing. That's for taking off.'

'Naughty Kate.'

'Single Kate. She must have been young when she had Chloe.' I stopped to do the sums. 'Twenty-four. Maybe she felt she had some catching up to do after her divorce.'

The drawers lower down had T-shirts and jumpers arranged by colour, rolled rather than stacked, organised as precisely as if she'd known they'd be scrutinised by strangers. I checked there was nothing caught in the folds or underneath the clothes or even under the drawer liners. Then I took out each drawer and checked underneath it, and along the sides and back.

'Think she was hiding something?'

'You never know.'

I carried on searching, checking between layers of clothes, looking in every box, every container, patting down the clothes on hangers to check there was nothing in the pockets. There was no way to know what I was looking for until I found it. I had searched chaotic and dirty houses, derelict buildings, squats and sheds: this was at least clean. But it was also frustratingly normal.

Right at the back of the wardrobe, though, there was something that gave me pause: a plastic bag folded over. I opened it and sat back on my heels. 'God.'

Derwent was tipping the contents of the bin into an evidence bag. He glanced up, distracted, and half of it fell onto the floor. 'For shit's sake.'

'Come and look at this,' I said.

'What?'

'Clothes.' I was holding the bag at arm's length, the back of one gloved hand to my mouth.

He came over and peered into the bag, then recoiled. 'Fuck. That stinks.'

It was a strong and brackish smell, like unwashed exercise kit or dirty bed sheets.

I squeezed the bag, shuffling the clothes around inside it without touching them. 'Looks to be a top, skirt, bra, knickers. A whole outfit.'

'A whole outfit that she couldn't be bothered to wash?'

'Or she had some reason for keeping it like that.' I offered him the bag. 'I don't want to take them out in case we lose trace evidence, but look at her underwear.'

He leaned over. 'Ripped.'

'Badly.' I closed the bag again carefully. 'Why would you leave a bag of unwashed, torn clothes in your otherwise immaculate wardrobe?'

Derwent looked down at me, his face grave, but he didn't say what he was thinking. He didn't have to. 'Bag it up.'

I edged the bag into a brown paper sack. It might be connected with what had happened in the house and it might not, but I wanted to know whose DNA was on the clothes and how it had got there.

Derwent retrieved the scraps of cotton wool and other rubbish that had tumbled away from him. I pointed out a stray button and a needle that was silvery invisible in the pile of the carpet. The more we took now, the less chance there was that we'd miss something important, but clogging up the lab with irrelevant material was not going to make us popular.

Derwent headed to the study while I dealt with the en-suite bathroom. It was clinically clean. The SOCOs had been here too but the dusting of fingerprint powder had caught only smudges and the wide swinging arc of a cloth used to polish glass. The air smelled of bleach and something else, more acrid. I bent over the sink and inhaled gingerly: definitely stronger. Drain cleaner, used for legitimate drain-cleaning purposes rather than destroying evidence. The bathroom cabinet was so well organised that I could see at a glance there was nothing of interest in it. One container held spare razor blades with plain black casings, not the pastel colours of women's toiletries. Which meant nothing, I decided. There was no other sign of a man having lived in the house. Kate herself could just as easily have used the blades. Similarly, the stack of unused toothbrushes still in their packets didn't mean she had frequent visitors, despite what Oliver Norris had suggested. She was the sort of person who stockpiled essentials like toothbrushes. There was a basket under the sink filled with rolls of toilet paper, and I'd found at least two of everything in the bathroom cabinet. Everything spoke of planning, care, preparation, organisation. It didn't suggest chaos, terror, impending disaster. It didn't make me think she had fled in a hurry after killing someone downstairs.

It didn't make me think she had left at all. At least, not by choice.

'What have you got?' I stood in the doorway of the study, mainly because it was very much a one-person space. The computer was gone from the desktop, leaving a labelled void behind, and some of the files and folders were missing from the shelves, the spaces tagged to show that it was the police who'd removed them. Otherwise it was the same as the rest of the house – organised and orderly.

'Nothing.' Derwent didn't bother to look up from the filing cabinet he was flicking through. 'But Liv's got the good stuff already.'

'Is there anything about her daughter?'

'A fuck of a lot of correspondence with the local educational authority.' He was skim-reading it. 'This goes back a long way. She had a fight to get Chloe educated around here. She wanted her to stay in mainstream education and the local council didn't want to have to pay for the extra learning support.'

'What's does it say about Chloe?' I was curious about her. She had been distant but lucid when I spoke to her. And shock could do that to you.

'Speech delay. Developmental delay. Attention deficit disorder. Anxiety. Oppositional defiant disorder.' Derwent snorted. 'That just means you don't like doing what you're told.'

'What else does it say?'

'Depends who you ask. According to the Council, she was fine. According to her mother and the educational psychologists she consulted, Chloe needed a full-time classroom assistant to help her, extra tuition, extra time for tests . . .' Derwent sighed. 'Makes you realise how lucky you are if your kid is normal.'

'I don't think we're supposed to say normal any more. There's no such thing.'

'Bullshit.' He pushed past me and disappeared into the bathroom.

I listened to him rooting through the cupboards even though I'd already searched there. 'Did you find a passport?'

'In a drawer.'

'Cash?'

'Nothing significant.'

'Jewellery?'

'No. But she's not wearing much in the pictures I've seen of her.' Derwent reappeared. 'Anyway, do you see this as a burglary?'

'No, I don't.'

'Come and look at this.' He led me back into the bedroom and opened the French windows. A waist-high railing ran across the space. It was dark now, the lights on in the houses all around. The rain had stopped for the time being but the air was sweet with it and night scents rose up from the gardens that stretched as far as I could see. The trees were plumy with leaves and from where I stood the gardens blended into one enormous space framed with houses, the walls and fences invisible.

'We need to ask the neighbours if they saw anything.' I had a perfect view across to the houses behind, to the domestic dramas playing out in brightly lit windows. Life going on, as it tended to.

'Especially at the back. We think she went out the back door,' Derwent said. 'The dog took us to the back fence, through a gate and along an alley that runs between the gardens. We went left. We got one . . . two . . . three gardens along – that house.' He pointed. 'Twenty-two Constantine Avenue, if you were wondering. We took the dog into the garden and it got excited about the fox shit. And then . . . nothing.'

'Who lives in that house?' It stood out because the lights were off.

'It's unoccupied. The neighbours said the owner is in a nursing home. I had a look at the doors and windows, but it looked secure.'

'Access to the front of the house?'

'There's a gate. *You* could climb it.'

'Even me? It must be easy. But could you get a body over it?'

'Very possibly. And if you didn't want to, you could pick the lock in about ten seconds.'

'Did the dog seem to think someone had done that?'

Derwent shrugged. 'The dog had lost interest by then.'

'But our killer could have parked in front of the unoccupied house and taken the body away in his car.'

'He could indeed.'

'It seems like a lot of trouble, though. If you want to move the body, why not take it out the front door?'

'With all the neighbours watching?' Derwent shook his head. 'What you don't know about that house is that there's a front garden.'

'Is there?'

'With a high hedge.'

'Now you're making more sense.'

'So it's worth dragging a dead weight all the way over there if you know the area.'

'If you do,' I said. 'You'd have to know it was unoccupied, though, and about the gate. You'd have to be local.'

'Mm.' Derwent stared out at the houses across the way where the silent scenes played out, as unreal as television. 'I might not know where to find Kate Emery's body but I do have some idea where to start looking for her killer.'

6

Monday mornings are the same the world over, no matter the job or the city. It was a pale and bleary-eyed group of detectives who gathered in the meeting room for an early briefing about the Putney crime scene. I'd seen Una Burt outside the room, pacing up and down, eager to get started. I wished I could feel as keen. I tried not to yawn, my jaws quivering as I fought it back. Georgia Shaw was sitting near the front of the room in a grey trouser suit, silver Tiffany heart earrings, her fair hair sleekly groomed.

I would not allow myself to glower at her. I was better than that.

'Hi.' Liv Bowen slid into the seat beside me, immaculate in black, her hair folded into a complicated knot at the back of her head. She was a detective constable and a good one, and she was my friend. I felt myself relax.

'Hi, yourself.'

'You look knackered. What time did you leave the scene?'

'Getting on for one.' And then I'd gone back to my empty flat. I hadn't gone to bed straight away. I'd stopped for long enough to eat a bowl of cereal while I watched the news headlines. That already represented something like a victory. One: I had bought cereal. Two: I owned milk that hadn't gone off. Three: I'd remembered to eat them. I sensed that Liv would be underwhelmed, so I didn't bother to tell her about it. She lived in domestic harmony with her girlfriend in a pretty little house near Guildford and she had long since despaired of my sketchy home life. I also didn't tell her how I'd wandered through my flat looking at all the tidy rooms where nothing had moved since the cleaner left two days before. The tracks of the vacuum cleaner were still visible in the carpet. You spent a few hours judging someone else for how they lived and it gave you perspective on your own life, whether you wanted it or not.

The investigation had been on the news, but the details remained under wraps. The media only knew it was a murder investigation. The report was heavy on footage of police officers searching the area in the rain, lifting drain covers, poking bushes with sticks. I had been on screen for a split second. The camera had lingered on Georgia's fair hair.

I could get to like working with Georgia if she took some of the unwanted attention off me.

'How did you get on?' I asked Liv.

'Bits and pieces. Background stuff.' She shrugged. 'Nothing you could call an obvious motive to kill Kate Emery.'

'That's a shame.'

'I thought so.'

Derwent took the seat in front of me with a sigh. He barely nodded hello, which didn't surprise me. He wasn't a morning person.

He wasn't an afternoon or evening person either.

'Right.' Una Burt marched in and put her folder down on the desk. 'We're here to talk about Kate Emery. She's a forty-two-year-old mother of one, who lived at Valerian Road in Putney with her daughter, Chloe Emery. Chloe is eighteen. She was staying with her father and his family for the last few days. She left London on Wednesday and returned yesterday afternoon. Five days.' She looked around the room meaningfully. 'When Chloe left, everything was normal. When she returned, the house was covered in blood and her mother was gone. We need to know what happened to Kate Emery in those five days, and we need to know where she is now. Who wants to start?'

'I can fill in some of her background,' Liv volunteered.

'Go ahead.'

'Kate Emery has lived at that address for twelve years. She moved there after her divorce from Brian Emery, Chloe's father. She had custody of Chloe, who went to the local state schools.'

'Mainstream education?' Burt checked.

'Yes, although with support. Chloe has some educational disabilities,' Liv explained to the rest of the room. 'Kate was a stay-at-home mother for the majority of the last twelve years. She started her own business four years ago. It's called Novo Gaudio Imports. She was importing traditional herbal supplements for childless couples to boost their fertility.'

'Did she have a medical background?' Burt asked.

'She was a nurse before her marriage. She'd let her registration lapse so she was no longer allowed to practise. The imports were classified as dietary supplements rather than medical ones so she was able to supply them legally.'

'And did they work?' Burt asked.

'Lots of grateful customers left feedback on her website. I don't know how many of them were real,' Liv said. 'Many of them seemed very similar in tone, but then there probably isn't that much to say about getting pregnant. At least, there are probably lots of things to say about it, but not on a website selling fertility drugs.'

I made a note of it all the same. *Unsatisfied customer?* I was still at the stage of being grateful every month for the definitive proof that I wasn't pregnant, but I could understand something of the terrible hunger for a child. I'd seen it in others and I feared it. There wasn't much I could do about it when I was single and likely to remain so.

60

'How was the business doing?' The question came from Colin Vale. I could see he was straining to get at the papers, to scrutinise the accounts. I might have felt guilty that he always got landed with every boring, repetitive task involving hours of paperwork or scouring CCTV, but it made him happy.

'I can't say for sure because I don't have this year's accounts and the computer guys haven't analysed her PC yet,' Liv said. 'I have the impression it wasn't doing as well as she'd hoped. She had a lot of stock in her house. Her initial sales were good but they had tapered off over time – the profits for last year are a long way down on the previous year. I looked up the company name and found a pretty damning thread on an infertility message board – Don't use these, they're rubbish, waste of money, that kind of thing. There were multiple users complaining about the lack of results and quite a lot of responses were from people saying they wouldn't try them as a result. Kate actually posted a message asking for the customers to apply to her for a refund, but she said she would only pay up if the thread was deleted. That did not go down well at all, as you can imagine. Then there were a few messages in defence of the Novo Gaudio products. Again, they read very much like the positive comments from the website and the users were pretty sceptical about them. The accounts have all been suspended for "abuse of the website's terms and conditions".' Liv looked up and smiled. 'That means they were fakes. Sock puppets, they call them. Kate got caught out lying about her products.'

'So she was struggling to make ends meet,' Burt said.

'Well, no. Not really. Her current account was in credit. She had a small savings account – I think she invested a lot in the business but there was a tiny bit of cash left over.' Liv leafed through the documents in front of her. 'She was getting something like three grand every month from a personal bank account. I haven't traced it back yet but that could be Chloe's dad.'

'Chloe's eighteen,' I said. 'Would he still have been paying to support her?'

'Worth asking.' Burt nodded to me. 'Get the address from me after the briefing. You can talk to him.'

I nodded. 'I was going to ask if I could. Chloe came home early from her visit and I'd like to know why. She wouldn't tell me.'

'Or couldn't,' Georgia said. 'She seemed quite intimidated.'

Intimidated? I knew exactly what Georgia was implying and so did the rest of the room. She didn't look in my direction, and it took a practised back-stabber to slide the knife in without checking for a reaction.

'I think it's far more likely she was in shock,' Una Burt said, coming to my rescue, much to my surprise. 'Maeve is only ever intimidating when she means to be.'

'How was Kate paying the mortgage?' Pete Belcott asked. I didn't like Belcott but I recognised that he was a good police officer when he could be bothered and on this occasion he'd asked precisely the right question.

'She wasn't paying a mortgage,' Liv said. 'I haven't found any payments to a bank or mortgage company. Which is why I'd say she wasn't in desperate need of cash. She could easily have borrowed against the value of the house, even to shore up her business.'

'Did she have any other payments into her current account?' I asked.

'Nothing significant. Refunds for things she bought and returned. A transfer from the savings account, for a few hundred pounds.' Liv shrugged. 'What were you looking for?'

'Another source of income. One of the neighbours mentioned that she had a lot of gentlemen callers when her daughter was away. I was wondering if it was professional or strictly amateur.'

'If she was on the game she might have been cash only. A lot of them are. They're not the kind of people who file detailed tax returns.' Belcott looked around the room. 'I mean, that's what I hear.'

Chris Pettifer snorted at that, but it was a pale imitation of his usual mockery. He'd aged ten years in the last few months. He hadn't been the same since we'd lost a team member. Maybe he blamed himself.

I knew he blamed me.

'We didn't find much cash when we searched the house,' Derwent said. 'No safe. Nothing in the teapot, even.'

Burt's attention swung around to Derwent, and it was like seeing an artillery piece wheeling into position. 'Yes, tell us about what you found out.'

Derwent cleared his throat. 'Um. We searched the property—'

Burt interrupted. 'Who's "we"?'

'Me and Kerrigan.'

'What about the dog?'

'Oh, yeah. That was before. It didn't find much, to be honest with you.'

I resisted the urge to kick the back of his chair. *Get it together. You're making both of us look bad.*

As if he'd heard me, he sat up straighter. 'If you have a map of the area, I can show everyone the route the dog picked out.'

Of course Una Burt had a map of the area – a satellite photograph of it, in fact, and it was on her laptop so it could be projected on the wall behind her. Derwent got out of his chair and sloped up to the front of the room, the picture of a schoolboy who hasn't done his homework properly. As he'd done the previous evening, he described where the dog had alerted and why it was possibly significant.

'What do we know about the owner of this property?' Una Burt tapped the house three gardens over.

'He's a pensioner. His name is Harold Lowe and he's been in a nursing home for a few months according to the neighbour. I don't know of any connection between him and Kate Emery.'

'Is the house obviously unoccupied?'

'Yes,' Derwent said slowly, thinking about it. 'But the house is in pretty good condition and the garden is fairly neat. The neighbour I spoke to still cuts the grass for him and trims the hedges. He has a key to the gate but it's not a very secure lock.'

'Any CCTV nearby?'

'Not that I saw. It's a nice residential road. No one that I spoke to saw anything out of the ordinary but I'd like to go back there and try again when we get a better idea of when all of this took place. It's hard to pin people down when you're asking about a five-day period.'

'We can narrow that down a bit,' I said from the back of the room. 'The last sighting of Kate Emery that I've heard about was Oliver Norris, the neighbour who was with Chloe when she discovered the crime scene. He told me he saw her on Friday evening. The only other sighting I heard about was Norris's wife, and she saw Kate on Wednesday night.'

There was a ripple of interest around the room. Norris was just a little too involved to be believed without question.

'Did anyone else see her on Friday?' Burt asked.

'Not as far as I know.' I waited but there was nothing from the front of the room. 'Georgia, did you find any neighbours who remembered seeing Kate?'

'Oh – no. No, I didn't. They couldn't remember. No one noticed anything strange.' It sounded weak and she knew it. 'I didn't really get to talk to that many people. DS Kerrigan sent me home.'

'It was getting late.' *I was doing you a favour, you stupid bint.* 'We'll go out again today and see if we can get any corroboration of Norris's story.'

'All right. I don't want to assume anything at this stage.'

64

Burt frowned. 'I'm not sure how Friday fits in with what we know about the cat. But then, I don't know how much the cat . . . er . . .'

'Shits?' Derwent suggested, sitting down again.

'Quite.'

'The other thing we found that might help us narrow down when she disappeared,' I said hastily, 'was a receipt in the kitchen bin. Someone went shopping on Thursday and bought a lot of food.'

'A week's worth for a normal person,' Derwent said with a glint in his eye. I ignored him.

'It was all put away but not eaten. There were no wrappers in the bin – nothing to say she'd used anything she bought.'

'That'll be a time-stamped receipt,' Colin Vale said happily. 'I can check the CCTV from the supermarket. Make sure it really was her who went shopping. See if she was alone. That kind of thing.'

'Good idea. We're getting a list of transactions from her bank, aren't we? Try and find her on the CCTV in every shop that would have it. I want to see her and I want to see if anyone was with her, or following her,' Burt said. 'I want to know if she looked tense or if she was the same as ever. I want to know if there was anything strange about the last twenty-four hours before she disappeared.'

'Did you find anything else in the house?' Colin Vale asked. 'A passport? Bank cards?'

'We found her passport and her wallet,' I said. It had been in the kitchen, on top of the microwave, complete with her bank cards and gym membership and supermarket loyalty cards. 'No mobile phone, though we've asked her service provider to let us know if it's in use. No keys.'

'You'd want the keys,' Derwent observed, 'so you could shut the front door without making a big noise and drawing attention to yourself. If you'd killed her, I mean.'

'The more I hear the more I think we're right to treat it as murder,' Una Burt said gravely. 'What else did you find that might be of interest?'

'A bag of dirty clothes,' I said.

'I know Kerrigan's not exactly domesticated, but I didn't think she'd get excited about laundry.' It was a whisper, but a loud one, and it came from Pete Belcott.

'It wasn't laundry.' It was Belcott's habit to be rude to me but I absolutely refused to let him ruffle my feathers, especially when I was senior to him now. I described where I'd found the clothes and the condition they had been in. Una Burt's eyebrows were raised.

'Sexual assault?'

'Potentially. I think we have to be careful about it, though. She might have kept them as a souvenir of a particularly – er – passionate encounter.' I felt the heat rise in my cheeks as everyone in the room turned to look at me, with the exception of Derwent. 'I mean, I wouldn't. But you never know.'

'Indeed.' Burt made a note. 'But it's of interest.'

'Even if she was raped,' Chris Pettifer said, 'it doesn't get us all that much closer to a killer, does it? If she killed him, that would be something else.'

Burt checked her watch. 'I'm waiting to hear back from the forensic team about the blood. Keep working on the basis that Kate is the victim for the time being. We need motives and suspects and we're already a few days behind the killer. I can't waste any more time.'

'That's the thing,' I said. 'There's no obvious reason for anyone to want to kill her. Everything we've found out so far points to her being a person who minded her own business, who worked hard, who was determined but slightly unscrupulous and maybe a little unwise, but it doesn't add up to a motive.'

'There's the ex-husband,' Derwent said.

'Yes, but why kill her now? They divorced over a decade ago. It doesn't make sense.'

'She was a bit lively in her personal life,' Georgia Shaw said.

'According to one neighbour,' I pointed out. 'But she was attractive. Maybe she was playing two men off against one another and it went wrong. Maybe she made the wrong person jealous.'

Una Burt nodded. 'I'll mention it when I do the press conference later. If I appeal for her boyfriends and associates to come forward in confidence, we might get a better picture of what was happening in her life. What do we know about local suspects? Anyone of interest?'

'I checked with the local coppers,' Belcott said. 'It's a quiet area. They couldn't think of a similar incident locally in the past five years.'

'Oliver Norris told me we should look at a guy called William Turner.' I said it quietly, knowing Belcott would take it as a criticism of his work, and maybe it was. Fairness made me add, 'I don't think he can be relevant, but Norris said he lives nearby and knows Chloe. He was arrested for attempted murder a few years ago but never charged.'

'Why not?' Burt asked.

'Insufficient evidence, I think. I'll look it up and speak to the SIO before I go back to Putney.'

'You should certainly speak to him. Get some idea of what he's like. I don't want to ignore anything at this stage.'

Speak to SIO I wrote in my notebook, so Burt could feel reassured that I was listening to her.

'So where does this leave us?' Burt looked around the room.

'I'd like to know more about Oliver Norris,' I said. 'He's a bit too helpful and he keeps coming up with important information at the precise moment we need it.'

'And you said he was paranoid about explaining why his fingerprints might be all over Kate Emery's bedroom,' Derwent said. 'Nothing suspicious about that, is there?'

'He's ultra-religious, though.'

'So? Repressed.'

'Not necessarily,' Chris Pettifer said.

'But possibly,' I said. 'I didn't like him.'

'Whoever did this was at ease in the property,' Derwent said. 'They knew where to find drain cleaner. They knew where they could shower off the blood. They knew where to take a body so they could dispose of it without being seen, and they were strong enough to handle a body. This wasn't a stranger who blundered in off the street. This was someone with a plan and they executed it pretty perfectly.'

I nodded. 'As far as I can see, only one thing went wrong for them. If Chloe hadn't come back early, no one would even know yet that Kate Emery was gone.'

7

I was on my own when I arrived at William Turner's address, and glad to be. Georgia had gone to collect CCTV footage from the local shops and show Kate Emery's picture around, trying to reconstruct Kate's movements before the attack. She had gone with bad grace.

'It feels like admin.'

'That's exactly what it is.'

'It's not going to help us find who killed her.'

'You don't know that.'

'But I want to see William Turner.'

'Do you? Because I don't.' I picked up my phone. 'It's going to be more of a waste of time than looking for CCTV, I promise you.'

'He sounds interesting. Oliver Norris thinks he's the devil incarnate.'

'I wouldn't put too much faith in anything Norris said to us.' I started dialling the number I'd found for the SIO in the Turner case.

'Then we should talk to him again.'

'About what? The weather?' I leaned back. 'The next time we talk to Norris, we need to know exactly what happened to Kate Emery so we can find out how his version differs from the truth. At the moment, all I can say to him is that I don't believe him. I've got nothing to throw at him. When the forensics come back, we'll see if there's anything to make him feel uneasy, but as things stand we have to let him go about his business. And you should do the same.'

She had gone, but she hadn't liked it. I had other things to worry about, like William Turner. I thought about him on the drive to Putney, and the incident that had earned him his reputation. The SIO had remembered the case well. It wasn't the kind you forgot.

I found a parking space on the other side of the street from Turner's house and walked across. I would have liked a second to collect my thoughts but there was a young man standing in the doorway, smoking a tiny, pungent roll-up. He watched me stop at his front gate, and his expression was wary under a veneer of insolence. He was mixed race and had the kind of good looks that suited a sullen expression: high cheekbones, a full mouth, a face saved from being too feminine by a square jaw and strong, dark eyebrows. What was it Oliver Norris had said? Good looking and he knows it? He had close-cropped hair that showed off the shape of his head, and skin like honey. He wasn't big – slight was the word that came to mind – but he was wiry and I thought he was probably stronger than he seemed. He wore a grey V-necked T-shirt with jeans that were skin-tight and ripped at the knee. His feet were bare.

'William Turner?'

He took a long drag before he replied in a slow, husky drawl that I thought he'd probably practised. 'That depends. Who's asking?'

I held up my warrant card and he stepped down from the doorway to inspect it, moving with feline grace.

'Maeve Kerrigan,' he read.

'Detective Sergeant Maeve Kerrigan,' I said. 'I'm part of the team investigating what happened up the road.'

'Yeah, what did happen? I saw all the excitement. Everyone coming and going. Very intriguing. Nothing much ever happens here.' He flicked the butt of his cigarette away then folded his arms across his chest, pushing his biceps with his fists to make himself look bigger.

'Do you know the residents of number twenty-seven?'

'A little. I know what they look like.' He had stepped back a bit and found some high ground on a loose brick that was by the gate so he could stare into my eyes. His irises were light brown, almost gold, like a lion. Like a predator. The hairs stood up on the back of my neck. Humans were still animals when all was said and done.

'But to speak to?'

'No. You know what London is like. No one knows their neighbours.'

'Depends on the area.'

'And the neighbours.' He laughed softly. 'No one wants to know us so we don't know them. That's why you're here, isn't it? Because someone told you to come and talk to me. Because I'm the local scum so if something's happened in the street it must have been me.'

'It's my job to talk to potential witnesses. You live in this street and I'm told you spend a lot of time out here watching people come and go.'

'You're told that.' A slow smile spread across his face. One of his front teeth was crooked, overlapping the other by a couple of millimetres, and it was strangely charming. 'Let me guess. Who could have told you? So many suspects. This is like doing your job, isn't it? I can see why you like it. It could have been Narinder across the way, but I think she likes to see me out here. She's always watching.' He lifted a hand and waved. I turned in time to see a curtain fall back into place in the house opposite. 'It could have been the bitch next door but she was away for the weekend. Anyway, she's too snobby to talk about me. She likes to pretend we don't exist. So who

71

hates the fact that I dare to show my face in public?' Turner stroked his chin, pretending to ponder it. He had a few days' worth of stubble but it was sparse and fine. 'Who doesn't like me talking to his daughter?'

'Mr Turner—'

'Got it, haven't I?' He leaned out so he could look down the street, towards Oliver Norris's house. 'I've tried to explain it to him. It's not me making the running. Bethany's the one who talks to me. It's not as if I'm all that keen on hanging around with a fifteen-year-old. That's the kind of thing that could get me in trouble.' He took a tin out of his back pocket and set it on top of the gatepost. The sweet raw smell of tobacco floated out of it when he popped it open and picked out a cigarette paper. His hands were shaking very slightly as he made the roll-up. It was thin, with no filter, and the back of my throat ached at the thought of smoking it.

'Mr Turner, I do need to talk to you. I wonder if we could go inside.'

'We could go inside.' He ran his tongue slowly along the edge of the paper to glue it together. 'But you'll have to put up with my mother if you do that. There's a reason why I spend a lot of time out here and if you go in there you'll find out what it is.'

'I can cope.'

'I'm not sure I can.' He lit the cigarette and drew on it, coughing as he exhaled. 'What a terrible rollie. It's an embarrassment. I usually do much better than that.'

'It's bad for you, you know.'

'No shit, Sherlock.' He picked a shred of tobacco off his lower lip. 'I like to live dangerously.'

'I spoke to DCI Gordon,' I said softly.

Turner went very still. 'That was quick.'

'I'm investigating a serious incident.'

'You didn't say what it was.'

'No, I didn't.'

72

'Is it murder?' He pulled at his lower lip again, nervously this time.

'Why would you think that?'

'Because. Because of the fuss. Because of the guys in white suits going in and out. I didn't see a body bag.' He over-balanced and almost fell off the brick.

'There wasn't one.'

'So what happened?'

'We don't know yet.'

'You don't know?' His eyebrows went up, sky-high. 'Doesn't usually stop the cops from talking to the press, does it?'

'In your experience.'

'In my very unpleasant experience.' It was warm in the sunshine but I could see goosebumps on Turner's arms and he shivered. 'You're right. I don't want to talk about this out here. Come in.'

At his invitation, when he was good and ready. I recognised it for a power play and tried not to feel irritated. Derwent would have found some reason for saying no but I followed Turner to the door, where he stopped.

'Just so you know, my mum is upstairs and I'd like her to stay there.'

'I might need to speak to her.'

'No. No, you don't.' He swallowed. 'She won't be able to help you, anyway. She's not – she doesn't notice things. She doesn't go out. She doesn't look out the window. She doesn't even know anything's happened.'

'I still might need to speak to her.'

He bit his lip, then went into the house. It was cooler inside, the air still. A fly buzzed somewhere, the sound swinging from loud to soft and back again. There was an all-pervading smell of vinegar and lemon and the place was absolutely spotless.

'You need to take your shoes off,' he threw over his shoulder and padded into the sitting room. I did as I was told and followed him, blinking against the sunlight that streamed into the room. It was neatly furnished with a leather sofa and armchair, and a couple of small tables. What was mainly remarkable, though, was what I couldn't see when I looked around. No ornaments. No books. No cushions. No rugs on the wooden floor.

Turner coughed again, his chest heaving. The hollow at the base of his throat deepened as he fought for air. 'Sorry. Need my —'

He dug in his back pocket and pulled out an inhaler, handling it with the practised skill born of long usage. He turned away from me before he used it and I took the hint: this was private. I was intruding on a personal battle. I sat down, acutely aware of the wheezing, terrified in case it stopped. I knew, in theory, how to resuscitate someone, but that didn't mean I wanted to do it.

'Sorry,' he managed.

'It's all right. Take your time.'

'It happens now and then.' Five words and three breaths to say them. I winced and took my radio out of my bag, holding it on my knee in case I needed to call for help in a hurry, for him rather than me. Suddenly the room made sense to me: hard surfaces. Wipe-clean leather upholstery. No dust. Vinegar and lemon because someone used homemade cleaning products instead of mass-produced chemicals. Nothing left to chance.

He stood with his back to me, his shoulders hunched, his head hanging down. The wheezing lessened, the breaths coming more regularly. Between his shoulder blades, the fabric of his T-shirt had darkened where he'd sweated through it.

'Sorry about this,' he said for the third time.

'You don't need to apologise.' He was watching me out of the corner of his eye, I realised. There was something sly about it that put me on my guard; it was as if he was assessing the impact of the attack on me. 'What triggered that? Do you know?'

'I'm not very good at taking my medicine. I forget.'

Maybe you should try a bit harder, since it could actually kill you.

'Was that a particularly bad one?'

'Normal.' He leaned against the chimney breast and ran a hand over his head. 'Happens all the time. Anything can trigger it. Perfume. Chemicals. Dust. Change in temperature. I've got shit lungs.'

'All the more reason not to smoke.'

'That's what they say.'

'But you keep smoking.'

'I'd give up if I wanted to live.' His eyes were fixed on mine, hungry for a reaction. I shrugged.

'Most people do.'

'I thought you'd know by now I'm not like most people.'

I laughed. 'What are you, twenty? Twenty-one?'

'Twenty.' His voice was flat.

'I've never met a twenty-year-old who didn't think they were exceptional. You saying that tells me you're just like everybody else.'

'Hey,' he said, affronted.

'Hey yourself.' I leaned forward. 'Look, I appreciate the effort you're putting into this but you're not going to impress me or shock me or whatever it is you're trying to do. Drop the attitude and I'll make this as quick as I can.'

He dug his hands into his pockets and shrugged. 'OK.'

'I'm here because your name came up when we made enquiries with the neighbours. I am not accusing you of anything.'

Turner's mouth tightened but he stayed silent.

'I know you know Chloe Emery. How would you describe your relationship?'

'I only know her to speak to.'

'Have you ever visited her house?'

'I don't remember.'

'You don't remember,' I repeated.

'No, then.' The amber eyes flicked away from me, darting around the room for inspiration. 'When we were younger, maybe.'

I sat back in my chair. 'For someone who managed to avoid being charged with attempted murder, you're a terrible liar.'

The smile spread over his face. 'I wasn't charged with attempted murder because I didn't do it.'

'Remember, I've spoken to DCI Gordon.'

Turner sat down slowly on the arm of the sofa. 'What did he tell you?'

'Everything he found out about you and Ben Christie. Which wasn't much. Why wouldn't Ben give evidence against you, William?'

'Because I didn't do it.'

'The incident happened in an alley behind some shops. You were there and Ben Christie was there and Ben ended up with a stab wound in his stomach. It doesn't take a great leap of imagination to guess what happened.'

'You could guess, but you'd be wrong.' Turner's breathing was still a little fast but his eyes were bright; he was enjoying this.

'What about the text messages on his phone?'

'What about them?'

I opened my notebook to read out the exact words. '"u know wot u did" "Time 2 make it right" "u can't back out now" – what was that about?'

'I don't remember. Nothing much. Teenage shit. Maybe he spilled my drink or borrowed a quid and didn't pay it back.' He yawned. 'You know you're talking about something that happened four years ago. I can't be expected to recall all the details.'

'He was your friend and he almost died. Of course you remember it,' I snapped.

Turner lifted his hands and looked at them, turning them

over to examine the palms. 'I was covered in his blood. Did you know that?'

'I'm not surprised. He was very badly injured.'

'It was so hot, his blood. It got everywhere. Under my nails. On my shoes. I dream about it sometimes.' He looked up at me again. 'I saved his life. I called the ambulance.'

'You stabbed him.'

'Not me. I found him. I helped him.'

'You met him in the alley near your school and you stabbed him.'

'Did DCI Gordon tell you about the forensics?' Turner asked, his eyes intent. 'Did he tell you about the knife?'

'Yes. He did.'

'Whose knife was it?'

It was a kitchen knife, an ordinary one with a serrated blade, the kind you might use for cutting up vegetables. Mrs Christie had identified it as one from her house, and cried as she did so.

'It belonged to the Christies, but—'

'And whose fingerprints were on it?' Turner asked.

'Ben Christie's.'

'Not mine.'

'No. But there are ways of staging that.'

'I didn't have to. I never touched it. Did they find my DNA on it?'

'No.'

'I've read up on DNA. They can do amazing things these days, can't they? A skin cell or two, that's all they need to identify someone beyond doubt. And every contact leaves a trace.'

Edmond Locard's maxim. It was the basic principle of all forensic investigation – that criminals left traces of themselves at crime scenes and crime scenes left traces on the criminals themselves. I wasn't used to having a suspect quote it at me.

'So they say. But—'

'There was no trace of me on the knife. I never touched it. I never held it. I didn't stab him.'

'You said yourself you were covered in his blood.'

'That was after he stabbed himself,' Turner said dismissively. 'That proves nothing.'

'Why would he stab himself?'

'You need to ask him that.'

DCI Gordon had done precisely that, over and over again. Christie had refused to say. All he had mumbled, over and over again, was that it wasn't anything to do with William Turner, and no one had been able to prove him wrong.

'You mean you don't know? You were there.' Along with two other teenagers who swore they'd seen Turner helping Christie, calling an ambulance on his phone, cradling his friend and comforting him.

'I was too late to stop him. I tried. I saved his life. A suicide is a terrible thing.'

'Says the man who doesn't care if he lives or dies.'

'Which reminds me.' He took out his tin of tobacco again, opening it on his knee this time. 'Almost time for another coffin nail.'

'Will-i-am. I wish you wouldn't call them that.' The voice came from behind me and I jumped; I hadn't heard anyone approach. A thin, withered woman stood in the doorway holding a cloth with gloved hands.

'Mrs Turner?' I stood up. 'I'm DS Maeve Kerrigan. I'm here to ask some questions about what happened up the road.'

'I don't know anything.' Her eyes were fixed on her son who was concentrating on his cigarette. 'Don't do that in here, William. You'll drop bits of it everywhere.'

'Then you can sweep them up.' He winked at me. 'Got to give her a reason to live, don't I?'

Mrs Turner sighed. 'You're terrible.'

'You love it.'

She squeezed the cloth in her hands, still watching him. It

was as if I didn't exist. I could see what William had meant when he said she didn't notice anything that happened outside their home. DCI Gordon had been forthright about her. 'She can't imagine her boy doing anything wrong. She thought I was a bully and a liar. Little Willy never did anything to hurt anyone.' A snort. In his opinion, Mr Turner had been fully justified in doing a runner before William was born. 'She had money because her parents were very well off – they bought the house, for instance – but money isn't everything, is it?'

I had agreed that no, it was not and Gordon had laughed. 'It helps though.'

'Sometimes.'

'Well, Turner didn't stick around to see his son. Maybe the boy would have turned out better if he'd been around. He had too much attention, that was the problem. He thought he was the centre of the universe because, for his mum, he is.'

'Do you know Kate Emery, Mrs Turner?' I asked.

'Who?'

'The lady who lives at number twenty-seven. She has a daughter, Chloe, who's almost the same age as William.'

'Oh. I know her a bit. Not properly.' She was folding the cloth over and over, mindlessly. 'She used to be a nurse.'

'Once upon a time.'

'She helped me with William once, when he was younger. He had a bad attack and I ran out into the street in a panic. She helped me before the ambulance came. She was nice then. But I don't know her.' She blinked. Her eyelids and the end of her nose were pink and looked raw, as if she'd been crying. She had none of her son's looks, and I couldn't imagine that she'd ever been attractive. Mr Turner had to have been a stunner.

'You still haven't said what happened,' William Turner said. 'Is Chloe OK?'

'Physically.'

79

'So that leaves her mum.' A muscle tightened in his jaw. 'Let me guess. She was stabbed.'

'Why would you say that?'

'Because you're asking me about something that happened four years ago, that was thoroughly investigated at the time, as if it's suddenly important.'

'Well, it might be.' I stood up. 'I can't tell you what happened at number twenty-seven yet. At the moment we're still investigating. But I can tell you that we'll need a sample of your DNA and your fingerprints.' And while they were at it, I was going to apply for a warrant to search his house.

'Am I a suspect?'

'You said yourself you couldn't remember if you'd been in the house. We need to rule you out.' *Or in.* 'That's why we need your prints and your DNA.'

Turner nodded. 'Then come back and get them. I have nothing to hide.'

'We'll see,' I said, and left.

8

I stepped out of the house with a profound feeling of relief that evaporated instantly. Derwent was leaning against the bonnet of my car, his legs crossed at the ankle, his hands in his pockets.

'What are you doing here?' I demanded.

'Waiting for you.'

'For any particular reason? Or because you missed me?'

'Funny.' His mood was like a black cloud hanging in the air around him. 'I recognised the car. Who were you talking to?'

I came closer so I could speak more quietly. 'William Turner. And his mother.'

'And did he ping your freak-o-meter?'

'I'm not sure. He was trying hard to impress me, so there was a lot of showing off.'

'I bet he was,' Derwent said softly. 'How old is he?'

'Twenty.'

'And he still lives at home.'

'He has bad asthma. I doubt it would be safe for him to live alone. Plus, I imagine he's on benefits. He doesn't work.'

'What a prize.'

'You wouldn't have liked him.' *But then you don't like anyone.* I tried again. 'Why are you waiting for me?'

'Harold Lowe has given us permission to look around his house.' Derwent held up a set of keys and shook them at me. His expression, if anything, had darkened.

'I don't see how that's a bad thing.'

'He said that he knew Kate Emery well. She used to bring him cakes, cook him meals, that kind of thing.' Derwent's mouth tightened. 'Guess how she used to come round?'

My spirits sank. 'Through the back garden?'

'Got it in one. And get this: she used to use it as a shortcut to get to the shops. She had a key to the side gate and everything.' He stood up and stretched. 'So what the dog told us doesn't mean much, does it? Back to square one. No body, no suspects and no ideas.'

'Still no sign of the body.'

'They're looking. They've been out on the river, checking the places the bodies usually wash up. But if she went in the water, she'll be long gone. All that rain.'

I shuddered, thinking of the cold grey waters of the Thames. Countless bodies had disappeared into it, never to resurface. 'Risky, throwing a body into the water, though. There's always someone watching in a city like this.'

'You'd think so.' Derwent yawned. 'She's probably in an outhouse somewhere, or a ditch.'

'Or some leafy bit of countryside where she won't be found for a year or two.'

'By a dog walker who will never get over the shock of Rex digging up an actual human bone to chew.' Derwent grinned. 'That's one reason why I'm never getting a dog. It's not as if I need more corpses in my life.'

'This one would be nice to find.' I was looking at Kate Emery's house where there was a uniformed officer standing guard. Flapping tape still cordoned off the house. 'Where would you dump a body if you killed someone here?'

'I wouldn't. I'd leave it where it is. Move a body and you contaminate your car or van. You transfer trace evidence to the body and the car, and yourself. Your risk of being discovered goes up massively. Unless you've got an amazing place to hide it, the body will be found eventually. There's no good reason to take the body away.'

'Unless you know you left evidence of yourself on the body and you're not sure you can clean it up.'

'What do you mean by that?'

'If Kate was raped before she died. Or after.' I said it calmly, professionally, not allowing myself to imagine her pain, her fear, the moment when she realised she was going to die.

Derwent nodded. 'There is that. She put up a hell of a fight, by the looks of things.'

'But it wasn't enough.'

'Not this time.' He turned away abruptly and I wondered if he was thinking about Melissa, who had been attacked over and over again by her handsome husband. Some cases were too close to home, for both of us.

We could have taken the shortcut to Harold Lowe's house – through the bloody hallway at number 27, across the garden, through the gate and down the alley – but Derwent wanted to take the long way round, by road, in my car, which would take a couple of minutes. It seemed like unnecessary hassle to me but I went along with it. The only way to survive working with Derwent was to pick your battles.

'Is it the house?' I asked.

'What?'

'Kate Emery's house. Does it bother you? The blood?'

'Nah.' He leaned back in the passenger seat, folded his arms and closed his eyes. 'Drive slower.'

'Seriously? You usually complain about how slowly I drive.'

'I'm tired.'

'Well, it's not naptime.'

His answer was a snore. I hit the brakes a bit harder than

I needed to at the next junction and he startled awake, his hands flying up.

'What?'

'Why are you sleeping?'

'Because I'm knackered.' He did look tired, I thought, with shadows under his eyes that weren't usually there. 'Thomas hasn't been sleeping well.'

'He has to get used to the new house.'

'It's not that. He's been having nightmares. Night terrors, actually.'

'What's the difference?'

'It's like sleepwalking except he's in bed. Screaming.' He shivered. 'It's fucking creepy. He can be sitting there with his eyes open, shouting at the top of his voice about monsters and people chasing him, and there's nothing you can do to comfort him. He doesn't even know you're there.'

'What does Melissa think?'

'She wants to take him to see a sleep specialist.' He sighed. 'I think she's overreacting but I can't say that, can I? He's not my kid. Google says it's normal at Thomas's age.'

I pulled up outside Lowe's house, on the road. The high beech hedge screened the front of the house completely from anyone walking past. 'What did you say he screams about?' Monsters?'

'Monsters, baddies, someone watching him, you name it. I put the light on to show him there's no one there but he's not conscious really, so he doesn't register it. You have to wait for him to calm down by himself and go back to sleep and it takes hours.' He yawned so widely I heard his jaw crack. 'It's happening two or three times a night. And in the morning he doesn't remember any of it.'

'Maybe moving house will sort it out.'

'Maybe. The flat was too small for the three of us. That didn't help. But Melissa thinks it might make it worse. He's had a lot of disruption in the past year.'

'Yeah, but with a happy ending. He got away from his dad, didn't he?' Mark Pell had beaten and intimidated his wife until she took Thomas and ran away to London, to what should have been a safe place. It wasn't her fault that it had turned out to be the opposite.

Derwent nodded soberly. 'That could be part of the trouble, though. He must miss his dad. Melissa never let him see any of the violence. He didn't know about her injuries. As far as he's concerned, his mummy and daddy loved each other very much and then Mummy took him away. Daddy disappeared out of his life from one day to the next.'

'But you're there.'

'It's not the same.'

'Isn't it? He adores you, you know that.'

Derwent put a hand up to his eyes, rubbing at them with his forefinger and thumb. 'Fuck's sake. I'm not crying. My eyes are watering because I'm tired.'

'Yeah, of course. I think we drove past someone chopping onions, actually. That's probably it.'

'Don't take the piss,' he mumbled.

'Wouldn't dream of it.'

'I want to look after him. That's all. And I don't know how to make it better for him.'

'It's a phase.'

Derwent squinted at me. 'What do you know about it?'

'That's what my brother says about every annoying thing his kids do. Everything's a phase. In a month's time he'll be sleeping beautifully and you'll have something else to worry about.'

He thought about it. 'Thanks, mate.'

'Any time.' I got out of the car and looked up and down Constantine Avenue. The houses were detached, set back from the road and there were no pedestrians. It was quiet, and private. 'This is going to be rubbish for witnesses.'

'Come on.' Derwent led the way through the gate and

85

paused to scan the gravel in front of the house. 'What do you think? Tyre marks?'

'None to speak of.' I crouched down, trying to see. 'Nope. There isn't enough gravel for that.'

'Typical.' He looked up at the house. It was a 1930s house with ugly aluminium-framed windows that had probably been put in four decades after the house was built. It had a general air of being unoccupied. The curtains were drawn in every window and weeds had sprouted through cracks in the steps. Some rubbish had blown in from the street and tangled in the undergrowth. 'You'd know it was empty, wouldn't you.'

'Empty or that it belonged to someone elderly.' I followed him through the front door, working my hands into my gloves as a precaution but also because I really didn't want to touch anything. I stepped over the slithery pile of post and junk mail on the doormat, wrinkling my nose. 'It stinks in here.'

'Not as much as the nursing home did.' Derwent looked back at me. 'When I get old, I'm going to Switzerland to end it all. No way do I want to drag out my days staring at the walls surrounded by a load of drooling vegetables.'

'It can't have been that bad.'

'Whatever you're imagining, it was worse.' He strode into the kitchen, snapping with energy now that we were working again, the hunter's instinct overriding fatigue. I tried and failed to visualise him as an old man. Impossible to think of him being calm, sitting quietly, staring at the walls. He'd burn the place down first.

The living room curtains were faded and worn, the material grubby on the edges where Harold Lowe had pulled them closed night after night. I pushed one back to let some more light in, revealing a room full of the kind of furniture my grandparents liked: dark mahogany tables that were cloudy with dust, over-stuffed armchairs with heavily textured uphol-stery, a wood-framed sofa that was so far out of fashion it had come back in. Dust and fibres floated in the light that slanted in, as thick as mist, and I thought of William Turner's antiseptic home. I believed he had asthma – no one could have faked the attack he had experienced in front of me – but clean homes made me suspicious, on the whole. A lot of people became surprisingly house-proud when they had something to hide.

Derwent poked his head in. 'Anything strange?'

'Nope.'

'Upstairs, then.'

'Does Harold have any family?'

'No. He's on his own.' Derwent's mouth thinned. 'Poor old bugger. He was so pleased someone had come to see him. The house is going to be sold to pay for his nursing home. God knows what they're charging for it.'

'So what happens to all of this stuff?'

'No idea. Charity? He doesn't want to come home, he says. I think he was lonely here.'

'Well, that's something, isn't it? Maybe if you're ninety-odd and you don't want to live on your own any more you don't mind being in a home.'

'Maybe.' Derwent didn't sound convinced.

I went up the stairs first and glanced into the first bedroom: Harold's own, the bed stripped, the mattress covered in overlapping stains. The room next door was a study, followed by a bathroom and a separate lavatory. The air was stale, the rooms dusty and worn out, the smell of pine still surprisingly strong in the bathroom. There was something tragic about the things he'd left behind – a brush with yellowing bristles, a cracked bar of soap, a face cloth hanging stiffly at an angle over the edge of the sink where he'd left it to dry. Kate Emery's house had been the same. Life, stopped.

'Whoever buys this place is going to have to gut it,' Derwent said. 'Keep the walls and start again with the rest.'

I was about to answer him as I pushed open the door to

the last room at the back of the house, but the words evaporated. I stood for a second, my brain trying to work out
what was bothering me. It *smelled* wrong, that was it. The
room smelled, but not of stale air and old clothes like the rest
of the house. And I knew better than to override the feeling
that something wasn't right.

'What is it?' Derwent was right behind me, jostling me,
trying to see.

'Wait.' I put a hand up. 'Someone's been in here.'

The curtains were drawn at the window but there was a
gap that let some light into the room. It was a bedroom, the
bed covered in a pink candlewick bedspread, the cream carpet
worn and thin underfoot. I edged forward and crouched to
look under the bed. There was a knotted condom on the
carpet, curled up, forgotten. That was the smell I'd caught.

'This should be good for DNA.' I straightened up. 'I'm not
touching it. I'll let the SOCOs recover it.'

Derwent drew back the bedspread carefully. There was a
pale green sheet on the bed with a ghostly white mark in the
exact centre.

'I don't think Harold has been banging his brains out in
here,' he said. 'So the question is, who has?'

'More than one couple.'

'What do you mean?'

I pointed. 'Semen stain. On the floor, we have a condom.
When the semen is inside the condom, it's not generally all
over the bed.'

Derwent grinned. 'In your experience.'

'Yes. I know what I'm talking about.'

The grin widened. 'Is that so?'

'I don't want to shock you, but I have had sex. A few times,
actually.'

Derwent was inspecting the rest of the room. 'Not for a
while.'

'What makes you think that?'

88

'I know.'

'You are so creepy. Of course you don't *know*.'

'You haven't.' He glanced at me. 'But when you do, I'll know.'

'No, you won't.'

A slow, emphatic nod.

'You're disgusting.'

'It's like a sixth sense.' He tapped the side of his head. 'I see things.'

'I'm pretty sure sight is one of the basic five.'

He recovered with barely a flicker. 'Look, all I'm saying is, you can't hide that kind of thing from me. I know you too well. You're not getting any and you haven't been for a long, long time. So when you do, I'm going to notice the difference.'

'You're deluded. And perverted.'

'Just observant. Anyway, it could be one couple. Maybe they ran out of condoms and took a chance.'

'Kate had keys to this house. Who else did?'

Derwent shrugged. 'No one, as far as I know. The neighbour only has a key to the garden. Harold didn't mention anyone else.'

'There was no sign of anyone breaking in. We have to assume Kate was using the house or letting someone else use it.'

'Or someone stole her keys.'

'Either way, we need to know who was here. And why they were using this room.' I nudged the curtain back, noticing a fragile curl of ash that ghosted along the sill, and a sticky mark where something round had rested. 'That's a hell of a good view of Kate's house. Maybe that's why they chose this room.'

'Or it's a complete coincidence. It can't be connected with her murder or they'd have done a better job of cleaning up. You'd have to be as thick as pigshit *and* you'd have to know nothing about criminal investigation to leave this place as it is without even attempting to get rid of the sheet, not to mention the rest.'

'Maybe they meant to. Maybe they didn't have time. Chloe came back early, remember? She wasn't supposed to be here until Tuesday. Maybe they thought they could come back and clear up at their leisure, but then there were police everywhere and they couldn't take the risk.' I looked around. 'Remember, if it wasn't for the dog leading us here, we probably wouldn't have known about the house. Kate's keys were gone, along with the keys for this place. There was nothing to send us over here. They probably thought they could leave this stuff here forever. They gambled and lost.'

'So this counts as us being lucky.' Derwent rubbed his forehead with the back of a gloved hand. 'Excuse me if I don't rush out and buy a lottery ticket.'

9

I left Derwent with Kev Cox and Una Burt, trying to justify why we'd trampled all over a house that was suddenly vital to the investigation. From the looks on their faces, ignorance was not going to be an adequate defence. Burt in particular had a wild look in her eyes that was as close to panic as I'd ever seen in her. She was presiding over a murder investigation with no body and no suspects, after all; it wasn't a reputation-maker. And through no real fault of our own, we'd lost an opportunity to watch and wait for the perpetrator to come to us. Whatever the forensic evidence said – assuming we hadn't compromised that too – there was nothing to compare to catching someone red-handed.

It wasn't only cowardice that made me slip away. I wanted to speak to Chloe Emery again, this time alone. I didn't think that Georgia had put her off the previous day – I doubted Chloe had even noticed she was in the room – but it couldn't hurt to try a more casual approach.

I rang the doorbell at number 32 and waited. It was Morgan Norris who came to the door, his expression forbidding. I thought for a moment that he wasn't going to let me in but then the scowl faded and he clapped a hand to his head.

91

'You're the police officer who was here yesterday. Sorry, I didn't recognise you. Your hair was . . . um . . . different.'

I let that go without acknowledgement. The difference humidity made to my hair could be measured in yards. 'I'm sorry to bother you. I wanted to speak to Chloe again.'

'Have you found anything?' He glanced up the stairs as he spoke, wary of being overheard.

'It's a routine follow-up. No news.'

'That's good, isn't it?' He fiddled with the chain on the back of the door, frowning at it as if it was important. 'There's hope.'

Hope could be far more destructive than grief. I didn't say that to him. I smiled instead.

'Is Chloe upstairs?'

'I believe so.' I started to move past him and he put his hand on my wrist. 'Wait. Eleanor wants a word first. She's in the kitchen.'

I was about to say no. He was holding on to me firmly, but not tightly, and his hand was very warm against the soft skin on the inside of my wrist. I objected on principle to being grabbed. If he could feel my pulse under his fingers he would know my heart was pounding.

But my reaction was nothing to do with Morgan Norris. I wasn't scared of him.

And I didn't want to miss out on a chance to speak to Eleanor Norris again just because I was offended by some uninvited manhandling.

Norris tilted his head to one side. He had dark eyelashes, several shades darker than his hair, and they made his eyes look lighter. It was attractive, and he knew it. 'Please.'

'All right.' I twisted my wrist out of his grasp but without drama. I knew he would never have touched a male DS and it annoyed me but there was nothing I could do about it.

'I want to apologise too,' he said quickly.

I had already started towards the kitchen. I stopped and looked back at him. 'For what?'

92

'Calling you names yesterday. It was a stupid joke and I was sorry as soon as I said it. We were all under a lot of strain.'

I genuinely couldn't think what he meant at first. 'Oh – when you said we were the filth, you mean?'

'Yeah. I'm not proud of it.'

'I've heard it before. I've heard worse.'

'You weren't at all like what I was expecting.'

I frowned. 'Expecting?'

'When they said a detective would come round.' He shoved his hands in his pockets, doing the awkward little boy act. 'I was expecting someone tougher. Older.'

'Great.' I managed to get a world of I-don't-care into my voice. 'Shall we get on with this?'

'Yes, of course. Sorry.' He looked upset, sincerely so, and I revised my impression of him: maybe it hadn't been an act after all. Maybe he genuinely did feel awkward about what he'd said.

But I couldn't quite believe he was unsure of himself when he'd had the confidence to take hold of me. My wrist ached. That was psychosomatic. It was the memory of having to fight for my life that was flooding my body with adrenalin, not real, actual pain. It wasn't fear of where I was or what I was doing. It was a useless leftover, learned behaviour from experiences I wanted to leave far behind me. That wasn't who I was any more.

I squared my detective sergeant shoulders and lifted my chin and walked into the kitchen as if every step took me further away from the past. *The past can't hurt me any more.*

I knew it was a lie, but it was a comfort all the same.

Eleanor Norris had her back to me. She was leaning over the kitchen table, reading a newspaper. 'Who was it?'

'DS Maeve Kerrigan,' I said. 'We met yesterday.'

She actually jumped at the sound of my voice, whirling

around with one hand to her throat, her eyes wide. Her gaze tracked over my shoulder to where Morgan Norris stood.

'Calm down, Eleanor. It's just a routine visit. She's not even here to see you.' There was an undercurrent of irritation in his voice. Something about Eleanor invited it: the pink-rimmed eyes, the small voice, the ostentatious meekness.

'You gave me a fright. I didn't hear two sets of footsteps, that's all.' She tried to smile. 'Everyone creeps around here in their socks. I need to get hobnailed boots for them for Christmas so I can keep track of them.'

'I came to see Chloe,' I said. 'But Morgan said you wanted to speak with me first.'

'Oh. Yes.' A look passed between them that I couldn't read. Norris went over and started leafing through the newspaper.

'I wanted to say that Chloe is welcome to stay here as long as she likes,' Eleanor said. 'I – I hadn't thought about it last night. I should have said it from the start. Of course she can rely on us.'

'That's a very generous offer,' I said slowly, choosing my words with care. 'It's quite difficult to accommodate someone in your home, especially when you don't know how long they might stay with you.'

Norris laughed. 'Eleanor knows that. She's already got me.'

'But you're family.' I bit my lip. 'Look, the family liaison officer can give you more information—'

'Her? I sent her home,' Eleanor snapped. 'She was a very stupid, offensive woman and all she did was make cups of tea in *my* kitchen.'

'Offensive?' I said, puzzled.

'She didn't quite understand about Eleanor and Oliver's commitment to their church,' Morgan Norris said. 'She called them God-botherers.'

'Oh. Well.'

'Because Oliver invited her to join us in prayer,' Eleanor

94

said. 'She obviously has no idea how much God could help her in her work.'

'It's a difficult job,' I said diplomatically, thinking that Eleanor Norris was a nightmare and the FLO had probably skipped out of the house when she got her marching orders. 'If she was here, she would tell you what I'm about to tell you. It's natural to want to make everything right again in the aftermath of a crime. It's easy to make commitments that you could find yourself regretting. And Chloe is an adult.'

'How ridiculous. She couldn't survive on her own with her limitations.'

'Maybe not. There are other options, though. After all, she's not an orphan. Her father—'

'She can't go and live with him.' Morgan Norris looked up from the paper again. 'It's out of the question.'

'Why not?'

'She's terrified of him.'

'What makes you say that?'

'She said it herself. Last night.' Eleanor folded her arms. 'I asked her if she wanted to see him and she was beside herself. She begged me not to send her away. Of course I said she could stay here until she wanted to leave.'

'Did she say why she was scared?'

'No.' Eleanor turned to her brother-in-law. 'She didn't, did she?'

'She said she didn't want to go to his house again,' Norris said. 'She wouldn't say why.'

'His *house*,' I repeated. 'So it's not that she doesn't want to see him.'

'I can only tell you what she said. You'll have to ask her what she meant.'

'I just wanted to reassure her.' Eleanor was back on the verge of tears. She had obviously been chewing over what I'd said to her, preparing to disagree with me. I had the feeling

95

she was the kind of person who would keep returning to an argument until she felt she'd won. There was a word for them.

Exhausting, that was it.

'I didn't mean to say the wrong thing. And anyway, it's not wrong to say she can stay as long as she likes. I really think she should. I prayed about it. I asked for God's guidance.' Her eyes narrowed. 'But you probably think that's strange.'

'Not at all.' I meant it. My mother had garlanded my childhood with novenas and holy days and special intentions, with holy water and decades of the rosary and prayer cards for specific pious purposes. I was very familiar with the concept of praying for guidance. And it reminded me of something that had caught my attention the previous day. 'Your husband mentioned that he'd invited Kate Emery to your church. Did she ever come?'

I thought for a moment that Eleanor was going to faint. Her face went white, her lips bloodless. She put out a hand to the back of the chair beside her. 'He did *what*?'

'He said he invited her to your church,' I repeated, but diffidently.

'There's no way he would have done that. He'd have told me if he had.'

'That's part of the deal, isn't it, Eleanor? You invite poor sinners to join you in Christ.' Morgan reached out and put his hand on her shoulder. 'It's nothing to worry about.'

She pulled herself together with a visible effort. 'Even if he had, she certainly wouldn't have come. She had no interest in anything spiritual. Quite the opposite.'

'She did come.' Morgan looked uneasy. 'I think it was when you and Bethany were away with your mum. A couple of months ago.'

'What? Why didn't Oliver tell me?' Her eyes narrowed. 'And how do you know about it? You weren't there, were you? You've never gone to a service.'

'She came over here before they left. Oliver drove her.'

'But that doesn't make any sense. She was a sceptical person. She would only have come to mock us.'

'Well, she never went back, did she?' Morgan turned a page in the newspaper. 'So it can't be that much of a big deal.'

I was going to have to talk to Oliver Norris again, and the white-haired preacher. I suppressed a tiny sigh at the thought. 'Right. Was that everything?'

'The car.' Morgan spoke without looking up. 'Why did you want to examine it?'

'Routine enquiries.'

He glanced at me. 'So you've been examining all the cars on the road, have you?'

'Not all.'

'Why Oliver's?'

'I can't tell you that.'

'Did you find anything?' Eleanor was trembling, I noticed, her knuckles white as she dug her fingers into the chair back.

'I can't tell you that either.'

'If they'd found anything, they'd have taken the car away,' Morgan said, losing interest. 'There was nothing to find.'

He was right about that. The car had been immaculate, the boot recently vacuumed. The material that lined it was still slightly damp, according to the SOCO who had gone over it for me.

'Who cleaned it out?' I asked.

'The guys at the car wash near the dump. Oliver took it there after we got rid of the garden rubbish. They're Polish or Russian or something – not very much English, anyway. But you can speak to them if you like. They'll tell you it was muddy and full of leaves. They charged him extra for cleaning it because it was so filthy. There's always some reason why they need to charge extra, but they do a good job.'

The SOCO had sprayed the entire car including the inside of the boot with Luminol, a chemical that made traces of blood fluoresce under the right light. She'd promised me that, despite the cleaning, she'd have found traces of blood if they'd been there to find. And if there had been as much as a speck of blood, I would have arrested Oliver Norris then and there. I couldn't explain why I disliked him so much but I wasn't ready to write the feeling off just because his car seemed to be clean. Not when his wife was under so much stress she was coming apart at the seams. Not when his brother was fishing to find out if Norris was a suspect.

I left the two of them in the kitchen and headed upstairs with the intention of persuading Chloe to leave Oliver Norris's house as soon as possible. I could hear voices and followed the sound to the bedroom where I'd seen Chloe the previous day. As I got closer there was a sudden burst of laughter, quickly stifled in a flurry of shushing. I tapped on the door gently.

'Wait!' There was a scuffle from inside, and then a voice said, 'Come in.'

It wasn't Chloe's voice, I thought. Bethany's.

I put my head round the door. The two girls were lying on the floor. Chloe's face went as blank as a sheet of paper when she saw me. Bethany's expression jumped from wariness to surprise.

'Sorry. I thought it was my mum.'

'I wanted another word with Chloe.'

'We didn't think it was – we thought – you went to talk to my mum. We thought you'd left.' Bethany scrambled to her feet, shaking out her long, loose dress, and I saw she had been lying on a mobile phone. She saw me looking at it. 'It's not mine. I'm not allowed one. It's Chloe's.'

I looked down at Chloe, who was still lying on the floor. 'Can you sit up and talk to me, please, Chloe? And Bethany, do you mind leaving us for a few minutes?'

Bethany flashed me a hostile look, then turned to her friend. 'Do you want me to stay?'

'That's not an option, I'm afraid.' I held the door open. 'As I said, I won't be long.'

She trailed out past me, muttering under her breath. I smiled at her, unmoved, and shut the door firmly. She might dress like something from the nineteenth century but she was a normal teenager under it all.

'What do you want?' Chloe sat down on the chair she'd occupied the previous night, pulling her legs up again so she could hide behind her knees.

'Did you get the medication I brought over last night?'

A nod.

'I didn't find the envelope you were asking about.'

Her face went taut with tension. 'It must be there. It has to be.'

'We took some papers from your mother's study on the second floor. I'll check to see if it's got caught up with them. Is it important?'

A nod. 'I need it.'

'Then I'll check very carefully to see if we have it.'

She managed a smile.

'I have a couple of questions to ask, Chloe. Why did you come home early from your dad's house?'

'I don't want to talk about it.' She was more focused today, less blank. No more helpful, I noted.

'I'm going to talk to him tomorrow.'

'So?'

'So I'd like to know your side of the story before I hear his.'

'He doesn't know.'

'Know what?' No answer. I tried again. 'Was it something someone said? Or something they did?'

No answer.

'Why doesn't your dad know about it?'

'He wasn't there.'

'He'd gone out?'

'No, I mean he wasn't there.' She looked up. 'He was away.'

'But you were there to see him.'

She shrugged. 'It was business, he said. Important.'

'When was he away?'

She thought about it. 'He left on Friday morning. He came back on Saturday evening.'

I made a note. 'Do you know where he was?'

'No. He didn't say.'

'OK. You know, I understand that you don't want to talk about what happened in your dad's house, but it was something that really upset you, enough that you didn't want to stay there even after your father came back, and that makes me think it's something the police should know about.'

Her eyes went wide. 'No, no. It was . . . family stuff.'

'An argument?'

Her eyes slid away from my face. 'Yeah. I said some things I shouldn't have. I got in trouble with my stepmother. I don't think she likes me very much.'

'OK,' I said. I might have tried to convince her she was wrong but I knew there were a lot of wicked stepmothers out there. I'd reserve judgement on the second Mrs Emery until I met her. 'Was there anything else you wanted to tell me? Has anything else occurred to you that you think I should know?'

She shook her head.

'Do you have any message for your father? Anything you'd like me to pass on to him?'

'No.'

Time to see if I could get a reaction. 'If he asks about you coming to live with him for a while—'

'He won't. I've told him. I'm not going. I'm *never* going.' She was shivering.

'Have you spoken to your father?'

'No. I've sent him a text.' She looked up at me. 'Can you tell him I really mean it? Tell him to stop calling me and sending me messages too. I don't want to talk to him and I don't want to see him. Tell him that. Tell him.'

*

100

I didn't see Bethany straight away when I came out of the bedroom. She was sitting on the stairs, a few steps down, crouching like a cat. 'Hey.'

'Hi,' I said, surprised.

'I wanted to talk to you.'

'Go ahead.'

'It's about Chloe.' Bethany glowered at me. 'You need to leave her alone.'

'I can't, I'm afraid. It's a murder investigation. I don't get to leave people alone.'

Pure shock on her face. I'd thought it was common knowledge that we were treating the case as murder but it shouldn't have surprised me that the Norrises had kept the girls away from the news. If Bethany had no phone she almost certainly didn't have internet access either.

'Murder. So you think—'

'We don't know anything for sure yet. Don't say anything to Chloe about it.'

'I have to.'

'No, Bethany, please.'

'I'm not going to *lie* to her for you.'

'I'm not asking you to lie, I'm simply asking you not to use the word I used.'

Her expression was venomous. 'You people always underestimate her. When are you going to tell her if I don't?'

'When I know for sure what happened.' I sat down on the top step. 'Look, if it's a murder investigation it gets all the resources the police can throw at it. You know the forensic team have been working here since Sunday. You've seen the uniformed officers in the area, and the detectives. If it wasn't a murder investigation we'd find it very hard to commit so many people to finding out what happened. We're going to work as hard as we can to find out what happened in Chloe's house and why. And it helps us to assume the worst but that doesn't mean Chloe has to think that way.'

'I still think you should tell her.' That small stubborn face; I remembered her winding her father up about Chloe's cat. A born troublemaker.

Or someone who still believed in right and wrong. I faintly recalled what that was like.

'I will tell her when it's the right time. This isn't the right time.' I waited for a second. 'Bethany, do you know what happened at Chloe's dad's house? Do you know why she came back early?'

'No idea,' she said instantly.

'I think you have a very good idea.'

'Not really.'

'I think Chloe's told you exactly why she couldn't stay there.'

'You can't make me talk to you.' She stood up. 'This isn't even a proper interview. And I don't have to tell you anything.'

'No, you don't.' I was determined not to show frustration with her, or disappointment, mainly because I knew she was looking for a reaction. 'Thanks for your time, Bethany.'

'Is that it?'

'Unless you have anything else to say.'

She shook her head and went past me again, heading for the bedroom where I'd left Chloe.

'Bethany?' She looked back at me. 'Not a word, remember?'

The door slammed behind her.

Making an exit, teenager style.

10

Derwent slept all the way to Oxfordshire, snoring uninhibitedly in the back seat. I didn't really mind, not that he'd asked me. It gave me some time to think about Chloe, and her absolute reluctance to say what had driven her away from her father's home. It had to be something that she was ashamed of. Something she wanted to keep secret. The question was whether it was something she had done or something someone had done to her.

Emery lived outside Lewknor, a small village between High Wycombe and Oxford, slap bang in the middle of an area of outstanding natural beauty. The traffic was light and we made good time, sliding down from the high ground of the Chilterns to the rolling green countryside that was still unspoilt, still postcard-perfect. When the satnav told me we were a couple of hundred metres away from the house I found a place to stop. It was a narrow road where the houses were a long way away from each other and surrounded by high walls or tall hedges. This was private, moneyed territory, the sort of place where you could convince yourself nothing bad ever happened.

'Hey. Wake up.' I reached back and shook Derwent's knee until he came back to himself, his eyes screwed up against the light. 'We're here.'

'Shit.' He winced. 'My mouth tastes like something died in it.'

I threw a packet of chewing gum at him and he caught it in his left hand even though I could have sworn he wasn't looking. There was nothing wrong with his reflexes, anyway.

'Have we got any water?' He leaned forward so his forehead pressed against the headrest.

'*We* don't. I do.'

'Please, Kerrigan.'

'I love it when you beg.' I handed him the bottle though, watching as he emptied it in one long series of gulps.

'Thanks.'

'You're welcome,' I said, surprised that he'd bothered to say it. That was how low the bar was set: simple courtesy could shock me.

'What a shit day.'

'We've had worse,' I said, truthfully.

He grunted. 'Burt wants to get rid of me.'

'That's not news. She's never liked you.' Justifiably. Derwent wasn't in the business of making anyone's life easier. Una was inclined to take it personally.

'Yeah. But I'm actually thinking about it.'

'What?' I twisted around in my seat so I could see him properly. 'Not really.'

'I don't think I can be bothered any more.'

'Look, I know Burt is annoying, but the boss will be back soon—'

'It's not about that.' Derwent sighed. 'This wouldn't be any easier if Godley was in charge.'

'What is it?'

'I don't know.' He looked away from me, staring out of the window as if he was going to have to sit an exam on the view.

It was a lie, I thought. He did know. He just didn't want to talk to me about it. And why should he? He frequently threw himself into my private life with all the delicacy of a Labrador bounding into a stagnant pond, but it wasn't something I encouraged.

Even so, I couldn't ignore it.

'If you ever want to talk about it—'

He shook his head, popping some gum into his mouth. 'It's nothing.'

'Is it Melissa?'

His eyelids flickered. *Gotcha.* 'She doesn't like the job.'

'Why?'

'The hours. The stress. The fact that I don't talk to her about what we do. She says I shut her out.' He glanced across at me. 'She's right. It's deliberate.'

'I don't blame you. There are things civilians don't want to know, even if they think they do,' I said. 'You're protecting her.'

'I'm protecting myself. I don't want her to know about the things I think about.' He slid down so his knees were jammed against the passenger seat, as if he needed the pain to counterbalance the ache inside him. I'd been there. I knew the signs. 'You see enough of the ways people hurt each other and you start to believe that's all there is.'

'You wanted to be with Melissa because she was the light in the darkness,' I reminded him. 'That's what you said to me before you got together.'

'It's making it worse.' He said it without looking at me. 'I can't stop thinking about something bad happening to her or Thomas, or both of them, and how I couldn't live with it.'

'That's what happens when you love someone. That's the price you pay.'

'I'll lose her because of it.'

'Not if you explain—'

'I've tried.' His voice was harsh. 'I can't tell her the truth. I don't want to make her as scared as I am.'

'But—'

105

'Every night, I get Thomas's clothes ready for the next day. I put out his uniform if he's going to school. I put out his little jeans and a top if it's the weekend. Socks. Pants. Every stitch he's going to be wearing. Melissa thinks it's sweet.' He swallowed. 'It's because I need to know what he's wearing in case he goes missing, or in case someone kills him. Every night I think about what it would be like for him to be gone. Preparing for the worst. And Melissa stands there smiling at me, thinking I'm playing Daddy.' He took out his phone and flicked to the photos, skimming through them. 'She thinks it's so sweet the way I take pictures of him. She doesn't know I'm getting a record of his face. Left profile, right profile, full face. Updated every couple of months, so if he disappears, there's a recent set of pictures they can use.' Thomas's face flashed by on the screen, turned to the camera and away, smiling and serious, muddy and clean. 'Who thinks like that? Who looks at a beautiful kid like Thomas and imagines him dead?'

'I would probably do the same,' I said. 'It's natural. We've done those investigations. It's only that you've never had anyone to care about before.'

'I would die for them.' He slid his phone back into his pocket. 'But I can't say that to Melissa.'

'You have to be honest with her or it's not going to work out.'

He shook his head slowly. 'I can't do it. She says I put up a wall between her and my job, and she's right. But that wall is there to protect her, not keep her out.'

'Have you said that to her?'

He smiled, a brief flash of the old Derwent. 'I think it would make her even more determined to get me to quit. She'd like me to do a nicer job.'

'Like what?'

'You name it, she's suggested it. Something nine to five.' He stretched, yawning. 'I'd only have to be scared of dying from boredom.'

106

'I can't imagine it,' I said.

'Me neither.'

Life was so complicated, I thought. Melissa had fallen for Derwent because of what he was: the alpha male in his prime, strong and aggressive, able to defend her and her child. She had trusted him because he was a police officer. She loved what he did and who he was, I was sure of that. And then she ran up against the reality of his job. He wouldn't be easy company to live with, whether you understood him or not, but she couldn't understand him the way I did. I saw what he saw. I heard what he heard. She couldn't begin to guess why he came home snappy and withdrawn, or why he was short with her now and then.

But you couldn't change him. You'd destroy everything that was good in him if you tried to make him into something docile and peaceful. She'd kill their chance of being happy together unless she accepted him for what he was.

'Where's the house?' Derwent asked, his tone of voice indicating that the conversation was now over.

'Two hundred metres that way.'

'Better try and look awake.' He got out of the car, stretched, and then opened the passenger door so he could sit in the front. 'Let's go.'

I drove the short distance in silence and parked in front of the house. It was made of the local honey-coloured stone and came complete with a Range Rover squatting on the drive and a climbing rose over the front door. *Too good to be true.* I wondered if I would think that if I hadn't known about Chloe running away.

Derwent squinted up at the house. 'What does Emery do?'

'Carpets, apparently. You should ask him about it, since you're looking for a new career.' I got out of the car before he could come up with a comeback.

Emery must have been waiting inside the door because he opened it before I even had a chance to knock. He was small with thinning dark hair and a round face. His daughter looked very like him, I thought, but by a lucky quirk of genetics, on her face the features were perfectly proportioned. His version was less successful.

I introduced myself, and Derwent.

'Come in, come in.' He held the door open, directing us to a sitting room to the left of the front door. It was more of the same perfect country life: squashy sofas, a wood-burning stove, heart-shaped willow wreaths, a vase full of wildflowers on the windowsill. There would be an Aga in the kitchen, I thought, and a dog or two somewhere about the place.

'Can I get you anything? Tea? Coffee? I was going to have a coffee myself.' He had a slightly hurried, stuttering delivery that was quite charming.

'Not for me.' I took out my notebook and sat on one of the sofas, waiting for Emery to sit too. Derwent stood near the door. *This isn't a social call.*

'So, you've come all the way from London to talk to me.' He perched on the edge of the sofa opposite. 'Very thorough of you.'

'We wanted to ask a few questions.'

'I'll do anything I can to help.' His right knee was jiggling. 'Not that I can really think of much I can tell you about Kate. We got divorced a long time ago and I haven't been part of her life since then.'

'When did you split up?'

'When Chloe was six. Twelve years ago, it would be. God, it doesn't seem that long.'

'What happened?' Derwent asked.

'It was my fault. We were happy.' He shrugged. 'Well, as happy as we could be, given Chloe's issues. I'd recently been promoted. Money was tight for us up until then, because Kate gave up work once Chloe started having problems at nursery. We didn't know there was anything wrong until they flagged it up. Kate devoted herself to Chloe from that point on. She was a good mother, I always said that.'

'But not a good wife?' Derwent suggested. Emery flinched.

'No. That's not true. She was fine. I wasn't a good husband.'

'In what way?'

'I was busy. Working hard. And – well, I met Belinda while we were married. Belinda is my current wife.' He glanced at me, shamefaced. 'It was messy. When Kate found out, she asked me for a divorce. I went along with it. There was nothing else I could do.' He dropped his voice. 'According to my current wife, Kate took me for a ride. I agreed to pay her the amount she said she needed, but maybe if I'd had a better lawyer he'd have negotiated a more favourable settlement for me. But then again, I didn't want Chloe to suffer because we couldn't make our marriage last.'

'I've seen the bank statements,' I said. 'You were pretty generous.'

'Well, I increased it over time. When I was making more money, they got more. It only seemed fair.'

'Many men wouldn't have done that,' Derwent said. 'Not without a court order.'

'I wanted to do what I thought was right.' He pressed his lips together. 'Having a child like Chloe – it was even more important to give her the best possible start in life.'

'And in the nicest possible house?'

'Oh. Kate moved there after we split up.' Emery shrugged. 'I never went there. Not until—' He broke off.

'Until?'

'Until about three months ago. She asked me to come and meet her at her house. She wanted to talk to me about Chloe's future. Her prospects, now that she's finished school.'

'Was it a pleasant discussion?' I asked.

'It started off that way.' A nervous smile. 'She wanted me to give Chloe a large sum of money to set her up for her adult life. Belinda – that's my wife – thought we should draw a line under funding Chloe after she turned eighteen. I'd agreed to another year initially. Trying to find a compromise. I knew

Bel wouldn't like the idea of handing over a lump sum.' He looked like a man who spent a lot of time between a rock and a hard place.

'So you talked.'

'We did.' He licked his lips. 'I asked about the house. About her business. She seemed to be very well off. But she said she was short of money and she couldn't support Chloe on her own. I mean, we are both her parents. If Kate was paying for Chloe, I felt I should be too. But Belinda didn't see it that way.'

'What happened?' I asked.

'We argued. Well, that's not really true. I told her what Belinda thought and she told me Belinda needed to stay out of her life. I mean, it was a bit unreasonable of Kate. It does affect Bel and the boys too. I can see both sides, but no one else seemed to be able to do that. Kate got quite angry with me. She told me to— well, she told me to grow a pair.'

I darted a look at Derwent, who was struggling to keep the corners of his mouth from turning up.

'How did you leave things?'

'I said I'd talk to Bel. What else could I do?'

'And did you?'

He took a deep breath. 'I didn't actually tell her I'd seen Kate. I told her what I'd decided, which was that I'd continue to pay for Chloe until she was twenty-one. If she was at university, I'd be funding her studies. Even though she's not capable of that, I'm not going to deprive her.'

'And did you tell Kate?'

'I emailed her.'

'Did she reply?'

'Ye-es. She was a bit disappointed. If I've learned anything it's that you can't please everyone.' He trapped his hands between his knees. 'Look, my wife doesn't know about me going to see Kate and I don't want her to know.'

'Is she here?' I asked.

'She's upstairs, resting.'

'We'll probably need to speak to her too.'

'Oh.' He looked awkward. 'I don't know if she'll agree.'

'Why's that?'

'She didn't know Kate. They never actually met. She doesn't want anything to do with all this.'

'We'll keep it brief.'

Emery swallowed nervously. 'She's not— don't think she's always— Kate brings out the worst in her, basically.'

'It can be difficult to cope with ex-wives,' I said. *It can be fatal.* 'How does she get on with Chloe?'

'Fine. Bel's absolutely wonderful with her. Wonderful. They're great pals.' A big smile. 'The daughter she never had, I suppose.'

'You have stepsons, I gather.'

'Oh yes. Nathan's fourteen and Nolan's eighteen. They go to boarding school.'

'Were they here at the weekend?'

He nodded. 'They come back one weekend in three. It's nice for them. A bit of a break. I don't think they'd want to be here all the time – too boring for one thing, with just their mum and me. It's a bit remote here for teenagers.'

'So they were here, and Chloe was here,' I said slowly, 'and your wife was here . . . but you weren't.'

'Oh.' He laughed. 'No. Very unfortunate timing. I had a business meeting.'

'In London.'

'Yes.'

'And you stayed overnight.' I tapped the end of my pen on my pad. 'It took us fifty-three minutes to get here from central London through weekday traffic. I wouldn't have thought you'd need to stay away.'

'Well, it was two meetings. One late on Friday, one early on Saturday morning.'

'A business meeting on Saturday morning.'

'Business breakfast.' He patted his stomach. 'I should really try to avoid that sort of thing. You can eat a hell of a lot of saturated fat that way without even noticing. My heart won't thank me for it in a few years.'

'What is it you do, Mr Emery?' Derwent asked.

'I run my own business supplying and fitting carpets. We work with developers, mainly. My team have just done all the carpets for a development of two hundred flats in Nine Elms. We're talking about that sort of scale of job.'

'Impressive,' Derwent said softly. 'But I wouldn't have thought it was the kind of thing that involved meetings at weekends. I mean, in our job, we work weekends without even thinking about it because we have to, but if I had a choice about it, I wouldn't.'

'What can I say? I love my job.'

'And you probably take home a bit more cash than we do,' Derwent said.

'It's very unfair really. The police, teachers, nurses – I mean, you're the ones making a valuable contribution to society. All I do is keep people from having cold feet.'

'So what was the big carpeting emergency on Saturday morning?'

'A supplier.'

'What's the name?' I asked.

He rubbed the top of his head with the heel of his hand. 'They're an Indian company. I don't see why it's important to involve them.'

'Mr Emery, your ex-wife was murdered some time between Wednesday and Sunday,' I said coldly. 'You need an alibi more than you need to avoid upsetting your supplier.'

He gave a sigh. 'All right, then. I'll get you the details. They'll be able to confirm where I was.'

'Thank you.' I leaned forward. 'And while you were gone, Mr Emery, what happened here?'

'What do you mean?'

'Why did Chloe run away? She wasn't supposed to go, was she?'

He blinked. 'No. She was supposed to stay until today. I'd taken the day off work yesterday to spend it with her. Another plan that didn't quite work out.'

'Why did she go?'

'I have no idea. She hasn't told you?'

'She hasn't said anything.'

'When I came back on Saturday she was quiet. That's all I can tell you. I tried to bring her out of herself – I thought we could all go to the cinema in Oxford, and then out for a meal. But she said she wasn't hungry and there was nothing she wanted to see. She went to bed, in fact. The rest of us watched a film together – something the boys found on Netflix. It was all right. Kept us occupied.'

'When did she go?'

'Very early Sunday morning. I was up at six – we have a chug and a cockapoo, Betsy and Tyler, and I had to take them out for a walk. I can only think she left right after me, because the alarm was off and no one would notice the door opening and closing. They're used to me going in and out in the morning.'

'How did she get to the train station?'

'Not the train. She'll have got the coach. It stops near here on the way to and from London. There are loads of them – they run a twenty-four-hour service. Nothing easier than getting back to London from here.'

A creak from upstairs made him jump. 'That'll be Belinda. She must be up.'

'Great,' I said. 'We can speak to her now.'

He stood up, rubbing his hands on his shirt as if his palms were sweaty. 'I'll let her know you're here. I'm sure she'll want to help but – well, she might take a bit of persuasion. I'll try to hurry her along.'

'Take your time,' Derwent said, and held the door open

113

for him. We listened to him making his way upstairs, followed by the low murmur of a quiet conversation. It was too indistinct to be able to pick up any words, and Derwent closed the door softly.

'Are you wondering what I'm wondering?' he murmured.

'Probably. Why did it take Chloe Emery so long to get home if she left here at six in the morning? She didn't get off the train in Putney until after three.'

'That,' Derwent allowed. 'That's worth wondering. But that wasn't it.'

'What, then?'

He looked genuinely bewildered. 'What the fuck is a chug?'

11

The second Mrs Emery was physically different in almost every way from her predecessor. Tall where Kate had been of average height, Belinda Emery had a mane of black curls and an impressive bosom. For a large lady, she was light on her feet; I didn't hear her approaching the door. She flung it open as if she was expecting to catch us doing something we shouldn't have been doing. I was, in fact, trying to get Derwent to stop holding forth about designer dogs and speculating on what a Chihuahua/pug cross might look like, so I was more than pleased to see her.

'Mrs Emery?' I ventured.

A brisk nod. 'Brian says you want to speak to me. I can't imagine why. I don't know anything about what happened. I never met the woman and I didn't want to.'

'Your husband mentioned that.'

She seemed to swell. 'Did he, indeed? Well, I hope he told you what she wanted him to do. Fund her lifestyle indefinitely. As if she was entitled to enjoy the benefits of his hard work. She wasn't even with him when he set up the company. She contributed *nothing*. Why should she take a share?'

'I thought the money was for your husband's daughter,' Derwent said. 'Isn't that where it was going?'

Belinda Emery delivered herself of a world-class eye roll. 'Oh, *apparently* that's where it went. But it's not as if Brian ever asked to see receipts. "Chloe needs this. Chloe needs that. Chloe wants to try horse-riding. Chloe needs a holiday." Money was what she wanted and Chloe was the way she got it.'

'Chloe does have some learning disabilities—' I started to say.

'Do you know how many educational experts she had to consult before she found one who'd say that?' Belinda demanded. 'There was nothing wrong with that girl when she was a child and there's still nothing wrong with her now that she's an adult. She's not the brightest – that I will admit – but her main problem was her mother. That woman kept her isolated. She made her dependent. She wouldn't let her make her own way in the world, because of course if Chloe was able to live on her own and get a job – lead a normal life – poor little Kate would have to start working for a living.'

'I've interviewed Chloe,' I said, 'and I didn't find it all that easy to talk to her. And I have to say, I didn't think she was faking anything.'

'Oh, she's learned to play the part well enough. But if you catch her off guard, you get a very different Chloe.'

'Would you say you know her quite well?'

'I've seen a lot of her,' she said evenly. 'Over the years. It used to be some weekends and the occasional holiday, but now she's not in school any more she can come and stay regularly. Especially when it suits Kate.'

'I suppose it's nice for her to spend time with her father and stepbrothers.'

Belinda shook her head pityingly. 'That's not what it's about. It's about Kate keeping my husband under her thumb. Intruding into our lives. That's what she does. She's never let go of him – not really. Why didn't she change her name when they divorced? She's not Mrs Emery any more, but of course she clung on to it for dear life, along with her direct access to poor Brian's bank balance.'

'It must be hard for you.' I put as much sympathy as I could fake into my voice.

'Well, it has been. It's been a challenge all the way.' She caught sight of herself in the mirror over the mantelpiece and paused to fluff her hair, pouting at her reflection. She reminded me of a giant doll, her eyelashes standing out in spikes, her lips glossed to a high shine. 'I'm not the sort of person to walk away from a challenge, fortunately. And I would never let Brian down. I made it my business to get to know Chloe really well, so I could encourage her to lead a normal life.'

'How did Chloe feel about that?' Derwent asked.

'She was grateful.'

'Was she?' He folded his arms. 'I hear she ran away Sunday morning, early doors. What was that about?'

'Some sort of teenage drama.'

'Do you know that or are you just guessing?'

Belinda sighed. 'You have to understand, Chloe needed to grow up. She didn't like me telling her that. She's lived in a bubble her whole life and I'm the only one who's tried to burst it.'

'What did you say to her?' I asked.

'Nothing.' Belinda blinked at me, all affronted innocence. 'I only said what I would say to any girl her age, which was that she has a responsibility to conduct herself in a modest way. She needs to understand that men will make assumptions about her if she dresses in revealing clothes. It's like leaving your handbag in your car – it's your own fault if it gets stolen. You can't expect people not to take advantage.'

I almost choked from sheer rage. Derwent shot me a warning look then turned back to Belinda.

'You're talking as if something happened. Did someone attack Chloe?'

'No. Absolutely not. She was here the entire time. She didn't go out. It was general advice for her. The weather was warm last week when she arrived and she was wandering around in very short shorts and a T-shirt and no bra. Completely unsuitable, as I pointed out to her. I would never have dressed that way when I was her age. And frankly, I think it's irresponsible of Kate to let her go about the place dressed like that. I tried to explain to her that she wouldn't get any sympathy from anyone if something terrible happened to her, and she took offence.'

I was surprised my voice sounded calm when I spoke. 'It's quite an offensive thing to say.'

'Oh, don't be ridiculous. Everyone knows it's true even if you're not supposed to say it. There's a distinct lack of common sense about it. You cannot allow girls to engage in risky or sluttish behaviour in the name of equality. It's asking for trouble.'

What a good thing you have sons, I thought. Their picture was on the mantelpiece in a silver frame: handsome, fleshy faces, tanned from holidays, one smiling, one not.

'Do Nathan and Nolan get on with Chloe?'

Instant, absolute ice. 'Why would you ask that? What did Chloe say?'

'Nothing. We're trying to get a full picture of what happened over the last few days, that's all,' I said.

'Well, you can leave my children out of your picture. They had very little to do with Chloe. As you can imagine, they didn't have much in common with her. They are both highly intelligent boys. Nolan is extremely creative and Nathan has a gift for mathematics. They didn't want to spend a lot of time with Chloe since she couldn't engage with their interests.'

'I'd like to speak with them,' Derwent said.

'Certainly not.' She was quivering with outrage. 'I have done my level best to save them from being exposed to the complications of Brian's private life. There was no reason for them to meet Kate and they never did.'

'They might be able to shed some light on Chloe's state of mind.'

'They are teenage boys. They don't even know their own state of mind.' She shook her head. 'I will not allow you to disrupt their lives because of this. I don't give a hoot about why Chloe left here on Sunday morning, except that I thought it was rude of her to go without so much as a thank you. If I never saw her again, I wouldn't particularly care. She's not my family and I'm not going to pretend I care about her just because you're probably judging me for being a wicked step-mother.' There were tears standing in her eyes. So she was capable of emotion after all. It was a shame that emotion was pure self-pity.

'We're not here to judge you.' From the tone of Derwent's voice, though, it was clear that he had judged her, and not kindly. 'We're here because Kate Emery has disappeared. From the state of her house we know something terrible happened there. It *is* a murder investigation.'

'You don't understand, do you? I don't care who killed Kate,' Belinda spat.

A noise in the doorway made me look round: Brian Emery. Very quietly, he said, 'I really think it would be helpful if we all calmed down.'

Belinda was far too angry to notice he was there. 'I don't care if she's dead. I don't care if you never find her body. The only thing that surprised me about it was that it took so long for someone to decide to murder her. I'd have done it years ago.'

'Brian Emery has interesting taste in women, doesn't he?' Derwent settled down in the passenger seat. 'Goes to show money and sense don't go together.'

'She's terrifying.' I smiled and waved at the pale face in the window: Brian Emery, watching us go as if we were his last chance of salvation. 'But I can't quite make it all fit together.

119

You don't get to run your own business and make a huge success of it if you're a total doormat. It's not as if property developers are notoriously easy clients.'

'People can be different at home and at work.'

'Oh yeah?' I glanced sideways at him. 'So when you're at home with Melissa you're really quiet and gentle, is that it? I'd never have guessed.'

'I'm not talking about me.' *So back off*. 'I don't quite believe he's as meek and mild as he seemed to be. I imagine it's useful for him to pretend to be that way. Belinda's not the kind of lady who likes to be challenged. But he had a big old argument with Kate, didn't he?'

'Well, she shouted at him. We don't know if he shouted back.'

'And we don't know if he was really happy about giving Kate money all the time. It was causing him problems in his marriage, wasn't it? I wouldn't want to sign up to anything that would get me in trouble with Belinda.'

'He could have given Kate the lump sum she wanted. That would have ended it.'

'Would it? Kate kept coming back to him. She was tapping him for more and more money. I doubt it would have been the end.' Derwent rubbed his face. 'What do we think about Chloe? Why did she run away?'

'I don't know. It could have been as simple as a row between her and Belinda. God knows, I wouldn't want to spend any time under the same roof as her.'

'Why wouldn't she tell you about it though?'

'Embarrassed? Maybe she thought it was her fault that her stepmother didn't like her. I'm tempted to apply for a restraining order to keep Belinda away from her. No wonder Chloe doesn't want to go and live with her dad.'

'Do you think Belinda had a point?'

My hands tightened on the wheel. 'About not dressing in revealing clothes because men can't control themselves?'

'About Chloe being much more capable than Kate would ever admit.' He reached over and patted my knee. 'Calm down, dear.'

'Keep your hands to yourself,' I snapped.

'Temper, temper.'

I shook my head. 'You're so annoying.'

'Famous for it,' Derwent agreed.

'I don't know if Chloe is faking. I don't think she is. But . . .'

'What?'

'She's friends with Bethany Norris, and that girl is nobody's fool. I don't really understand their friendship but they seem close.' I bit my lip, remembering the two girls laughing on the floor of Bethany's bedroom, and how the light had died in Chloe's eyes when she realised I was watching them. 'Maybe Chloe is more capable than Kate allowed. Remember the files of paperwork in Kate's study? She did seem to go through a lot of specialists, as Belinda said.'

'Well, there's your next job. Collect up all the papers from the study and have a good look through. See if you can talk to any of the people who assessed Chloe and didn't give Kate the answers she wanted.'

'What are you thinking?' I asked.

'It did suit Kate that Chloe was dependent on her.'

'And you think Chloe might have resented it?'

'It's possible. What if she wanted to spread her wings? What if she didn't like being kept at home?'

'I wouldn't have liked it,' I said, thinking about it.

'Me neither.'

'But she could have left. She is an adult now.'

'She might not have known that. She might have thought she needed to stop her mother interfering in her life once and for all. She's a pretty girl, isn't she?'

'Stunning,' I agreed.

'And according to Belinda she dressed provocatively.' Derwent held up his hands. 'Which is completely her right

121

and I'm not saying she shouldn't have. If anything, I wish more women dressed that way.'

'Men like you are the reason they don't.'

He whistled. 'Harsh, Kerrigan. Anyway, my point is that she could have recruited someone to help her. Someone to do the deed while she was miles away. Someone who could have camped out in Harold Lowe's house and waited for the signal to go in and slaughter Kate Emery.'

I thought about it. 'It's possible. But it's not easy to find someone who's prepared to kill for you, is it?'

'People kill for all sorts of reasons – you know that. Sex. Money. Shame. Frustration. Fear. No shortage of any of them in Kate Emery's life, as far as I can see. You heard what Belinda said. She was surprised it took so long for someone to kill Kate.'

I nodded. 'All it needed was for one person to have had enough.'

12

'Where shall I put this?' Georgia Shaw was standing beside my desk, holding a box of files.

'Anywhere.' I sounded snappy, even to myself. I looked up from the letter I was reading and tried to smile. 'Sorry. I don't mean to be rude. I'm just trying to get my head around Kate Emery's life and it's confusing.'

'It's fine,' Georgia said in a tone that made me feel it wasn't fine at all. 'That's the last box. Do you want me to start going through it?'

'No. I'd better do it myself.'

Her mouth tightened before she turned away and I suppressed a sigh. Did I really have to explain that it wasn't that I didn't trust her? That she didn't know what she was looking for and neither did I? That boring paperwork was a huge part of the job and sometimes it meant spending an entire morning reading through the mind-numbing admin of a stranger's life?

'Georgia.'

'Yeah.'

'Can you make some calls for me? See if you can get hold of any of these people and if they'll speak to us.' I handed her a sheaf of letters. 'The addresses are old, I'm afraid. We're going back ten or fifteen years. It might take a bit of time to track them down.'

'Who are they?'

'Psychologists who saw Chloe Emery when she was a child. Kate took Chloe to see quite a few before she felt she got the correct diagnosis.'

Georgia frowned. 'OK, but what does this have to do with whoever killed her?'

'I don't know yet. It might be a complete waste of time. It's bothering me, that's all.'

'Great.' Georgia said it under her breath as she turned away. I went back to my paperwork, but not before I caught Liv Bowen's eye and shared a meaningful look with her. Liv got it. Georgia didn't, yet. But I wasn't ready to write her off. I had to be fair.

I was trying to make sense of a bank statement when she came back.

'OK. I've got hold of this lady: Raina Khan. She's still at the same address and she says you can come round this after-noon at three.'

'Oh, well done. Do you want to come with me?'

She brightened. 'Yes. Definitely.'

'Any luck with the others?'

'Not so far, but I'll keep trying.' She headed off with a spring in her step.

'You're so good at motivating people, Kerrigan.' Derwent, leaning over my desk, murmuring so Georgia couldn't hear. His breath tickled my neck and I twisted away.

'I learned it all from you, obviously.'

'Obviously. Does she remind you of yourself when you were a lowly detective constable?'

'Nope.'

'You were so sweet before you became all cynical and embittered.'

I rolled my eyes. 'That happened about five minutes after I started working with you.'

'Sexual frustration will do that.'

'Frustration, certainly.' I swivelled on my chair so I was facing away from him. 'Do you mind? I'm trying to concentrate.'

'Found anything?'

'Besides the psych info? I found this.' I flattened it out and showed him.

'A life insurance policy. For Kate?'

'Yep.'

'Who's the beneficiary?'

'Chloe.'

'How much?'

'Half a million quid.'

Derwent whistled. 'Is it valid?'

'All she has to do is claim it once the death certificate comes through.'

'It would help if we had a body, wouldn't it?'

'Without a body, we have less chance of proving Chloe was involved in her mother's murder,' I pointed out. 'It might be worth the wait for the death certificate in those circumstances.'

Derwent frowned. 'If this was the reason Kate was killed, Chloe would have had to know about it and plan her mother's murder. That's a lot to ask of any eighteen-year-old, let alone one who isn't the sharpest knife in the drawer.'

'Well, she could have known about it fairly easily, because it was in this envelope.' I showed Derwent. It had CHLOE written across it in the clear, distinctive handwriting I recognised as Kate's. I flipped it over and read the sentence scrawled across the back: *In case I get run over by a bus!*

'It wasn't sealed. She could have read it. Everything Chloe might have needed was in here – her birth certificate, her passport. Kate planned for a time when she wasn't around, so Chloe didn't have to go looking for anything. And Chloe asked me about it on Sunday night, and on Monday when I spoke to her. She knows it's important.'

'Life insurance and plans for what might happen in the event of her sudden death.' Derwent rubbed his chin thoughtfully. 'Either Kate was highly organised or she knew her life was in danger.'

'This is jokey,' I said, tapping my finger on the envelope. 'This doesn't suggest to me that she knew what was coming. The house was very organised too. Nothing out of place. Some people are just like that. *You're* like that.'

'I like to know where to find things. I don't have an envelope for anyone to open in the event of my sudden death.'

I shivered, suddenly spooked. 'Don't talk about it.'

He grinned. 'Feeling nervous? Someone walking over your grave?'

'Stop,' I said quietly, and for once, he did. I slipped the envelope into an evidence bag and started filling in the details. 'Of course, it wouldn't have to be Chloe's idea to kill her mother and claim the life insurance policy. If she'd told someone about it, they might have come up with the plan. All she had to do was play along.'

'Who?'

'I don't know. Her dad? Her stepmother?'

'It's possible. Maybe they recruited Chloe rather than the other way round. Or maybe Chloe isn't so dim after all.'

'Do you think we should bring her in?'

Derwent thought about it. 'Not yet. Save that for when we know a bit more. At the moment she has no idea we're interested in her and I think we should try to keep it that way for as long as possible.'

'What if she runs?'

'She won't.' He sounded certain. 'She has too much to lose if she goes.'

*

126

It was raining again when we arrived at Raina Khan's address, a narrow townhouse in a back street of Pimlico, near the river. The building was shared between different businesses: an interior design company in the basement and on the ground floor, a solicitor's office on the first and second floor, and Raina Khan's consulting rooms at the top of the building.

'It would be the top,' Georgia complained as the psychologist buzzed us in.

'It's always the top.'

I was amused to see how the different businesses had laid claim to their share of the communal spaces: flowers and a scented candle on the ground floor, files stacked in boxes on the first and second floor where they didn't have time for fripperies. And on the third floor there was a child-sized chair with a fat, sagging teddy propped up in it. It set the tone nicely.

I knocked and the door opened immediately. 'You're the police officers. Come in, come in. Take a seat. Let me pour you some tea. It's an infusion, not tea. Herbal, very good, very relaxing.'

I blinked against the light and the onslaught of hospitality; somehow I hadn't been expecting either. The room ran the length of the building, with windows on either side and a view of rooftops stretching into the distance. Seagulls whirled around outside the windows like scraps of paper caught in the wind. The room was crammed with art and books, with batik wall-hangings and carved wooden furniture, and the overall atmosphere was as welcoming as the woman who worked there.

Raina Khan was tiny, her long hair streaked with grey, her eyes very bright. She wore a dark red dress and flat ballet shoes, and she didn't stop moving or talking for as much as a second while we settled into low, squashy armchairs.

'If you're hungry you must have a biscuit. I made them with my last client – he's a regular, very sweet, loves making

127

things. He does better when he's doing something with his hands, you know? He needs that tactile element in everything. Kneading dough is wonderful. Pressing out biscuit shapes – terrific. It's all about feeling what he's doing, taking time, learning to control his movements. It's very soothing, baking. You can't rush it. I have a minuscule kitchen but I can make a surprising amount in it. People tell me they're very good, these biscuits. Go on, have one.'

She put a tray on the coffee table: small cups of steaming, aromatic liquid and a pile of dry-looking biscuits. I took a cup and sipped it, tasting mint and something else, something bitter but somehow wholesome.

'Good?'

'Yes,' I said, and it was the first thing I'd managed to say since we arrived. 'Thank you for seeing us, Dr Khan.'

'You can call me Raina.' She sat down, shaking her wrist to settle her collection of silver bracelets into place. 'Which one of you is Georgia?'

'Me.' Georgia waved. She had taken a bite of biscuit and seemed to be struggling slightly.

'And so you are?'

'Maeve Kerrigan. I'm a detective sergeant.'

'And you're investigating a murder. Kate Emery.'

'That's right.'

'I'm surprised that you want to see me.' She blinked a couple of times, inviting me to explain.

'It's not directly connected with what happened to Kate – background information, really. Do you remember seeing Chloe as a patient when she was five or six?'

'Oh yes. I remember it very well, and I remember Kate. I saw them four or five times.' She sighed. 'Poor woman. I read about it in the paper but I didn't realise it was her until yesterday. The name – I recognised it but I couldn't quite remember her. Then I checked my files when Georgia rang me, and of course it all came back.'

128

'Was there something in particular that made them stand out?'

She hesitated, flexing and rubbing her small hands as if they were stiff or cold. 'Well, every child is different, and every parent is different. That's the first thing to know. So there's no typical family that walks through my door for help. Some people are very accepting and positive. Some people want me to be wrong about their child. They get angry when they hear a diagnosis. It's understandable.'

'Was Kate angry?'

'She was when she came. She was annoyed that people weren't taking her seriously. I remember her sitting in your chair while Chloe played in the corner here. She had tears in her eyes, talking about how she'd struggled on Chloe's behalf.'

It felt strange to think of Kate sitting exactly where I was, in a room that probably hadn't changed much in twelve years. A large wooden doll's house stood in the corner Raina indicated. The furniture inside was jumbled up, the dolls upside down or poking out of the windows. I imagined a small Chloe playing with it while her mother talked about her, complained, wept a little. Would the child have noticed? Or would it all have gone over her head?

'Is that normal?'

'Oh yes. Many people find it hard to get the system to acknowledge their child's needs. It can be frustrating.'

'So why did Kate stand out?'

'It was a combination of things.' Raina smoothed her skirt, pursing her lips. Lines fanned out from her mouth. I couldn't begin to guess her age but she looked at least seventy at that moment. 'Do you know Chloe's medical history?'

'No.'

'It was a difficult birth. A forceps delivery, in the end. Chloe was in neonatal intensive care for some time afterwards. Birth trauma can have a permanent effect on a child, or it can kill, or it can have a negligible impact. Kate was very concerned about Chloe's development, always, and she felt the medical establishment were much too casual about the effect of the traumatic birth on her child. She was a nurse, you see, so she was familiar with how doctors and nurses spoke about patients, and parents. She didn't trust any of them.'

'Was she right to be concerned about Chloe?'

Raina pulled a face. 'It's hard to say. By the time I saw her she was certainly struggling with gross and fine motor skills. She found it difficult to communicate and to concentrate. She struggled to make eye contact. She was very shy and lacking in confidence as well as social skills. But I wasn't sure that it was attributable to the traumatic birth. Kate wanted to find labels for Chloe's condition. She had done a lot of research and she wanted me to say that Chloe was going to be permanently affected by what had happened to her. Chloe was . . . borderline. I believe that's what I said in my report.'

'Why would she want you to say Chloe was more incapacitated?' Georgia asked.

'Because of money. You can claim extra funding with a firm diagnosis. But also because sometimes parents just want someone else to see what they see. And sometimes it's to know why. If you know why your child isn't what we think of as normal, you can be angry about that specific thing. If you can't find any specific reason for your child to be different from other children, you might worry that it was your fault.' Raina frowned. 'With Kate, though, it was almost an obsession.'

'Did you ever meet Brian Emery, Chloe's dad?'

'Never. I asked if he could sit in on what turned out to be our last session but he didn't come. Kate told me he was in denial about Chloe's condition. I felt – and I may have been misjudging her – that she didn't want him there. She was traditional about it. She had given up work as soon as Chloe's problems became apparent. I remember her saying it was Brian's job to keep a roof over their heads and food on the table, and it was her job to cook the food and look after

Chloe.' Raina shrugged. 'Old-fashioned. I told her she was selling herself short and she didn't like that at all.'

'Was that why they stopped coming?'

'They didn't come to an appointment one day. I called, left messages. No answer. Then I got a letter from another practitioner saying he had taken Chloe on as a patient and asking for my notes. That was that. I hoped Kate found what she was looking for.'

'So you thought it was more about Kate's needs than Chloe's,' I said.

'Definitely. She needed Chloe to need her. I had the impression that she enjoyed the attention she got because of Chloe being as she was. Ordinary wasn't good enough for her. She wanted extraordinary, even if it was in a negative sense of the word.' Raina sighed. 'Most parents want their children to be normal. To fit in. Kate was the opposite.'

'But she wanted Chloe to stay in mainstream education.'

'Yes, she did. You see, if Chloe had been in a special school, she wouldn't have stood out at all. In a mainstream school, with neurotypical children, she was the centre of attention. So much pity from the other parents, so much kindness, so much help when she needed it.' Raina narrowed her eyes, looking very wise. 'Kate was very good at appearing to be helpless, when she was really quite a capable person.'

'Would you describe her as manipulative?' I asked.

'Yes.' Raina smiled. 'That's not always a bad thing. Many very successful people are able to influence other people's behaviour.'

'And in Kate's case?'

The smile held for a second, then disappeared. 'In Kate's case, I was concerned. I wrote back to the psychologist who took over from me, confidentially, to share with him my findings about Chloe. I told him that I felt Chloe was capable of more than Kate allowed. I felt it was likely to cause problems in their relationship as Chloe got older; that lack of

131

independence, of freedom – it can suffocate, you know? It can cause resentment and heartache for no good reason. I wanted them to be able to rely on each other. It's like two trees growing together.' She knotted her fingers together. 'It's much better for them to be pruned so their branches don't tangle. Then if one sickens or falls, the other can continue to thrive. But pruning is hard on the trees. If we asked them, they would prefer to be tangled together.'

'Did you say that to Kate Emery?'

She nodded. 'The last time I saw her. She said she wasn't going to sicken. She said she would never let Chloe down. And I said that wasn't the point. I told her she couldn't know what the future was going to hold.' Raina gave a long sigh. 'It gives me no pleasure at all to know that I was right.'

13

The Church of the Modern Apostles was a square, cream-painted building set back from the South Circular Road. It looked like a former bingo hall. A billboard outside read 'Christians: Keep the Faith . . . But Not From Others!' I walked up to the main door. It was uncompromisingly closed, with a padlocked chain wound around the handles inside the door. I stood on the steps for a moment, looking at the cars glittering in the strong morning sun. I recognised Oliver Norris's Volvo beside a van with a *What Would Jesus Do?* bumper sticker, so I knew I was in the right place.

There had to be another way in.

At the side of the building, I found another door, this one with a ramp leading up to it and a sign that read 'OFFICE'. This door opened easily and I found myself in a narrow corridor decorated with posters. *You are not too bad to come in – you are not too good to stay out.* It smelled musty, like a school locker room. *The best things in life aren't things.* My footsteps sounded uncertain on the tiled floor and I made myself walk confidently. *It's hard to stumble when you're on your knees.* Derwent would have liked that one.

That, in itself, was a good reason for not letting him come along.

There was a murmur of voices coming from a room at the end of the corridor. I walked down and tapped on the door.

'Come in.'

I recognised the deep, warm voice immediately. Gareth Selhurst was standing in the middle of the room, facing a desk where a woman was working. She was in her thirties, with threads of grey in her dark hair. Her hands were poised above the keyboard of her computer: I had interrupted them in the middle of some dictation, I guessed.

'Can I help you?' This time Selhurst sounded sharp and distinctly less welcoming.

'DS Maeve Kerrigan. We met on Sunday.'

'At Oliver's house. I remember.' He was shorter than I'd expected now that I saw him standing up, but the hair was magnificent, a white mane swept back from a high forehead. 'It's official business, I take it.'

'I'm afraid so.'

'You'll want to speak to Oliver.'

'Actually, I'd like to start with you.'

His eyebrows drew together. 'Me?'

'I have a few questions,' I said firmly. I glanced down at the woman, who was watching us closely, her mouth hanging open. 'Here, or in private. Whatever you prefer.'

Mr Selhurst preferred to talk in private. He led me down the corridor to a small, spotless kitchen. I waited for him to offer me a cup of tea or a glass of water, but he looked around as if he'd never been in the kitchen before and wasn't sure how any of it worked. He folded his arms and leaned back against the counter.

'We can talk here. I can't give you much time, I'm afraid. I'm needed elsewhere at ten.'

'That's fine.' I took out my notebook and sat down on a stool in the corner, beside a table with a chipped laminate top.

'I really don't see how I can help you anyway, if it's about Oliver's poor neighbour.'

134

'Did you know her?'

'I met her. Briefly.'

'Once? More than once?'

He pulled a face. 'More than once.'

'Twice? Three times?'

'I don't recall.'

'Where did you meet her?'

'She came to worship with us once. She wasn't ready to hear God's call, I'm afraid.'

I waited, my eyebrows raised.

'She found it hard to let go of her preconceptions. To lose herself in talking to Christ, our saviour.' He smiled. 'We are an evangelical church, Miss Kerrigan. We sing and make music. We pray out loud. When the spirit moves us, we pray in tongues. Christ is a very real presence in our gatherings. He heals us, he speaks to us and through us. He walks ahead of us and we follow in his footsteps. He cleanses us of our sins and our faults when we beg him for salvation. When he dances, we dance.'

'And Kate didn't dance.'

'No. She was full of doubt and confusion. The devil had a firm grip on her.' His lip curled. 'She wore immodest clothes. She questioned many of the things we see as truths, such as a man's place as the head of his family. She, of course, had a broken marriage. I pointed out to her that if she had come to God earlier, she and her husband could have stayed together, in the proper relationship between man and wife. The head of every man is Christ, the head of a wife is her husband, and the head of Christ is God, as St Paul said.'

I was very glad Derwent wasn't there to hear that. 'It's not a very popular opinion in this day and age.'

'This godless age,' Selhurst thundered, slipping into preacher mode. 'At least in our spiritually bankrupt country. There are countries in the world where the word of God holds sway, where people have turned to him for help in times of need.

It is my constant prayer that the same feeling will sweep over this nation, this once-great Christian country, and wash all of the unworthy away. The bible tells us that a great flood happened before. There are many recent prophecies that it will happen again, that a wave will come and destroy the south of England. It's sheer arrogance to think it won't, that we can behave as we wish without angering God.' He leaned forward. 'You're not married, I see.'

'No.'

'Are you a Christian?'

'I was brought up a Catholic,' I said.

Selhurst physically recoiled. 'Well, that's not quite the same thing.'

'I'm sure it's not.' I checked my notes, secretly pleased to be the embodiment of all that was unholy. 'So Kate came to church here on one occasion.'

'I asked her not to return until she was ready. She was a disruptive influence. People were inhibited by her presence. It's a small congregation, still, but then the church hasn't been here for very long. In a group of fifty, one discordant presence stands out.' Selhurst shook his massive head. 'We must leave our earthly concerns behind when we enter the house of God. Lose ourselves in the Lord. We must not be self-conscious in the presence of God, but conscious only of him.'

In other words, she had interfered with the collective hysteria that Selhurst relied on to make his congregation feel euphoric.

'And she never returned.'

'No.'

'You said you'd met her more than once. Did you speak to her after that?'

'I went to her house a number of times, with Oliver. Kate was reluctant to speak to me, but Oliver convinced her.' He shook his head again. 'There are none so deaf as those who will not hear. As I explained to Oliver, it can take many

136

visits before a heart is opened to God, but it was worth fighting.'

'Even though Kate wasn't really interested.'

'Kate wasn't the only one we were concerned about.'

It took me a second. 'Chloe? But she's—'

'She was never baptised. I prayed and prayed for Kate to see that she was stopping her daughter from receiving the greatest gift there could be. God was waiting to help her, his arms open wide, and Kate was stopping her from going to him.'

'And does Chloe want to be baptised?'

'Kate said she did not.' He closed his eyes for a second and sighed. 'I always left her house exhausted, feeling I had battled hand to hand with the devil. Do you believe in evil, miss?'

'Yes, I do.' I said it without hesitation, and meant it.

'Kate was full of evil. I saw it in her, and I heard it.' He leaned forward. 'I *know* evil.'

'When you say she was evil—'

'No!' He slammed his hand on the counter. 'I said no such thing! I said she was full of evil. The devil was strong in her. He countered my arguments. I am but a man and although God was with me, guiding my path, he was stronger than me.' He leaned back, apparently drained, and murmured, 'But I would have succeeded. I know I would. God conquers all. Jesus cleanses us of all our sins, no matter how dark.'

'What's all the shouting about?' Oliver Norris was standing in the doorway, crisply dressed in a polo shirt and chinos. He was looking at Gareth. 'Practising for Sunday?'

'I was talking to this lady about the devil,' Gareth said gruffly, pointing at me.

When he saw me, the colour drained from Oliver's face under his tan. 'It's just a simple prayer ceremony. It should help.'

'Help who?' I looked from him to Gareth, who was rolling down his shirt sleeves as if they were his main concern.

137

'We conduct special ceremonies now and then for people who are very much in need of prayer. There will be one on Sunday. I think Oliver assumed I was speaking about it.' Gareth smiled at me. The preacher was gone: the man remained and he was gentle, normal – pleasant even. 'It's very effective. Of course Kate will be on our mind and in our hearts.'

'Did you want to talk to me?' Oliver had shoved his hands into his pockets and was tensing his arms so his triceps flickered.

'Please,' I said, standing up. 'I won't take up too much of your time.'

'Take her through to the main hall,' Gareth said. 'Show her where we worship. I think she'd find it interesting.'

Oliver looked as if he wanted to argue but he nodded. I followed him, heading in the opposite direction from the office. He held open a door for me and ushered me through. I found myself on a red-carpeted platform facing a huge room about half-full of gold-framed chairs. It felt more like a convention hall than a church to me, but then I was used to pews, statues of saints, banks of candles, the Stations of the Cross and the red glow of the sanctuary lamp. This had two projection screens and a pair of chairs on the raised platform, with a keyboard and drum kit on the right. There were big loudspeakers on either side of the platform and a soundboard at the back of the room. Oliver flicked some switches and lights went on at the sides of the room and all the way down the centre.

'This is where we have our services. We dim the lights in the main body of the church when they're going on, of course.'

I walked to the centre of the platform and looked out, imagining a sea of faces focused on me. There were no distractions here – no pictures, no aphorisms. No banners promising eternal life. Here you were alone with your God and your fellow worshippers, abandoning yourself to religious bliss. Or damnation, depending.

'What's that?' I pointed at a large square structure below the platform, in front of the first row of chairs.

'That's where we carry out baptisms and other ceremonies.'

'In it?'

He nodded. 'Total immersion. It symbolises rebirth, whether that's in Christ or in good health or simply a fresh start. All our members are baptised once they've repented and placed their faith in Jesus, even if they were baptised as children. It's a wonderful celebration that unifies the whole church.' His voice was toneless, as if he was reciting something he'd said before but his mind was elsewhere.

'Mr Selhurst said you have a small congregation.' I stepped down and started walking along the aisle, Oliver following me as if he couldn't let me get too far away.

'Small but growing. We have over thirty regulars but the door is always open if anyone else wants to join us.'

Gareth had said there were fifty in the congregation. I suspected he had a tendency to exaggerate for effect.

'We have visitors from other communities, of course,' Oliver went on. 'We are part of the Modern Apostles movement. There are two hundred thousand of us in Asia, half a million across Africa, the same again in South America.' He reeled off the numbers fluently. 'The new world has a lot to teach us in Europe about faith. They've kept the flame burning brightly even if we've allowed it to dim.'

'Do you preach?' I asked. He looked disconcerted.

'Me? No.'

'You sound very practised. Very persuasive.'

'I do all the public relations for the church. I write press releases, do the website – that sort of thing.'

'And it's a full-time job?'

He nodded. 'It's not only this church. I'm based here but I work for other churches in the Modern Apostles movement. There's one in High Wycombe, one in Haywards Heath, one in Leighton Buzzard that Gareth planted before he was directed

139

to come to Putney and start a new congregation here. We have national conferences every three years and I'm involved in organising them.'

'What did you do before?'

'I worked in the PR department of a major pharmaceuticals company.'

'So you're used to selling hope.'

His face flushed. 'I always wanted to help people, if that's what you mean. But we've healed more people here than the pharmaceuticals company ever did.'

'Literally healed them?'

'The lame walked.'

'The blind saw?'

He gave me a half-smile. 'Not quite. Not yet, anyway. But God can do anything.'

We had reached the back of the hall. It was piled with boxes. I glanced in one and saw groceries.

'We run an unofficial food bank. Everyone contributes what they can and once a month we distribute them to those in need in the area.'

'That sounds useful,' I said.

'I don't understand why there's such hostility to Christianity when we just want to help people.' The words came out with surprising force, as if he'd been suppressing them for too long.

'What kind of hostility?'

'People mock us for how we pray and for our beliefs.' He shook his head, still angry. 'We get called names. You hear things on the radio or on television – slighting comments. And no one says a word! If you said these things about Muslims or Jews, you'd be hounded. But Christians are fair game.'

'You have to turn the other cheek, as I understand it.'

'I get tired of it.' A glance. 'Why are you here?'

'I'm still finding out more about Kate. She came here.' I shrugged. 'It might be relevant, it might not.'

'She only came once.'

'So Mr Selhurst said. He said he argued with her.'

He nodded unhappily. 'Kate was . . . disrespectful. I thought I was doing the right thing in asking her to come. Gareth told me I hadn't done anything wrong, but I wondered if I should have checked with him first.'

'Was he angry with her?'

'Gareth doesn't get angry. Not about personal things. He allowed God to speak through him and Kate was scared by what he said.'

'What did he say?'

'That hell was waiting for her if she didn't change her ways. That she had one choice to make because after her death there would be no more choices. That she had let herself fall into evil and God would help her out but she had to want to be saved.'

'And she didn't like that.'

'She called him a patronising old lizard.' Norris sighed. 'I tried to intervene.'

'He said that other people were upset.'

'Everyone was.' Norris swallowed. 'People were unsettled. They didn't feel they had been able to pray. After I took Kate away, some of our flock asked Gareth to lead another service straight away. They wanted to purify our church. Kate was like pollution among us.'

I whistled. 'Strong words.'

'Strong feelings.' Norris frowned, not looking at me. 'But that was the end of it. She didn't come back.'

'Was there anyone in particular who asked about her? Anyone who wanted to know her name, or where she lived?'

'You don't think someone here harmed her. That's impossible.'

'It happens. And Mr Selhurst said she was full of evil.'

'But that's not her fault. We *prayed* for her. We wouldn't *hurt* her. That's not God's way.'

141

He looked genuinely appalled at the idea. I backed off. 'Mr Selhurst said he spoke to her again a number of times. With you.'

'Gareth wanted to convince her to let Chloe join us. She was obviously interested – she talked to Bethany about it all the time. Kate wouldn't even let her walk through the door. That was one reason why I asked Kate to come and see what our services were like. I thought it would show her we weren't happy-clappy types. But it only confirmed all her prejudices. She didn't want to believe. She didn't want to know.' He looked unhappy. 'She wasn't ready, maybe. Her mind was closed.'

I had made up my own mind too. 'I'm going to need names and addresses for everyone in the congregation.'

'You're wasting your time looking for Kate's killer here.'

'I hope so. But I have to do my job.'

'Can I say no?'

'It would be helpful if you didn't. I want to run background checks on them. I need to make sure you don't have anyone in the congregation with a history of violent or unstable behaviour. If I don't find anything, I won't bother them.'

He sighed. 'Come to the office. Stella can print them off for you.'

Stella – the dark-haired woman – did, shuffling the pages together and sliding them into a folder for me as Gareth Selhurst and Norris watched. I noticed her long-sleeved, shape-less top, her ankle-skimming skirt and the flat shoes she wore that were like Eleanor Norris's. I was probably breaking all sorts of rules by wearing trousers in the church, I thought, not to mention the two-inch heels. On the other hand, there were long days when I might be prepared to admit that high heels were evil.

'That's everything for the moment.'

Gareth smiled, all benevolence. 'I'll pray for you, child.'

'There's no need,' I said.

'There's every need. We all need prayers. Especially those of us who walk in evil ways.'

'Because of my job?' I said, wary.

'I think you know what I mean.'

The easy option was to smile and say nothing. Mentally I tossed a coin and decided to be difficult. 'No, I don't.'

'Don't you find your spiritual life is rather lacking? Like Catholicism itself?'

'Not often.'

He smiled a little wider. 'The Church of Rome will fall, my dear.'

'It's lasted a long time without falling.'

'It's riddled with corruption. You only have to look at the things they've done.'

'The things that some of them did.'

'Too many. Men who were supposed to be of God. Men tainted and rotten with sin.'

I tucked the folder under my arm and smiled back at him with equal tolerance and just a hint of condescension. 'If I've learned one thing doing this job it's that evil can be anywhere. Even here.'

And on that note, I left.

14

It was early on Friday morning – so early that the houses on Valerian Road were all dark. The moon was bright in a faded sky, hanging on to the end of the night like a lover. I followed Derwent's car into the street and pulled up a little way away from Kate Emery's house. Una Burt had parked and was walking back up the street towards us, on her phone, co-ordinating her teams. At four thirty we were an hour into the working day already, I'd had something less than three hours' sleep and I didn't feel tired in the least. I was running on adrenalin.

I had returned from the church of the Modern Apostles and stepped into a whirlwind. The preliminary forensic reports were back, Una Burt informed us, and in spite of the fact we didn't have a body, we had a good reason to bring some suspects in for questioning. I'd spent the rest of the day on background checks, finding out as much as I could about them. We needed to walk into the interviews knowing not just what questions we were going to ask, but how they were going to answer.

My mood dipped fractionally at the sight of Georgia getting out of Derwent's car. Una Burt had divided us into teams: Derwent with Georgia and Chris Pettifer with me. I walked quickly to where the others were assembling. Pettifer made room for me. Derwent was brooding at his phone and ignored me. Georgia was huddled in her jacket, standing close to him. Her mascara was already on, I noted. I wondered what they'd found to talk about in the car on the way over. She had tried to find out more about him on the way back from Pimlico and I'd found myself reluctant to say too much about him, about times we'd worked together, about our history of stepping all over each other's lives.

I didn't want her to take my place.

'Ready?' Una Burt turned her phone away from her mouth. 'The others are in position.'

We nodded. The best time to call on a suspect was unannounced, early in the morning. No warning. No time to prepare. No time to get word to anyone else. No *Fly, all is discovered*. Or rather, no *Get your story straight because you've got some questions to answer*. We very definitely hadn't discovered all. The forensic report had kept me awake during my brief night's rest as I tried and failed to make the pieces fit a pattern.

'I don't think we're going to have any problems with bringing them in. They're not known and they have no warnings – but obviously, take care.'

My stab vest was digging into me but it wasn't optional. Houses were full of weapons, and more than one officer had been injured that way. It happened when you least expected it. That was another reason for wanting to have surprise on our side and for knocking on doors at dawn. Sleepy, confused, half-dressed people were generally docile.

It was such a still morning, the slightest noise carried. A metallic sound made me turn to check behind me. It was a key turning in a stiff lock and the rattle of a chain. It came from the house nearest us: number 6. William Turner's home. The door opened and Turner stepped out, taking up his regular position against the frame. He already had a cigarette between

145

his lips, the lighter cupped in his hand. A worn denim shirt, jeans, bare feet: it looked like the tail end of his day rather than the start of it. He looked up and froze.

'Fucking hell. To what do I owe the pleasure at this time of night?'

I leaned over the garden gate and hissed, 'Keep your voice down. We're not here for you.'

'Is that right?' He flicked his lighter and bent his head to touch the flame to the end of the cigarette. It flared and caught, the loose tobacco burning unevenly. Then he narrowed his eyes at me. They were bloodshot, the skin around them puffy from lack of sleep. He was young and pretty enough that the slight hint of a dissolute life made him more attractive, not less. 'Arresting someone?'

'Nothing so exciting.'

'Oh, come on. At this time of day, it has to be something good. I might ring round the newspapers. Tip them off that something is happening. They love to be the first to hear about a new development, don't they?'

My jaw had clenched. The papers had been full of Kate's picture – the windswept one from the beach – and long, speculative articles for the past few days. I had been here before. Slowly, subtly the focus would shift from 'murder investigation' to 'police incompetence'. The last thing we needed was their attention at this stage, when we were still groping in the dark – when we were taking a chance and hoping it paid off.

'If you tip anyone off, your life won't be worth living. This isn't a game, Mr Turner. This is a murder investigation.'

'Found a body, then?'

'Still looking. Maybe we should come and see if it's down the back of your sofa.'

He held up his hands. 'Nothing to do with me.'

'Then don't make me make you prove it.' I stared at him for a moment longer, until he looked down at his feet and nodded.

Behind me, a clatter of knocks on a front door made me jump. Turner stood on tiptoe to see better, his mouth falling open, the laidback slouch forgotten.

'Who are you looking for?'

'I can't tell you that.'

'Not Chloe. You need to leave her alone. You can't harass Chloe. It's wrong. It's like shooting fish in a barrel. She doesn't know anything anyway.'

'No one is harassing anyone,' I said, irritated. 'We're trying to find out what happened to her mother.'

He shook his head. 'I know how the Met works. Find a suspect, make a case.'

'Well, it didn't work on you, did it?'

'Not for want of trying.' He swallowed. 'Seriously, you wouldn't fit her up.'

'Seriously, I wouldn't.'

After a second, he nodded, and I turned away to see lights coming on in the houses on either side of the road. Morning had officially broken on Valerian Road.

At number 32, the door was standing open, the hall beyond it full of people. All of them seemed to be talking at once.

'You can't just barge in here in the middle of the night, uninvited.' That was Oliver Norris, bare-chested, his pyjamas slung low on his hips. Eleanor was literally clinging to him, her eyes wide with shock, her hair all over the place.

'They can do what they like,' Morgan Norris drawled from halfway up the stairs. 'Isn't that right? That's the message here.'

'We'd like to talk to both of you.' Una Burt looked from Oliver to Morgan, as implacable as ever.

Up at the top of the stairs, Chloe made a noise like a whimper. Bethany caught her hand and held it, tight enough that I could see her fingers bleaching the blood from Chloe's skin.

'What do you want to talk to us about?' Oliver blustered.

'What could you possibly think we can tell you? I've answered your questions already.' He noticed me and jabbed a finger in my direction. 'Her. I spoke to her. Twice.'

'These relate to developments in our enquiries,' Burt said blandly. 'And we feel they're best answered in a formal inter- view. So we're here to arrest you.'

'Arrest us?' Morgan Norris was wearing sleep shorts and a T-shirt and should, by rights, have been feeling self-conscious. He looked anything but, leaning against the wall, completely at ease.

'Yes.'

'So we need solicitors.'

'This is crazy,' Eleanor wailed. 'This has nothing to do with us. Chloe—'

'Leave Chloe out of this.' Oliver Norris shrugged his wife off. 'It's to do with me. And with Morgan, apparently.' He looked over his shoulder at his brother. 'I don't know what you've done, Morgan, but when this is over you're going to have to find somewhere else to live.'

'Not the time, Ollie.' Morgan yawned and pulled his T-shirt up so he could scratch his stomach. 'Any objection to us getting dressed before we come with you?'

'No, but you're going to have to do it with one of my officers watching,' Burt said.

Morgan grinned at me. 'Do I get to pick which one?'

'No,' Derwent said flatly before Una Burt could answer. He was glaring up at Morgan as if he was willing him to drop dead then and there.

'Shame.' Morgan looked back at Burt. 'Will you be searching the house?'

'I have a warrant to do so, yes.'

'Then you'd better know I have some pot in my room. Not much. About five quid's worth.'

'Morgan,' Oliver snapped. 'For God's sake.'

'It's not a big deal unless they choose to make it one,' he

said. 'And I'm sure they have more important things on their minds.'

'DI Derwent will accompany you to your room. You can show him where it is.' Every now and then I realised that DCI Burt knew exactly what she was doing. For the first time, Morgan Norris looked mildly uneasy. I'd have felt the same way if I was going to be confined in a small space with Josh Derwent when he was in that sort of mood.

'But I don't understand.' Eleanor was looking from her husband to her brother-in-law. 'What does this have to do with us? With both of you? What have they found?'

'I don't know and I don't care.' With poorly concealed irritation, Oliver moved her out of his way. 'I'm going to call Gareth and my solicitor and get all this sorted out. With any luck, I'll be home for lunch.'

It would take some luck, I thought. We'd hang on to them for as long as we could, and make the most of getting to search the house. There was a twenty-four-hour window before we had to charge them with anything, and I was inclined to use it.

'Get dressed first. You'll be going to the local police station and you'll get one phone call once you're booked into custody,' Una Burt said, completely calm. 'It's up to you who you decide to call. Mrs Norris, is it? Could you gather everyone apart from your husband and brother-in-law in the living room? That would make it easiest for us to search the premises without causing too much disruption.'

'Disruption?' She laughed hysterically. 'That's one word for it. You're tearing my life apart.'

'It's part of the investigation.'

'You don't care, do you? You don't care that you upset people. You're like the Stasi. Give you a little power and you take it as far as you can.'

'That's enough, Eleanor,' Oliver said wearily. 'I must apologise.'

'Don't you dare apologise for me. Don't you *dare*.'

'Mrs Norris,' I said. 'Eleanor. Come into the living room and have a seat. You too, girls.'

They started to make their way down the stairs, self-conscious and bewildered. Chloe's head was hanging down so I couldn't see her face. Eleanor Norris muttered something and darted towards the kitchen. Chris Pettifer blocked her, massive and bull-necked.

'Whoa. Where are you going?'

'I don't—' She put a hand to her head. 'I need coffee.'

'I can make you coffee,' he said. 'You just sit yourself down in here.'

Yes, why don't you sit down in the room full of cushions rather than the room full of knives. I winked at Pettifer over the top of Eleanor's head and steered her into the living room. The girls followed and sat down at the very end of the sofa, huddled together like birds on a wire. Eleanor collapsed into an armchair as if her legs had given way. I could hear footsteps upstairs, people moving around, the low rumble of conversations.

'Are you all right?'

'Yes. Shocked,' Eleanor mumbled.

'We'll get you that coffee. Chloe? Bethany? Do you want anything?'

A double headshake. I had the impression that they were still holding hands but I couldn't quite see. And was that strange, anyway? I tried to remember how I'd been with my friends when I was a teenager and came up blank.

That feeling – coming up blank – was going to become very familiar to me over the next couple of hours as I went through Oliver Norris's house. Searching was one of my specialities, but even I couldn't find anything if there was nothing to find in the first place. I let the girls and Eleanor get dressed once we had finished with their bedrooms, mainly so I could search Oliver's desk in peace. It was in a corner of the living room, set into an alcove beside the chimney breast, with shelves above it and a small filing cabinet wedged underneath it. There was barely room for my legs under the desk when I sat in the chair and I wondered how he managed. With some difficulty I levered out the drawers of the filing cabinet (unlocked, I noted) and flicked through each one. Insurance documents, bills, the family's passports, a tax return that made me whistle and showed there was decent money in pushing God . . . Nothing that made me sit up. I turned my attention to the shelves, lifting down books so I could flick through the pages. They had titles like *Bound Together: A United Church* and *The Spirit-Filled Vessel: A Voyage into Faith*. Page-turners, I was sure.

As I lifted down the last two, I saw there was a box on the shelf, slightly dog-eared and crushed from being hidden behind the books. A dozen condoms, the same brand as the ones I'd found in Kate Emery's and Harold Lowe's houses. I was peering into the box to discover there were only two left when footsteps made me twist around. Eleanor, who had pulled herself together enough to brush her hair as well as getting dressed.

My first instinct was to hide the box, but I thought better of it.

'Do you recognise this, Mrs Norris?'

She looked at it, uninterested. 'No.'

'Do you know what it is?'

'I can read.'

OK then. 'Do you know how it came to be on this shelf?'

'No.' She looked at me levelly, her face impassive.

'Who uses this desk?'

'My husband.'

'Anyone else? Your daughter, maybe?'

'No. Just Ollie.'

'Do you ever look on these shelves, or in the drawers?'

'Ollie looks after all our affairs. I don't need to. I cook and clean and take care of Bethany. Those are my responsibilities.' She gestured. 'These are his.'

151

'And – sorry if this is an intrusive question – do you use condoms with your husband?'

She flushed. 'It is intrusive and I'm not going to answer you.'

'But you've never seen these before. And you didn't buy them.'

'No.'

'Aren't you wondering where they came from?'

'I don't wonder about my husband. I trust him.' She said it as if she expected me to argue the point.

'May I ask Bethany about them?'

'About what?' Bethany slid around the door with such speed I thought she had been there for a while. 'Condoms? Where did you find them?'

'How did you know what they are?'

Bethany gave her mother a withering look. 'I shop in Boots. I've seen plenty of them. Ribbed. Multi-coloured. Extra-large— Ow!'

Eleanor had grabbed her daughter's arm. 'Are they yours?'

'No. Of course not.'

'Mrs Norris, please.' *Or I'm going to have to arrest you for ABH on your daughter . . .*

She got the message and let go. Bethany rubbed her arm, wounded. 'How could you even think they'd be mine?'

'I'm going to need to take the box away for forensic examination,' I said. 'So if you do know anything about them, Bethany, now would be the ideal time to say.'

'I told you. I don't.' She turned away. I wondered if I was imagining that she looked uneasy.

'We're going to need to take the car away too.'

'But you already checked it,' Eleanor protested.

'They gave it the once-over, but now they want to have another look at it.' *Look at,* in this context, meaning *take apart.*

'You know, I don't understand any of this,' Eleanor said.

'Why you would want to question *Morgan* about Kate, why you're asking questions about some old condoms, for God's sake – why you're even *here*. It's ridiculous to think that Ollie had anything to do with her disappearance, and Morgan never even *spoke* to her.'

'Are you sure about that?'

'I think so.' Eleanor wrapped her cardigan around herself and shivered. 'I mean, I thought I was. Now I'm not sure about anything.'

Join the club. It took a lot of self-control to think it and not say it.

15

It was quiet in the office. I tracked Una Burt to the meeting room where she was monitoring the live feed of Derwent's interview with Oliver Norris. I'd already called her with the bad news: with the exception of the condoms, we'd found nothing much of interest in Norris's house.

'How's it going?'

'It's interesting,' she said, muting the sound. On the screen, Norris was sitting with his legs crossed, his arms folded, his entire demeanour screaming that he was offended. Derwent was leaning across the table, talking. The tilt of his head told me he was making trouble. 'I don't think they're going to be sending each other Christmas cards.'

I grinned. 'There's a shock. What about Morgan?'

'He's in Interview 2.' Burt frowned. 'Tricky customer, isn't he?'

'I don't know yet. He seemed pleasant enough whenever I spoke to him.'

'He's been asking if you're going to interview him.'

I had been flicking through my notes but now I stopped. 'And?'

'I think you should.'

I relaxed a little. 'If you're sure.'

'I don't know why he's particularly interested in speaking to you, but I know you and he doesn't. You're a good interviewer. If he underestimates you, so much the better.'

'Thank you.' I couldn't keep the surprise out of my voice.

Burt looked sideways at me. 'You weren't expecting me to say that.'

'No.'

'You're doing a good job.' She said it stiffly, as if it didn't come naturally to her to praise anyone, but she said it. Even if it was only what she'd learned on her most recent management course, I'd take it.

I walked into Interview Room 2 behind Chris Pettifer, whose height and general bulk made the room feel smaller. Morgan was staring up at him with undisguised disappointment when I stepped into view.

His face lit up. 'There you are. I've been wondering when someone sensible was going to turn up.'

I ignored that. 'Did you want a solicitor to be present?'

'I don't need one.'

'I'm going to ask you again when I start the interview, OK?'

'For the benefit of the tape.' He had been leaning back on his chair so the front legs were off the ground. He let it slam back down with a thud and winced. 'Sorry. That was a bit loud, wasn't it? A bit over-dramatic.'

I put some evidence bags on the floor beside my chair then sat down. Beside me, Pettifer put a folder on the table and flipped open a notebook.

'Taking notes too? Very thorough.' Morgan sat up, trying to read upside down. Pettifer tilted the notebook so he couldn't quite see the page. 'You're going to have to forgive me for being curious about all of this. It's my first run-in with a murder investigation.' His eyes were bright, his expression artless.

'Most people we meet aren't all that familiar with murder investigations,' I said.

'I can't really see why I've been dragged into this one.' He pushed up the sleeves of his sweatshirt. 'The solicitor thing was to wind up Ollie. He's not going to be enjoying this one bit.'

'And you are?' Pettifer growled.

'Aspects of it.' Morgan's eyes stayed on me as he said it. It wasn't the first time an interviewee had tried to flirt with me and I was more than capable of ignoring it. I checked the tape recorder was properly set up and started it. The CCTV in the room would have been recording from the moment Morgan walked in; if he claimed we'd intimidated him or tortured him there would be evidence to show that we hadn't done anything of the kind. But the tape was our evidence. The tape transcripts were used in court, if a case got that far. I'd never yet had to feel embarrassed when reading out something I'd said in an interview and this was going to be no different, I told myself.

I read out the usual preamble, stating who we were and where we were, the time, the details that anchored our conversation in the investigation. Morgan listened politely.

'Do you know why we wanted to speak with you?'

'I don't have the foggiest idea.' His voice was totally sincere. There was no hint of tension in his body, in the carriage of his head, in his bright blue eyes. He looked about as stressed as if we were embarking on a meditation exercise.

'We're investigating the murder of Kate Emery. Do you know who that is?'

'Yes, of course.'

'What was your relationship to Mrs Emery?'

He shifted in his chair. 'Um – temporary neighbour. I've been living nearby for the past couple of months.'

'Did you know her?'

'No.'

'Did you ever speak to her?'

'No, I don't think so.' He frowned, looking down, taking

his time about it. 'I'd remember, wouldn't I? I was vaguely aware of her because her daughter spends half her life in my brother's house. She's friends with my niece, Bethany. So I knew who she was and what she looked like. Not that I'd have recognised her from the photograph of her you released to the media. Couldn't you have done a bit better?'

The answer was no, we couldn't. I had scoured the house for more recent, clearer pictures, and came up empty-handed. Single mothers didn't really have anyone to take pictures of them. Colin Vale had diligently tracked her across various shop CCTV systems and got some smudgy images of a thinnish, smallish woman in a tracksuit, her hair hidden by a beanie cap, running errands.

'It could be her. It could be your nan,' Derwent had said, unimpressed, and Colin had taken offence, but Derwent hadn't been wrong.

'What made her different in real life?' I asked now. 'Why wouldn't you have recognised her from the image we have.'

'Um . . . what's the etiquette on talking about how attractive murder victims were?'

I waited.

He sighed. 'OK. She was attractive and she knew it. Very nice figure. Nice smile. Bit of a glad eye. You can always tell when women look at you when you're walking towards them. The ones who aren't interested don't look, or half-look, or look away straight away. The shy ones look down. The ones who are keen make eye contact, and keep looking.'

Or they need a new glasses prescription and they're wondering if they should recognise you, I thought. Or they're wondering if you're going to grab them, pull them into an alleyway and rape them. But OK, imagine it's because they want to shag you.

Oblivious to what I was thinking, Morgan Norris smiled. 'Whenever I walked past her, Kate kept looking.'

'And you never spoke to her.'

'I'm not looking for a relationship at the moment. Nursing a broken heart.' He smiled. 'I don't really feel as if I have a lot to offer anyone. No job prospects and no income, living in my dear brother's house, one step away from being on the streets – not a catch, am I?'

'Were you ever in her house?' I asked, ignoring the invitation to make him feel better. *Find someone else to dry your tears.*

'What, burgling it?' He laughed. 'I didn't know her, so no. I was never in her house.'

'You knew Chloe, her daughter,' Pettifer said.

'Yeah, I did. I do. I mean, I know her well enough to have a brief conversation with her, when she's not locked away with Bethany, scheming. The two of them stay in Bethany's room most of the time. I didn't realise for weeks that Chloe was a bit special because I never heard her say anything except hello and thank you and goodbye.'

'So you wouldn't have been in Kate Emery's house for any reason.'

'No. I said no.' He looked from Pettifer to me. 'Why?'

'Our crime scene examiners spent a lot of time in Kate's house looking for trace evidence, fingerprints, DNA – anything that could help us find whoever harmed Kate.'

'Yeah, I know that. And I know that you took my DNA and my fingerprints. I cooperated fully because I had nothing to hide. If you found something, it's a mistake. Cross contamination. Something of mine that Chloe took home by accident.'

'If it was trace evidence, you could be right,' I said. 'But it's not.'

'What is it?' The laidback amusement was gone. He was alert and wary now.

I took the folder Pettifer had brought into the room. For the benefit of the tape, I said, 'I'm showing Mr Norris a folder containing a series of photographs.'

'What's this?' He leaned forward. 'Fingerprints?'

158

I let him leaf through the pictures which showed a wooden surface and the fingerprints they had recovered.

'Those images are from Kate Emery's bedroom,' I said. 'That's the back of the headboard of her bed. The report suggests that the person who left those fingerprints had put his hand on the top of the headboard, curling his fingers over the top. And those fingerprints are a match to yours. Your right hand, to be specific.'

He looked at the images for a long time, considering his response. The fingers in question were drumming lightly on the surface of the table. Eventually he looked up. 'Is it worth telling you I helped her to move the bed once?'

'Not if it's not true.'

He opened his mouth to say something and I held up my hand. 'Before you say anything, you should know that, from the angle, we are sure that you were in the centre of the bed, facing downwards. And then, of course, they did find skin cells and body fluids there that matched Kate's DNA. The reason you left fingerprints was because you had touched her intimately.'

'And in English?'

'Your fingers had been in or near her vagina,' I said. *Clear enough for you?*

Very slowly, he closed the folder and leaned back in his chair. 'OK. Should we start this again?'

'I would like you to tell me the truth about your relationship with Kate,' I said evenly.

'You could have given me a heads-up before I started lying.' He shook his head. 'I should have known better than to try and trick you. I didn't think there was anything to link us. No one knew about it.'

'About what?'

'We had a fling.' He managed a rueful smile. 'I wouldn't even call it a fling, actually. It was a spur-of-the-moment thing. A one-off. I'd been for a run and I was on my way back,

159

sweating like a horse, tired – I mean, not at my best. She called me in. She said there was a spider in her bathroom and Chloe was away and she was terrified. So of course, like an idiot, I run up the stairs to deal with the big bad spider. Only I was the one who got caught.'

'What happened?'

'She – well, she seduced me. She was wearing a shirt with buttons on it and most of them were undone. She had the most amazing tits. Sorry,' he said, seeing the expression on my face. 'I couldn't help noticing. I was meant to notice them. I was in running shorts and there's not much you can hide in them. It had been a while since I'd been with someone and I was horny and she took advantage of that.'

'You didn't want to have sex with her.'

'No, I did. I mean, I did at that moment. I hadn't been planning it. And I wouldn't have wanted it to happen that way if I had been planning it, because I'd just run six miles and I wasn't able to give it my best shot.' A sheepish look at Pettifer. 'I wasn't surprised she didn't invite me round again, if you know what I mean.'

Pettifer's face was about as expressive as a slab of granite. For the first time, Norris looked uneasy.

'Tell me what happened after you had sex. Did you stay?'

'No. No way. I had a shower and got dressed again and left.'

'Where did you shower?'

'Downstairs. There's a shower room near the kitchen. She told me I could use it when I asked. She wanted to use her bathroom. I think she was a bit pissed off and she wanted me out of her life.'

Of course it had been downstairs, where Kate's killer had washed away the blood. Of course he had found a way to put himself there, using the shower. An explanation for any evidence we found. Something a barrister could use to create doubt in the minds of a jury, if he ended up in the dock.

160

'When you say she was pissed off with you, what do you mean?'

'I mean she was disappointed in my performance. And I think I offended her by saying something I shouldn't have.'

'Which was?'

'That we shouldn't have done it. I blurted it out. I was – well, I was still inside her at the time.' He winced. 'If I'd known I was going to have to recount the whole experience to the police I would have handled things differently.'

I was still stuck on what he'd said. 'Why did you say you shouldn't have done it? You were both single, both consenting adults.'

'I know.' He pulled another face. 'This is going to sound really weird. As if the rest of it wasn't, I mean.'

'Go on.'

'Eleanor. She didn't like Kate. At all. They were obviously very different. They'd made different choices in life. Eleanor disapproved of Kate, but I think she envied her too.'

I frowned. 'So why wouldn't she have wanted you to pursue a romantic relationship with Kate?'

'Um. Because Eleanor thinks of me as her property.' He grinned. 'I know it sounds strange but she's never liked any of my girlfriends. I met her first – did you know that? I was the one who introduced her and Ollie.'

'Did you have a relationship with her?' I asked.

'Nothing serious. She was saving herself for marriage. To my brother, as it turned out.' A smirk. 'But I don't think she's ever quite given up on me. And she *hated* Kate. She'd probably have kicked me out for immoral conduct and being a bad influence on Bethany.'

'So you had sex with Kate,' I said. 'Once?'

'Once.'

'Did you use a condom?'

A muscle tightened in his jaw. 'No. She didn't mention it and I didn't have one on me. Is that illegal now?'

161

I ignored the question and made a note. 'Was it consensual?'

'Was it— what the hell are you implying?'

'I'm not implying anything. I'm asking if Kate wanted you to have sex with her.'

'Yes. Yes, she did. She initiated it.'

'I don't believe you.'

He looked wary. 'Why not?'

'Because you lie when it suits you. You've lied to me several times already in this interview, haven't you? And then you changed your story when you got caught out.'

'Oh, come on.'

'Do you remember what Kate was wearing on the single occasion you and she had sex?'

'Not much by the time I was finished with her,' he snapped.

'Before that.'

'No. Not in detail.'

'The shirt with buttons – you remember that, don't you?'

'Yeah. I mean, sort of.'

'Is this the shirt?' I picked up one of the evidence bags from beside my chair and flattened it out so he could see what was inside. The shirt was unbuttoned. Two of the buttons dangled by threads and a third was missing.

'It could be.'

'Was she wearing a skirt or trousers? Jeans?'

'I don't remember.'

'Did she go up the stairs in front of you?'

'Yes. Yes, she did.'

'So you were looking at her walking in front of you.'

He rubbed his mouth with a hand. 'Yes. OK. It was a skirt.'

'This skirt.' I laid it on top of the other evidence bag: a navy-blue cotton A-line skirt.

'Looks like it.'

'The forensic testing we did showed that your DNA was on the inside of the skirt. Your seminal fluid was all over it.'

He shrugged. 'So?'

'So was she wearing it when you had sex?'

His face twisted. 'Do you want all the details or something? Does this turn you on?'

'I'm trying to get your version of events, Mr Norris. At the moment we can't ask Kate for her story. All we can do is look at the evidence. Your account so far doesn't match up with the evidence we've got.'

'I'm telling the truth.' He was staring at me, his eyes locked on mine.

'You said you took her clothes off, but that's not true, is it? You took off enough clothes to be able to have sex with her.'

'Look, no one was lighting any candles or scattering rose petals on the bed. It was a quickie.'

I put another evidence bag on the table: a plain white bra, lightly padded. There was a very small brownish mark on the edge of the left cup: Kate Emery's blood. 'Is this the bra she was wearing?'

'I have no idea.'

'Your DNA was on it.'

'Then it must have been.'

'Tell me about the blood.' I held the bag so he could see it: a smudge, nothing more.

He shook his head. 'I can't.'

'Did you hurt her?'

'No. Not deliberately. Not as far as I was aware.'

'Did you scratch her?'

'I might have.'

'Did she scratch you?'

'I don't remember.'

'This is the last item we found. It's a pair of knickers. I don't know if you can see their condition through the evidence bag.'

He glanced at them briefly, then stared back at me. 'Say it.'

'They're ripped. Did you rip them?'

'Yes. I did.' He leaned forward, dropping his voice. 'Come on, Sergeant. You must have had sex like that in your time. Down and dirty, anything goes. If you haven't, you've been missing out.'

'I'm going to ask you again if the sex was consensual.'

'And I'm going to tell you again, that it was. It was what she wanted. She told me to do it. She was begging me to tear her clothes off and fuck her.' He threw himself back in his chair, irritated. 'What was I supposed to do? Say no in case she got herself murdered and I got accused of rape?'

'She kept the clothes. She didn't wash them.'

'Maybe she wanted a souvenir.'

'A souvenir of what, by your own account, wasn't very good sex.'

'I don't fucking know, do I? If I knew why women do the things they do, I wouldn't be single.'

'Don't you think it's possible that she kept them because they were evidence of an unwanted sexual encounter? That if she made a complaint of rape against you, she'd be able to produce the clothes to help prove her story?'

'Is that what *you* think?'

'It's what I suspect,' I said.

'You've made up your mind. You haven't even considered that Kate was pissed off with me. If she wanted to frame me, this would be a good place to start, wouldn't it?' He turned to Pettifer. 'You're a man. What do you think?'

'I think your explanation doesn't hold together very well.'

Morgan nodded, biting his lip. To give him his due, he wasn't panicking. 'Did she make a complaint? To the police, I mean?'

'No.'

'Did she tell anyone she'd been raped?'

'Not as far as we know,' I admitted.

'So all you have is a bag of dirty laundry and suspicious minds. And I have to defend myself against an accusation that no one has even made.'

164

'You can understand why we need to ask these questions,' I said.

'Oh, I can understand it all right. You don't have a clue what happened to Kate and you're hoping I'll incriminate myself.' He leaned forward. 'Not going to happen.'

'Did you talk to Kate again after this incident?'

'No. Kept my distance. I wanted to apologise to her for having been a sweaty mess but I thought it would look as if I was asking for a rematch or making excuses, neither of which I wanted to do. It wasn't hard to avoid her and that's what I did.'

'And then Kate disappeared.'

A slow nod. 'Yeah. That was a shock. But it didn't have anything to do with me.' He had recovered his composure quickly, I noticed: the anger had disappeared as completely as if I'd imagined it. 'You know, I think you're looking at this from the wrong perspective.'

'Go on,' I said.

'If she was yanking strange blokes off the street to shag their brains out, she probably wasn't exhibiting very good judgement. She didn't *know* me. She knew who I was, but she didn't know if I was a good guy. She might have picked up the wrong kind of person in a bar or on a train or something. Or – or a plumber. An electrician. Someone who came to her house. She was living dangerously.'

'When was the last time you spoke to her?'

'When I was leaving the house after I had sex with her. This would have been about six weeks ago. I said "Thank you for having me" and she didn't so much as crack a smile.' He shrugged. 'That was when I wrote her off completely. No sense of humour, no chance.'

I had never met Kate Emery but I was sure she had been a long way from heartbroken about that.

*

'What did you think of that?' Pettifer asked.

I dropped my notes on my desk and stretched, feeling all the small muscles along my spine complain. I tensed up in interviews and it wasn't good for me. 'I think he raped her.'

'You'll never prove it.'

'Nope. And he knows it.' I shook my head. 'There's something about him that's not right. Objectively speaking, he's attractive, physically fit, sort of charming . . . but I wouldn't go near him. Too arrogant. He's the kind of person who sends unsolicited dick pics and gets all hurt when you're not impressed.'

'Talking about me again?' Derwent slid across the room on his desk chair. 'Except you can't be. You know that the ladies are always impressed with my dick pics.'

'If they're not expecting much, it's easy to impress them, isn't it?' I said.

'Who are you talking about? Morgan?' Derwent revolved slowly on his chair. 'I don't like him either. I thought he was a turd.'

'He admitted that he and Kate had a one-off fling,' Pettifer said.

'He couldn't do much else, could he?' Derwent looked at me. 'But you don't believe him.'

'He said it was rough sex, but consensual.' I shrugged. 'Without Kate, I can't prove anything.'

'He also said he was shit in bed.' Pettifer sniffed. 'He's an arrogant sort. If he was making it up, he'd have said he was amazing, wouldn't he? Especially when he was trying to flirt with you, Maeve.'

'There's a shock,' Derwent said. 'Kerrigan is a creep magnet.'

I put my foot on the seat of his chair and shoved, hard, so he rolled a few feet away. 'It's a good point, *Chris*. That's a strange thing to make up. But I can't see any other reason why she'd keep the clothes.'

'Did we find any other DNA in the house?' Pettifer asked.

166

'Three other men. We haven't identified them yet. There's nothing on the system,' Derwent said. 'It fits with what Oliver Norris said about her having visitors.'

'Living dangerously,' I said. 'Most murder victims do, one way or another.'

Pettifer went back to his desk but Derwent propelled himself around to sit beside me. He leaned on my desk, staring into the distance.

'How was Oliver Norris?' I asked eventually.

'Inconclusive.'

'Still a suspect?'

'Very much so.'

'What did you make of him?'

'I don't know.' Derwent rubbed his eyes with the heel of his hand. 'Watch it, if you like. Let me know what you think.'

'I will.' Very casually, but because I had to know, I asked, 'How did Georgia do?'

'Fine.' He got up and walked away. Over his shoulder, he said, 'But I missed you.'

By the time I'd decided how I should respond, he was long gone.

16

Metropolitan Police
RECORD OF INTERVIEW
Visually Recorded Interview

Person interviewed: Oliver John NORRIS
DOB: 05/12/71
Place of Interview: Colton House, Westminster
Time commenced: 1235 hours
Time concluded: 1430 hours
Duration of interview: 115 mins
Interviewing Officer(s): DI Josh DERWENT,
         DC Georgia SHAW
Other persons present: Mr John PACKARD,
         Solicitor, JPL Solicitors

**All persons present introduced themselves.
Tape procedure explained.
Mr NORRIS confirmed he had had sufficient
time for legal consultation. Advised of ongoing
right to legal consultation. Caution given,
explained and understood.**

DERWENT: Do you know why you're here?

NORRIS: Because you want to talk to me about Kate Emery. That's what you said when you came to my house in the middle of the night. It was completely unnecessary.

DERWENT: It's routine. Tell me about Kate.

NORRIS: She was my neighbour.

DERWENT: Just a neighbour or more than that?

NORRIS: What are you implying?

DERWENT: I think you knew her a bit better than you're letting on.

NORRIS: I knew her. [inaudible]

DERWENT: Could you repeat that?

NORRIS: I was friendly with her.

DERWENT: How friendly?

NORRIS: I – does my wife need to hear about this?

DERWENT: Go on.

NORRIS: We were . . . close.

DERWENT: What does that mean?

NORRIS: No comment.

DERWENT: That's not how it works, Mr Norris. You can't opt out of answering the difficult questions. Did you have a sexual relationship with Kate Emery?

NORRIS: No.

DERWENT: No?

169

NORRIS: Not really.

DERWENT: What does that mean?

NORRIS: [inaudible]

DERWENT: Shall I tell you what we've found, Mr Norris? Would that be helpful?

[Silence]

DERWENT: The forensic service can say with a high degree of certainty that your DNA was on and inside this used condom, along with Kate Emery's skin cells and body fluids. Do you know where we recovered that?

NORRIS: No.

DERWENT: It was in number twenty-two Constantine Avenue. That house belongs to a man named Harold Lowe.

NORRIS: I don't know him.

DERWENT: Have you ever been in that house?

NORRIS: No.

DERWENT: Are you sure?

NORRIS: I – I can't.

PACKARD: My client is very distressed.

DERWENT: My colleague will give you a tissue, Mr Norris. Would you like some water?

NORRIS: [sniffing] No.

DERWENT: How do you explain the used condom in Harold Lowe's house?

NORRIS: I know this looks bad. It is bad. I should never have done it.

DERWENT: What did you do?

NORRIS: OK. I'm going to tell you everything that happened. Everything. I'm not going to lie any more. I was very taken with her. Obsessed. Out of my mind. I knew it was wrong. I've been married for a long time and I've never been unfaithful. I've never wanted to be. Marriage is a sacred union and I love my wife. That's the whole point. I love her. I don't want to hurt her. I don't want her to know . . .

DERWENT: Know what?

NORRIS: I got to know Kate. I got to know her better than Eleanor realised. I spent quite a bit of time with her. I got in the habit of popping round when Eleanor was out and Chloe was round at our place. I was lonely, I suppose. She was good company and she was fun. I started off thinking that I was there because I wanted her to join our church, but I was wrong to use that as an excuse. It wasn't true. She let me talk about God and prayer and so forth, but it wasn't why I was there and I knew it. I should have walked away from temptation but I was weak. I was weak.

DERWENT: Did you have an affair with her?

NORRIS: Not at first. Then – then I couldn't help myself. But I didn't want Eleanor to find out. I couldn't think about what would happen. It would destroy her. You mustn't tell her.

DERWENT: When did it start?

NORRIS: After she came to our church. I wouldn't have—

I couldn't have encouraged her to come if we'd already been— but it was only a few times. Five. Six, maybe.

DERWENT: Explain to me why you were in Harold Lowe's house.

NORRIS: I was worried that Eleanor would see me going into Kate's house. I thought I could come round the back way, but Kate said she had a better idea. She had a key to the house on Constantine Avenue. She told me we wouldn't be disturbed. Otherwise we could only meet when Chloe was away, or out, but it was too risky. I wasn't always able to get away when Chloe was out, so it was . . . frustrating. But when we had the house, we could meet there and Kate could keep an eye on her house so she'd know when Chloe got back.

DERWENT: And you met there for sex.

NORRIS: Yes.

DERWENT: Did you drink while you were there? Smoke?

NORRIS: No.

DERWENT: Did you have sex without a condom?

NORRIS: No. Never. I had no idea we'd left one behind, obviously. I thought we'd been pretty careful about tidying up. Kate cleaned the room we used. It was wrong to use someone else's house, especially for that, but it seemed like the only option.

DERWENT: Apart from not having an affair.

NORRIS: Apart from that. But we had decided to end it. She had decided, actually. I was sorry, but it was a relief too.

172

DERWENT: Tell me about the last time you spoke to Kate.

NORRIS: I went round to her house last week. She asked me to come over. Chloe was out with Bethany at the cinema. Eleanor was at choir at the church. I said I had a sore throat so I had to stay at home.

DERWENT: When was this? What night?

NORRIS: Monday.

DERWENT: Time?

NORRIS: I don't know. Eight? Eight thirty? We had a glass of wine. I brought a bottle over.

DERWENT: How did she seem?

NORRIS: She was a bit on edge. I felt I was in the way. I – well, I got annoyed with her.

DERWENT: How annoyed?

NORRIS: I didn't shout or anything.

DERWENT: Were you physically violent?

NORRIS: I didn't *hit* her, if that's what you're suggesting. I was hurt that she wanted to stop seeing me. I was angry with myself for not being strong enough to end it. I didn't want it to stop. We were in her kitchen, drinking wine, and I said I'd go. I was in a bit of a huff.

DERWENT: Was that the end of it?

NORRIS: No. She apologised. And then we kissed. And then – then she – um – she performed a sex act on me.

DERWENT: A sex act.

NORRIS: Oral sex.

DERWENT: That's surprising, considering the conversation she'd initiated about breaking up with you.

NORRIS: Things progressed. Obviously.

DERWENT: But she'd told you she didn't want a sexual relationship.

NORRIS: I know. And I would never have forced her.

DERWENT: What did she say afterwards?

NORRIS: Nothing. I mean, she laughed it off.

DERWENT: She laughed.

NORRIS: She told me she thought I should get home. She said she'd see me soon. And I left. That was the last time I saw her.

DERWENT: You said you saw her on Friday evening.

NORRIS: Yes. That's right. Standing in her window. When I say it was the last time I saw her I mean it was the last time I saw her to speak to.

DERWENT: Right. So not the last time, in fact.

NORRIS: I suppose not.

DERWENT: Did you watch Kate, Mr Norris?

NORRIS: Watch her?

DERWENT: Did you go to the house on Constantine Avenue without her? Did you go there when you knew she had visitors?

NORRIS: No.

DERWENT: The thing about Harold Lowe's property is

that it's behind Kate Emery's house. There's a very good view, isn't there? If I was spying on someone who lived in that house, it's the ideal location. You said you were obsessed with her. Did you watch her?

NORRIS: No.

DERWENT: Did you fantasise about her?

NORRIS: No.

DERWENT: Did you resent her for rejecting you?

NORRIS: No. Not at all.

DERWENT: When my colleague interviewed you, you said she had male visitors. You'd noticed them. You implied that you disapproved. Was that because you were jealous?

NORRIS: It was her life. I had no claim on her.

DERWENT: You see, I can imagine you needing to see what they did when they went into the house. I can imagine you needing to watch them through the windows. I can imagine Kate not getting round to closing the curtains, so you had a grandstand view of all the men she wanted to touch her. She didn't want you, even though you were just as good as them.

NORRIS: I didn't watch.

DERWENT: You saw them arrive. You imagined what they were doing. You watched. It made you even more obsessed. And then, finally, you'd had enough. You'd risked everything for her and she didn't want you. She invited you round to her house, but not for sex, not like the other men. She wanted to break up with you. She gave you oral sex out of pity, to shut you up.

175

NORRIS: [inaudible]

DERWENT: It meant nothing to her, did it? It meant everything to you. You'd broken your marriage vows and she didn't care. You betrayed your faith for her.

NORRIS: No.

DERWENT: You were hurt and embarrassed.

NORRIS: No.

DERWENT: You went away and instead of feeling better, you felt worse. When Chloe went to stay with her father, you knew Kate was alone. You wanted her to respect you, not laugh at you. You wanted her to be as passionately attracted to you as you were to her. You're a handsome man. Why didn't she want you?

NORRIS: [inaudible]

Derwent leaned into the room. 'Well?'

I took off the headphones. 'Remind me never to let you interview me. How many times did you make him cry?'

He shrugged. 'You play, you pay. If he didn't want to talk about getting sucked off in his neighbour's kitchen, he shouldn't have done it in the first place.'

'That was nice. Romantic.'

'A special moment,' Derwent agreed.

'He was very forthcoming, wasn't he?'

'Wouldn't shut up. The whole confessional thing. Bless me, Father, for I have sinned.'

'That's Catholics.'

Derwent shrugged. 'Same difference. Talking seemed to make him feel better about it.'

'In fairness, he couldn't deny the condom.'

'Nothing like a bit of DNA to make people feel chatty.'

'Of all the things to forget about, that's a big one. If he killed her, he made her body disappear without a trace – you'd think that would be a lot harder than remembering to clean up after yourself.'

'If it hadn't been for the dog we wouldn't have gone near Harold's house, though. Going back to clean up would have been riskier than leaving it alone.' Derwent sounded distracted. 'Go back to disposing of the body.'

'What about it?'

'I think he had to have help. She's an adult woman. At the very least he had to carry her through two gardens and along an alley. He needed a car. He needed to find a place to put the body – somewhere that was so well chosen, we haven't found it yet. And he needed to clean the car out.'

'There was no trace of Kate in the car,' I reminded Derwent. 'They're looking at it again, but either he did a great job or it wasn't that car.'

'So he could have had an accomplice.'

'I think he'd have needed one.'

'Morgan Norris?'

'It's possible. I wonder if he knew his brother had had sex with her too.'

'He said he didn't when I asked him. I wouldn't want to be Morgan when he gets home.'

'They obviously have very similar taste in women. Or they compete for them. Did you know that Morgan and Oliver's wife had a thing before she got together with Oliver?'

'A thing?'

'According to Morgan, it was all very innocent, but I wouldn't necessarily believe anything he says.' I stretched. 'I did notice they were at ease in each other's company. I suppose she wouldn't have let Morgan stay in the house for so long otherwise, Christian charity or not.'

Derwent checked his watch. 'Burt's doing a press conference in a minute. Want to come and watch?'

177

'I want to finish Oliver Norris off.'

'That's what Kate Emery said.'

'Get out.' I threw a pencil at him and he sauntered off, chuckling. I put my headphones back on but before I started the video again, I looked for Kate's picture. It was pinned up on the wall, fuzzy from being blown up to A4 size. Dark hair in the corner of the picture was Chloe's, though someone had cropped her out. Kate was squinting, her face screwed up. Her hair had blown across her nose and mouth, but she was smiling. Full of life. She had been attractive enough to make men abandon their principles, break their vows, humiliate themselves to please her. She had stuck up for her daughter in the face of institutional indifference. She had started a business and tried to make it work. She had done her best, I thought.

Or she had used strangers for sex, and tormented her pious neighbour for her own amusement, and pestered her ex-husband for money, and victimised her daughter because she needed her to be dependent on her. Two totally different pictures. Two sides of the same coin.

Except that in Kate's case it was heads you lose, tails you lose. Whether she was good or bad, she was dead. It didn't really matter whether she had done anything to bring it about. The only person responsible for Kate's death was the person who killed her. I wasn't going to sit in judgement on her. The only reason I needed to know what she was like was so I could work out why she'd died.

17

'I'm not saying it was a complete waste of time to get the two of them in for questioning but it doesn't get us that much further, does it?' Derwent looked around the room where the team were sitting. Most of us were slumped in our chairs, exhausted and fed up. Saturday morning. No weekend for us. 'All that we've got from it is that Kate had sexual relations with at least two of her neighbours.'

Una Burt nodded. 'That's not illegal and not necessarily a motive for murder.'

'If Eleanor Norris knew about it, it might have been,' I observed.

'But did she?'

'I don't think so.' I tried to remember how she had been the first time I'd met her. Nervy. Tense. Shocked. Not like someone who was braced for the horror of an investigation. 'She was still ironing her husband's shirts. I don't think she'd have been doing that if she'd known he'd cheated on her.'

'What about if Norris had found out about his brother?' Georgia said. 'He could have killed Kate in a jealous rage.'

'But let Morgan stay in his house?' Derwent frowned. 'He'd have started off by kicking him out. And I thought he looked properly shocked when I mentioned it.'

Colin Vale cleared his throat. 'I do have one new lead. I was going through the information we got from Kate Emery's bank. She was living right at the edge of her income, incidentally – she had a fair amount coming in but she dipped into her overdraft every month and she only paid off the minimum on her credit cards.'

'So she was depending on Emery's financial support,' I said. 'Even though it was really intended for Chloe.'

'Unless she had some other source of income that was going into a different bank account. I haven't found anything to suggest that.' Colin smiled happily. 'What I did find was a direct debit she cancelled last week. It was a business name I didn't know so I asked the bank for more information. Turns out it's a small storage company in Roehampton. She had an account with them. It's paid up to the end of this month.'

'Storage space for her products?' I suggested. 'If she was trying to save money that would be one place to start.'

'Maybe. But the timing's interesting,' Burt said. 'Anything that happened right before she died could have triggered her murder. Maeve, take Georgia and check it out. See if you can find out what she was keeping there.'

I was more than glad to go, even with Georgia in tow. I would take any excuse to get out of the office and the slow death of hope that we'd be ending this investigation any time soon.

In the car park, Georgia went to the passenger door of the battered Vauxhall pool car.

'Do you want to drive?' I asked.

She looked terrified. 'No, that's OK.'

I unlocked the car, wondering if I'd scared her and if so whether it was worth trying to mend fences. I hadn't tried very hard with Georgia and I couldn't work out why.

I was putting my seatbelt on when the door behind me opened. Derwent swung himself into the back seat.

'What the—'

'Get out of here before Burt notices I'm gone.' He was

keeping low, peering out through the window as if he was worried about snipers.

'You must have something better to do,' I said, not moving.

'Nope. Only boring paperwork.' He reached around the side of my seat and pressed down on my thigh. 'This leg is for the accelerator – that's the pedal at the end of your foot. Pushing it makes the car move.'

'Don't touch me.' I adjusted the rear-view mirror so I could glower at him.

'Most of the inspectors I've worked with never went out on enquiries,' Georgia observed. She was transformed, her eyes bright as she stared back at Derwent.

'I'm not like most inspectors.'

'He says, as if that's a good thing.'

'Oh, cheer up, Kerrigan.'

'Get out of the car.'

'No.' In the mirror his eyes were steady, daring me to argue.

Georgia tried, not very hard, to suppress a giggle. I debated whether I should order both of them out of the car, or just get out myself and leave them to it. In the end, I reversed the car out of the space and drove to Roehampton in silence.

I almost overshot the road that led to the storage company and had to make a sharp turn. Georgia braced herself on the dashboard and Derwent swore.

'Sorry.' I concentrated on driving up the narrow lane between the high walls of two industrial units. The entrance to the storage company's yard was concealed around a bend and led into a small yard with a row of garages on one side. The car lurched over the old, broken concrete, loose stones crunching under the wheels as I parked outside a Portakabin with a tattered sign in the window: OFFICE.

'You'd never find this unless you knew it was here,' Derwent commented. 'We passed two other storage companies on the way here – big places with proper car parks and lifts. Why pick this one?'

'Cheaper?' I suggested.

'It wasn't, though. She was paying a couple of hundred quid a month.'

'For this?' Georgia wrinkled her nose. 'That seems a bit steep.'

'Maybe it was the customer service that sold her on it.' I was looking at the elderly man who was standing on the steps of the Portakabin. He yawned and scratched his belly through the thin T-shirt that was stretched over it. His tracksuit bottoms were perilously low-slung, his trainers unlaced. You couldn't have said his expression was welcoming. I got out of the car and walked over to him, Georgia beside me.

'What's your name, sir?'

'Yawl.' He spelled it for me. 'First name's Martin. I ain't got no criminal convictions so don't bother looking.'

'I didn't say I was a police officer.'

'I knew you were Old Bill as soon as I saw you. Even pretty girls like you can't hide it.' He leered at Georgia who smiled as if she was genuinely pleased by the compliment. 'What have you done now, Martin, I thought to myself. What do they want with an old bloke like you? I ain't done nothing wrong, miss.'

'Do you know this woman?' I showed him Kate Emery's picture.

'Why?' He looked past me, watching Derwent, who was wandering around inspecting the garages like a dog trying to decide where to wee.

'Never mind why. Do you know her or don't you?'

'I know her.'

'How?'

'She rents one of the units here.' He scratched his head, long nails raking through his lank grey hair. 'Katie, that's her name. Nice girl.'

'When did she rent it?'

'I'd have to check.' He frowned. 'No, I do remember. Three months ago. She said she only wanted it for three months.'

182

Three months. I glanced across at Derwent to check whether he'd heard and he nodded slightly.

Yawl was still talking. 'She wanted to pay me in cash, but I wasn't having that. She tried to argue with me but she needed the unit and she could tell I wasn't going to back down. People think they can fuck you off because you're running a small business but I know what I'm doing. Bank details, direct debit, all in my account in advance, and then I know who you are and I know how to find you. I've got to be able to protect myself, don't I? I've got to know you are who you say you are. I had a little incident once with the tax man – a mistake on my part, nothing illegal – so now I've got to keep proper records. Once Her Majesty's Revenue and Customs have you on their list you never get off it again. It's harassment of small business people, really, when they're letting those crooks in the City get away with murder.'

'She cancelled the direct debit last week,' I said.

'Three months, see? She meant it.' He spat on the ground but well away from me: habit, not an insult. 'End of the month, everything goes, then. If she doesn't come back for anything, it's mine. They don't get one day for free off me. Clear it out and clear off, that's what I say. I'm not running a charity.'

'When was she here last?' I asked.

'Wednesday last week.' The answer came too quickly for my liking.

'You're sure about that.'

'I know my business.' He looked defensive. 'Always been good at knowing when things happened. Dates and times, type of thing. Ask me what day Christmas is this year. Go on, ask.'

Derwent snorted. 'I couldn't give a monkey's about Christmas, Martin. Which unit is hers?'

He pointed to one on the end of the row of garages. The door was closed with a chain that ran through the hasp. It was padlocked.

'Do you have a key for the padlock?'

'No. It's hers.'

'What did she use it for?' Georgia asked.

'Storing things.'

'What sort of things?'

'I dunno. I never asked.'

I raised my eyebrows. 'And you never noticed her carrying things in and out? Come off it, Mr Yawl.'

'She didn't use it for much,' he said reluctantly. 'She was here most weeks but whatever she was keeping in there, it wasn't bulky. It was small enough to go in a bag. I had a look in when she was coming and going, you know, when the door was open, to make sure it wasn't anything *illegal* that was going on in there, because you never know these days, do you, and these are my premises and at the end of the day it all comes back to me, doesn't it?'

'And what did you see when you looked in?' I asked patiently.

'Nothing. The freezer, that's all.'

'The freezer?'

He nodded. 'That unit's got a freezer inside. A big one. A chest freezer. That's why she wanted it. Urgently.'

Derwent rattled the door. 'If you don't have a key, how are you going to get in here to clear it out?'

'I've got bolt cutters. I warned her. I warn everyone. If you don't take your padlock away with you when you're finished using it, I cut it off. But she's got until the end of the month.'

'I don't think she's going to be back, mate.' Derwent hit the door with the heel of his hand and it echoed, as if the space behind it was empty. 'You couldn't get us the bolt cutters, could you? You can blame us if she comes back and gets angry about it. I'll give you a receipt.'

'All right.' He turned round to shuffle into the trailer and I nudged Georgia.

'Go with him. Get him to show you the paperwork for the unit. Make sure it matches up with his story.' I could tell she

184

didn't want to go but she nodded and hopped up the steps into the trailer.

'A chest freezer,' Derwent said behind me. 'Call me paranoid but I don't like them.'

'It explains why she came here rather than using a bigger storage company. They don't tend to have things like chest freezers hanging around.'

'It doesn't explain why she needed it. Unless her stock needed to be kept frozen.'

'She's been running the business for years, though. She'd have had to have it somewhere else if it did need to be frozen. And why would she have known she only needed it for three months? Why was she coming and going with a small bag?'

Derwent was working his hands into blue gloves. 'I don't like any of this, to be honest with you. I can't smell anything bad through the door but we're still a body down on this murder inquiry. I'm not opening the freezer. You can do it.'

'My hero.' I got out my own gloves as Derwent collected the bolt cutters from Martin Yawl.

'I can take it from here. No need for you to watch,' he said briskly, patting the old man on the shoulder.

'I'd like to see, though.'

'I'm sure DC Shaw would appreciate your help with the paperwork.' Derwent shook his head. 'Pretty girl, but she does get confused now and then.'

Yawl hesitated, clearly torn.

'Go on, mate.' There was no warmth in Derwent's voice despite the 'mate' he tacked on to the end. It was an order, and Yawl took heed.

'I'll go and check on how the lady's getting on.'

'Good plan.'

Derwent waited until Yawl had gone inside before he turned his attention to the chain. It was a heavy one and he struggled to cut it.

'Do you want me to call the fire brigade?'

185

'No, I do not.' He glowered at me as he shrugged off his coat and jacket, thrusting them at me. 'Hold those.'

'Maybe a saw would be better.'

'These will do the job.' He hefted the bolt cutters and bent down to inspect the chain.

'Maybe it's your technique. Martin could give you a few tips.'

He straightened up. 'Kerrigan, you're not helping.'

'I'm only saying, if he can cut through a chain like that, you'd think it would be possible for you to do it. Unless he's a lot fitter than he looks. Or, I suppose, if you're not as strong as you thought.'

He frowned at me. 'Still angry I came along?'

'Livid,' I said crisply. 'Not that I want to talk about it in front of DC Shaw.'

'Oh.'

'Come on, get on with it. That chain's not going to cut itself.'

It took him a minute and some swearing through gritted teeth but eventually the chain gave way. I had used the time to get a few evidence bags from the boot of the car, spreading one on the ground.

'Finally.' I waited while Derwent pulled the chain through the hasp and set the padlock on top of the evidence bag.

'Good thinking.'

'In case we find something.'

Something. A body was what I meant, and what he understood.

He lifted up the garage door, sliding it back. I had taken out my torch already and now I shone it around the bleak interior. It was a concrete box three metres wide and four metres deep, and it was almost empty. It was cold and smelled of dust but not noticeably of decay. In the corner, at the back, the chest freezer squatted, humming quietly. It was not a new one. I shone my torch along the cord to where it was plugged in. The socket was cracked and there was no switch to turn it off; I wouldn't have dared to try to pull the plug out myself.

I moved towards the freezer, my eyes on the floor in case I walked through something that could turn out to be important evidence.

'At least it's still on.' Derwent nodded towards the freezer. 'It's when they're switched off that things get messy.'

'So you're going to open it after all.'

'Not me.' He literally stepped back, holding his hands up, as if I was going to force him. 'I've got a phobia.'

'That must be nice.' I bent down to look at the edge of the freezer before I touched it. There was an indentation in the middle, the natural place where you would put your hand if you were opening the lid. If Kate Emery's fingerprints were on there – or someone else's – I didn't want to smudge them beyond recovery. I handed Derwent the torch and used both hands to prise it open, staying well away from the middle. I steeled myself, pushed the lid back and held it up. He shone the torch over my shoulder, sweeping it around the interior of the freezer. Frost bulged from every surface, indented on the bottom where something rectangular had been resting.

'Nothing.'

'Not absolutely nothing.' I pointed to the frost on the bottom of the freezer. There was a mark, a smudge that was less than a centimetre long. 'Shine the torch there. What's that?'

He leaned in. 'It looks like blood.'

'Doesn't it, though.'

'Maybe that's just our suspicious minds.'

'Maybe. It could have been there for years. This freezer hasn't been defrosted since the last Ice Age by the looks of it.'

He straightened up. 'I'm calling Kev Cox anyway. If that's blood, I'd like to know who or what it belongs to. We can worry about how it got there later.'

187

18

I got back to my flat at seven, tired, hot and annoyed. It had been a long day and ultimately a frustrating one. There weren't any forensic officers free to come and retrieve the evidence from the yard; it wasn't a priority when there had been a shooting in Brixton and two bodies found in a flat in Acton. After a couple of hours of waiting, Kev had called me to put it off until the following day. I'd gone back to the office and endless paper shuffling, scanning through mobile phone records until my eyes ached. Net progress: nil.

I plugged my phone in so it could charge and stripped off my clothes, stepping into the shower while it still ran cold enough to make me shiver. It was worth it to feel the grime of Martin Yawl's storage unit sluicing away. A cold drink, laundry, trashy TV; my plans for the evening were not ambitious. It was a good thing, I told myself as I pulled on a T-shirt and shorts, that I didn't have to factor anyone else into my plans. There would be no argument about going out, or what to watch on television or who had drunk the last Diet Coke.

It was no good. I couldn't fool myself even if I was able to fool anyone else. I was lonely.

Still, actually going on a date was unthinkable. I wasn't ready for that.

I wasn't ready to let go of the thought that maybe – just maybe – Rob might reconsider his very abrupt departure from my life. It was strange how I could be totally rational and even cynical most of the time, but when it came to Rob I still believed in happy ever after. That was love, though – that blind faith that everything would come right in the end. I had been slow to love him, slow to trust him, and even when it was absolutely clear that he had betrayed that trust, I was reluctant to accept it.

And there was something to be said, all things considered, for being alone. If he didn't come back, it made it so much easier. I could put off making those decisions about when to have children, if I even wanted to have them. I could work all the hours there were in the day without worrying about anyone minding. I could be free.

I was halfway through my drink, staring into the fridge as if looking at shrivelled mushrooms and a waxy piece of cheddar might cause inspiration to strike (it was going to be toast for dinner again, and I knew it) when I heard the low purr of my mobile from the hall. Una Burt's name flashed on the screen.

'Boss.'

'Maeve, I've had a call from Oliver Norris. He says the girls have gone missing.'

'The girls?'

'Chloe and Bethany.'

'When you say missing—'

'They were at home this morning but sometime after lunch, Mrs Norris realised they'd gone out. It's out of character for Bethany to leave without telling her mother she's going.'

'So they've been gone for a few hours.'

'At least five or six.'

'Have the locals been informed?'

'They're all looking out for them.'

They would be. As a fifteen-year-old, Bethany Norris

189

counted as a child. She would be categorised as a high-risk misper – police slang for missing person – even without the connection to a murder investigation, or the fact that she was on her own with an adult who had special needs. If it came to that, Chloe would be a high-risk misper too. They made a distinctive couple, I thought. It should be easy enough to find them if they were wandering the streets of London.

'So what can I do?'

'Go and talk to the Norrises. Reassure them. See if they'll talk to you. I know Bethany is only fifteen but she's a smart girl. Oliver Norris sounded much too worried to me. I want to know why he's in such a panic.'

'Do you think they might have gone because they feel guilty about something?'

'It had occurred to me to wonder.' Burt paused, uneasy. 'They weren't on our list of suspects, were they?'

'They weren't off mine, but there was no evidence to link them to Kate's death. Chloe wasn't even in London, was she?'

'Unless that was deliberate.'

'It was very convenient.'

'I'd like to know where the girls are, Maeve. I'd like to know they're safe and then I'd like to hear why they've run away without leaving as much as a note behind.'

'OK. Just me?'

There was a tiny pause. 'I didn't think you'd mind.'

Because everyone else was busy having a life.

'It's fine.' I was worried about Chloe and Bethany too. I remembered them holding hands while we searched the house. I remembered the look of terror on Chloe's face when we'd turned up at the Norrises' house to make arrests. I'd thought it was the early hour and the general upheaval, but I was re-evaluating it, and fast. 'I'll be there as soon as I can.'

All the lights were on at Oliver Norris's house, blazing a distress signal across the street. I rang the doorbell, hoping that Una Burt had told them I was on my way. Whether she had or not, Eleanor Norris snatched the door open, the hope dying on her face as she saw I was alone.

'No news,' I said, sincerely apologetic.

'I just thought . . .' She swallowed. 'Sorry. Come in.'

'Thanks.' I paused for a second in the hall. 'We've got lots of people out looking for them. Not only the local police – it's gone out across the Met. Every briefing will include their pictures and descriptions.'

Eleanor nodded but she didn't look particularly comforted. And really, I could understand it. The girls could be anywhere with a few hours' start.

I followed Eleanor down to the kitchen, where Morgan Norris was standing by the window, looking out into the dark garden, tapping a car key on the countertop mindlessly.

'I should go out and look for them.'

'Ollie's only just come back,' Eleanor said.

'So? He didn't find them, did he?' He glanced back over his shoulder and saw me. 'Oh. It's you.'

'I came to see if there was anything I could do.'

'Don't you think you've done enough?' He turned around fully, folding his arms across his chest: angry, I thought, despite the way he'd smiled and flirted through his interview.

'I'm doing my job.'

'That's convenient for you, isn't it? You can use it as an excuse for terrifying two young girls into running away. How do you think they felt, seeing me and Ollie dragged away at dawn, not knowing where we were or what was going to happen to us?'

'We hardly dragged you,' I said drily. 'And you were back by the end of the day. I don't know what you told them about it, but there was nothing to scare them away.'

'I didn't tell them anything. I wasn't allowed to.' He shot a vindictive look at his sister-in-law. 'I knew it would be better to fill in the details than to leave them thinking the worst.'

191

'I didn't want Bethany to hear the details of how that whore seduced you, and if you had any sense, you wouldn't have wanted it either. You should be ashamed of yourself.' Eleanor was shaking, I noticed.

'I'm sure you're right. It might have been slightly awkward to tell Chloe what happened too, since it was her mother I fucked.'

'Morgan!'

'Oh, come on, Eleanor. We're all grown-ups here, aren't we?' He was watching her as if he was interested in seeing what kind of reaction he could provoke. I felt chilled without knowing why. 'That's what we did. You couldn't say it was making love or whatever phrase you like to use.'

'There's no need to be crude.'

'You know, I don't like Ollie much, but I feel fucking sorry for him sometimes. I can almost—'

She stared at him, hurt and angry. 'Almost *what*?'

'Nothing.' He smiled. 'Nothing, Eleanor dear. I'm sure you're the perfect wife in every way.'

'Stop going on about it. And stop talking about – about being with her. I don't want to think about it.' Eleanor turned away, her face pale.

Morgan looked at me. 'Is this what you wanted?'

'I wanted the truth.'

'And you got it. How much further did it get you? Any answers? No? Thought not.'

I passionately wanted to know whether Oliver Norris had confessed to his wife too. 'Was there much discussion of your trip to the police station? Would the girls have overheard you talking about it?'

'No.' Eleanor looked wretched. 'I waited until Bethany was at school before I spoke to Morgan. And I haven't even seen Ollie. He came back so late he slept on the sofa, and he had already left for work before I got up. I rang him when I realised the girls were gone.'

192

'So where is he now?'

'He was having a shower.' She looked up at the ceiling, listening. 'I can't hear the water running any more. I'm sure he'll be down in a minute. He's been driving round looking for them. He was so upset when he got back.'

'It's strange he didn't manage to fill you in on his interview,' Morgan said silkily. 'Almost as if he'd been avoiding you.'

She whirled around. 'Shut up. You don't know anything about it.'

A clatter on the stairs made me look round: Oliver Norris, smelling of shower gel and deodorant, his hair slicked back. He was buckling the belt on his jeans. He hadn't even waited to put on his shoes, as if my presence was an emergency.

'Why is she here?' The question was addressed to his wife but I answered.

'To see if there was anything I could do to help. And to ask if I can search their rooms.'

'The police have already checked they're not here.'

'I want to search for anything that might tell us where they've gone.'

'The answer's no.'

My eyebrows shot up. 'Even if it helps to locate them?'

'I don't want you poking around in my house. If you want to search, get another warrant.' He pushed past Eleanor to get to the fridge. She was standing stock-still, apparently shocked into immobility by the mere sight of her husband, and she staggered a little when he knocked into her. He didn't pause to see if she was all right, or apologise.

'We've been talking about the girls,' I said calmly. 'Do *you* know why they ran away?'

'No.' He twisted open a bottle of water, managing to make it look like a threat.

'Where did you go, Ollie?' Eleanor asked. She wasn't even looking at him, as if she didn't dare. She went to the cupboard and found a glass, setting it on the table near him.

'The school. Around the neighbourhood. Over to Richmond and back by New Malden.' The anger broke through in his voice. 'They could be anywhere by now, though.'

'They can't have gone too far,' I said. 'They don't have a car, so they'll be on public transport or on foot, and if it's public transport we'll be able to track them easily enough. We're looking out for them to use a bank card or their phones. We will find them.'

'I bet that's what you always say.' Norris poured the water into the glass and gulped at it again. 'But kids go missing every year.'

'Sometimes they don't want to be found, which makes it all the more important to find out why they disappeared in the first place.'

'If we knew that, we'd tell you,' Eleanor said. 'We don't know. There was no reason for it. Except that of course Chloe must have been disturbed by what happened to her mother. It's awful. I've been having nightmares about it and I didn't even see anything.' Her hand went up and clawed at her neck where the stress rash was starting to show. I wondered if it was caused by me, murder, or her husband, or if it was the effect of all three combined.

'We should never have let them spend so much time together.' Oliver Norris sat down at the table. 'We shouldn't have let Chloe stay in this house.'

'It was the Christian thing to do—' Eleanor broke off and flinched as her husband picked up the half-full glass of water and hurled it against the wall, where it smashed.

'It was stupid, Eleanor, and I said as much.'

'Jesus, Oliver, there's no need for that.' Morgan picked up a dustpan and brush and set about clearing up the glass.

'Fuck yourself.' Norris stood up, patting his pockets. 'I'm not staying here. I'm going out again. Where are the keys?'

I was sure that Morgan Norris had them in his pocket but

I didn't want Oliver Norris driving around when he was so stressed he was on the very edge of reason.

'Sit down, Mr Norris. You can't achieve much on your own. You've already looked in all the places you thought the girls might be. It's better for you to wait here in case we need to get hold of you, or in case they come back.'

'I can't just *wait*. What if something happens?'

'What sort of thing?'

'What if Chloe did something to her mother and she takes it into her head to do the same to Bethany?'

Eleanor was shaking her head. 'No, she wouldn't. She couldn't.'

'The truth is, you don't know what she's capable of doing, Eleanor. You never thought about that before you invited her into our lives.'

'She had nowhere else to go.'

'I'm not talking about that. Before her mother died. Long before. You thought it was a good idea for Bethany to spend time with her.'

Tears filled Eleanor's eyes and her voice came out thickly, clotted with upset and anger. 'Chloe accepted her for what she was. She didn't bully her or try to change her. She didn't want Bethany to drink or smoke or flirt with boys. She was young in her ways and she loved Bethany and I didn't see any harm in it. And neither did you, Ollie, or if you did, you didn't say it.'

'You said you thought they were spending too much time together,' I said. 'Why was that?'

'They're too close,' Oliver Norris said. 'They live in each other's pockets. They spend their time whispering together. Bethany shuts us out.'

'Bethany isn't all that different from other teenagers,' I said carefully, avoiding the word 'normal'. 'But most of them have mobile phones and access to the internet. They spend most of their time communicating with their friends even if they're not actually with them. But you said they're close . . . are they in a relationship?'

'What?' Oliver looked baffled as Morgan threw his head back and laughed.

'Nothing like sticking the cat among the pigeons, is there? She's asking if your daughter's a lesbian, Ollie. Try to expand your mind to imagine such a thing.'

'That's a disgusting suggestion.' Norris had gone red. 'Eleanor, tell her.'

'They were friends. That's all. There was nothing strange or perverse about it.'

Perverse. I was glad Liv wasn't with me.

'What about you?' Time to put Morgan Norris on the spot. 'Did you ever think that might be the case?'

'Me? No. But I didn't know them all that well,' he said. 'If I had to say, I'd guess they were both more interested in the lad down the street.'

'Turner?' Oliver Norris stood up so quickly his chair tipped back. His brother caught it before it could hit the ground and set it back down delicately.

'The one who's always smoking on his front step. I saw them talking to him a few times.'

'Bethany was talking to him? I forbade her to go near him.'

'So her being in his house wasn't allowed.' Morgan pulled a face. 'Naughty Bethany.'

'She was in his house?' Norris started for the door and I stuck my hand out, planting it in the centre of his chest. He collided with it hard enough to jar my arm and wind himself a little.

'You don't talk to him, Mr Norris. Leave that to me.'

'Is that an order?'

'It's good advice and you should take it.'

He said something under his breath that sounded a lot like *fuck that* and went to pass me. I didn't go so far as to trip him up deliberately, but I certainly didn't move my foot out of his way. He plunged across the room and went down on one knee. I was right behind him, murmuring in his ear that the only thing that would happen if he went over to Turner's house was that he'd end up getting arrested, by me, for breach of the peace, and he'd spend the night in a horrible police station cell that smelled of sick, listening to the regular prisoners screaming threats against themselves and others, while Turner got on with his life and none of it would help Bethany in the slightest . . .

Something I said got through to him. He shook his head, getting to his feet slowly.

'I never liked him. I never wanted him here.'

'I know.'

'I said he was trouble.'

'You did.'

Oliver Norris turned to me and his eyes were haunted. 'Can you go and see him? Make sure that my little girl isn't there? Make sure he doesn't have her?'

'That was the next thing on my list,' I said.

19

My head was ringing, the sound vibrating through the bones of my face. I lifted my head, half-panicked and wholly confused, then fumbled under my pillow for my phone. I squinted at the screen. Half past nine. An hour since I'd got to bed.

And it was Derwent calling me, on a Sunday morning.

No way.

I put it down on the bedside table and buried my head in the pillow again, listening to it humming in a frenzy of bad temper until it went silent. I was probably imagining that it sounded angrier when it started ringing again, though I knew he'd be swearing up a storm. The third time the phone rang I gave in.

'What is it?'

'Where the hell are you?'

'In bed.' I still had my eyes closed. 'I told Burt I'll be in later.'

'Yeah, so she said. But you need to get here now.'

'What? Why?' I stuck the heel of my hand into my eye socket and rubbed gingerly. My throat felt raw and every bone in my body ached. 'I was up all night.'

'This is important. Unless you want to miss it.'

'Miss what?'

'The mark on the inside of the freezer at the storage company.'

'Blood?' My eyes came open properly.

'Dead right. Want to go for two out of two?'

'Kate Emery's blood?'

'The very same. So we're going over to the storage company to check it out and ask Mr Yawl a few more questions.'

'Who's we?'

'Me and DC Shaw.' He said it too casually.

'You fucker,' I muttered.

'What was that? Sorry, I didn't quite catch it.' I could hear the grin in his voice.

'When are you leaving?'

'Half an hour.'

I groaned. 'I'll never make it.'

'Then I'll see you there.' It wasn't a question, and I couldn't even mind too much that he'd taken it for granted I would turn up. I'd have had to be a lot more than tired to stay in bed when, at long last, we'd caught a break.

I walked into the yard of Martin Yawl's storage company holding on to my cup of bitter petrol-station coffee as if my life depended on it. I should have been tired – I *was* tired – but I felt alert. The place hadn't changed since we'd been there the previous day, but it seemed completely different now that the Met had arrived in force. The crime scene examiners were currently crawling over every inch of the storage unit Kate Emery had rented, while Martin himself sat in his miserable office watching as the team bagged up his paperwork, his ancient computer and anything else that could possibly help to disentangle the knots of the case.

Derwent jumped down the steps of the trailer and crossed the yard.

'What the fuck happened to you?'

'I was up all night looking for the girls.'

'I know that, but I'd still expect you to look a bit less . . .'

'Less *what*?' I snapped, knowing it was a mistake to ask.

'Undead.'

'Thanks. Thanks a lot.'

'That's why you join CID, Kerrigan – so you don't have to stay up all night looking for people.'

'The teams got swamped. Three high-risk mispers in addition to the girls, plus two domestics, plus a burglary. There was no one left to look for them so I went out by myself. You'd have done the same.'

He flashed a grin at me instead of answering, and made a grab for my coffee. I jerked it out of his reach.

'No way. Get your own.'

'It's bad for you. Bad for your ulcer.'

'So is stress, and yet you're still here.' I gulped a mouthful of it: too hot and it tasted of burnt cardboard. *Pry it from my cold, dead hands.* 'I have a warrant to search Oliver Norris's house if you're interested in joining me.'

'He made you get a warrant?' Derwent shook his head. 'What a cock that man is.'

'He doesn't like us.'

'And I don't like him. Doesn't he want us to find his daughter?'

'He thinks he can do it himself.' I stifled a yawn. 'What have I missed?'

'It's a tiny amount of blood. You saw it.'

I nodded. 'A smudge.'

'But it's definitely Kate's. And it's not from a scrape – it looks like it leaked into the ice over time. They found more when they took the ice off the side of the freezer. So it's a fair guess that this is where the body was.' Derwent counted on his fingers. 'Last sighting is Friday of last week, according to Norris. Give him the benefit of the doubt. Yesterday, which was Saturday, there was very definitely no body in the freezer.

That leaves a week for someone to come and drop the body here, then retrieve it and move it wherever it is now.'

There was a faded sign on the wall, promising that the place was constantly monitored by CCTV. 'No cameras?'

'Not one. Martin says he doesn't need cameras because he's always here.'

I looked at the miserable prefab in horror. 'Does he live here?'

'No, but I think he sleeps here sometimes. He spends every waking hour in the office and when he's not here, that gate's locked.'

I twisted to see it: ten feet high and topped with razor wire.

'He says no one could have interfered with the gate's lock without him noticing, and no one could have come in or out without him seeing them when he was here.'

'He was pretty sharp when we were here yesterday,' I said. 'He heard the car straight away.'

'And this morning.' Derwent stretched. 'He says no one has been here in the past week except his regulars. Pettifer is getting in touch with all the other customers to check they're all above board and not homicidal lunatics.'

'She could have met him here,' I said, shivering.

'She could have met him anywhere.' Derwent ran a hand over his head. 'That's what bothers me. We're looking at all these men who knew her – her ex, her neighbour, his brother – and we have no idea what we don't know. We only know about them because we've fallen over some lucky evidence. What about the blokes we haven't come across? The ones who didn't grab the headboard or leave their DNA in compromising places? The ones who can vanish a body to a chest freezer and out again without the human guard dog spotting them, or getting caught on CCTV, or making a mistake?'

'They will have made a mistake.' I sounded certain about it, slightly to my own surprise. 'We just need to spot it.'

They will have made a mistake. Easy to say. Harder to

believe when the white-suited technicians emerged from Kate Emery's unit shaking their heads. They had swabbed and photographed and measured every inch of the place, and found nothing. There were footprints: mine and Derwent's and Martin Yawl's and a pair of size five trainers. Kate Emery had worn size five shoes, I confirmed when Kev Cox asked. He sucked his teeth.

'Maybe she walked over to the freezer and tidied herself into it. To be helpful, like.'

'What about Yawl?' Una Burt had demanded, her face strained.

'They only found his footprints in the doorway,' Georgia said. She had spent most of the morning with Yawl, listening to his interminable explanations of how he conducted his business. 'He said he looked in after we left.'

'That's consistent with what we found,' Kev said happily. He was the only person looking remotely cheerful. He liked it when the facts lined up neatly, when the evidence confirmed people's stories. And I should have too, because what I wanted was the truth, not a convenient suspect I could call a killer.

Una Burt sighed. 'So this is a dead end.' The skin around her eyes looked bruised, up close.

'Looks like it,' Derwent said. 'Now what?'

'There's the search warrants for Oliver Norris's house.' I was so tired, I felt as if the ground was moving under my feet.

'You should go home,' Burt said. 'There's no point in exhausting yourself.'

'I know.' I could leave it to the others for a day and the world wouldn't end. It was always there, though – that fear that I'd miss something I should have seen, that someone would get away with murder because I was indulging myself with a luxury like sleep. And it was worse now that I was a sergeant. One step up the ladder and the view was giving me vertigo.

I blinked the tiredness away. *Focus*. Search the houses. Go home. Sleep like the dead. Get up and do it all over again.

'We can do the search in Valerian Road.' Georgia smiled at Derwent.

'You can probably manage it by yourself, if it comes to that.' Derwent looked at his watch, so missed Georgia's glare.

'I'd like to do it,' I started to say, but Burt was frowning at her ringing phone. She held up a finger and moved away to answer it.

'Are you sure you're all right?' Derwent said, leaning in too close to me.

'I'm tired. Someone woke me up early this morning.'

Burt returned. 'DNA results on the sheet from Harold Lowe's house. Contributions from Chloe Emery and an unknown male.'

'So Chloe was using the house too,' I said. 'Nice.'

'Her mum had the keys. She must have nicked them. When you're a teenager, you'd give a lot for a house of your own,' Derwent said, his expression remote. Trotting down memory lane, I assumed.

'Who was she with?' I said.

'She spent a lot of time with that boy down the road, Oliver Norris said.' Georgia looked at me with a frown. 'What was it – Turner?'

'Didn't we get a DNA sample from him?'

Blank faces all round. I rubbed my forehead, wondering if I'd forgotten to put the request through.

'We can get it now,' Derwent said. 'We're going to Valerian Road for the searches, anyway. Might as well drop in on Turner and see what he has to say for himself.'

'Then I'm definitely coming with you,' I said.

'We can manage,' Georgia Shaw said.

'I'm sure you can.' I smiled at her. 'But he likes me.'

*

I should have known better.

I stood on the doorstep and hammered on the door with the side of my fist, not for the first time. Derwent leaned against the gatepost, his hands in his pockets, smirking.

'I'm glad you think this is funny.'

He shrugged. 'You have to laugh, don't you?'

'Not really.' I shaded my eyes to look down the street. At least Georgia had gone into number 32, armed with her search warrants. An audience of one was bad enough.

I bent down and peered through the letterbox. Turner was sitting on the stairs, rolling a cigarette.

'Open the door, William.'

'What do you want?'

'A chat.'

'Mum said you were here last night. It's beginning to feel a lot like harassment.'

'It's not harassment,' I said patiently. 'And where were you last night?'

'Out.'

'Where?'

'With some mates.'

'What time did you get back?'

'Dunno.' He leaned back against the step behind him. 'She said you asked to search the house.'

'It's routine.'

'It doesn't feel routine to me.'

'I'm worried about Chloe and Bethany, William. You can understand that, can't you?'

'They'll come back.'

'Are you saying that because you know where they are and you know they will be back or because you want it to be true?'

'I don't know where they are.' He sniffed. 'Is that what you wanted to talk to me about?'

'That and some other things. I need your DNA.'

He had been licking the edge of a cigarette paper, but he stopped. 'Why?'

'To rule you out.' *Or in.* 'I told you we'd be needing DNA from you.'

'I thought you'd given up on that.'

'Nope. And I could lift it from one of the cigarette ends you've scattered around out here, but I'd rather do it properly so there's no mistake about it. You don't have a problem with giving me a DNA sample, do you?'

He sighed. 'Look, I'm cooperating.'

'So open the door.' My patience was running out.

Slowly, with bad grace, he uncoiled himself and came down to open the door. He leaned against the frame, his face sullen.

'You haven't found the girls.'

'No.'

'But your priority is coming round and bothering me. That makes sense.'

'There are other people looking for them,' Derwent said. 'Have you heard from them since yesterday morning?'

'No.'

'Are you in a relationship with either of them?'

'No.' The amber eyes moved from Derwent to me. 'I told you that already. Don't you two talk to each other?'

'As little as possible,' I said, truthfully. 'Are you going to let us in?'

'Not unless I have to.'

'Then we can take your DNA here.' I took out the kit we used for taking samples and showed him the tool like a large cotton bud inside a plastic case. 'I need to swab the inside of your cheek.'

'Why don't you want us in your house, sonny?' Derwent was frowning.

'I just don't.'

'Makes me think you have something to hide.'

'You can think what you like,' Turner said.

205

'Is your mum here?' I asked.

'She's at her knitting club.' He grinned. 'I still don't want you in my house.'

I was tired of the bickering. 'Open wide.'

He did as I asked and I swabbed his cheek carefully. A car drove past, slowing almost to a stop. Turner's eyes went dark and I glanced over my shoulder.

It was Oliver Norris's Volvo. He was driving in the company of two other men I didn't know. There was something about a car full of men that always made me suspicious but I fought the feeling down. Sunday: they would be coming back from church, more than likely.

I was expecting them to park near Norris's house but the car carried on down the street, turning at the end, out of sight.

'Has he spoken to you?'

'Norris? No.'

'He thinks you know something about where the girls might be.'

'Him too?'

'They spent a lot of time with you.'

'Only because I'm always here.'

'Why don't you have a job?' Derwent, the question bursting out of him as if he couldn't hold it in any more.

'Bad lungs. All winter, it affects me. I do a bit now and then but cash-in-hand, like, or I'd lose my benefits.'

'Couldn't have that.'

'I'm entitled to them.'

Derwent's mouth twisted but he let it go, to my relief.

'Do you know any reason why they would run away, William?' I asked.

'No.'

'Were they in a relationship?'

His surprise was comical and, I thought, unfeigned. 'No. No way. Just friends.'

'All very friendly round here, isn't it?'

'You have a dirty mind.' He gave me a long, appraising look and I heard Derwent snort.

'William, if I find out you know something about the whereabouts of either or both of those two girls, I will make it my business to have you prosecuted for whatever charges I can dream up.'

'Yeah, OK. I believe you. But I don't know anything you'd find useful.'

'Do you have a car?'

He looked wary. 'Yeah. It's that Corsa. The blue one.'

I made a note of the registration number. 'Don't go anywhere, Mr Turner. I don't want you disappearing. And stay away from the Norrises unless you're trying to cause trouble.'

'Tell them to stay away from me.'

'I already did.' I frowned. 'Look, if anyone bothers you, you have my number. You can get in touch with me—'

'I'll cope.' He stepped back into his house and shut the door in my face.

I turned back to Derwent.

'Don't say anything.'

'Not even that it's nice to see you haven't lost your touch?'

'Not even that.'

20

Eleanor Norris let us into her house, her face pale but composed. The house smelled of cooking, of lamb and rosemary and roasting potatoes, and I caught Derwent sniffing appreciatively.

'I thought you'd be at church,' I said.

'I didn't go. I didn't want to. In case they came back, I mean. I prayed here.' She pointed to a well-worn bible that was lying on the hall table, as if she'd put it down to answer the door.

'Is that where your husband is?'

'He should be back by now,' she said vaguely. 'Lunch is ready.'

'I'm surprised you're cooking, given that Bethany is missing.'

'There's nothing strange about celebrating God's love in a time of hardship. He has her in his hands. What can we do but praise his name in company and fellowship?'

'What indeed?' I murmured.

'Besides, we always give Gareth lunch on a Sunday, and anyone else who needs to eat with us. Gareth says we need to share God's grace with anyone who needs it.'

How convenient for Gareth.

'Is DC Shaw upstairs?'

208

She nodded.

'We'll try not to take too long.' I started up the stairs, followed by Derwent. Glancing down I saw that Eleanor had picked up her bible again and was already immersed in it, her lips moving as she read.

We separated on the landing. Derwent headed into Bethany's room and I went to find Georgia in the room Chloe had been using.

'Anything?'

She leaned out of the wardrobe so she could see me. 'Nothing out of place. I don't know how much stuff she had but she doesn't seem to have taken much with her, so they weren't planning to stay away long.'

'Or it wasn't planned at all,' I said, pulling on gloves to open the drawer in the bedside table. It contained the medication I'd found in Chloe's house. I went through the boxes methodically, counting. She had taken one box with her – and all the contraceptive pills she'd had. I frowned.

'What's wrong?'

'Just wondering . . .' I went out and back down the stairs to the kitchen, where Eleanor was sitting at the table, her head in her hands, still reading the bible.

'Did you take any of Chloe's things? Her medication?'

She was lost, her eyes half-focused. 'No.'

'What about the pill?'

'Oh, that.'

'Yes, that. Did Chloe take it with her?'

'No. We don't agree with contraception of any sort. Abstinence is the best contraception there could be.'

'So you *took* it?'

'She couldn't have it in this house.' Eleanor placed a bookmark in her bible and shut it. 'We had to think about Bethany. That wasn't the example we wanted her to set our daughter.'

'No wonder she ran away,' I said, unable to stop myself. 'You were supposed to be providing her with a safe place to stay. It wasn't your job to monitor what she did with her own body.'

'She was under our roof. She had to obey our rules.'

'You don't even know why she was on the pill. It could have been for lots of reasons. And even if it was because she was sexually active—'

'Oliver and I had to do what we thought was right.' Her face was stubborn.

'Kerrigan!' The shout came from upstairs: Derwent. He thundered down the stairs, vaulting the last four or five steps to gain a half-second. As he dragged the front door open he threw over his shoulder, 'Call for back-up.'

'What's going on?' I was talking to the air; he was running down the street at house-on-fire speed. I looked up the stairs and saw Georgia peering down from the landing, her face pale. 'What's happening?'

'I think DI Derwent saw something out of the window.'

No shit. There was obviously no point in asking what. I followed him out to the middle of the road and shaded my eyes so I could see in the dazzling sunshine. Oliver Norris's car was parked at an angle across the road, near William Turner's house, which was not good at all.

Also not good: I could hear Derwent shouting. I put my hand down to get my radio and found nothing. I'd left it in the car.

'Georgia!'

She appeared in the doorway, looking wary.

'Have you got your radio?'

A nod.

'Then call for some back-up, quick as you can. And then come and help.'

'Help? With what?'

'Whatever Derwent has got tangled up with.' I was backing away, impatient to be gone but I couldn't leave Georgia when she was looking pinched and shocked, when she was still –

still – not calling for back-up, when her hands were shaking so much that I could see it a mile away. 'Come on.'

'But I don't have any body armour or gas.'

'Neither does he,' I said. I had no faith in her and I couldn't wait any longer. 'Just – just do your job.'

Every instinct told me to run as fast as I could and jump straight in to whatever situation lay behind Derwent's call for help, but my training and experience overrode it. I went low, behind the parked cars on the opposite side of the road from William Turner's house, until I had a decent vantage point and I could see what Derwent had seen.

Oliver Norris was standing in the front garden, his hands clenched into fists. Two men flanked him, both heavy with muscle, one older, one younger. Norris was talking, trying to hold Derwent's attention. Derwent stood astride a huddled figure that lay on the ground and the expression on his face was pure death: *I dare you to try it.* He was in shirtsleeves: no baton, no CS gas, no radio. All he had was his rank and his absolute belief in his ability to control a volatile situation. And his knowledge, of course, that I was right behind him.

On the ground: a man barely recognisable as William Turner, his face a blur of blood, his body curled in on itself in a way that spoke eloquently of pain received and pain that was yet to come.

Norris was leaning in, shouting in Derwent's face, distracting him from the men who presented the greater threat. Derwent shook his head, looking like a bull tormented by a fly. Even as I watched he yelled, '*Get back.* That is an *order.*'

There were situations where you could shout your way out of trouble; I didn't think that this was one of them.

'This is nothing to do with you.' The tendons were standing out on Oliver Norris's neck. On edge. Something to prove. Reckless.

'It is now,' Derwent said. He glared around, making eye contact with all of them. 'Go on. Fuck off, the lot of you.'

211

'He knows where my daughter is.' Norris was shaking.

'No, he doesn't.'

'Is that what he told you?'

'Yeah, it is.'

'And you *believed* him?'

Derwent shrugged. 'Why shouldn't I?'

'We saw you taking his DNA. He's a suspect.' The older man's eyes were cold, unblinking. 'You're too soft, you police officers. Too scared of losing your jobs to do them properly.'

Derwent laughed. 'You're talking to the wrong officer about that, trust me.'

I was almost starting to believe Derwent might have the situation under control when the younger man spat a gobbet of slime that landed on Turner's chest. I doubted he'd even felt it but Derwent snapped.

'Don't you fucking spit near me.'

'Watch your mouth,' Norris said.

Derwent snorted. 'Like fuck I will.'

Quick as lightning, Norris punched him. Derwent had time to flinch away from it but not enough time to dodge it completely, and Norris's fist caught him high on his cheek. He lost his balance for a second, staggering back, almost tripping over Turner. I could see the confidence coming back to Oliver Norris and his muscled pals, the balance of power shifting as easily as that. Derwent was only one man, after all, and there were three of them. Three against one didn't seem fair at all.

It was time to improve the odds.

The rules on the street were simple and I'd learned them the first time I stepped out in uniform: never lose face. Never show weakness. Never back down once you've fronted up. And never look as if you don't know what to do.

'Assault on a police officer. This just got a lot more serious,' I said, strolling up to the garden gate. I had jammed my hands in my pockets to hide the fact that they were shaking. 'Ever heard of joint enterprise, boys? When one of you does some-thing, it's the same as if you all did it. So if this lad dies, you're all up for murder. And if one of you hits a police officer, you're all in the dock.'

'Look, help me get him into the car,' Norris said to his friends. 'I need to know what he knows.'

'You mean you didn't get him to talk before you beat him to a pulp?' I clicked my tongue. 'Schoolboy error, Mr Norris. Always get what you want before you do the damage.'

'Kerrigan,' Derwent said, his voice tight, because it was all right for him to risk injury and worse but he didn't like it when I did the same. I moved my hand, drawing it out of my pocket so he could see the car key fob in my palm.

I cocked my head. 'Do you hear that? Sirens. Back-up for us.' I looked around at them. 'Where's your back-up, boys?'

Norris's heavies glanced at one another, an unspoken message passing between them. *This is more trouble than it's worth.*

'Don't listen to her,' Norris said, his voice edged with desperation. 'You have to help me.'

The younger one moved then, vaulting over the garden wall and setting off down the street at a pace that was a bit too fast. He pulled his hood up as he went. I let him go. We'd catch up with him another time.

Anyway, I was more interested in getting out of this in one piece.

Turner groaned. Derwent reached down and hauled him to his feet, drawing one of Turner's arms around his shoulders. Upright, he looked much, much worse, his head lolling, his nose swollen, his mouth a bloody blur. I pressed the button that unlocked my car. It was parked ten feet from the garden gate and I had to hope Derwent had noticed where it was parked or, at the very least, might have seen the lights flash when I unlocked it.

It played out as smoothly as if we'd discussed it beforehand, planned it out and practised it. Derwent shouldered his way past me to manhandle Turner into the passenger seat of my car. It would be easier to deal with Norris when he was gone, I thought.

But in the meantime, Derwent had left me to face him down alone.

No problem.

'What are you doing?' Norris demanded. He stepped up, crowding me, his face in mine. 'You can't take him away.'

'I can't leave him here. He's not safe.'

'You're damn right he's not.'

The big older man had lost patience. He jostled Norris out of his way and took hold of my shoulders. I twisted out of his grasp.

'Don't touch me.'

'Don't tell me what to do, miss.'

'When we run you through the box, what are we going to find? Outstanding warrants? Or are you out on licence? Either way, I hope you've got a bag packed.'

'Kerrigan.' Derwent, behind me. I backed away from them, going around the car, making for the driver's seat. Priority one: rescue Turner. Priority two: get every officer to safety. Priority three, in very small print at the bottom of the list: arrest the men. Someone would get around to it sometime.

I looked for Georgia and saw her cringing on the pavement on the other side of the road, holding on to her radio like a talisman, her face paper-white. There was no time to get her into the car too. I slid into the driver's seat and started the engine, listening to the wheeze and rattle of Turner's breath, hoping it was his injuries and not another asthma attack. Eye contact with Derwent and a meaningful look in Georgia's direction; I saw him start towards her before I began to reverse, cursing the narrow street and Norris's Volvo blocking the roadway. Something hit the roof of the car with a bang that had me ducking: Norris himself hammering his fist on the

214

metal, his face contorted with rage. I locked the doors in the nick of time and Norris tugged at the handle as if he was going to break it off. The big man was moving to block my way out; it was now or never.

I spun the wheel, careless now, and accelerated away. I checked the rear-view for the other two, seeing the men running after me as Derwent guided Georgia to the other car. I tore out of Valerian Road on to the main road and saw the blue lights closing fast, carving through the traffic. How long had it been since we summoned them? It felt like forever.

'What . . .' Turner shifted in his seat, bleary-eyed. 'What's happening?' He sounded slurred but coherent.

'I'm taking you to hospital.'

'My face . . .' He put his hand up and I caught it.

'Don't touch it.'

He groaned. 'Fuck, it hurts.'

'I'm not surprised.' I turned down a side road and another, trying to remember the maps I'd studied of the local area.

'Where are we?' He peered out of the window. 'Where are we going?'

'Hospital,' I said again. He was definitely concussed. 'You need a doctor.'

He gave a bubbling sniff and stared at me out of his one working eye. The other one had swollen shut already. 'Is it bad?'

'They'll patch you up.' He had a fractured eye socket, I guessed. His nose was definitely broken. They had targeted his face deliberately. I could imagine Oliver Norris taking pleasure in it, destroying the looks of the man who'd intrigued his daughter. 'But you need to get it looked at now.'

'I need to talk to you first.' His breathing was still laboured.

'Do you have your inhaler?'

'Yes. No.' He patted his pockets and found it. 'But I don't need it now.'

'Just in case.'

215

'Yes.' He put his hand up to his face again, his fingers trembling, and I took hold of it gently but firmly.

'Trust me, you don't need to touch your face. It'll only make things worse.'

'Can I see what they did?'

'I don't recommend it.' I put his hand down on his knee. 'What do you want to talk about?'

'Chloe. I should have told you before.' He winced. 'Can you stop the car for a minute?'

I should have said no, really; he needed to be treated and anything he said to me could be challenged in court. This was far from an official interview. What was more important: the legal side, or finding out where the girls had gone? *Toss a coin* . . . I cut down a narrow alley and stopped. It was a dead end, not overlooked, no houses.

'Where are they, William? Where are Chloe and Bethany?'

'I don't know.'

I felt the disappointment in my gut. 'Oh. I'd hoped—'

'No, I told you. I don't know. That's what I said to the men back there – to Norris and the others. I haven't heard from them since they disappeared and it's driving me crazy.' He clenched his fists. 'If anyone harms her, I'll kill them.'

He was probably too weak to punch his way through a wet tissue at that moment, but I didn't doubt him.

'You love her.'

'Of course I do.' He sniffed and coughed as the blood ran down into his throat. A fine spray dusted the inside of the windscreen.

'Do you know Harold Lowe?'

'Who?' Unfeigned confusion.

'Twenty-two, Constantine Avenue.'

He shook his head again, but this time I didn't believe it.

'Did you go there? With Chloe?'

He closed the single eye and sighed.

Bingo.

'Chloe suggested it.' He sniffed, his eyelids creasing as he rode a wave of pain. It had to be hard for him to think straight. Easier, on the whole, to tell me the truth . . . 'It was her idea. Her mum had the keys. Chloe took them.'

'Why were you there?'

'It was somewhere to go. Somewhere we could be on our own.' He touched the tip of his tongue to his lips, assessing the damage. 'We stayed at the back so the neighbours didn't see. And so Chloe could see when her mum got home.'

'What were you doing there?'

A one-eyed look, heavy with scorn. 'Can't you guess?'

'With Chloe.'

'She wanted it. I always liked her.' With a flash of exasperation he added, 'There's no need to look at me like that. If it wasn't me it would have been someone else. At least I was careful. At least I took care of her. I made sure she was on the pill. She didn't care if I used a condom or not. She didn't care about anything. I was the responsible one.'

Abuse? I wondered. That could turn a child hypersexual from an early age. But of course, Chloe wasn't a child. She was an adult with adult desires and a diminished ability to understand the consequences.

'If we asked Chloe, what would she say about her dad?'

'I don't know. I never asked her.'

I sighed, frustrated. 'So what do you want to tell me?'

'Why Chloe came back from her dad's house early.'

'Go on.'

'Because when she's there, her shitbag stepbrother comes into her room every night and puts his fingers inside her when he thinks she's asleep. And her shitbag father is too scared of his evil wife to call the cops on him. It's all an accident. All a misunderstanding. Fuck's sake.'

'Which stepbrother?'

'The older one. Nolan.' Under his injuries, Turner's face was a mask. 'I've never met him. I wish I had.'

217

There was something in the way he said it that made me shiver. 'That's what we're for. So you don't have to deal with these things on your own.'

'Excuse me if I don't think the cops are worth bothering with.'

'Is that why you dealt with Ben Christie yourself?' It was a shot in the dark. If he confessed to harming Christie I was screwed, because I hadn't cautioned him. I was all too aware that would shut him up. Anyway, a half-decent defence lawyer would get the whole case thrown out, caution or no caution.

'Why bring him up?'

'Because I think you have a history of taking the law into your own hands and I think you're not afraid to use violence when it suits you.'

'I never touched him.'

'What about Kate?'

'I never touched her either.'

'Did she know about you and Chloe?'

'No. Definitely not.'

'She wouldn't have approved.'

'I don't know,' he said, wary. 'I presume not.'

'Because you do see where I'm going, don't you? Kate's dead. Her body's probably in the river or dumped somewhere out of the way to rot. Now Chloe and Bethany are in the wind and we have no way of knowing if they're safe but we do know they're running from something. And usually, that means one of two things – they're scared or they're guilty.'

'I don't know why they ran away,' he mumbled.

'Would you do anything for them, William? Would you dump a body for them? Would you let yourself get beaten to a pulp for them? Would you die for them?' I leaned over. 'Would you kill for them?'

'I didn't do anything wrong.'

'We'll be taking your car for forensic examination, to see if you moved Kate Emery's body for the girls. And we'll be finding you on CCTV. We'll know where you went and what you did. We'll take your phone and track everywhere you've been since Kate Emery died.' I smiled. 'Whether you cooperate or not, we'll find out what happened and what part you played. Your best chance – your only chance – is to talk.'

'I've said all I have to say. I've told you the truth.'

'Where are they, William?'

'I don't know. They didn't ask me to help them. I didn't move any bodies or drive them anywhere.'

'Let's get you to hospital.' I glanced across at him, observing the tremor in his limbs, the pallor of his skin where the blood wasn't coating his face, the general wretchedness of his demeanour. There was the tiniest glint in his eye, though. He felt in his pocket and pulled out his tobacco tin, to my complete lack of surprise.

'Not in my car.' I started the engine. 'And put your seat-belt on.'

21

I was in a cubicle with Turner when the curtain rattled back. I looked around, expecting to see a nurse, and found a grim-looking Derwent instead. He pointed at me.

'You. Out here. Now.'

'I don't want to leave Mr Turner alone,' I said. He was still hovering on the border between victim and suspect and I wanted to make sure he didn't disappear.

'That's why I brought him.' He moved to one side so I could see Chris Pettifer, who nodded at me. There was a hint of apology in his expression and the tentative way he edged into the cubicle.

I looked back at William Turner. 'I won't be long.'

He managed a tiny nod. He was looking worse by the second as the blood clotted around his nose and on his forehead. His right eye was still swelling and it looked as taut and shiny as a ripe plum. Someone had informed his mother but he'd asked – begged – for her to be kept in the waiting area, and I'd backed him up. The last thing I needed was her having hysterics over him, at least while I had to listen to it.

I followed Derwent into the busy area outside the cubicles where the nurses and doctors were hurrying up and down.

'Not here,' I said, on instinct. From Derwent's expression, it was going to be a bollocking; it didn't need to be public.

'This way,' he said, stalking out through a door marked 'No Entry'. No one stopped him.

No one would dare.

I followed him through the door and found him waiting for me in a darkened, empty corridor.

'Why is this bit shut up?'

'They can't use the beds in this section of the hospital. Not enough staff. Cutbacks.' Derwent leaned against the wall, his hands in his pockets, his eyes glittering in the half-light. Oliver Norris had left his mark. The bruise on his cheek was darker now, unmissable. 'Well?'

'Well what?'

'Well, where would you like to begin?'

'You start. Tell me why you jumped into the middle of that confrontation when you didn't have your radio or any protective equipment with you,' I said.

'Because that kid was about to get his head kicked in.'

A complete answer.

'You could have been killed.'

'You could too.' His glowering increased a notch. 'There was no need for it. I had it under control.'

I laughed. 'Oh, I see. Sorry. You're annoyed that I didn't leave it up to you to deal with a volatile situation single-handed. I should have hung back and let you be a hero.'

'You put yourself in harm's way for no reason.'

'I was there to help you. To back you up.' I frowned. 'Speaking of which, what happened to Georgia?'

'She's around here somewhere.'

I wondered if he hadn't noticed her freezing in terror and completely failing to be of any use. 'Was she OK?'

He shrugged. *I don't know and I don't care.* 'Now tell me the rest.'

'What do you mean?'

'What took you so long? Why did we get to the hospital before you and Turner did when I had to explain what had happened to a hundred coppers and their dogs? I managed to get out of arresting Norris myself but it still took a good half hour to get out of Valerian Road. So where were you?'

'Turner wanted to talk to me,' I said.

'Wanted to? Or did you take the opportunity to question him when he was so out of it he couldn't manage to lie to you?'

'Of course not. I'm not you.'

'I wouldn't do that,' he said softly.

'You would. In a heartbeat. You wouldn't think twice about it.' I sighed, frustrated. 'Look, he had some information he wanted to share with me. It's hearsay but it's interesting. Apparently one of Chloe's stepbrothers was molesting her and that's why she came back to London early.'

Derwent frowned. 'So no one was expecting her.'

'Nope.'

'Worth a word with the stepbrother.'

'That's what I thought.'

He contemplated me for a second. 'All right. What else?'

'What do you mean?'

'Telling you that would have taken two minutes. Three, if you were being extra-chatty.'

'Um, he also told me that he was in a relationship with Chloe. He used to hang out with her in Harold Lowe's house.'

'Is that so? Why did he tell you that?'

'I asked.'

'And he just told you.'

I looked at him warily. 'I didn't do anything wrong.'

'So what did you do?' Derwent asked, his voice soft. 'Did you threaten him?'

'No. Nothing of the sort.'

'Did he talk?'

'A bit. Enough.'

'But it's unusable, Maeve. You know that, don't you?' Another step closer. 'If he's charged with anything, you've given him a nice angle to exploit. You didn't caution him.'

'He's not going to be charged, *Josh*. He hasn't done anything wrong, except for pissing off Oliver Norris.' I stood up very straight, flattening my shoulder blades against the wall. I was getting annoyed now. 'What I mainly wanted to know was what Chloe told him about her stepbrother, which is not admissible as evidence. You know that, don't you?'

'Don't get smart with me.'

'Don't take me into a deserted corridor to bully me, then.' My anger blazed white-hot. I didn't usually let it out at work, and never at Derwent. For one reason, he gave it straight back.

'I'm not bullying you. I'm looking out for you.' He leaned forward, jabbing a finger too close to my face. 'Do you really think Burt isn't looking for a reason to get rid of you? Do you really think she won't hang it on you if this case goes bad? Don't you see that you're in the firing line now you're a sergeant? You actually have some responsibilities now, believe it or not, and there are consequences for fucking up. I can't protect you any more.'

'Stop poking at me,' I said, knocking his hand away. 'As if you ever protected me anyway. What I recall is me getting you out of trouble, more than once.'

He bit his lip, suddenly sheepish, letting me see a rare flash of the charm that could persuade anyone to do just about anything. 'I remember. Once or twice.'

'Several times,' I said. 'And I think you are massively over-stating how angry Burt would be. She doesn't hate me that much. Why would she want to get rid of me?'

'Because she knows if you go, I'll go.'

The words hung in the air. Derwent looked as if he wished he could unsay them. I was too surprised to stay angry. 'What did you say?'

223

'Nothing.'

'That wasn't nothing.' I closed my eyes for a second. 'I got Turner to agree to give me a statement. He'll repeat what he told me in the car. He's willing to cooperate fully.'

'And if he's the killer?'

'There isn't one shred of evidence to suggest that he is.'

'Doesn't mean he isn't who we're looking for.'

'I know.' I tilted my head to one side, considering him. 'You know, talking to him like that is exactly what you'd do. Why is it OK for you to do it and not me?'

'You're not me,' Derwent said. 'And you shouldn't try to be me.'

He pulled open the door and disappeared through it, leaving me on my own in the empty corridor. A tap dripped somewhere, too loud in the silence he left behind him. Slowly, thoughtfully, I found my way back to William Turner. He had his eyes closed and I nodded at Chris Pettifer to let him know he could go. He stopped beside me.

'You OK?'

I didn't want to think about how I looked. 'Long day.'

He hesitated as if he wanted to say something else, then went out, pulling the curtain closed behind him.

'It's you.' Turner hadn't opened his eyes, I would have sworn.

'Yeah.' I sat down in the chair by the bed and sighed, feeling exhaustion settle in my limbs.

'Are you going to go and see Nolan?'

'Yes.'

'Are you going to arrest him?'

'Not unless Chloe makes a statement about what he did. No Chloe, no case.'

His knuckles shone white for a second as they tightened on the blanket that was spread over him. 'Can you scare the shit out of him?'

'Probably.'

A gleam of amber from Turner's eye. 'I'm glad I told you about it.'

'Me too.'

'I would tell you if I knew where Chloe was. I meant what I said. I want her to come home.'

'Me too,' I said again.

22

Brian Emery's face fell when he saw me standing on his doorstep, and I suppose I couldn't blame him for not rolling out
the welcome mat.

'What do you want?'

'Are Nolan and Nathan here?'

'The boys?' He swallowed. 'What do you – what have you
heard? Did Chloe—'

'No, Chloe didn't. She's still missing, as you probably know.'

He sagged. 'I thought there might be news, when I saw the
car. I thought – if they'd found her – I thought she might be
with you. But then I saw that it was only the two of you and
I thought you wouldn't have come yourselves if there was
good news. There would have been a phone call. I was
expecting – I was hoping for a phone call.'

I felt myself soften towards Brian Emery. He was hollow-
eyed, his hair seeming thinner than the last time I'd seen him,
the cuff of his jumper stained with something that looked like
grease.

'I promise you, we've got the best people out looking for her
and Bethany, and they won't give up until they find the girls.'

Beside me, Pettifer shifted his foot on the gravel, a subtle
movement with a message for me. *Don't make any promises*

226

we can't keep. I liked having him with me. He was a solid presence, stable enough to trust. Plus, he had driven from London while I curled up on the back seat. I wasn't a fan of in-car napping usually, unlike Derwent, but I was too tired to carry on.

It was far better to have Pettifer with me than Georgia, but I still didn't want to think about the look on her face when, in the corridor of the hospital, Una Burt had told me to take her with me to Lewknor and I'd said no, so firmly that Burt hadn't so much as tried to argue with me.

'Are the boys here?' I asked again. 'I spoke to their school and they said they were at home for the weekend.'

'We wanted to have them here. My wife wanted them here. I think – all of this has left her very upset. It's worrying for all of us.' His eyes were wet all of a sudden and he rubbed at them. 'Sorry.'

'No need to apologise. I do need to speak to both of them, I'm afraid.'

'I'll need to get my solicitor.'

'It's not a formal interview,' I said. 'Any appropriate adult would do.'

'I'm not taking that chance,' Brian Emery said, and for the first time I recognised the steel in him that had made him a successful businessman. Then he smiled. 'It won't take long to get him here. He lives five minutes away.'

The solicitor arrived exactly eight minutes after Brian phoned him, sweating slightly in cords and a checked shirt with a green sleeveless fleece over the top. He was a big man and he made the sitting room feel small when he appeared in the doorway. 'Sorry. Gardening. Anything for Brian.' He stuck out a hand that was still damp from being scrubbed and I pretended not to notice the soil that was lurking under his nails.

'DS Maeve Kerrigan and DS Chris Pettifer.'

'Harry Miles.' He was fifty-something with curling grey hair that started far back on his head but finished well below

227

his collar, as if to compensate for coming up short at the front. He was still handsome in a florid, well-fed way. I looked into his shrewd blue eyes and I knew better than to underestimate him even if he wasn't a criminal solicitor.

'What is it you want with the boys?' he asked.

'We're investigating the death of their stepsister's mother.'

'Kate,' Brian Emery interjected.

'Quite.'

'Their stepsister has disappeared.'

'Very upsetting,' Miles said. 'But I don't see why you want to speak to the boys.'

I turned to Brian Emery. 'Does Nolan have a car?'

His throat worked as he swallowed. 'At school.'

'Has he used it recently?'

Miles was watching me. 'Brian?'

'He, uh . . .' His eyes were pleading with me. 'You've spoken to the school.'

'I have.'

Emery gathered himself together and turned to his friend. 'Nolan has been suspended. He left school late last night. The groundsman noticed his car was missing at midnight. He got back at half past two and tried to sneak in unobserved. They were waiting for him.'

'Where had he been?'

A helpless shrug. 'We collected him this morning and he didn't say anything. He's been in his room ever since. Nathan doesn't know either.'

'He's here too?' Miles checked.

'We brought him home as well, but only for the weekend. Nolan's suspended but the head told me it's very unlikely he will be allowed to return to the school.' From the look on Emery's face it was the end of the world.

'Let's speak to them,' I said. 'Nolan first, if you don't mind.'

'What's going on?' Belinda Emery, in velour tracksuit bottoms and a mismatched sweatshirt. I didn't think she'd brushed her hair. Her face was pale, her eyebrows patchy where she hadn't drawn them in.

'They want to speak with the boys.'

'Well, they can't.' Her nostrils flared. 'Stop them, Harry.'

'I think it would be better to let them interview them here, Belinda. The alternative is the local police station.'

'*What?*'

I nodded. 'He's right. But I'd rather talk to them here too.'

'This is harassment.' She looked from Miles to her husband. 'Can't you do something?'

'I think we need to let them do their jobs,' he muttered.

Her face twisted. 'You're pathetic.'

'Belinda . . .'

'This is all Chloe's fault. Your daughter is *ruining* my son's life,' she spat.

'What do you mean by that?' I asked.

'Isn't it obvious?' she snapped.

'Not to me. Which son do you mean, for starters? You said life, not lives. So which one?'

Her face darkened. 'I don't want to talk to you any more.'

'Fine.' I looked at Harry Miles. 'Nolan first, then Nathan. We'll wait in the sitting room.'

It took Harry Miles ten minutes and a lot of swearing to get Nolan downstairs and into the sitting room. He had a fine, deep voice and the house was small enough that we could catch almost every word. I almost felt sorry for Nolan when he shuffled into the room behind Miles. He looked bewildered and paranoid, as if all his worst fears were coming true one after another. I found, though, that I didn't much mind being the personification of his worst nightmares when I thought about what William Turner had told me. Nolan sat down where Miles told him to and I tried not to dislike him for the sheer amount of money he had spent on his clothes. He wore expensive trainers, designer jeans, a branded sweatshirt, a fat metal-strapped diver's watch. He was holding his phone and it was, inevitably, the latest iPhone, although the screen was cracked and the casing was battered.

'Put that down,' I said, pointing to the coffee table, and after a moment he did so. Trained to obey instructions. Posh schooling was good for some things.

I knew he was eighteen but he looked older, his face bloated and red. He had a long straight nose and full lips; there was potential there for him to improve if he got a better haircut and lost some weight, but I couldn't tell which way he would go. When he looked at me, his eyes were sullen.

'Nolan, do you know why we want to talk to you?'

'No.'

'It's about Chloe, your stepsister.'

He laced his fingers and looked at Harry Miles for guidance. Miles looked back blandly.

'Where did you go last night, Nolan?'

'What?' He hadn't been expecting it. 'Nowhere.'

'You left school before midnight and you got back at half past two.' I looked up from my notes. 'That's a long time to be nowhere.'

'It's nothing to do with Chloe.' His face was reddening. 'It was . . . personal.'

'Go on.'

'I'm not saying any more.'

'Did you go to London, Nolan?'

'No.'

I turned to Pettifer. 'Do you think he thought of changing the plates?'

'I doubt it.'

'So we'll get him on ANPR.'

'What's ANPR?' Nolan's eyes flicked from me to Pettifer.

'Automatic number plate recognition software. It means we can trace anyone who's been using major roads,' Pettifer said. 'We've got cameras everywhere.'

It was a slight exaggeration, but Nolan believed it. 'I didn't go to London.'

'Where, then?'

'Oxford.'

'Where in Oxford?'

'I don't want to get into trouble.'

'You're already in trouble,' I snapped. 'Where did you go?'

'A house off the Iffley Road.'

'Why?'

'To buy drugs.' He dropped his head down to his chest and took two or three deep breaths.

'For your personal use?'

'Don't answer that,' Miles said and Nolan looked up at him, surprised.

'What kind of drugs?' Pettifer asked.

'E.'

'Ecstasy?' I checked.

'Yeah.'

'Have you taken it?' If he had, there was no point in going on with the interview.

'No.'

'Where is it?'

'Upstairs in my room.'

Which meant I was going to need to seize it before I left. Nolan was making work for me with every answer he gave. 'How did you know where to find a dealer?'

He looked at me as if I was crazy. 'They're on Facebook.'

Of course they were. 'Why didn't you say this before?'

'I'd get expelled. There's a no-drugs policy at my school.'

'But according to your stepfather, you've been expelled already,' Pettifer said.

'Yeah, but it's not my fault really, so much, at the moment. They don't know where I was. So it's not so bad. I could get into another good school, probably.' He snorted. '*Brian* will pay any money to get me out of the house.'

231

'Now, now.' The chill in Harry Miles' voice turned the air around them to ice.

'Tell me about Chloe,' I said.

Nolan's face darkened. 'I don't like her.'

'Why not?'

'She tells lies. She said to my mum that I'd been groping her.' His fingers clamped together: white plump hands, bitten nails. Ugly hands.

'Had you?'

'It was her imagination. She was half asleep.'

'Was this the last time she was here?'

A nod.

'Were you in her room?'

'Yeah. I went in to – to borrow something. She woke up and started screaming.'

'What time was it?'

'Two?'

'In the morning?'

'Yeah.'

'What did you want to borrow at two in the morning?' Pettifer asked, frank disbelief on his face.

'Wait a moment. Has Chloe made a formal statement?' Harry Miles asked smoothly.

'No.'

'So you're fishing.'

I smiled at him pleasantly. 'I wanted to know why she ran away the last time she stayed here. Something sent her back to London in the early hours of Sunday morning. And I heard from a friend of hers that it was because of Nolan here.'

'That's not evidence.' Miles turned to Nolan. 'You don't have to answer any more questions.'

His face was red, his neck flushed too. 'She made me out to be a pervert. She told my mum I was a freak.'

'Was it the first time you'd done it?' I asked.

He glared at me, his eyes hostile. 'I'm not going to say yes

232

because then that's like saying I did it. And I'm not going to say no because that's like saying I did it a lot.'

'It's not a riddle. I want you to tell me the truth.'

'I'd never touched her before, and I didn't touch her then.' He looked straight at the bridge of my nose as he said it: a liar's trick.

'Then why was she so upset? Why did she run away very early in the morning without talking to anyone?'

'Because she knew she was going to get shit from Mum.' A smile that didn't reach his eyes. 'Mum was fucking livid when she went whingeing to her. And it is her fault, really, because she's always wearing skimpy clothes and acting like a slut.'

I unclenched my jaw to say, 'I thought nothing happened.'

'Er, what?' He looked over to Harry Miles for reassurance and got a cold stare.

'So what was her fault?' I asked. 'If nothing happened, I mean.'

Silence.

'Do you have enough for the moment?' Harry Miles asked me.

'I think so. I'd better have a word with Nathan too.' I smiled at his brother. 'Just to be fair.'

'Nathan doesn't know anything.' Nolan sniffed, his eyes suddenly wet. 'Nathan thinks it's funny that I've been expelled. He did last time too.'

'You've been expelled before?'

'Three times.' Another sniff. 'Mum says it's their fault for not understanding me.'

He was lucky to be rich, I thought, as Nolan shambled out of the room, his head down. If he'd been born poor, he'd have been in prison early and often. But Brian's money would pay for good schools, fine solicitors, top briefs, sympathetic psychologists' reports, expensive rehab. And Nolan would go on taking drugs and taking advantage of women, taking what he wanted, assuming it was his right.

Nathan was a cut-down version of his older brother, wide-eyed and childish rather than sullen but with the same drawl, the same expectation that what he wanted was what should happen, the same veneer of manners over a self-centred personality.

'Why do I have to talk to you? I was watching TV.'

'Because it's police business.' Harry Miles glared at him. 'So answer their questions unless I tell you not to.'

In fairness to Nathan, he did his best, but he couldn't add much to what Nolan had told us. Except one detail he added to my picture of Chloe, a detail that, much to my surprise, corroborated what Turner had said.

'She showed me her – you know. Tits, I suppose.' He giggled.

'On one occasion or more often?' I asked.

'Once. I didn't ask her to. She was jumping on the trampoline and she saw me watching her. She got off and she lifted up her top.'

'What did you do?'

'Nothing.' He looked scandalised. 'I'm fourteen.'

'Did you tell your parents?'

'No.'

'Nolan?'

'No way. He'd have taken the piss out of me.'

'Do you know why she did it?'

He wrinkled his nose. 'Because she's mental?'

When he left the room, Harry Miles behind him, I fell back against the perfect cushions and groaned. 'What the hell was going on in this family?'

'Nothing good.' Pettifer got to his feet with a grunt. 'Do you know what surprises me?'

'What?'

'That there was only one murder. I can think of two or three candidates and I've only just met them.'

23

I walked into the office on Monday morning in a Monday-morning mood, and I wasn't the only one. I could hear Derwent holding forth even before I got through the door. He was in Una Burt's office, the door closed, but the view through the window told me he was furious.

'What's going on?' I asked Liv.

'No idea.'

The two of us stood and watched for a minute, like tourists on safari watching a bloody kill. I tried to pick out individual words. Derwent was doing all the talking – well, shouting. I moved to see Una Burt's expression: bored, largely. She caught sight of me and beckoned to me imperiously.

Shit.

I trudged across to her office and opened the door. Derwent wheeled around.

'Oh, you've made it into work, have you?'

'I'm not late,' I said, knowing that I wasn't, resisting the urge to check my watch anyway. 'What's up?'

'They NFA'd Oliver Norris.'

NFA stood for No Further Action; it meant that the coppers who'd arrested him had decided there was no point in charging him or investigating further.

'How come? William Turner was in shreds. Not to mention that he hit you.'

'Yeah, I did notice that.' The bruise was bluish purple and looked painful.

'Josh decided not to make a statement about it.' There was no judgement in Una Burt's voice but Derwent took it badly anyway.

'Only because I thought it would be a waste of time to get him charged with assaulting me. He'd beaten the tar out of Turner.'

'And you didn't want to have the bother of getting him prosecuted for punching you,' Una Burt said. 'Very understandable.'

'Look, I had more important things to do.'

'Didn't Turner give a statement?' I had left him in the hospital, dozing, compliant. 'I thought Norris would get charged with GBH.'

'He said he didn't see who hit him.' Burt shrugged. 'You can see his point. He has to live in the street. Not much fun when you've accused one of the neighbours of something that carries a heavy sentence.'

'He has to live with a neighbour who was prepared to beat him to a pulp. I'd say that's worse than a little social embarrassment.'

Una Burt sighed. 'There's nothing we can do about it, Maeve.'

'We witnessed some of the attack,' I said. 'What if we make statements about it?'

'If Turner isn't going to cooperate the CPS aren't going to be all that keen to take it to court. It's hard to explain why the victim doesn't want to give evidence in a case like this. It makes juries think they're not being told the whole story and they don't convict.'

I turned to Derwent. 'What about you? You could make a statement now. That bruise has come up lovely.'

236

He raised a hand to it, defensive. 'Yeah, I could. But realistically he's not going to be held in custody for thumping me, is he? He'll be out on bail in an hour or two and we'll be back to square one.'

'So he's back at home?' I bit my lip. 'What about Turner?'

'They kept him in overnight but I think they'll be releasing him today. He didn't need surgery. It was concussion they were worried about.'

'I think someone needs to pay Norris a visit to remind him to stay away from Turner,' I said.

'I volunteer,' Derwent said grimly.

'That's not a good idea,' Una Burt said.

'Oh, come on. I'm not going to pick a fight with him. But he's not going to listen to Kerrigan asking him nicely not to cause any trouble, is he?'

'Much as it grieves me to say it, he's right. Norris isn't the sort of man who pays much attention to women at the best of times.'

'Fine,' Burt said. 'But go with him, Maeve. And I don't want to get any complaints about your behaviour, Josh. I'm still filling out forms from the last time.'

Derwent blinked, innocent. 'I told you, that was all a misunderstanding.'

'You did say that, yes.' She flipped open a file and started reading. 'Off you go.'

I parked a short distance from Oliver Norris's house and walked back with Derwent. In spite of the horrors the street had seen, normal life was reasserting itself. This was the Valerian Road Kate Emery had known – window cleaners, Ocado delivery vans, scaffolders slinging metal poles and bad language about as they built a framework around a house.

Normal, privileged, middle-class life.

And behind door number one: blood-soaked carpets, blood-stained walls.

Behind door number two: bruised knuckles, empty beds, the word of the Lord.

Behind door number three: fractures, stitches, fighting for breath, fighting for life.

What private hell would I find if I knocked on door number four? Or five?

It was Oliver Norris himself who came to the door.

'What do you want?'

It took me a second to respond. I was distracted by the way Norris looked: his hair dishevelled, his eyes puffy and red as if he'd been crying. Stubble darkened his chin and a sour smell emanated from him: rank sweat. He was squinting at the sunlight as if he hadn't slept much, or at all. Somewhere in the house, music was playing: a gospel choir. Even as I noticed it, the sound was turned up.

'Is everything all right, Mr Norris?'

'Yes, of course.' He seemed to pull himself together. 'What can I do for you?'

'We popped round to give you a few words of advice,' Derwent said. 'About Mr Turner.'

Norris nodded. 'I thought you might.'

'You need to stay away from him. Don't talk to him, don't look at him, don't cross to the same side of the street as him. Pretend he doesn't exist.'

'Is that it?'

Derwent didn't move or speak, but something in his expression made Norris take a step back. 'OK. OK, I get the picture. I'll ignore him.'

'You've been very lucky not to be charged with some serious, serious offences. If there's any reason for Mr Turner to make a complaint about you, I will make sure that you are prosecuted properly and promptly for anything I can think of.'

'Noted.' Norris cleared his throat. 'Sorry about your face. It looks painful.'

'About as painful as your hand, I'd say.'

Norris looked down at his knuckles, flexing his hand. They were swollen and bruised, his skin scratched. 'Yeah. I made a bit of a mess of myself yesterday. Lesson learned.'

'I hope so,' I said.

He flicked a look at me and I wasn't imagining the hostility. I had challenged him and he had lost, after all. I was surprised I hadn't been struck down by a bolt of divine lightning.

'Thanks for calling round.' He started to close the door and two things happened: the choir fell silent and I stuck my foot in the door.

'Hold it. What's that?' There were six, maybe seven seconds of silence before the organ thundered into life again, and in that time I heard, very clearly, the sound of sobbing.

'I didn't hear anything,' Norris said.

'Someone is crying,' I said.

'I heard it too.' Maybe Derwent had and maybe he hadn't, but he wasn't about to let me down. 'What's going on?'

Norris's shoulders slumped. 'I'd hoped – I wanted – look, she got back very late last night. I don't think she's in any condition to speak to you.'

'Who got back? Bethany? With Chloe? Where were they? Why didn't you tell us?' The questions were tumbling out of my mouth and Derwent brushed the back of my hand with his knuckles, so subtly that Norris would never have noticed it.

'It's Bethany. Bethany came home.'

'Not Chloe?'

He shook his head.

'When?'

'Eleven – twelve. Some time like that.'

'Did you tell anyone? The police?'

'No.' Norris shook his head. 'I rang the officer we'd spoken to about her disappearance but he wasn't on duty. I did leave a message for him.'

Which he would have received in four days, given the usual

239

shift pattern: two earlys, two lates, two nights, four off. I couldn't keep the edge out of my voice. 'They are still looking for her. And Chloe. Didn't it occur to you that Bethany might be able to help us find Chloe?'

'She doesn't know anything.'

'She knows more than I do about why Chloe disappeared in the first place. She knows where she last saw Chloe, and when. She might know where Chloe intended to go.'

'We need to speak to her,' Derwent said, cutting across me. 'Right now.'

'She's not well enough.' Norris started to close the door again. 'She can't.'

'I'm going to have to insist,' I said.

'And I'm going to have to insist on you leaving us alone.' Norris's face had gone red.

'Ollie.' Eleanor appeared behind him and put a hand on his shoulder. 'It's all right.'

'Let me handle this.'

'Of course.' She bowed her head. 'I didn't mean— but if they need to speak to her.'

'She's in no condition to speak to anyone. I don't think she can.' Norris's shoulders sagged. 'She hasn't said anything at all since she came back.'

'I could sit with her,' Eleanor murmured. 'She wouldn't be on her own.'

'Please,' I said, despising myself for begging. 'For Chloe's sake. Bethany wouldn't want her to be in danger.'

Norris looked at me, unseeing, for a long moment. Then he nodded.

'I'll go and tell her you're here.' Eleanor stopped, one foot on the bottom step of the stairs. 'She's in bed so I think we would prefer a female officer to speak to her.'

'Of course,' Derwent said. He sounded polite but the muscle flickering in his jaw told a different story. 'I'll wait while DS Kerrigan speaks to her.'

'I think that's best.' Eleanor carried on upstairs. Norris moved back to allow us inside the house, his face stony.

'If you upset her—'

'That's the last thing I want to do.'

He snorted. 'I'm sure.'

'Sounds as if she's already upset,' Derwent commented. 'Given that she was crying.'

'She's exhausted. We're all exhausted.' Norris shook his head. 'This whole thing has been a nightmare. What happened to Kate – of course we had to let Chloe stay with us. But if I'd known how hard it would be – and Bethany going missing . . . I mean, she has to be our priority. I'm sure you can understand that.'

'I understand,' I said shortly. *I understand that you're trying to protect your daughter and you don't give a shit about Kate's daughter. So much for Christian charity.*

'Can we take the clothes she was wearing?' I asked.

Norris's eyes flickered. 'I think Eleanor's washed them. In fact, I know she has.'

It was a blow but I dredged up a smile. 'Never mind. It's surprising what survives a trip through the washing machine.'

'I'll get evidence bags from the car and let everyone know Bethany's been located.' Derwent headed out of the door and I could tell Norris was itching to shut it behind him.

'Detective? You can come up,' Eleanor called.

I went past Oliver Norris fast enough to feel a breeze, just in case he changed his mind. Eleanor was standing in the doorway of her daughter's bedroom.

'Don't take too long. She needs to rest.'

Bethany was curled up in bed, a small shape under the covers. I edged around the bed until I could see her face, her eyes tight shut, her expression pure misery. The curtains were drawn in the room and I could barely see her. I tweaked one back a few inches and she winced.

'Sorry, Bethany. Only it's a bit dark in here.'

She looked thin, her face flushed and feverish. Without glasses, her eyes looked vulnerable, defenceless. Her lips were chapped but a full glass of water stood on the bedside table.

'Has she been checked over by a doctor?' I asked, crouching so I could feel her forehead. It was hot and she flinched away from my touch.

Eleanor shook her head. 'She was fine. She didn't need a doctor. She needed rest.'

'Bethany, I need to ask you if you know where Chloe is.'

Her whole body shuddered and she screwed her eyes tight shut.

'Where did you last see her?'

No answer.

'She could be in trouble, Bethany. In danger, even. We need to find her urgently.'

'And what are you doing about it?' Eleanor's voice was too loud in the gloom. 'Apart from bothering my daughter, I mean.'

'There've been appeals on social media and the local news. She's going to be featured on national news bulletins today.' I checked my watch. 'It'll be on the one o'clock news.'

'But it's two days since she disappeared.'

'Vulnerable people go missing all the time.' I stood up. 'We were balancing Chloe's need for privacy with her safety. Especially given her current situation. There's going to be a lot of media interest in her disappearance. That's why we really need to know why she left and where she was planning to go.'

'If Bethany doesn't know she can't tell you.'

'I appreciate that. Anything she knows might help.' I crouched again. 'Bethany, where did you go? Where were you hiding?'

No answer.

'Were you together?'

She gave the tiniest of nods.

'All the time?'

Another nod.

'So when did you leave her? Or did she leave you? Did someone help you to hide? Did you argue?'

Tears were sliding out from under her eyelids.

'Bethany, please.'

'That's enough,' Eleanor said, leaning over her daughter as if she needed to shield her from me.

'But I need to—'

'No. I'm sorry. You need to leave right now.'

'Bethany, you know you can talk to me. You're not in trouble and neither is Chloe. We need to make sure Chloe is somewhere safe.'

Bethany buried her face under the covers and gave a low wail that made the hairs stand up on my arms.

'Go now. Please. Go,' Eleanor said.

'I'll come back soon, Bethany,' I said. *And hopefully I can speak to you without your mother intervening.* I didn't know if she'd been afraid to talk in front of Eleanor but I had to assume it was part of the problem.

The hall downstairs seemed full of people but there were only three; it was just that they were all large men. Oliver Norris, Derwent, Morgan Norris. The latter looked up as I came down the stairs and grinned.

'Well, if it isn't Juliet Bravo.'

'That was her call sign, not her name,' I said.

'The thing I like about you is your passion for accuracy.' Morgan gave the word *passion* full value, lingering over it, and I felt a chill ghost over my skin. I don't know how I looked, but it made Derwent move between me and Morgan, crowding him. Morgan held his ground until the last possible minute, then fell back. 'All right. It's all right.'

'I apologise for my brother,' Oliver said from behind me.

'There's no need.' I wanted to get out of the house: it was stifling, the air fraught with tension. 'If Bethany wants to talk to me, I'll make myself available. Any time.'

'Even in the middle of the night?' Morgan asked, then raised his hands as Derwent twisted to glower at him. 'God, can't a man ask a simple question?'

'Not if it's you.'

'You don't like me, do you? I can tell.'

I'd often thought it would be easier to work with Derwent if he wore a lead, so I could drag him out of trouble. I was starting to think a muzzle might not be such a bad idea either. I cleared my throat.

'I think we're finished here.'

It was by no means immediate but eventually Derwent tore himself away and followed me out of the house. He waited until the door closed behind us before he took hold of my arm just above the elbow, pulling me close to him so he could murmur in my ear.

'I don't want you going back there on your own. Not for any reason.'

'He wouldn't do anything.'

'I'm not so sure.' Derwent looked back over his shoulder. 'I don't like him. And I don't like his brother. If you're going to that house, you're going to take me along.'

'Even if it's the middle of the night?' I asked, imitating the way Morgan had spoken.

'Especially then.' A shake of my arm. 'Promise me.'

I promised. I had to. I knew Derwent well enough to know he'd never have let go of my arm until I did.

We stopped on the way back to the office so I could get petrol. I bought coffee for Derwent while I was paying. It wasn't so much a peace offering as avoiding a bigger, worse argument about leaving him out.

He wasn't waiting in the car. I suppressed a sigh and looked around, eventually spotting him. He was pacing up and down near the car wash, on his phone, deep in conversation. I moved the car so it wasn't blocking the pump any more and leaned back in my seat, thinking about Kate Emery and Morgan Norris and how much I'd like to arrest him for killing her if I could find one speck of evidence against him.

I was sipping coffee when a dark figure appeared on the periphery of my vision and my heart jumped into my throat. I glowered up at Derwent, who yanked open my door and leaned one arm on it. He braced the other on the roof of the car, looming over me. Personal space was not a concept he respected.

'You gave me a fright,' I snapped. 'What do you want?'

'They think they've found Chloe.'

The relief made me feel weak. 'That's brilliant. Two for two.' Then I saw the expression on his face. 'Not brilliant?'

'They need us to go out to Surrey.' It seemed to take him a long time to say the next bit. I wouldn't have minded if he'd never said it. I knew what was coming and I didn't want to hear it. 'They've found a body.'

24

Surrey was a big county but we were in luck, if you wanted to call it that: the body was just beyond the M25. I parked behind a black mortuary van on a country lane that felt as remote from London as the moon. The sun shone, the birds sang in the trees, the weather was picnic-perfect.

Silently, I stood by the boot of the car changing into welling-tons. It was soft going at the crime scene, I'd heard. Glancing along the line of vehicles I saw Una Burt's car and the patholo-gist's BMW. *The gang's all here . . .*

'Ready?' Derwent asked.

I nodded and started down the lane. He kept pace with me, shortening his stride to match mine, a solid presence at my elbow though he knew better than to try to talk. I could hear a plane humming towards us, louder and louder. Heathrow Airport was nearby, I reminded myself. We weren't so far from civilisation as all that.

A uniformed officer checked our credentials and made a note of our attendance at the scene on her clipboard. She directed us through a scrubby bit of woodland.

'It's about five minutes from here. You'll see them when you get out the other side of the trees.'

The woodland was criss-crossed with desire lines, suggestions of paths rather than established routes, overgrown with grass and weeds. The sunlight shone through the leaves, breaking through in tiny patches here and there that spangled the ground. It was like being underwater, cool and green and hushed. It should have been a pleasant place to walk.

'Who found her? Was it a dog walker?'

'I didn't ask,' Derwent said.

We were a long way past joking about it.

The officer had been right: it was easy to see where we needed to go once we emerged from the treeline. We cut across a small grassy field to where Una Burt stood, a little way away from the others. As I got closer I could see the field's boundary was composed of low bushes with an occasional tree, the spaces between filled with white clouds of meadowsweet and thick stands of nettles. On the other side of that a shallow stream dragged itself sluggishly over rounded stones. The water level was low, the banks choked with greenery. The white suits were ankle-deep in the water or crawling around on the banks, measuring and sampling. *Too late. Too late.*

I forced the words down and made myself greet the chief inspector. 'Boss.'

'Where is she?' That was Derwent, getting straight to the point.

Burt pointed wordlessly, and I saw: lying on the grass face up, her head tilted back and away from us, her hair wet and tangled like weeds. Chloe, but not Chloe any more now that the life had left her. She was naked, her body pale against the grass. There was a streak of mud on one thigh but aside from that I couldn't see a mark on her. Her legs were together, her arms by her sides.

'Did someone pull her out of the stream?' Derwent asked.

'The guy who found her. He dragged her out of the water, then realised she was dead and there was no point in doing

CPR. He had chest pains afterwards. We had to call an ambulance for him.'

'Is he local?'

'He owns the land. Nothing strange about him being here.'

'Why here?' I said, looking around. 'It's a walk from the road and it's in the middle of nowhere.'

'It's not as remote as all that,' Burt said. Another plane was approaching. She pointed up. 'Flight path.'

The three of us tilted our heads back, watching as the plane went over. The landing gear was down, the great engines roaring. Hundreds of people would be on board, oblivious to what lay beneath them, untouched by it.

'I suppose most people wouldn't choose this area for their country walk,' I said, when the sound had died away.

'We'll be looking for Kate Emery's body around here too – I've got a cadaver dog coming along later.'

'It's definitely Chloe, I suppose,' Derwent said. 'We're sure about that.'

'It's her,' I said, certain.

Burt nodded. 'No doubt about it, though we'll need her father to do the formal ID.'

It hit me with physical force so I struggled to breathe, not to sob: *Not a phone call, Mr Emery; it'll be a personal visit from grave-faced officers, bringing you the worst news of all, and there's nothing you can do to stop it.*

Una Burt was looking at me, doubt in her eyes. 'Are you all right?'

I nodded, somehow. To my eternal relief her phone rang and she turned away to answer it. Derwent's hand was on my arm, squeezing slightly too hard.

'Pull yourself together,' he murmured so only I could hear it.

It wasn't the done thing, to be emotional at a crime scene. Not unless it was a child. You could care about children. It was all right to cry about their innocent broken bodies. It

248

was strange if you didn't, in fact – a sign you'd burned out, that it was time to change jobs and do something other than homicide investigation. But it wasn't all right to cry about young women who had struggled to find their way, who had been victims since the day they were born. I bent over, pain lancing through my stomach.

'The fuck is wrong with you, Kerrigan.' He stepped back, though, pulling me with him, standing in front of me so I was shielded from the other officers while I tried to control my breathing. I didn't know whether I was going to cry or be sick for a few seconds. I didn't know which would be worse.

'I'm OK,' I said at last, not looking at him.

'Do we need to up your medication or something?'

I shook my head. 'I thought we'd find her.'

'We did.'

'You know what I mean.'

'Obviously.' His voice was cold. 'It's not your job to mourn for her, Kerrigan. It's your job to get the fucker who put her here.'

Another plane passed over, scoring the sky. It was shatteringly loud. I used it as an excuse to walk away. You couldn't expect Derwent to understand an emotional connection with a victim; I didn't know why I had thought he would.

The pathologist was finishing, writing some notes. I waited at Dr Early's elbow until she looked up and her narrow face softened to a smile.

'I didn't know this was one of your cases, Maeve. It's a long way off your usual patch.'

'It's connected to another case.' I couldn't make myself smile back, and the pathologist's grin faded. 'I know you won't have any firm answers yet, but can you tell me when she died?'

'Not with any degree of accuracy.' Dr Early flipped back through her notes. 'There's no sign of decomp yet, so I don't think she's been here for long, but she could have been kept somewhere. There's considerable post-mortem lividity on her back and legs. If I had to guess, I'd say she was in a confined space for some time after her death, curled up with her knees to her chest.'

'A confined space. Like a car boot?'

'Exactly.'

'So she didn't die here.'

'I can't tell you that yet for sure, but I would say not.'

'How did she die?'

'I can't tell you that either but between us, my money is on drowning.'

'Drowning?' I shivered. 'Could it have been an accident?'

'She has bruising on her arms and shoulders. I would say not an accident. She was held down.'

'Could one person have done it?'

'Not if all the bruising was inflicted at the same time.' Dr Early frowned at the body. 'She didn't fight much. It looks as if she was easy to subdue. I've taken scrapings from under her fingernails but I'd be surprised to get anything from them.'

'The water won't help.' Derwent, who was watching my face.

'That's right,' Dr Early said. 'Being in the water will have washed a lot of evidence away. But she had quite long nails and none of them are broken. I'd have expected her to snap one or two if she was fighting for her life.'

'Maybe she went along with it,' I said. 'She was biddable. She'd been brought up to do what she was told.'

'I'm wondering about her level of intoxication. Fighting is instinctive when you're threatened. Mainly people don't fight back because they can't. I've sampled the fluid in her eyeball to see if she was drugged or drunk.'

Derwent winced. 'Jesus. You couldn't just take some blood?'

'The vitreous humour is more stable.' Dr Early gave him a savage smile.

'Was she sexually assaulted?' I asked.

'I haven't observed any damage. I've taken swabs, of course.'

Dr Early glanced back at where Chloe lay. 'I'll know more after the post-mortem. I'll do that tomorrow. Come along if you like.'

I absolutely did not want to see Chloe Emery's body peeled apart, no matter how scientific and professional the process might be.

'We'll be there,' Derwent said, and I caught the emphasis. *Don't think you're going to skip out on this one, Kerrigan.*

'They're going to move the body now.' Dr Early glanced at me. 'Do you want to get a closer look before they take her away?'

I felt I had to. I felt I owed it to her, and to her mother, and her father who was waiting for a phone call that would never come.

I stepped carefully on the mats the forensic team had laid down so my boots didn't tear up the soft mud, and looked down at Chloe, at her face. Mainly the dead bodies I saw belonged to strangers, people I'd never seen moving and talking and smiling. People whose lives had ended before I ever knew they existed. I never got used to seeing the utter absence that was death. The spirit that had made Chloe what she was had departed. It was why I couldn't reject the religion that ran through the tapestry of my childhood like a gold thread, even if it was fashionable to forget it, even if I didn't always agree with the specifics. There was a comfort and a certainty to it, a calm acceptance that life went on after the body faltered and fell. I stood by Chloe Emery's body and I prayed for her soul.

Later that day – much later – I stood outside Oliver Norris's house again. This time I had Georgia with me. It was Una Burt's idea. I knew Derwent had kicked off about it and I knew he had got nowhere. It was hard for me to mind when Burt had said, in no uncertain terms, that Georgia and I didn't need protecting from anyone. That was the message I had wanted him to absorb for years, after all.

And now I was at the house, ringing the doorbell. Eleanor came to open the door. When she saw me, she faltered.

'What is it?'

'Where's Bethany? Still in bed?'

'Yes.'

'Has she said anything yet?'

'No.'

'I need to talk to her.'

Eleanor shook her head. 'You can't. She needs to rest.'

The kitchen door opened and Gareth Selhurst came into the hall, his face grave. 'Are you all right, Eleanor?'

'Yes, but they want to talk to Bethany.' She was holding on to her elbows, her fingers digging into her arms.

'I hope you explained it's impossible.'

'Of course.'

'It's not impossible,' I said, losing patience finally. 'It's an essential part of a murder investigation.'

Selhurst came forward, pushing Eleanor behind him. 'You must understand that our only wish is to help.'

'In that case, move out of my way and let me speak to Bethany.'

'I don't understand the urgency.' He smiled. 'It's late. You may be working, but Bethany is resting. Why don't you come back tomorrow?'

'Because I need to speak to her now.' Confrontation wasn't getting me anywhere. Trickery might. I dropped my keys so they clattered on the hall floor, sliding behind Selhurst and Eleanor. They both looked down – it was a reflex; they couldn't help it – and while they were distracted I ducked past the preacher, heading for the stairs. Georgia was right behind me. The door to Bethany's room was closed but I pushed it open. Bethany was exactly where I'd left her, her eyes closed. Her breathing was uneven and I knew she wasn't asleep. I switched on the light.

'Look at me, Bethany.'

She didn't move.

'Look at me.'

Slowly, reluctantly, she opened her eyes.

'We found Chloe, Bethany.' I waited to see what her reaction might be: hope first, then fear. 'I'm sorry, but it's not good news.'

'Is she—'

'She's dead.' That was Georgia, from the doorway.

'It's not true.' Bethany looked up at me, her face pinched. 'It's not true.'

'I'm afraid it is. Someone found her body earlier today in woodland near Heathrow Airport.'

She started to sob, her body shaking.

Oliver Norris slammed into the room, pushing past Georgia without so much as a sideways look. 'You can't do that. You can't tell her that kind of thing.'

'It's the truth,' I said quietly. 'She deserves to know the truth.'

'She deserves to know what happens when she doesn't trust people who are trying to help her.' There was that edge in Georgia's voice again, and it was frustrating to know that Bethany could have helped us, and Chloe, but I couldn't let her take it out on the girl.

'I think you thought you were doing the right thing, Bethany. I think you thought you were doing what Chloe wanted you to do. But now we need to find out who did this to her. Who harmed her, Bethany? Who dumped her body as if it was nothing more than rubbish?'

'Leave her alone. She can't help you.' Oliver Norris's face was white. 'You're torturing her for no good reason. You want someone to blame because you didn't find Chloe in time to save her, and you're picking on Bethany.'

'That's not it,' I said. 'We never had a chance to find Chloe. I don't feel like I need to blame anyone. But I do feel, very strongly, that we need to find the person who killed her.'

'Bethany could be in danger,' Georgia said and Oliver made a movement towards her as if he wanted to hurt her for even thinking such a thing. I wished she hadn't said it out loud, even though I'd been thinking – and hinting – the same thing.

'Georgia, can you go downstairs and wait for me there?'

I thought she was going to argue with me, but she went, her face mutinous. I waited until she was gone before I spoke again.

'Bethany, you're the only person who can help us work out what happened to Chloe. You need to talk to us. To your parents, even. Someone you trust. You can't hide from this by keeping silent and hoping it goes away. Sooner or later you're going to have to talk about what happened.'

'Please. Leave.' Oliver's voice was brittle with tension. I didn't want to go, but one look at Bethany's face told me I hadn't got through to her – that she wasn't ready or able to talk yet.

I walked out past him and stood in the hall, waiting. He closed the door behind him and glared at me.

'You shouldn't have talked to her like that.'

'I've spent the afternoon with Chloe's dad. He had to identify her body.' He had wailed in my arms, grief tearing at him like a wild animal.

Oliver flinched. 'I'm sorry.'

'It was hard.'

'I didn't know,' he said.

'Know what?'

'That you cared so much. I thought it was just a job.'

'Sometimes it is.' I looked down, embarrassed to have shown how much it got to me. 'Sometimes it's a lot more than that.'

Georgia was waiting for me on the doorstep and I didn't blame her for avoiding any further conversation with Gareth Selhurst, who was brooding in the hall. She shook her head as she handed me my keys and anger made the blood sing in my ears. I waited until we were both in the car, the doors closed.

'What's the problem, Georgia?'

'You sent me downstairs as if I was a *child*. That's not how you treat a colleague. It's disrespectful.'

'You don't get my respect as a right. You have to earn it,' I said icily. 'And you were completely unprofessional in there.'

'Don't you dare lecture me about professionalism. You of all people.'

'What does that mean?'

'You disappear off with a suspect and take your time about getting him to hospital, and when he gets there, oh look, he's eating out of your hand.' She glared at me. 'I don't know what you did but I have some ideas about it.'

I shook my head. 'You're way off.'

'Am I? DI Derwent didn't think so.'

For a brief moment she was in real danger. I felt the anger surge up and it was only the fact that I knew she wanted me to lose my temper that enabled me to keep it. 'I've talked to DI Derwent about it. And I'm glad you brought him up because I've been meaning to discuss him with you. You hung back when DI Derwent needed back-up. You were more worried about saving your own skin than helping a fellow officer.'

'I was running comms.'

'That is a very grand way of saying you called for help.'

'Well, *someone* had to keep their head. The two of you were behaving like this was the Wild West. You don't do that. You call for back-up. You wait. You don't take stupid risks.'

'No, you calculate the risks and you behave accordingly. You put yourself in harm's way. That's the job, Georgia, and if you don't like it, you shouldn't be trying to do it. And if you won't do it properly, I don't want to work with you.'

'Standing between the monsters and the weak.' It was a police officer's saying, the job in a nutshell, and most cops didn't say it with a sneer in their voice.

'If you like,' I said coldly. 'It's a lot better than bullying

255

the weak because they didn't do what you wanted them to do. Bethany is as much of a victim as Chloe and if she doesn't trust us, she'll tell us nothing.'

She pressed her lips together. 'Did you mean what you said about getting rid of me?'

'I—' I shook my head. 'I don't know. I don't want to work with you if I can't rely on you.'

'Give me a chance.'

'I already did,' I said softly.

'Then I'm going to have to tell DCI Burt about what you did with Turner. About how you behaved.'

'Is that it? That's what you've got?'

'She won't be pleased with you.'

'Possibly not,' I acknowledged. 'But she'll understand why I did it. Una Burt is a cop, not an administrator. She's not your teacher and she's not your mother. She plays by the rules because she has to, but she wants to win. She believes all that guff about standing between the monsters and the weak, Georgia, because when you get down to it she's just like me.' I started the car. 'I'm leaving it up to you to decide whether you want to stay on the team or not. You pick.'

'What if I decide to stay?'

'Then you'd better make sure you do the job.'

25

I stood outside the morgue watching the clouds scud across the sky on a stiff summer breeze that plucked at my clothes and ruffled my hair. It was one of those times when I would have liked to be a smoker, to have a reason for standing there on my own. The door opened behind me, and Derwent stepped out.

'All right?'

'Yeah.'

'You made it all the way through.'

I half-laughed. 'Were you hoping I wouldn't?'

'Nope. I thought you'd be OK.'

'OK is debatable.' I risked a look at him, expecting to see judgement on his face, or pity, and unsure which I'd prefer.

What I got, naturally, was neither. He was frowning at the middle distance. 'No one enjoys it. Maybe the pathologists do, but no one normal.'

'I know that. I've been to enough PMs.'

'It's different when it's someone you know.'

'It makes you realise we're all just meat.' I was trying not to think about it: the organs and how they fitted together, the surprising untidiness of what was inside a human being once you unpacked it.

Derwent winced. 'You're making it very hard for me to look forward to the next time I eat steak and kidney pie.'

'She was alive on Sunday.'

'Yeah.'

'While we were poking around the storage unit and dealing with Turner and Oliver Norris. While I was interviewing her stepbrothers.' I swallowed. 'What if something I did or said made it too risky to let her live?'

'It's possible.'

'Oh, thank you very much for the comfort.'

'What? You know it's true.'

'She was drugged.'

'Diazepam.' Derwent frowned. 'Enough to make her drowsy and confused, the doctor said.'

'So she had less chance of fighting him off,' I said, biting off the words. 'She was slight, wasn't she? I don't think she would have caused too much trouble even if she hadn't been drugged, but someone didn't want to take the chance.'

'If she was drowsy and confused, maybe she didn't know what was happening.'

'It explains the lack of defensive wounds.'

'Three broken ribs,' Derwent said, and I shivered.

'I wish I'd done more for her. I should never have left her with the Norrises.'

'She was an adult. It was her choice.'

'Still. The obvious place for her to be was with her dad.'

'And she wouldn't go near him,' Derwent said.

'She was afraid of her stepbrother.' I thought for a second. 'Maybe not afraid enough.'

'Why do you say that?'

'Nolan had a car. He went missing from school. Maybe he was supposed to pick her up and take her somewhere.'

'And he killed her instead?'

'It's possible, if she was blackmailing him into helping her. Maybe he decided it was too risky to let her live.'

'Wouldn't it be more likely that he'd have strangled her or beaten her to death?'

'He's not all that athletic. Maybe he didn't want to take the chance of her fighting him off.' Her lungs had been saturated with clean water – no dirt, no grit. 'Holding her down in a full bath would have done the job. He was out on Sunday night, according to his dad. And where she was dumped isn't a million miles from the M40, his road home.'

'Does his story about why he left school check out?'

'Funnily enough, the drug dealers don't remember him specifically and don't want to make any statements, helpful or otherwise. Of course, if they sold him the diazepam they're not going to say.' I sighed, frustrated. 'We could look for his car on CCTV in Oxford but he didn't go through the city centre. If we don't find him, that doesn't mean he wasn't there.'

'Bit weird that he chose that night of all nights to be out of school.'

'Coincidences happen. If he was looking for an alibi deliberately, he probably wouldn't have chosen the one involving illegal activity, expulsion and a gang of dealers as his main witnesses.'

'He might if he was a moron.'

'He might, and he might well be a moron.' I hugged myself. 'What about Morgan Norris?'

'What about him?'

'He's a predator.'

'Then he'd have raped her before he killed her.'

'Maybe he miscalculated. Or he decided we knew too much about his DNA to risk it. I spent a lot of time telling him about DNA. I might as well have held up a giant warning sign.' I shivered again. 'If she was living in the same house as her murderer, I'm not sure I can live with myself.'

'It's not about you. You weren't in charge of her just because

259

her mum was dead.' He frowned at me. 'Why does this bother you so much?'

'Because . . .' I swallowed. 'Because no one ever taught Chloe the rules. No one ever looked at her and saw a beautiful young woman who needed to know them.'

'What rules?'

'That your body is public property, if you're young and female. That men will take advantage of you, if they can.'

'Some men. Not all men.'

'It only takes one. And they don't always announce themselves until it's too late.'

'Is that why you dress like that?'

'Like what?' I looked down at my very plain trouser suit, my high-necked top. 'I'm at work.'

'I've seen you off-duty too. You dress like you don't want to be noticed.'

'And you dress like you have shares in North Face clothing. It's almost as if you want everyone to know you're an off-duty copper. So what?'

'It's interesting, that's all.'

'To you, maybe.'

'She wasn't raped.' Smoothly, he'd returned to Chloe. 'She didn't fight. She might not have known what was happening, if she was drunk or drugged.'

'I hope she didn't.' I could imagine her horror, as someone she'd trusted turned into something unrecognisable. A monster.

'Do you think it was the same guy who killed Kate?'

'I hope so, or we've got two to catch.'

Derwent grinned. 'It would be a lot neater.'

'Chloe trusted him, whoever he was. And Kate was taken by surprise, wasn't she?'

'That's how it looked.' Derwent rubbed his chin. 'Do you fancy another look at Kate's house to see if it gives us any ideas? I've got the keys.'

'Aren't we supposed to be going back to the office?'

'Burt will understand.' Off-hand, casual, infuriating. I felt sorry for Una Burt now and then.

'OK. Putney it is.'

We both parked right beside Kate's house, even though it wasn't coned off any more and the police guard was long gone from the door. The windows were boarded up against burglars and the press alike, the door taped off. Maybe I wouldn't have felt like parking in front of it either.

I walked over to Derwent, who was digging in the boot of his car for shoe covers and gloves. 'If you give me the keys, I'll open the door.'

He turned, rummaging in his pocket, looked past me and frowned. 'What's this now?'

William Turner was limping towards us at speed. His face was strained under the bruises, and one hand supported his ribcage.

'What's wrong?' I said.

'Bethany called me.' His chest heaved, the notch between his collarbones deeper with every breath. 'What did you say to her last night?'

'Why? What did she say?'

'Did you tell her it was her fault Chloe died?'

Derwent twisted to look at me, his eyebrows climbing.

'*I* didn't,' I said, thinking of Georgia, 'but she might have drawn that conclusion.'

Turner coughed. 'You've really upset her.'

'I'll go and talk to her.' I started towards the house.

'She's not there.' Turner was patting his pockets, not finding what he was looking for. No inhaler. Great.

Derwent stood up and took him by the arm. 'Let's get you home, fella.'

'Not yet.' He held up his phone. 'I just spoke to her. She said she couldn't live with herself. She said she'd called me to say goodbye.'

'Goodbye?' I repeated, stupidly. 'Where was she?'

'I don't know.'

'Did she call you?' I remembered that the Norrises hadn't let her have a mobile phone of her own. 'From a payphone?'

He shook his head, coughing again. 'She's got Chloe's phone.'

'Can you unlock your phone?' He did as I asked and handed it to me, his hands shaking. 'Get him some help, for God's sake,' I said to Derwent. 'He needs his inhaler and probably an ambulance.'

'I'll be OK,' Turner croaked, but his lips were turning blue.

Derwent half-dragged, half-carried him down the street to his house. I knew he wouldn't leave him until he was safe. I flicked to the recent calls on Turner's phone and found Chloe's number. I sent the contact information to my own phone but used Turner's mobile to return the call, hoping she'd pick up.

Praying.

And she answered. Instead of hello, I heard the wind whistling across the phone, and a sound that might have been a sob.

'Bethany?'

A long, nerve-shredding pause. Then: 'What – who is this?'

'DS Maeve Kerrigan. Bethany, where are you?'

'Where's William? Why are you ringing on his phone?'

'He gave it to me.'

'Gave it to you?' A sniff. 'Why?'

'To talk to you.'

'I want to talk to him.'

'He can't talk to anyone at the moment. He's gone home to get his inhaler. His breathing wasn't good.'

Silence. I listened intently, hearing the swish of cars. So she was near a road. That narrowed it down. *Fine detective work, DS Kerrigan.*

'I don't believe you.' Her voice was absolutely toneless.

'It's true. I've never lied to you, Bethany.'

262

Another silence as she considered it. 'Is he going to be OK?'

'One of my colleagues is with him. He's calling an ambulance for William. What about you, Bethany? Are you OK?'

A sob. 'N-no.'

'Where are you? You're not at home, are you?'

'No.'

'Where, then?' In the background I heard something that chilled me: a two-note, mournful train whistle. 'Bethany?'

It came again and this time I heard it too, carried on the breeze rather than by mobile phone signal. She had to be somewhere close to me, near the railway line.

And she'd called Turner to say goodbye.

Shit.

'Bethany, have you spoken to your mum?'

She was crying properly now. The sound from the phone was muffled.

'Where are you, Bethany? Please tell me. I'll come and find you.'

'No!'

'I'll tell you about Chloe. I'll tell you what happened to her.'

'You don't know.' It was a long wail.

'I know more than I did yesterday. I know how she died.' I closed my eyes for a second. 'I know it wasn't your fault. You were trying to help her, weren't you?'

'That's all I wanted.'

'You didn't know what was going to happen. You couldn't have known. You mustn't blame yourself. It's no reason to harm yourself.'

She laughed, a horrible, ragged sound that set my teeth on edge. 'That's not why – you have no idea.'

'Tell me, then.'

An ambulance swung into the street, the siren going, the lights blinking blue. I ran down the road to flag them down, pointing them towards Turner's house.

263

'What's that?'

'An ambulance.'

'For William?'

'Yes.' The two green-clad paramedics climbed out, shouldering their equipment, and hurried up the path to his front door. 'He was really worried about you, Bethany. I want to be able to reassure him. Can you tell me where you are?'

'No.' Her voice sounded distant. I was losing her, I could feel it. My shirt was sticking to me between my shoulder blades and under my arms.

'Keep talking to me, please, Bethany. There's nothing so bad that it's worth killing yourself for.'

'You have no idea. I shouldn't even be here.' She laughed again. 'You don't know what I am.'

'I know you're a clever girl. Too clever to think killing yourself will fix anything.'

Derwent appeared in the doorway of Turner's house, saw me and hurried over. He held up his car key and I nodded, following him to his car.

'It's too late to fix anything. But at least I won't feel anything any more. I shall be clean. Wash me and I shall be whiter than snow.' She laughed. 'That's how it's supposed to work.'

'It gets better, Bethany. Whatever it is that's making you feel this way, you'll feel better about it in time. You'll put it behind you.'

'No.'

I was leaning across to see the road atlas Derwent liked to have in his car: he was old school, no faith in satnavs, no interest in relying on his mobile phone. I pointed at the black line that ran through it, representing the train tracks.

'Why don't you tell me about it?'

'I wouldn't know where to start.'

'All right. Tell me about Chloe.' I spoke louder to cover the sound of the engine starting. 'Why did you run away with her?'

'I thought it would keep her safe.'

Derwent put his hand out to flick on the siren and lights and I grabbed it, shaking my head. I couldn't take the risk of spooking her.

'Safe from what?' The car swung round a corner and I grabbed on to the dashboard, bracing myself. 'Who was she scared of?'

'I can't tell you. I don't know.' She sounded distracted again as another train hooted in the background and suddenly I remembered something I'd heard on the radio about engineering work overrunning, causing travel chaos on the line into Waterloo. Engineering work meant the trains that did run would be extra-slow, extra-cautious, and extra-noisy. The drivers had to blow the horn to warn the men to clear the track.

'Go to the train station,' I said to Derwent, covering the phone.

'Is that where she is?'

'No.' That was all I had time to say before I had to speak to Bethany again. 'So she told you she had to go and you ran away from home with her, without asking any questions?'

'You don't have to believe me.'

'I don't believe you were following Chloe's plan, because I don't think Chloe was capable of coming up with one.' I waited and heard nothing. 'Or am I wrong about her? Was everyone wrong about her?'

'She was cleverer than she let on.' Another sniff. 'But it wasn't her idea. It was mine.'

It was the first thing Bethany had given me, the first indication that she could answer my questions. Progress, if she hadn't been planning to kill herself.

'What was your idea?'

'To hide. To wait.'

'For what?'

'For it to be over.' Her voice was fainter; I had to strain to hear her.

'For what to be over?'

265

'I can't tell you.'

We turned onto the main road and a river of red brake lights stretching into the middle distance: London traffic at its least helpful. I could see the train station and I popped open the door of the car before Derwent had actually stopped. There was a risk in asking any more questions, I knew, but it was a risk I had to take. I was running down the road towards the station, trying to keep my voice level.

'Bethany, I understand you might not like me asking the question, and I know it might be hard to answer, but do you know who killed Chloe?'

A van driver was inching forward, impatient even though the traffic was clearly going nowhere. As I ran by, he nudged the bumper of a car that was pushing in from a side street. The car's driver leaned out of his window, instantly incensed, and yelled something that for sheer offence took my breath away. The van driver shouted back.

'What was that?' Bethany sounded terrified.

'Nothing.'

'Is it to do with William? Is he OK?'

'He's fine. I'm not near him any more. It's nothing to do with him.'

There was a tiny silence. 'If you're not near him, where are you?'

'Bethany, I just want to make sure you're all right.'

Silence.

'Bethany?'

I was talking to dead air.

26

I got to the front of the queue to speak to the yellow-jacketed man from Network Rail by shoving and holding my warrant card up, making no friends.

'Where are the engineering works still going on? Show me.' I stuck my phone under his nose with the map on the screen.

'They're on the up line towards central London. That's why this station is closed and there's a rail replacement bus service in operation.' He'd raised his voice for the last bit; I did not appreciate him multi-tasking by addressing the queue of frustrated commuters.

'Show me exactly.'

He gave me an odd look but pointed at the map. 'About half a mile from here. Near enough to East Putney tube station. The District Line is running, if you want to try that.'

'Is there anywhere nearby that overlooks the tracks?'

The man shrugged but someone in the queue behind me said, 'Yeah, there is. There are two footbridges across the tracks, one on Oxford Road near the art college and one on Woodlands Way.'

Think fast. Guess right. She would want to be undisturbed.

'Which one is busier?'

'Oxford Road, I suppose.'

I ran, my phone to my ear to call Derwent. 'You still in traffic?'

'Yeah. I'll dump the car.' He sounded deeply tense. 'I can see you. Where are you going?'

'Woodlands Way near East Putney tube. It's a left off the Upper Richmond Road.' I could hear him flipping through the road atlas. 'There's a footbridge. There's another on Oxford Road, before that, but I think she's on Woodlands Way.'

'I'll check it out. Have you called it in so BTP can be informed?'

'You do it,' I said, short of breath already, and hung up. British Transport Police had jurisdiction over the railways and the land surrounding them. It was both courteous and correct to inform them about Bethany, but I wasn't going to wait for them to find her. The road noises – well, Upper Richmond Road was part of the South Circular Road and the traffic was pretty much constant.

I almost went straight past Woodland Way, in part because it wasn't an idyllic bosky grove but a narrow dead end that ran between some lock-up garages and a block of flats. Maybe the trees were on the other side of the railway line, I thought, racing down to where the District Line ran overhead. Beyond it there was a narrow bridge, blocked off for vehicular access and only really wide enough for bikes and pedestrians anyway.

There was no one on the bridge.

Fuck.

I stopped under the bridge, hearing a train rattle overhead, struggling to breathe. I'd guessed wrong. Derwent would get her, I told myself, wishing like hell I'd turned down Oxford Road. I'd run past it. I'd gambled and I hoped like hell Bethany wouldn't lose.

The phone purred to life in my hand. I answered with, 'Did you get her?'

'I was just going to ask you that. No sign of her.'

I closed my eyes for a second in despair. 'I thought she had to be around here somewhere. It's the obvious place. I could hear the trains.'

'I'll go back for the car and drive round the area. Try calling Bethany again.'

I hung up. Turner's phone was locked. I'd have to hope she was willing to answer a call from a strange number.

I walked across to the bridge as I waited for the call to connect. I could see the men who were working on the track a little way away, ten or twelve of them in hard hats and bright orange boiler suits. The parapet of the bridge was chest-high on me – high enough to prevent accidents, but not high enough to stop suicides. They came in handfuls, I knew, one inspiring another, and they caused chaos across the transport network. There were stations where it happened relatively often, where the fast trains went through in a blur of metal and noise and the difference between life and death was a split second. There was nothing the drivers could do. The human body was not designed for high-speed impact with a train.

A mobile phone chirped somewhere nearby and I looked around, trying to work out where the sound was coming from as it stopped halfway through the ringtone. Then I found myself listening to the voicemail message, the generic one from the phone company. Did teenagers even listen to voicemails? I killed it and hurried to the end of the bridge, where a high, sharp-tipped metal fence blocked off access to the embankment. There was a gate in the fence to provide access for the men who were working on the line, but it was padlocked. A fan of metal spread across the angle between the bridge and the fence to stop people climbing over the edge of the parapet and dropping down to the embankment – but Bethany was small . . .

'Scuse me, love.' It was a cheerful man in an orange suit, heading down to the tracks.

'Can you let me through this gate?' I was holding up my warrant card.

'Sorry, I'm not allowed to let anyone through. Health and safety—'

'It's an emergency.'

Something in my face or my voice convinced him he didn't want to get between me and what I wanted. He unlocked the gate and held it open for me. 'Stay away from the tracks and listen for the trains.'

I nodded. 'BTP are on their way.'

He looked very slightly reassured and then I forgot all about him as I edged down the steep embankment, slipping on the long grass. She couldn't be anywhere in plain sight or the men would have spotted her – although they were head-down, focused on doing their work in the intervals between trains. Overrunning was a disaster. They didn't have a lot of time for looking around.

I looked down the track, then back to the shadows under the footbridge. It was dark there, especially in contrast to the bright sunshine. I started towards it, wishing I had my torch. I could see something under the bridge, a small shape, a bundle of clothes. A split second after I started towards it, the bundle unfolded and turned into a girl.

'Bethany!'

'Leave me alone!' She stood up once she knew I'd spotted her and started to edge away from me, towards the track. Her hair hung in hanks around her white face.

'Look, I just want to talk to you.'

She shook her head.

'Please, Bethany, don't do this. I need your help.'

'I can't help anyone.'

'You know what happened.'

'No. I can't say anything.'

'Can't or won't?' I took a step closer to her. Behind me the long two-note call of a train sounded. I glanced back to see

270

the men clearing the track, standing to one side. The track was straight so I could see the train in the distance, the light on the front shining despite the sunshine. I took another sliding step towards the shadows.

'Bethany, whatever it is, it can't be that bad.'

'You have no idea.'

'No, I don't, but you could tell me. We could talk about it.'

'It's all in the bible. Do you know your bible?'

'Not as well as I should,' I said, trying to smile.

'For I know my transgressions and my sin is ever before me,' she recited.

'What sin, Bethany?'

'Deliver me from bloodguiltiness, oh God, oh God of my salvation and my tongue will sing aloud of your righteousness.'

'Kerrigan!'

I glanced up to see Derwent peering over the parapet. He looked furious.

'How did you get down there?'

I ignored him because the train was closer now, the sound increasing as my heart rate rose, and I'd just made the decision to try to grab her when she exploded into movement like a prey animal breaking cover. She ran as fast as she could towards the track.

'Bethany! Stop!' I sprang after her, not thinking about the train or the danger of slipping on the embankment. I knew what she intended and I wasn't going to have it; I wasn't going to let another teenager die while I did nothing. The train's horn sounded again, much too loud, much too close and Bethany hesitated for a second, her face flashing like a pale flame in the darkness. I reached out and caught her sleeve as she gathered herself to jump towards the rails. It was like being inside a hurricane as the wind and noise blasted around us; the train was seconds away. Then I was falling and so was Bethany and there was nothing I could do to save either of us. I think I screamed; I know Bethany did. Every muscle in my

271

body tightened, as if that would help . . . and we fell, tangled together, as the sound of the train broke over us like a wave.

It took a long couple of seconds for me to realise that we had fallen beside the track, not on it, and the train was passing by safely. The wind dragged at me – it was far too close. I was holding on to Bethany, half-lying on her, and I could feel the sobs wracking her body. My head was ringing and I felt weak, my knees and hands trembling. I wasn't planning to stand up until the train was gone but I wasn't altogether sure I'd be able to. It didn't matter. I crawled forward so I could see Bethany's face.

'It's all right. You're going to be all right.'

'Leave me alone,' she sobbed. 'Why couldn't you leave me alone? I don't want to be here any more.'

'This isn't the answer.'

She started to laugh while still crying, a hiccupping jagged sound that made me wince.

And then it was as if the bubble surrounding us had burst as the men reached us, running awkwardly in their heavy work boots: big hands helping to set us on our feet, guiding me up the embankment as I twisted to see that Bethany was following too, a jumble of accents around us – English, Eastern European, Irish, Jamaican, Glaswegian . . . London, basically. I felt giddy and knew that was shock, like the tremor in my joints and the frantic buzzing of thoughts that made my head feel like a jar full of wasps.

I looked up to see a BTP officer unlocking the gate, and Derwent standing behind him, his face sheet-white. I ignored that, needing to concentrate on Bethany, on making sure they didn't let go of her.

'Do you need an ambulance?' That was the BTP officer.

'I don't think she's injured but she's suicidal. She needs to be sectioned.'

He reached out and took hold of Bethany's arm, guiding her gently through the gate.

'All right, love. Let's get you into the car so you can have a sit down.'

Bethany was limp, unresisting. The BTP officer supported her for the few stumbling paces it took her to reach his car. I watched him fold her carefully into the back seat, glad that he was being gentle. She needed care, not anger.

'Do you feel up to giving us a statement?' The other BTP officer was beside me, his notebook in hand.

'Give her a chance,' Derwent snapped.

'No, it's OK.' I stood beside the officer and told him what had happened, as the workmen talked to the other officer and Derwent, then drifted back to work in ones and twos. The excitement was over. They'd be falling behind schedule. The work had to be done. I smiled thanks at them when I had the chance, especially the man who'd let me onto the embankment. He shook his head at me slowly.

'Warned you.'

'I take full responsibility.'

'You better, because I ain't gonna.' He gave a wheezy laugh and passed through the gate with a wave.

The BTP officer was serious, unsmiling and painstaking. This would mean paperwork, I assumed, and lots of it, so I let him take his time, ask his questions, tick his boxes. An ambulance arrived and they took charge of Bethany. They asked if I needed to be checked over and I said no. I had bruised a knee and pulled something in my shoulder, but it was minor. Better than being splattered over two hundred metres of track, anyway.

Behind me, Derwent fidgeted and paced until at long last the officer was finished with me.

'I'll write it up and send you the statement to approve.'

'Great, thanks.'

He went back to his car and finally it was only Derwent I had to deal with; I would have slightly preferred another train. I looked around for him and found him staring down the track, his expression remote. I walked over.

'I think that went well, considering.'

'Do you?'

'No one died.'

He looked down at his feet, frowning. 'When you went under the bridge, I couldn't see you. I could see the train coming. I could see the workmen by the track.' An assessing glance from under lowered brows. 'They thought you were fucked. You know that, don't you?'

'So did I,' I said lightly.

He went back to staring into the distance, unsmiling. 'Yeah. Well, I only had that to go on. And there was nothing I could do.'

'I was careful.'

'No, you weren't.'

'I'm here. I lived to tell the tale.'

'Because you were lucky. You're not going to be lucky every time.'

'Look, I'm not actively hoping to risk my life when I come to work, but if I have to, I will. That's the job.'

A muscle tightened in his jaw. 'When I was in the army, I watched people die in front of me. Friends of mine. It fucking *killed* me, Maeve. You don't know what that's like, and believe me, you don't want to know.'

'I know what it's like to lose a colleague. You might remember that.' I tilted my head to one side, considering him. 'These pals of yours – was it your fault that they died? Because if not, I think I still win this one.'

'It's not a competition,' Derwent snapped.

'Then why are you pretending you know more about this than me?'

'Because I've taken all the risks. I've done all the stupid shit to be brave, to prove myself, to make up for the fact that I was still alive and my mates weren't. I've been just as fucked up as you are now.'

'And now you're completely normal.'

274

'I could do without the sarcasm. I'm trying to help you.'
His nostrils flared. 'If you were drowning you'd be throwing
punches at the lifeguard.'

'You're not saving me from anything.'

'No. This is something you have to do yourself.'

I said icily, 'I'm coping fine.'

'By being the best little detective sergeant you can possibly
be.' He looked down at me. 'Do you know why I like working
with you?'

I thought about making a smart remark but shook my head
instead. I genuinely wanted to know.

'You do the job with all your heart. You really care. But
you need to let your head make your decisions, not your
heart. Your heart is big, but it's stupid as shit.'

I laughed because it was better than crying. He put his
arms around me and hugged me. If I'd been shorter he would
have rested his chin on my head, but he settled for leaning
his head against mine.

'I thought you were dead.'

'I know.' I tried to pull away but his grip tightened to the
point of being actually painful.

'You could apologise.'

'It wasn't deliberate.'

'You scared the shit out of me.'

'And myself. Please don't tell my mum.'

'I won't if you promise not to do it again.'

I patted his back feebly. 'I can't breathe.'

'If you *do* do it again, you'd better make sure you die.
Because otherwise I'm going to kill you.'

'Point taken.' I had another go at freeing myself with the
same result. 'You know this is edging towards assault, don't
you?'

'Yep.'

'You still haven't let go.'

'That's right.' He released me eventually and walked off,

back to the car. It was atrociously parked, at an angle with one wheel on the kerb.

'You know "drive it like you stole it" isn't supposed to apply to how you park. This looks like a classic decamp.'

'I was in a hurry,' he said. 'And if you don't like the way I drive, you can walk to the hospital.'

I hurried to catch up with him, hiding a smile. I was glad that he was being rude to me again. It was comforting.

It was normal.

27

At the hospital a Sri Lankan doctor with a heavy accent told us that we couldn't speak to Bethany, that she had been in distress and he had sedated her.

'When can we speak to her?' I asked.

'Not today. Maybe tomorrow.' He beamed at me as if it was good news.

'We really need to talk to her as soon as possible.'

'Tomorrow. The next day.' Another smile.

'It's just that it's a murder investigation.'

'Oh yes, I understand. But she's my patient now. We do what's best for her.'

If he had been my doctor I would have appreciated him standing between me and harm. As it was I had to resist the urge to kick something.

We were walking past the waiting room when Eleanor Norris leapt out at us like a wildcat.

'What did you do to my daughter?'

'DS Kerrigan saved her life,' Derwent said before I could answer her.

'She harassed her! She drove her to try to kill herself.' Eleanor glared at me with mad eyes. 'I'm making a formal complaint about your behaviour.'

277

'Good luck with that.'

I stepped back, my heel pressing on Derwent's toe hard enough that he'd get the message. *You're not helping.* Oliver came out of the waiting room, his face thunderous. He put his arm around Eleanor's shoulders.

'Leave them, darling. Don't waste your time on them.'

I ignored him. 'Mrs Norris, I understand why you're distressed.'

'Distressed? What you said to her was *wicked*.'

'If it helps, I don't think that's why she tried to harm herself.' I had been thinking about what Bethany said, trying to remember the exact words. If only it had been in an interview so I could have a transcript, complete with every um and ah. 'I told her it wasn't her fault that Chloe died and that she shouldn't blame herself. She said that wasn't why she wanted to kill herself.'

'Well, what then?' Eleanor hugged herself, the stress rash beginning to break out on her neck and chest. 'Did she say?'

I took a deep breath. 'Is it possible that she and Chloe might have acted together to murder Kate Emery?'

'What? *No!* Why would they?' Oliver demanded.

'If Kate wanted to keep them apart.'

Eleanor laughed harshly. 'If that bothered them, they'd have killed Ollie, not Kate. She always encouraged them to spend time together. She drove them places, paid for outings, let Bethany spend every spare minute in her house . . .'

I thought Eleanor was telling the truth. There was something matter-of-fact in the way she said it. She was silent for a moment, thinking about it. Then she burst out with, 'I wish *I'd* kept them apart. I should have listened to you, Ollie.'

He didn't speak but his fingertips bleached white where he was pressing them into her shoulder.

'Bethany said it was her idea for her to run away with Chloe. She said the idea was that they should stay away until it was all over. Do you know what she was talking about?'

278

Eleanor stared at us, her face blank.

'The investigation.' Oliver sounded certain. 'They were both finding it a tremendous strain to have you bothering them. Asking questions. Arresting me and Bethany's uncle, for God's sake – you don't have to think for very long about why they might have wanted a break from it all.'

'But she didn't say that to me on the phone. She didn't say that they'd run away so we would leave them alone.'

'No, well, she wouldn't. We've brought her up to be polite to her elders, even if they don't deserve it.'

I frowned, unconvinced. 'Bethany said something like *you don't know what I am* when I was talking to her.' I saw Eleanor start, her eyelids flickering. 'She said *I shouldn't even be here*. I think that was the wording. Can you tell me what she might have meant?'

Eleanor flushed deeply. 'No. No idea.'

'Mrs Norris,' Derwent said gently. 'Please.'

She looked up at her husband's face for a moment, communicating silently. He nodded and she turned back to us.

'I think she must have meant that we had great trouble when we were trying to conceive her. We tried for a long time. There were tests, clinics . . . it was humiliating. We were told there was no chance at all.'

'It was a miracle when Eleanor fell pregnant,' Norris said, squeezing her shoulders again. 'It was the happiest time of my life. We were concerned of course that she might not carry the pregnancy to term. We couldn't believe we could be so lucky, to beat the odds that way. But Bethany was fine. She was perfect.'

'She said it like it was a bad thing,' I said.

Oliver Norris shook his head. 'I don't know what she could have meant.'

'She was loved and wanted from the start,' Eleanor said. 'I've always told her so. I'd have done anything for a child – for her – and in the end all I could do was pray. We were desperate. We'd exhausted every other option.'

279

'And our prayers were answered,' Norris said with a smile that set my teeth on edge.

Derwent must have felt the same way. 'That's a hell of a burden to place on a kid, isn't it? Telling her she's a gift from God, or whatever it was you said to her. It puts her under a lot of pressure to be perfect.'

'I disagree,' Eleanor said coldly.

'Of course you'd find some way to make us look bad.' Oliver Norris was glaring at Derwent as if he wanted to murder him. 'You want to pin it on us. It's our fault our daughter is suicidal.'

'You've spent a lot more time with her than DS Kerrigan,' Derwent said with a glint.

'Look, none of us knows precisely why Bethany's here,' I said quickly. 'I think the best thing is to hear what she has to say.'

'I forbid you to speak to her,' Oliver Norris said.

'Mr Norris, it's not really up to you any more. She's an important witness in a murder investigation and we have to be able to talk to her.'

'Absolutely not. You've done nothing but harass my family since you started investigating what happened to Kate. And you don't seem to be making much progress with it, I might add.'

I felt my cheeks grow warm: Norris was right about that. And he wasn't finished.

'I think it would be best all round if you left.' He glowered at us both in a way that left no room for negotiation. 'If we can't see her, you certainly can't.'

'So what now?' Derwent asked as we walked out of the hospital.

'Well, we have one thing we didn't have before.' I showed him the mobile phone I'd picked up from the railway embankment.

'Is that Bethany's?'

'No, the Norrises don't approve of them, remember? This is Chloe's.'

'Nice one.'

'I thought so.'

'Have you looked at it?'

'It's locked. Password-protected. I was going to ask Bethany to tell me what the password was.' I turned it over in my hand: a Samsung Galaxy with a custom cover featuring a close-up of Misty the cat. 'Colin might be able to get something off it, but we'll probably have to send it to the lab to get a full forensic download.'

Derwent wrinkled his nose. 'I don't want Colin trying out his skills on this. Too important. If we send it off, I think we can get to the top of the list with a bit of badgering. Potentially, that phone can tell us a lot about where the two girls went and why they ran away.'

'What I'm wondering is why Bethany had the phone. We haven't found any of Chloe's stuff – her clothes, her wallet, anything that she took with her when she ran away. Just the phone, and we wouldn't have known about that if Bethany hadn't needed to use it.'

'Maybe Chloe gave it to her.'

'Why?'

Derwent shrugged. 'Because she knew we could track her if she had it.'

'We tried that. It was switched off.'

'See? They were aware that the phone could give them away.' He tapped his head. 'Savvy.'

'I'd believe that of Bethany. I'm not so sure you could say that about Chloe.'

'Maybe it was how Chloe was going to keep in touch with Bethany after they went their separate ways. She's kept in the dark ages, technologically speaking, isn't she?'

I nodded. 'No internet, no social media, no phone.'

'And Chloe couldn't exactly send her a postcard.'

'Makes sense,' I said. 'I still think it's worth searching Bethany's house again in case there's anything else she conveniently forgot to mention.'

'That'll need another search warrant.'

'I'll put in the request now.' I looked past him. 'Oh, that's not a good idea.'

Derwent turned to see William Turner hobbling across the car park towards us. 'For shit's sake.'

I moved to intercept him. 'William—'

'I want to see her.'

'If it's Bethany you mean, no one can see her. Not us, not her parents. She's in the mental health unit under sedation.'

Turner's eyes glittered and he turned away for a second, getting himself under control.

'What happened?'

'She tried to throw herself under a train.' The unembellished version, courtesy of Derwent.

'If you hadn't told us she was in trouble, she'd probably be dead,' I said. 'You saved her life.'

'Strictly speaking, DS Kerrigan saved her life,' Derwent said reprovingly, as if Turner had claimed all the credit. Then, magnanimous as ever, he added, 'But she couldn't have done it without you.'

'Why did she want to kill herself?'

'Good question,' I said. 'Actually, you might be able to help with that.'

I asked him the same questions I'd asked Bethany's parents – what Bethany had meant by saying they were staying away 'until it was all over' and why she'd said 'I shouldn't even be here'. To give him his due, Turner tried very hard to come up with an explanation but in the end he had to admit defeat.

'Sorry. If I knew I would tell you.'

I believed he was telling the truth. Derwent frowned at him. 'Last time I saw you, you were half dead. What are you doing walking about?'

'I discharged myself from A and E.' He stared Derwent down, the effect slightly ruined by the bruising that kept one eye from opening properly. 'I've spent enough time in there lately.'

'Well, unless you want to be heading straight back there, I'd stay away from Bethany Norris. Her dad is up there and he's spoiling for another fight. I'm serious. He'll do you some damage.'

'I need to talk to Bethany about Chloe.' Turner faltered as he said her name. 'I need to know what happened.'

'Join the club,' I said. 'But as I said, no one is talking to her at the moment. Doctor's orders.'

'When, then?'

'William, I don't think you'll be able to see her.'

'It's not fair. She'll want to talk to me, not you.' He sounded petulant and I caught that flash of arrogance I'd seen from him before: the kind of arrogance that had run rings around a good police officer when he'd been the main suspect in an investigation. I'd started to think of Turner as an ally when he was nothing of the kind, I reminded myself.

'You're way down the list, even if Bethany's parents are all right with you speaking to her.'

'You know they wouldn't want me to talk to her.'

'Yes, I do.' I kept my voice level and calm. 'I think you should go home.'

'You can't make me.'

'It would be very tedious to try,' I said. 'But a lot of things I do for work are tedious, and I still do them.'

He swung away from us, muttering something under his breath. Derwent took a step after him. I grabbed his arm and shook my head.

'Not worth it.'

'Little shit.'

'Oh, absolutely.' I watched Turner limp off across the car park. 'I wish we could use him, though. Bethany is far more likely to talk to him than to us.'

'You can win her round.'

'No. I think I've burned my boats with the Norrises. I doubt any of them are going to trust me from now on.'

'Yeah, but you don't trust them.'

'No, I do not.'

'Well then, let's get on with ruining their day,' Derwent said.

Ruining their day meant extending mine long beyond the point where I was ready to go home. I took a small team, including Pete Belcott, Liv and Georgia, and turned the house upside down. We found nothing useful, again, while Morgan Norris stood in the garden and smoked, watching us with thinly veiled hostility. I stayed away from him, sending Belcott out to talk to him whenever we needed to ask a question. It annoyed both of them, which was a win for me however you looked at it, since neither was a paid-up member of my fan club.

Searching the house was enough of a distraction that I didn't have to think about the way my knee throbbed, the way my shoulder ached – nagging reminders of what had happened earlier in the day. It could have worked out differently. I could have been in hospital myself, instead of at work, and that would still have counted as good luck.

'Are you all right?' Liv asked me quietly as I helped her lift the mattress on Bethany's bed to check there was nothing underneath.

'Fine. Why?'

'I heard what happened. Burt wanted to send you home.'

'There was no need.' I let the mattress fall back into place.

'You were brave.'

'It's only brave if you're scared.' I flashed a grin at her. 'Otherwise it's blind stupidity.'

'But you must have been scared.'

I thought about it. 'There wasn't time to be scared. I just needed to stop her.'

'Still.'

'Nothing bad happened.'

'It could have.'

'But it didn't.'

'I wouldn't have done it.'

'Yes, you would.'

But she shook her head and I thought she meant it. I didn't really want to think about it at all, let alone to consider whether or not I'd been reckless. I concentrated on the search, bringing new meaning to the word *thorough* as I combed through every room, every drawer, methodically hunting even if I didn't know what I was looking for.

By the time I got back to the flat I was clumsy with tiredness. It was quiet in the flat. Too quiet; the low hum of remembered fear that had been the background to my day buzzed in my ears. I put on some music to drown it out. I didn't really want to eat anything but I boiled water for pasta, conscious that I'd missed dinner. I'd been running on empty for too long. I was better than that. The new me had regular meals, wore ironed clothes, lived in a clean, orderly flat that contained more or less edible food. The new me could look after herself. Self-care, my counsellor had told me, was part of being a competent adult. Taking responsibility for my own life. Making good, healthy decisions. Valuing myself.

I burnt my tongue on the pasta when it was done, because the way I did self-care was a lot like self-harm.

28

The text message telling me to meet Derwent at a café on the high street in Putney was typically brief and didn't give much away. I braced myself, expecting the worst as I pushed open the door and scanned the room for him. He was right at the back, reading the paper, immaculate in a dark suit. A plate smeared with egg and ketchup told its own tale: I had missed breakfast, for better or worse. He glanced up and nodded to me, unsmiling. I ordered tea in a takeaway cup and a bacon sandwich and threaded through the buggies and pensioners to sink into the chair on the other side of the table.

'You look better than I expected.'

I raised my eyebrows. 'Is that so?'

'What did you get up to last night?'

'Not much.'

'I thought you'd have a hangover the size of a house.'

'I didn't even have a drink.'

'So what did you do to celebrate still being alive?'

'I finished work late. By the time I got home I only wanted to go to bed.'

Derwent frowned. The bruise on his cheek was fading to green, the edges blurring as it healed. His eyes were unblinking, surveying me at the same time as I stared at him. The waiter brought my breakfast and I took the interruption as a chance to change the subject.

'What are we doing here?'

'This.' He lifted the newspaper to reveal a cardboard folder that he slid across the table. I flicked it open.

'The blood-spatter report.'

'The preliminary one.'

'Where did you get it?'

'I was in the office this morning.'

'What time did you get up?' I asked around a mouthful of food.

'Six.'

'Seriously?' I stared at him, awed.

'Yes, seriously.' He shifted in his seat. 'I didn't sleep well.'

I thought about asking why but the expression on his face was a warning: *Stay out of it, Kerrigan.*

He tapped the folder. 'Have a read of that.'

'What about Chloe Emery?'

'Still waiting for lab results and phone records. In the meantime, you need to look at this.'

I ate my breakfast while I read about angles of spatter impact and points of convergence and inconsistencies and felt an ache start to tighten around my head. There was a lot of information in the report, a lot to absorb and interpret. And this was the preliminary version. I was glad it would never be my job to explain it to a jury. Eventually I looked up, frowning. *Inconsistencies.*

Derwent nodded. 'Exactly.'

'You wanted another look at the house.'

'No time like the present.' He was already standing. I picked up the end of my sandwich and my tea. He glanced at them. 'Good thing you got a takeaway cup.'

'I have worked with you before.' I led the way out of the café. I hadn't even bothered to take off my jacket.

*

287

Kate Emery's house was silent as the grave and about as appealing. It was a sultry day, the sky heavy with the promise of rain, but inside the house the air was chilled and unwholesome. I followed Derwent into the hall and closed the door gently behind me, avoiding the dried blood on the paintwork as best I could. Even with gloves, I didn't want to touch it, partly from legitimate concern about destroying evidence and partly because I was squeamish. It was more than a week since I'd been inside the house and it smelled foul: the ripe reek of decaying blood overlaid with rotting fruit and a bitter note of old cat shit. I put the back of my hand to my mouth as a precaution against the nausea swelling inside me.

'OK?' Derwent asked.

'I just need to get used to it.' I frowned at him. 'How come you don't mind it?'

'Smelled worse.' He'd left his jacket in the car, I noticed. I should have done the same. The smell would cling for the rest of the day, though it would catch in my hair as much as my clothes. Derwent was rolling up his sleeves. 'So?'

I looked around, at the dark smudges that told a story of violence and savagery written in Kate Emery's blood. 'Walk it through?'

'I thought you'd never ask.'

'Killer or victim?'

He took a coin out of his pocket and balanced it on his thumb. 'Heads or tails?'

'Tails.'

He frowned. 'I thought you'd go for heads.'

'Get on with it.'

The coin spun in the air and he caught it, then showed me. 'Tails.'

'Killer, then.'

'OK.'

'So where did it start?'

'The hall,' Derwent said instantly. 'Here. By the door.'

'Someone arriving. Someone unwelcome.'

'OK.' Derwent took up a position inside the front door. 'What happened?'

I pulled my pen out of my jacket pocket and held it up. 'Imagine this is a blade.'

'I'm feeling scared already.'

I mimed stabbing him, pulling the pen back and swinging it towards him a couple of times. He held his hands up, fending me off.

'Drops of blood on the ground and on the walls. Small wounds.'

I nodded. 'She was fighting the attacker off, wasn't she?'

'Trying to make some space for herself.' Derwent turned and started up the stairs, one hand trailing an inch away from the wall where there was a long streak of blood. 'So she runs up here.'

'And I catch up with her—' I took the stairs three at a time and reached out to grab Derwent's ankle as he neared the top. 'Trip her . . .'

He pitched forward, landed on his hands and flipped himself to the side, avoiding the actual bloodstain. He lay on his back and I bent over him to stab him again.

'You need to get a lot closer than that to inflict the kind of damage she sustained here. Look at the stains on the carpet.' He sat up and pointed. 'Body here. Attacker on top. Those look like knee prints on either side of the main bloodstain.'

He was right; there were two smudges on the carpet fibres where the blood had pooled under the attacker's knees.

'Lie down again.' I knelt carefully with one thigh on either side of his torso and pretended to stab him in the chest.

'Lower.'

'What?'

'She got up and ran from here. You just stabbed me in the heart. No one gets up from that.'

289

I shuffled back a little, moving down to his hips. It was inevitable, I think, that it felt as if we weren't acting out a murder any more. Embarrassment brought heat to my face. I couldn't look at him but I knew Derwent was laughing.

'All right, love, no need to enjoy it.'

'Shut up.'

He grinned up at me. 'Professionalism, Kerrigan.'

I stabbed him in the stomach with the pen, hard enough that he caught his breath and my wrist. He held it for a moment, looking up at me with a challenge in his eyes.

'You are supposed to be fighting me off,' I pointed out, in command of myself again. 'I was wondering when you were going to start.'

He let go of me and closed his eyes, his hands falling to the floor.

'She's getting weaker. You've injured her seriously now and she stays here for a while, bleeding into the carpet.'

'Agreed.' I stood up. 'Maybe I think I've done enough. I stand up and have a breather.'

'But she's faking.' He twisted, jumped to his feet and jogged into the bathroom. I followed and put the lights on. The blood screamed at me from every surface, darker now, just as horrible.

'Burt was right. This is a terrible place to try to hide.'

'She didn't have time to get any further away.' Derwent stood in the middle of the small room, his face sombre. 'Let's take it that you spend a fair amount of time here making sure you've done enough damage to kill her.'

'But she didn't die here, as far as we can tell.' I stayed in the doorway. 'How did that work? She was trapped. Then she ran past her attacker, even though she was bleeding profusely and had to be weak, disorientated – in no position to out-think anyone. Otherwise we wouldn't have the blood in the kitchen. Unless the attacker was injured, or incapacitated somehow, I don't see it.'

290

'More faking?' Derwent pointed to a concentration of blood beside and behind the toilet. 'If she lay here and pretended to be dead, maybe it looked as if the job was done.'

'Maybe.' I tapped the pen on my cheek, thinking about it. 'Or there were two attackers and they distracted each other.'

Derwent nodded. 'Which would explain the inconsistencies in the blood-spatter report. Two attackers, one taller than the other. Working together. Taking it in turns. Different blades. Different angles of attack.'

'Maybe one was trying to stop the other,' I said.

Derwent shook his head at me. 'Stop trying to make excuses for her.'

'For who?'

'Come off it, Kerrigan.'

I sighed. 'OK. Bethany and Chloe, working together or arguing, killed Kate.'

'And whoever helped them to get rid of the body turned on Chloe later. Maybe because he couldn't trust her to keep her mouth shut.'

It was plausible and I didn't like it. Not at all.

'We don't know it was them.'

'We don't know it wasn't.' Derwent leaned back against the door frame, squinting a little as he tended to when he was tired. 'Depends on how much you trust the blood lady to have got the report right.'

'I trust Kev Cox. He says she's good.'

'Well, then. What other explanation is there?' He waited for me to answer, and when I didn't, he raised his eyebrows. 'What?'

'I don't know.' I looked down at the bloodstain at my feet. 'Let's finish this.'

'OK.' He stepped away from the bathroom. 'Whatever happens, she makes it downstairs.'

'What about this: the killers go downstairs to clean up. While they're in the shower room . . . '

'She makes a move. She's holding on to the bannisters this time because she's half-dead.' Derwent ran down the stairs, dragged a hand up to the latch of the front door but stopped. 'For some reason she doesn't go out.'

I followed, looking over his shoulder at the smear of blood, at the lock underneath it. 'It makes sense if someone was chasing her. She wouldn't have had time to undo the locks.'

'But not if the killer or killers are scrubbing the blood off.'

'Unless there was something she needed from the kitchen.'

'More than she needed someone to call her an ambulance?' Derwent raised his eyebrows. 'I think not.'

'Maybe she was afraid to go out the front. Maybe she thought there was an accomplice waiting for her.'

'Maybe there was.' Derwent sighed. 'OK. For whatever reason, she doesn't go through the front door.' He turned and walked down the hall towards the kitchen. 'If you're chasing her, you haven't caught up with her yet, by the way. She has time to bleed all over the hall but no one attacks her here.'

In the kitchen he draped himself over the counter. 'She stops here for a rest.'

'Did we find her phone?'

'It was in her bag.'

'Maybe that's why she came in here. Maybe she was looking for her phone while she stood here and bled.'

'There's a landline in here too.' It was on the counter. 'She didn't try to call 999 from that either.'

'So she didn't want the police.' I swallowed. 'Because it was her daughter who was trying to kill her?'

Derwent shrugged. 'She makes it to the kitchen door, unlocks it, pushes the bolts back and opens it. You still haven't caught up with her, if you're chasing her.'

'I'm not chasing her. I can't be.'

'She runs out into the night, unobserved by any neighbours. She doesn't scream or call for help. She runs through the garden because there's no access to the street from here.'

Derwent stepped out onto the patio and looked down the garden. 'And then she disappears without a trace, despite having lost most of the blood from her body.'

'The rain didn't help us.'

'Nope.'

'She couldn't have got away,' I said. 'Even if they were distracted by cleaning up.' *They.* I'd almost accepted it was the girls. 'She'd have collapsed.'

'And their accomplice picked her up.'

'And took her to the storage unit until they were ready to dispose of her body.'

I shivered, thinking about Kate running for her life, too afraid to call for help. To see someone you love turn on you . . .

'Meanwhile I'm having a shower,' I said, pulling myself back to my role. 'I clean up after myself using only what's available to me in the house, so there's no chance of tracing me via anything I brought with me.'

'Clever you.'

'Sort of.'

'Yeah.' He came back in, frowning. 'This is either a highly organised, competent murder—'

'Or an absolute shambles,' I finished.

'Either everything went according to plan, or nothing did.'

'And if it was Chloe and Bethany, with the help of an accomplice, why did Chloe have to die?'

'They couldn't trust her not to talk.'

You don't know what I am – did she mean a murderer? It was possible.

I sat down at the kitchen table and propped my chin on my hand. Derwent leaned back against the island, watching me, not interrupting. Eventually I sighed.

'All of the evidence tells us a story but it doesn't make any sense and it's never made any sense. Every time we think we're making progress, we run into a brick wall.'

'I've noticed. So?'

'So maybe it's because we're being pointed at the brick wall.'

A clatter at the front door made my head snap up. I stared at Derwent, the two of us surprised into immobility. The front door closed and footsteps moved slowly through the hall: high heels clicking on the tiles, keys jangling. Derwent headed towards the kitchen door, as silent as it was possible for him to be. I was right behind him, my hand on my radio.

She was in the sitting room, opening and closing cupboards, trim in a black suit and spike-heeled black patent court shoes.

'Can I help you?' Derwent said. The woman whirled around, her eyes wide with horror. She was a total stranger, I registered, in the split second before she started to scream.

29

Neela Singh wasn't much reassured by the news that we were police officers rather than murderers waiting for a new victim. It took a long time for her to regain her composure enough to explain that she was entitled to be in the house – more entitled to be there than we were, in fact, because she was there at the request of the homeowner.

'I'm an estate agent with Miller Hamilton.' With a flash of pride, she added, 'We've been retained as the sole agents to bring this property to the market.'

'Congratulations,' Derwent said. 'You'll have buyers queuing down the street for this one, given what happened here.'

'You'd be surprised. Get it cleaned up, take up the carpets that are too stained, touch up the paintwork . . .' She flicked her hair so it fell smoothly down her back. 'This is London. Buyers want what they want. This is a sought-after area and a house in this location is always going to sell. A house this age is going to have history anyway, that's what I say. Plenty of people probably died here over the years. It's just that we know about this one and it's recent. But once the place is cleaned up no one will think twice about it.'

She was very pretty when she wasn't screaming her head off, and probably good at her job. She certainly didn't seem to be put off by the bloody smears all over the kitchen, which I put down to lack of imagination rather than heartlessness. The state of the house jangled my nerves though. I should have been used to it, but I wasn't.

Something else was bothering me, too. 'When you say you're here at the request of the owner, who do you mean? Kate Emery?'

'She's dead, isn't she?' She looked from me to Derwent. 'She was only the tenant. The house never belonged to her.'

'It didn't?' Derwent frowned. 'So who does it belong to?'

'A lady named Phyllis Charnock. I think she's Kate Emery's aunt? Between you and me, she's an old witch. She lives down in Cornwall somewhere in a massive house. She must be in her seventies.' Neela said it as if that was unimaginably old. She herself was probably twenty-five at the most.

'So she heard her niece was dead and decided to put the house on the market?' Derwent shook his head. 'People will never cease to amaze me.'

'No, that's the thing. She'd already decided to put it on the market. She retained us months ago. She'd given her niece formal notice to quit and everything.' Neela grinned. 'Can't deny it would have been easier to sell the house before someone was murdered in it. It's a good thing I like a challenge. But at least the tenant looked after the place. She renovated it, actually.' She ran her hand over the kitchen counter, avoiding the blood. 'These kitchens don't come cheap. That's a Corian worktop she put in and they cost a fortune. She's kept the house lovely. She looked after it like it was her own, she said.'

'So Kate wasn't pleased about moving out,' I said.

'This is the first time I've been able to have a proper look at the place. Every time I called round before she told me to bog off.' Neela rolled her eyes. 'I was just doing my job. It's not my fault her aunt wants to sell up. I know she's dead, but she could have been a bit nicer about it.'

'Do you have a phone number for Phyllis Charnock?' I asked.

'Yeah, of course.' She flicked through her folder of notes and found a page of contact information. 'But don't tell her I gave it to you, OK? She's a difficult client and I'm doing my best to stay on the right side of her.' A dazzling smile. 'So far so good.'

Within two minutes of starting a conversation with Phyllis Charnock ('*Miss* Charnock, please') I'd revised my opinion of Neela Singh from 'good at her job' to 'miracle worker'. Miss Charnock had apparently been waiting all morning for the chance to pick a fight with someone, and I was offering her a golden opportunity.

'It is impertinent of you to ask why I want to sell my property. It's my house and I am entitled to do exactly what I wish with it.' Her voice grated in my ear, granite-hard.

'Yes, of course. I was just wondering if there was a specific reason for selling it now. You haven't lived in it for some time, I gather.'

'I've never lived in it. I've barely even seen it. I don't like London. I inherited the house from my godmother.'

My godmother had left me a pair of earrings. I tried not to mind that it hadn't been a million-pound house.

'That was quite a legacy.'

'It was kind. Then again, she had no one else to leave it to. And of course I was grateful, at first, in spite of the tax implications. I rented it out for a time but that was a disaster. I thought it was quite a stroke of genius to invite my niece to live in it. After the failure of her marriage she had nowhere else to go. It made it much easier to have a tenant who could be trusted to keep an eye on the house.'

'Of course,' I murmured, looking around the living room at the tasteful wallpaper, the expensive curtains and the carpets that had to have been laid in the last couple of years. 'Was Kate paying rent?'

'Certainly not.' She sounded truly affronted at the suggestion. 'She was my only living relative and I felt it was my duty to help her. In return, she kept the house in a good state of repair and made whatever improvements she felt might be necessary.'

'She must have spent quite a lot of money on it.' More than rent, I thought. A lot more.

'That was her choice.' Her voice became even more severe. 'I never asked her to invest in the house. There was no suggestion on my part that she could look forward to owning the house one day. I helped her out of charity and family feeling, and it was a great shock to me that she didn't feel the same way.'

'Did Kate know you were planning to sell it?'

'She said she had no idea. She was living in a fool's paradise if she thought she could just *keep* the house. I set her straight.'

'She must have been very upset.'

'Oh, she was furious. She had the nerve to say she deserved half of whatever it fetched.' Miss Charnock snorted. 'I was very quick to tell her that she had no legal claim over it whatsoever.'

'But if she put in a new kitchen—'

'There was a kitchen already. And a perfectly good attic, which apparently she turned into a bedroom.' She said it as if no one had ever done a loft conversion before. 'Two of them living in the house and four bedrooms.' A sniff. 'Ridiculous. Her trouble was that she had champagne tastes and a lemonade income.'

Whereas you are bitter lemon all the way. 'When did you tell her you were planning to sell the house?'

'April. I gave her six months to find somewhere else to live. She'd had years to save her money,' Miss Charnock said peevishly. 'She might have known she would need a deposit for a house one day. But she spent the lot. Easy come, easy go. My brother was the same. He was penniless when he died.

298

Kate was only a child. One might have thought that growing up in poverty would have taught her to be more careful about money.'

I winced, imagining Kate coming up against this implacable lack of sympathy. 'Six months isn't a long time.'

'It was plenty of time. I had waited long enough. Her daughter is an adult now. I had done what I could for them. And there was no question of letting the daughter inherit it.'

'You mean Chloe.'

'I think that was the name. I only met her once, when she was eight or nine.' From her tone, Miss Charnock hadn't enjoyed the experience. 'A very unmanageable little girl.'

'Miss Charnock, you may not know this and I'm sorry to break the news to you over the phone, but Chloe died two days ago.'

'Oh.' She absorbed the news for a moment while I waited in respectful silence. 'Well, thank goodness for that.'

'Excuse me?'

'Her mother always said she found life difficult, that she couldn't cope on her own. If she couldn't be independent, what quality of life could she expect as she got older? And of course because of what happened to poor Kate she was in a very difficult position. She was slow, you know. She should have been in a home. That's what I said to Kate, when she said she wasn't able to live on her own.'

I frowned. That wasn't the impression I had had of Chloe. It seemed to me that everyone who knew Chloe – except her mother – thought she was far more able than Miss Charnock was suggesting. And Kate had had her own reasons for wanting Chloe to be dependent on her. I found myself thinking of all the specialists she had visited and discarded when their version of Chloe didn't fit in with Kate's narrative. She had remade her world to suit herself and the facts of her financial and personal situation had seemed like nothing more than an inconvenience.

'Chloe was a beautiful girl,' I said.

'Looks aren't everything. I couldn't let my inheritance go to an imbecile. If Kate had had a normal child it might have been different, but no.' Her voice sounded fretful all of a sudden. 'I have no one, you know. I'm on my own. My income has been very badly affected by low interest rates in the last few years. My investments aren't performing as well as I expected. I have to think of my future.'

'Of course.'

'I had thought – I mean, I expected that Kate would come down to look after me. But she made it very clear that she wouldn't do anything of the kind. After all I'd done for her, too. She needed to be with her daughter, she said. No family feeling for me whatsoever. I thought it was the least she could do, but she told me I could afford to pay for a nursing home.'

The vindictive edge in her voice was beginning to make sense. Selling the house was designed to punish Kate as well as reorganising Miss Charnock's finances. I got off the phone as quickly as possible, and not just because talking to Phyllis Charnock was depressing.

The clock was ticking for Kate, from the moment Miss Charnock announced she was selling the house. There would have been no possibility of negotiating with her aunt, I thought, even if they had been on good terms. Six months to find a home, having sunk all of her money into the house she thought she'd inherit. Her business had failed comprehensively. Chloe was still dependent on her and they were both dependent on Brian Emery's financial support. No wonder she was so keen to secure a lump sum from him.

And he'd said no.

In the kitchen, Derwent said something that made Neela laugh, a long peal of pure amusement. Either she had a very different sense of humour to me or he was trying harder than usual.

When I walked in I found him sitting at the breakfast bar,

his expression innocent. The only sign he had been misbehaving was that one of his knees was jumping, and only I would know it was a giveaway. I glanced at Neela, who was bright-eyed and inclined to blush as well as giggle. He couldn't help it, I thought. Especially when Melissa was turning out to be hard work. A little diversion here and there. Could I blame him?

I could, and I did.

'I think we're finished here,' I said coldly. To Derwent, I said, 'We need to get back to the office.'

The smile disappeared from his face. 'Why?'

Like I'm going to say anything more in front of your estate-agent friend. I raised my eyebrows at him.

He slid off the stool, coming to heel like a dog that knows it's pushed its luck too far.

'How was Miss Charnock?' Neela asked.

'I think she's enough to put off any buyer, even one who doesn't mind about the murder.'

'Yeah.' She sighed. 'I'm definitely going to earn my commission on this one.'

30

'Is that everything?' I asked.

'There's one more box.' Derwent dumped the one he'd been carrying on the floor and went out again.

Teetering piles of paper almost filled the meeting room table already. I started trying to put it in order, swearing under my breath at the scale of it all.

'What's this?'

I looked up to see Una Burt standing in the doorway. 'The files we took from Kate Emery's house and everything we've pulled together since. All the paperwork, basically.'

'Why?'

I rubbed my forehead with the back of my hand. 'Did you hear about the house?'

She nodded. 'Her financial situation was far worse than we thought.'

'Which makes me wonder if she was doing anything to try to get more money.'

'Like?'

'Extra work? Cash in hand? Something illegal? She knew about drugs. She had a supplier for the herbal stuff she sold as a fertility aid. Maybe she started importing something else. A dealer might have objected to her invading their territory.'

'Then where did the money go?'

I shrugged. 'She hid it too well. Or maybe Chloe went to find it and they followed her. Take the money, kill the only witness.'

Burt looked at the table. 'It's going to take you a while to go through all that on your own.'

'I was wondering if I could get some help – Colin, ideally. Or Liv?'

'They're busy working on Chloe's murder. But you've got Derwent.'

'I do.' I pulled a face. 'It might be more help if you took him away.'

Slightly unexpectedly, she laughed. 'All right. I'll find something for him to do to keep him off your back.'

I sat down at the table and began picking through Kate's life again, looking for any variations in the usual patterns. Most people had fairly predictable lives: a handful of jobs over the years, a couple of bank accounts, a dip into the red now and then. There was a rhythm to their spending: an uptick in December for Christmas presents and in July for holidays, paring outgoings to the bone in January. They paid off car loans and invested in their pensions and got a good deal on a new TV and the whole tale of their lives was laid out like the Bayeux tapestry once you knew how to read their financial documentation.

Kate's bank accounts told a different story.

'Find anything?' Derwent, leaning over my shoulder with a mug of tea. His, it became apparent when he sipped it a split second before I thanked him for making it for me.

'Cash.'

'What about it?'

I flipped back through the statements, pointing to the figures I'd highlighted. 'She started taking out cash in May. Phyllis told her in April the house was going to be sold. She gave her niece six months to get herself organised. I'd have expected

Kate to cut down on her spending and increase her savings so she could manage a rental deposit but she started taking out the maximum from cash machines between three and five times a week. Different machines, different places. Always the maximum.'

'So? Maybe she started using cash so she'd be more careful with her spending. Makes a difference when you see the money go, doesn't it?'

'But she never used it. All her spending was still on her debit and credit cards. Even small sums.'

'OK. So what was she doing with it? Paying someone off? Hiding it?'

'I don't know yet. But I know we didn't find it.'

'What else?'

'Nothing yet. Give me a chance. I've only just started.'

'You need some help,' Derwent said.

'Not from you.'

'Wasn't offering. Hold on a second.' He strolled out and a couple of minutes passed before Georgia appeared in the doorway.

'DI Derwent told me you needed me.'

I suppressed a sigh and filled her in on what we'd learned about Kate.

'So she had no money. Why didn't she get a job?'

'Doing what?'

'She was a nurse, wasn't she? Before she set up her company, I mean.'

'She'd let her registration lapse.'

'I think she was still working in that area, though, wasn't she?' Georgia started burrowing through the files, frowning. 'I'm sure I saw something when I was looking for the child psychologist reports. Here.' She handed me a letter on headed paper.

'A short-term contract at the Rosebery Clinic, whatever that is.' I checked the date. 'But this is from two years ago.'

304

'That's the last mention of a real job I found. If you're looking for work, you start off by going back to the places you've worked before, don't you? Unless you fucked up.'

'Absolutely.' I found my phone and called the number on the letter.

'The Rosebery Clinic, Anita speaking, how may I help you?' She sounded smoothly professional, her voice unapologetically posh.

I identified myself and explained I was ringing because of an active murder investigation. The silence on the other end of the line was charged with reluctance to get involved, but there was curiosity too.

'I'm not sure if we can help.'

'Is the Rosebery Clinic a medical clinic?'

'Yes, it is.'

'Specialising in . . .'

'Reproductive healthcare. Fertility, specifically.'

'IVF?' That was all I really knew about fertility treatments.

'Amongst other therapies. All of this information is available on our website. Now, if that's all—'

Other therapies. And Kate had been selling supplements to help couples with their fertility.

'Do you know of a woman named Kate Emery? Did you ever work with her?'

There was a tiny intake of breath. 'Hold on. Give me your number and I'll call you back.'

She hung up before I could ask anything else.

'What did she say?' Georgia's eyes were bright with interest.

'She's calling me back.' I stood up and paced around the room, too excited to sit still. 'I wish she'd hurry up.'

After a couple of minutes my phone rang: an unknown number.

'You were asking about Kate Emery.' No preamble, and this time Anita's voice was distinctly more down-to-earth. I could hear traffic; she'd obviously left the building to talk

305

to me. 'I saw in the paper she'd disappeared. Murder, you said.'

'It is a murder investigation, yes.'

'God, poor Kate.'

'You knew her.'

'She used to work at the clinic. She was a nurse there, donkey's years ago. Oh, it must be fifteen years ago. More. She quit when she found out her daughter wasn't well. Such a shame. She was a brilliant nurse.'

'Had you heard from her since?'

'A few times. It was hard for her to go out, you know, with her daughter.' A sigh. 'She was great fun, Kate. Trouble with a capital T. Always up to something. She'd do anything for a laugh. Play jokes on people. Say anything. Bold as brass, that's what I used to say to her.'

'What about boyfriends?'

'What about them?'

'Did she take risks with boyfriends? Sleep with people she didn't know?'

'I couldn't say. Is that what you've found out?' Avid curiosity.

'It's one line of enquiry,' I said. 'Did you know about her business?'

'Oh yes. I knew *all* about it. That's why I couldn't talk to you in the office. Kate came back to do a bit of work here a couple of years ago. Not nursing – reception work. I was off sick to recover from an operation and she covered for me. I was all right about it because I knew she wouldn't want to take my job, and she didn't. But she took something else. Our mailing list.'

'Without asking?'

'She didn't ask because she knew the answer would have been no. Then she started sending people letters about their fertility issues, selling her stuff. We had complaints from clients straight away. We had to send out letters of apology and our lawyer sent Kate a warning not to use the list any more. Management were furious. But I always thought it was her way of getting back at them for firing her.'

'They fired her before the theft of the mailing list came to light?'

'She was supposed to do six weeks here but she got fired halfway through the second week. She got caught going through the files. They're strictly confidential.'

'Which files?'

'Old ones from when she worked there. I don't know, maybe she was curious about patients she'd treated. But the requests got flagged up by the archive system. It's not like going through a filing cabinet. They're all computerised, you see.'

'What records were they, do you remember?'

'I can find out for you.' A pause while a lorry thundered past. 'Do you think it's relevant to what happened?'

'No idea,' I said cheerfully. 'But I'd like to know.'

'What did she say?' Georgia asked as soon as I got off the phone.

'I don't want to speak ill of the dead but Kate was downright unscrupulous about developing her business.' I told her about the mailing list.

'It's not a motive for killing her though, is it?' Georgia sounded disappointed.

'Probably not. You can't have everything.'

Georgia returned to the paperwork, speed-reading efficiently, commenting now and then on anything that struck her as unusual. Her comments were perceptive, I thought; she was good at this, even if she didn't have the right instincts on the street. Strengths and weaknesses. We all had them. The trick was to work with people who were strong where you were weak. Maybe that was why Derwent was so keen that I shouldn't become just like him. He needed me to be his conscience since he was entirely without one.

I was looking at a lab report when my phone rang again:

Anita. It was a short conversation. I sat for a minute after I hung up, thinking. Then I went looking for Liv.

'This lab report.' I showed it to her.

'What about it?'

'What are they talking about?'

'The needle.'

'What needle?'

'You should know. You collected it.'

I frowned at her. 'No, I didn't.'

'It came with all the rest of the stuff you collected from Kate Emery's house. I think it was from the bin in her bedroom.'

'I collected that,' Derwent said, coming over to tweak the report out of my hand. 'There was nothing in it. Cotton wool, used tissues.'

'And a button and a needle.' I shook my head. 'I saw the button and I assumed it was a sewing needle, but it wasn't. It was a *medical* one.'

'I thought you knew that,' Liv said, her face blank. 'That's why I sent it off for analysis. But it didn't have anything illegal in it.'

'No. It didn't.' And Liv hadn't realised the significance of it any more than I had, until I'd read the lab report.

Derwent frowned at me. 'But . . .'

'One phone call,' I said. 'Then we need to talk to the boss.'

'What have you got?' Una Burt looked up, expectant.

'Good news and bad news,' I said.

'What's the good news?'

'I've solved one mystery. When Kate Emery was temping at the clinic, she looked up one archived file. That file belonged to Eleanor and Oliver Norris. They were treated at the clinic for fertility issues when Kate was working there as a nurse.'

'When they moved in, Kate must have recognised them,'

Derwent said. 'As soon as she heard the story that Bethany was a miracle baby, she'd have known one of them was lying.'

'Why's that?'

'Oliver Norris is completely infertile,' I said. 'I've checked with the lab and they confirmed it from the used condom we found in Harold Lowe's house.'

'So Bethany isn't his daughter,' Derwent said. 'No miracle. And Kate knew it. Whatever Eleanor did to get pregnant – whether it was a donor or an affair – she didn't want her husband knowing about it.'

'Do you think Kate was blackmailing her?' Una Burt asked.

'Why else would she have looked them up on the system?' I said. 'It had to be more than curiosity. She must have known she was taking a risk, so it was worth it to her to forfeit her temporary employment at the clinic to find out about Eleanor. Her business was already in trouble then. She needed cash, urgently, and her ex-husband wasn't going to be any use when his wife was arguing over every penny he handed over.'

'But blackmail is a big step,' Burt said.

'Not for someone who was defrauding her customers. Not for someone who would stop at nothing to get money – even making out that her daughter was more vulnerable than she actually was, so her ex-husband would keep paying to support her. Chloe was far from helpless according to everyone but Kate.'

'Manipulative,' Una Burt observed.

'Desperate, maybe. She grew up in poverty, according to her aunt. She knew what it was like to be poor and she didn't want to go back to that. She had two bits of bad luck: she divorced Brian Emery before he made his fortune and she put all her money into the house. If she'd inherited it, she'd have been set up for life, but it didn't work out the way she'd planned.'

'Where was Eleanor getting the money to pay her off?'

'Oliver gets a nice salary from the church and I found

statements for a joint account among his papers. As long as Eleanor was careful, she could skim money off the house-keeping and keep Kate off her back. But if Kate got greedy or desperate, Eleanor wouldn't have had anywhere to turn.'

'Do you think Eleanor killed her?'

'No.'

'Who then? Oliver?'

'Not him either.'

'We wondered about the girls,' Derwent said. 'Bethany and Chloe working together. We ran through it earlier at the house. The blood-spatter evidence is contradictory at best. We thought two attackers might explain it.'

'But now I have a better explanation,' I said. 'And that's the bad news.'

'Go on,' Una Burt said.

'The reason we haven't found Kate's body is because there isn't one.' I paused as the chief inspector's face paled. 'Kate's still alive.'

31

'That's impossible,' Una Burt snapped. 'She can't be. You saw the house.'

'It was staged,' I said, almost apologetic. The time, the resources expended on a major murder investigation, the press conferences, the phone calls with senior officers: I could see Una Burt calculating the cost to her career and coming up with a figure that was unacceptably high. 'Among the items we removed from Kate's house was a needle. Liv sent it off to be tested for drugs. According to the lab, it was used to draw Kate's blood.'

'So?'

'Kate was a nurse. Kate knew how to draw blood, and how to store it. Her *body* was never in the freezer – but her blood was. And when she was ready, she took the blood out of the storage unit, thawed it, and covered her house in it. There was so much blood. No one could have survived losing so much in one go, so we've spent ten days looking for a corpse. She made it look as if she had been murdered and we investigated it as if it was murder.'

'Why? What good did it do her to be dead?'

'She left her life insurance policy for Chloe to claim once the death certificate was issued,' Derwent said. 'If she'd just disappeared it would have taken years to get the certificate. With us ready to confirm she was dead, the process would have been much, much quicker. Chloe was supposed to stay with her father until the insurance paid out.'

'Kate didn't know about Chloe's stepbrother molesting her. The plan started to fall apart as soon as Chloe came home. Instead of being out of the way, she was right in the middle of the investigation, surrounded by the very people Kate had been manipulating before she left.'

'And then someone killed her,' Burt said. 'But Kate being alive – and the blackmail – none of that is a reason to kill Chloe, is it?'

'Not directly. I don't see how it would benefit Eleanor Norris to kill Kate's daughter. That's why I don't think we should talk to the Norrises about the blackmail until we've tracked Kate down. She might have a better idea than us as to who killed Chloe and why,' I said.

'Where do we start looking?' Burt ran her hands through her short hair. 'She could be anywhere.'

'She left her passport behind,' Derwent pointed out. 'Makes sense. She wouldn't have wanted to leave the UK. She'd have been too far from Chloe, and we'd be more likely to spot her going. Crossing borders is risky. It would have been far easier to lie low in this country, especially since no one was looking for her.'

'So how do we find her?' I asked. 'A public appeal?'

'I don't think we should give away that we know she's alive yet. She might run again, for starters. And it might put her in danger,' Derwent said.

He didn't mean it as a dig but I felt it all the same; I still couldn't shake the feeling that Chloe's death was my fault.

'Sorry to interrupt.' Liv, leaning through the doorway. She was holding a printout. 'There's something weird about Chloe's phone records.'

'What sort of thing?'

'She didn't use it much for making or receiving calls – it was mainly texts and picture messages. After she disappeared, she started getting a lot of calls – like, thirty or forty – from payphones in Sussex and Hampshire.'

'All payphones?' I checked.

'Yeah. Different ones every time and all over the place. I haven't mapped it out properly yet but if it was the same person they were going around in circles.'

'Kate,' Una Burt said. 'When did the calls start?'

'Sunday.'

'After the public appeal to find Chloe,' I said. 'Kate must have been panicking.'

'Did Chloe answer any of the calls?'

Liv shook her head. 'Her phone was off.'

'Were there any voicemails?'

'Nope.'

'So either she couldn't answer her phone or she didn't want to,' I said. 'And somehow the phone ended up in Bethany's possession but she didn't answer the calls either.'

'Sussex and Hampshire are big counties,' Derwent said. 'Lots of people, lots of places she could be hiding out.'

'It's a start,' I said.

Colin Vale positively glowed when I informed him that Kate Emery was no longer a victim, but a suspect.

'Give me a live person to hunt for any day.' He wheeled his chair closer to his desk so his nose was practically touching his computer screen. 'Now, she didn't take her car so we don't know what she's driving or even if she is driving. She didn't take her phone. Let's make sure her bank accounts haven't been used.' He didn't even have to look up the number, dialling it with the fluency of a concert pianist. 'Ah, Miriam. DS Colin Vale here again. Yes, indeed, as usual! How are you today?'

313

Not banter. Please, save me from banter.

The expression on my face must have communicated what I was thinking. 'A quick enquiry, Miriam. Won't take long.'

It didn't, thankfully: she hadn't used any cards or made any payments since she disappeared. Colin hung up. 'So she's using cash. But you can't use cash for everything these days. She'll need another bank account. And you can't set up a bank account without proof of identification and proof of address.' He leaned back. 'Let's start with aliases. What's her maiden name?'

'Try Charnock.'

'Kate Charnock.' He logged on to a credit-rating service, and put in the name. 'Same date of birth . . . nothing.'

'Try Katherine Charnock. Try both spellings of Katherine,' I suggested.

'There's a Catherine Charnock in SW15. That's not her address, though, is it? Constantine Avenue?'

'That's Harold Lowe's house. She must have been using it as her alternative address.' I thought back to the pile of post in his hall, which I'd stepped over without a second glance. Stupid . . . but even if I'd seen the name I wouldn't have made the connection with Kate Emery. It had been a safe place for her to use as her address, better than any PO box. Untraceable.

More and more I thought that police dog had earned his Bonios.

'It's a Nationwide account.' He rang their call centre and explained what he wanted. They found her accounts within seconds. 'And that's active, is it? Whereabouts is she using her card? Where's *that*? Hampshire? Never heard of it.'

He was tapping a name into his computer as he spoke – Groves Edge. I leaned over his shoulder to see the results. It was a hamlet that consisted of a few shops and a handful of houses strung out along a minor road. He flicked between the satellite image and the map, zooming out so I could see how remote it was. Narrow country lanes. Not many houses.

The middle of nowhere. The largest settlement nearby was Lymington, and I'd never heard of that either, though it seemed to be a pretty seaside town.

'And she's used it to pay a sum of money to a lettings agent. All right. Thanks.'

'It's tiny,' I said. 'She'd stand out as a stranger.'

Colin was shaking his head. 'They always go rural. Never stay in the cities. It's so stupid. I know they want to get well away from other people, but if they found somewhere big enough and used cash all the time, they could lie low. We'd have no chance of catching them.'

'Lucky for us.'

'Indeed. Now to talk to the lettings agent.'

'I wonder if she's still there?' I said. 'Surely she'd run again once she knew Chloe was dead?'

'Speaking for myself, if anything happened to my kids, I'd be inconsolable. I wouldn't be thinking about getting away. I'd want to kill whoever hurt them. That would be my number one ambition.' He sounded matter-of-fact. I didn't doubt he would do exactly that.

'I never knew you had it in you, Colin.'

'You put everything you have into your kids. You'd do anything for them. Sacrifice anything.' He shrugged. 'I wouldn't hold back.'

'What have you got?' Derwent leaned on the desk beside me, making me jump.

'She's somewhere near a village called Groves Edge. It's in Hampshire,' I said. 'Straight down the A3.'

Derwent raised an eyebrow at me. 'Fancy a road trip?'

I was washing my hands when the door to the ladies' room opened. I looked up at the mirror and saw Georgia Shaw standing behind me, her face set.

'Are you OK?'

'You made fun of me.'

'What?' I twisted round to look at her properly. 'When?'

'When I suggested it might not be murder. The first night, when we were at Valerian Road. You laughed at me, and I was right.'

'DI Derwent laughed at you,' I said, and it was true, but guilt sent a chill over my skin. She *had* suggested it wasn't murder. I'd ignored her.

'You didn't exactly stand up for me. You sent me away.'

'That's right, I did.' I picked up a paper towel and started drying my hands. 'There was no reason at that stage to think you were right. We had no idea it was staged. And you didn't either.'

'No, but—'

If you'd stayed, Derwent would have ripped you apart and he'd have enjoyed it.'

'Why?'

'For fun.' I sighed. 'Look, I did you a favour by getting you out of his way.'

'You didn't want me to be around him.' Her eyes narrowed. 'Do you feel threatened by me?'

'Absolutely not.' I threw the paper towel in the bin and leaned back against the sink. 'But if you think I'm going to mentor you, you're mistaken. If you do your job properly – and it's a big if, considering how I've seen you behave – I'll back you up, every time. I've been looking out for you, believe it or not. I didn't say anything to Una Burt about how you froze on the street.'

'But you told her you didn't want to work with me.' Her bottom lip was quivering. 'You've always had special treatment on this team and you don't like sharing the limelight.'

'That sounds like something Pete Belcott would say.' I saw her eyes flicker: got it in one. 'Choose your allies carefully, Georgia. He's a shit.'

'And Derwent isn't?'

'He has his moments.'

316

'You act like you own him.'

'I most certainly do not.'

'Everyone knows you slept together.'

'No, that never happened. It was a rumour, that's all,' I said patiently. A rumour that Derwent hadn't done anything like enough to dispel. I had been angry that Georgia was challenging me, but I couldn't hold on to that feeling. I looked at her, flushed and struggling for composure, and I remembered what it was like to be the new girl on the team. To feel insecure all the time. To worry about opening your mouth in case you said the wrong thing. To wonder about people's loyalties, people's histories. To say the wrong thing without meaning to.

Don't try to be me. I'd thought I was doing enough by not being as hard on Georgia as Derwent had been on me, but that wasn't right either.

'I think we should start again. A clean slate.' I cleared my throat. 'You did a good job on the paperwork. Better than good. I wouldn't have found the Rosebery Clinic letter for hours, and I might have missed its significance.'

'Thanks.' She sounded wary.

'DI Derwent and I are going to look for Kate Emery in Hampshire.' I would regret this, I thought. 'Do you want to come?'

'Yes. Yes, I do.'

'OK. Good.' I hoped Derwent wouldn't mind. 'But watch yourself around Derwent. He's tricky.'

A glimmer of a smile lightened her expression. 'I've noticed.'

Fairness compelled me to add, 'He's a good person. I mean, if you expand your definition of good to include quite a lot of bad behaviour.'

'You trust him.'

'Never,' I said, and meant it.

'But you like working with him.'

'I wouldn't say that.'

317

She shook her head. 'I can't work it out.'

'I'm used to him. I know what to expect.' I checked my watch. 'For instance, I know that he is already in the car and if we don't get a move on, he'll leave without us. Let's go.'

32

We were twenty minutes into our journey when the heavy black clouds above us began to seep rain. Derwent flicked on the windscreen wipers as a flash of lightning made me jump.

'This is all we need,' he growled.

'It was forecast,' Georgia said from the back seat. 'Thunderstorms across the south-east. And a possibility of flooding.'

'No shit.' Derwent switched the wipers to their fastest setting as the rain poured down the windscreen in a near-opaque sheet. Water rattled on the roof of the car, so loud that I could barely hear the thunder, or Derwent swearing beside me. He slowed down a little, and then a little more, until he was only going approximately twice as fast as I would have liked.

'We're going to get soaked,' I predicted.

'Maybe it'll have stopped by the time we get there,' Georgia said.

Incorrectly, as it turned out.

Groves Edge would have been easy to miss in the best of circumstances: it was a straggle of houses and shops that flashed past the car in the strange, stormy half-light that was closer to dusk than it had any right to be halfway through a

319

July afternoon. Low buildings lined the main street: a teashop, a post office, two pubs, a handful of cottages with well-tended gardens. The rain had settled to a steady, heavy downpour that tore green leaves off the trees and plastered them onto the road. The gutters were rivers clogged with debris and every puddle sent a spray of water up from the wheels to smack against the side windows.

'Where are we going?'

'Crow Lane House.' I flattened out the map. 'Crow Lane is on the left in about a quarter of a mile.'

We were all watching for it and we still almost missed it: a gap in the high hedges that barely deserved to be called a lane.

'That's it,' I exclaimed.

Derwent braked hard, reversed, spun the wheel and accelerated up Crow Lane as leaves and twigs rattled against the side of the car. I thought of skeletons dragging bony hands against the paintwork and maybe it wasn't so farfetched; we were on our way to see a dead woman, after all . . .

'It should be up here, I think.' The scattered trees suddenly bunched together in a solid mass, dense and forbidding, and as the road turned towards it I saw a brick chimney through the leaves. The driveway was a narrow opening in the trees. Derwent shone the headlights on the gate and the ghost of words appeared, the paint faded to the point of invisibility: Crow Lane House in all its faded glory.

'Hop out and open the gate,' Derwent said to me.

'I don't think we should drive up to the house.'

A gout of water tipped from the leaves overhead and splattered on the windscreen.

'Yeah, why not,' Derwent said. 'It's a nice afternoon for a walk.'

'I don't feel like giving Kate a lot of warning,' I said. 'I don't want her to run again.'

'Where would she go?'

'I don't know. But do you really want to chase after her in this?'

He nodded. 'All right.'

'I'm glad the plan meets with your approval,' I said tartly.

'Don't be like that.' He opened his door and climbed out. I looked back at Georgia, who was biting her lip. *It's awkward when Mummy and Daddy argue in the car . . .*

I got out of the car and stared at him across the roof. 'Like what?'

'Snappy.'

'I'm not being snappy.'

'You're probably nervous,' Derwent guessed, accurately. 'Worried she won't be there. You put yourself under too much pressure.'

'Because you're completely relaxed.'

He grinned at me, his teeth very white in the gloom. 'Have you got your radio?'

'Of course.'

'What about you, Georgia?'

'Yep.' She pulled the hood of her anorak over her head and zipped it up.

'Did you tell the locals we were here?' Derwent asked me.

'They were completely uninterested.' Locating someone who had probably committed blackmail and fraud – even someone who had been, for a time, dead – wasn't the kind of thing that let you call in favours from another police force. Hampshire Constabulary had wished us well and left us to it.

Derwent grunted. 'As long as they know we're on their patch I don't mind them staying out of it.'

The three of us picked our way carefully up the drive. It was mud and stones all the way, and the rain made it as slippery underfoot as glass. The trees should have kept off the worst of the rain but it was a fickle kind of shelter. Every breeze sent heavy drops of water cascading down on us and

321

I was aware of the cold water seeping through my anorak across my shoulders and down my back.

'Careful now.' Derwent's voice was a breath in my ear as he put his hand on my arm. 'The house is close.'

We rounded the corner of the drive and saw it: a Victorian house, red brick and half-timbered, with bay windows and a front door set back in a large porch. It was grand at first glance and then less so as we got closer: damp streaked the brickwork and the coloured glass around the front door had a gaping hole in it, roughly boarded up. The trees came too close to the house, dense and overgrown as they were, and I felt uneasy, as if anyone could be hiding behind their bushy branches.

We stood for a second on the edge of the trees, not quite hiding but not announcing our presence either.

'Try the front. I'll go round the back.' He was gone, drifting over the uneven ground like a ghost. Georgia and I went up the steps side by side and I knocked on the door, the sound reverberating through the house. Somehow, even though I was confident we'd found Kate's hiding place, I wasn't expecting her to be there and the sight of a shadow approaching the door made the hairs stand up on the back of my neck.

The door opened and I held up my warrant card, conscious of Georgia doing the same.

'Kate Emery?' It was worth asking. The woman who stood in the doorway was dark-haired, not fair, and her hair was cut into a neat jaw-length bob with a deep fringe. She looked pale and tired. Her top and trousers seemed loose on her, as if she hadn't eaten much lately. I had been staring at photographs of her for the best part of two weeks and I would have walked straight past her in the street.

She nodded. There was no surprise in her heavy-lidded eyes. Resignation, I thought, and a degree of wariness. 'What do you want?'

'We want to talk to you, Kate. We need your help with a few things.'

'Help,' she repeated, her voice flat. 'Are you here to arrest me?'

'No,' I said, although it was a distinct possibility. 'We want to talk to you about Chloe.'

Something tightened in her face. 'Chloe.'

'You've heard about what happened.' I didn't phrase it as a question because I knew she had: the public appeal to find Chloe, the panicked phone calls to her number as Kate criss-crossed the local area, covering her tracks as best she could, not quite reckless with fear but close to it.

'That she's dead? I saw it on the news.' Her chin quivered but she held on to her composure, barely. 'I don't think I want to talk to you.'

'We're looking for the person who killed Chloe,' I said. 'You must want us to find them.'

A flash of anger made her pupils snap to pinpoints. 'Must I?'

'I assume so. She was your only child.'

'I'm aware of that.' Her eyes widened at the sound of footsteps crunching the gravel: Derwent, returning with less care to be silent and a lot more speed.

'Kate Emery, I presume.' He jogged up the steps and peered at her. 'You've changed. But then I suppose that was the idea.'

'Leave me alone.' She made to shut the door and Georgia stopped her.

'We can't do that, I'm afraid,' I said. 'We know you had your reasons for running away and we even know what some of those reasons were. But we need to hear your side of it.'

She looked at the watch that hung loosely from her wrist. 'You can't stay for long.'

'Got somewhere to be?' Derwent asked, and she glared at him briefly, then stepped away from the door and disappeared into the shadows of the house.

As I crossed the threshold I felt a chill that seemed to seep all the way through to my bones. The rooms on either side of the hall were dim. The air smelled of cold ashes and damp. I tried to imagine it blazing with life and warmth, sunlight streaming in through the big windows, the breeze from the river tossing the trees.

'Cheerful,' Derwent muttered in my ear and I nodded before following Kate into the room on the right of the hall: a sitting room. It was a pleasant enough room, or it would have been if there had been a fire in the hearth. The armchairs and sofa were upholstered in faded chintz that felt damp when I touched it. Kate seemed oblivious to the cold and when Derwent switched on a lamp she jumped, surprised at the yellowish light that flooded the room. We sat down, Georgia and me on the sofa, Derwent in an armchair that sagged under his weight. He leaned forward.

'So, Mrs Emery. Seems to me you have some explaining to do.'

'I don't have to explain anything to you.'

'That's not technically true, is it? You've got yourself into a right old mess, love. Why did you do it? Why fake your death?'

'I didn't.'

'Oh, come on. You left your house looking like an abattoir. You left your belongings, your keys, your phone. What else were we supposed to think?'

Kate shrugged. 'I can't help the assumptions you made.'

'People usually have a few reasons for pretending to be dead,' I said. 'They've done something terrible, they want to claim life insurance without the inconvenience of actually dying, or they're scared of someone. Which is it, Kate?'

'Insurance, obviously,' Derwent said. 'That would have been a hefty payout, Kate. Well worth losing a few pints of blood.'

'I didn't claim anything. I have a life insurance policy but so do lots of people.'

'You didn't get the chance to claim it.' Derwent smiled. 'I didn't come down in the last shower, Kate.'

324

'You can't prove it because I didn't do it. Are you arresting people for crimes they *might* commit now?'

'It's common sense, Kate. And if we put in a bit more work, we'll be able to prove it.'

'I doubt that.' She was tightly coiled like a snake about to strike. 'You're talking nonsense.'

'No, what's nonsense is expecting us to believe you'd stage your own death for no reason.'

'You're not being fair to Mrs Emery,' I said. 'I did mention some other reasons for wanting to disappear. Like having done something terrible. Like being afraid.'

Her attention switched back to me, her eyes unblinking. 'Afraid of whom?'

'Morgan Norris, for one?'

I thought she was going to be sick then and there. She swayed, then gathered herself together. 'What about him?'

'We found the clothes. Your clothes.' I tilted my head, considering her. 'But I think we were meant to find them. You didn't want him to get away with what he did to you.'

She didn't answer straight away. Then she said, 'He did it to scare me. And it worked.'

'Why did he want to scare you?'

'I don't know.' She was wary now.

'You were having an affair with his brother.'

I had the impression that something that had been held taut slackened within her: relief. We knew about the affair and not about the blackmail. 'You know about that.'

'We found some forensic evidence. And Oliver told us.'

'He was very forthcoming. He seemed proud of himself,' Derwent said. Kate's mouth curled into a smile, but not a pleasant one.

'I'm sure he was happy to tell you all about it.'

'One thing that's been bothering me.' Derwent leaned forward, his arms on his knees. 'Why did you make him use a condom?'

'What?'

'Oliver. Why make him use a condom? You knew he was shooting blanks.'

'I – I didn't. I couldn't have known.' She was on high alert again, her hands clasped together in her lap. 'It was healthier. For both of us. I always insist on it with all my partners. It's safer.'

'Morgan didn't wear a condom,' I said. Did we know about the blackmail or not? The tension had to be tormenting her. 'Because he raped you. You didn't get the chance to make him put one on.'

'Did you arrest him?'

'I've interviewed him but, without your testimony, I can't take it further. Believe me, I'd like to.'

'I can't help you.' Her face was shuttered, remote.

'He'll do it to someone else,' I said.

'That's not my problem.'

'All about the self-interest, our Kate,' Derwent said. 'It's what's best for you all the time, isn't it? You didn't even stick around to make sure your daughter was all right. You left Chloe behind, Kate. That's cold.'

'Don't you dare talk to me about my daughter. You have no right.'

Derwent carried on as if she hadn't spoken. 'Chloe's dead, Kate. DS Kerrigan and I went to her post-mortem. Someone killed her and threw her body away like she was nothing.'

'We don't know why it happened, let alone who did it,' I said. 'We've wasted a lot of time looking for your killer, but it hasn't got us very far with finding Chloe's.'

'How did she die?'

'She drowned.'

'Did they – did they hurt her?' she whispered.

'She had some injuries.' Pity made me add, 'But she didn't have defensive injuries. She wasn't assaulted. It looked as if she didn't fight.'

Kate pressed her hand over her mouth, physically holding back the sobs that shook her fragile frame. Her eyes filled with tears.

'Do you know what happened to her, Kate? Can you help us? That's more important than anything else at this moment.'

'We want to find the person or people who hurt your daughter,' Derwent said, his voice softer now. I'd known him a long time but I'd never got used to the way he could switch from flippant hostility to the purest kind of empathy. 'They don't deserve to get away with it. You don't want them to get away with it.'

'No.' She dragged in a breath, gasping a little. 'No, I don't.'

'So please, Kate, help us.'

'I can't.'

'Can't or won't?' I said. 'I don't understand. You obviously loved Chloe.'

'More than you can imagine. More than anything.'

'Then why won't you talk to us?'

She shook her head. 'I don't know anything.'

'She ran away with Bethany Norris and Bethany tried to kill herself after Chloe died,' I said. 'Why?'

'You'll have to ask Bethany.'

'Chloe was sleeping with William Turner, did you know that?'

Kate flinched. 'I – no.'

'They were in love.'

'Chloe didn't understand love.'

'William says she did.'

'I don't want to talk to you about that.'

I was starting to lose my temper. 'Why don't we talk about her stepbrother, Nolan? He sexually assaulted her. Did you know that? That's why she didn't stay with her father. She wasn't safe there. She wasn't safe anywhere.'

'Shut up. I won't listen to you. I won't.' Her expression was stubborn, unyielding.

327

Derwent stood up and jerked his head towards the hall. I followed him out, leaving Georgia to sit with Kate.

'We're not getting anywhere,' Derwent said, dropping his voice so it was barely audible.

'She knows more than she's saying,' I said. 'I know she does. Maybe she's afraid to incriminate herself. If she had a solicitor—'

'They'd tell her to go no comment.'

'Not if we promised to leave the fraud charges out of it.'

'What fraud charges? She's right, we've got nothing concrete against her on that. Not yet, anyway,' Derwent added. 'I haven't given up on it.'

'And the blackmail – if Eleanor Norris makes a complaint.'

'That's a big if. She'd have to tell her husband about it, for starters. We have no proof as it stands.' Derwent rapped his knuckles on my head. 'You're not getting this, are you? We've got a lot of guesswork at the moment, not facts. And she knows it.'

'She's going to run again if we leave her. I'm surprised she hasn't gone already.'

'We should arrest her. Keep her while we try to dig up some more on the insurance thing. There has to be something incriminating on her computer or in her papers. It's not as if we've been investigating this as an insurance fraud from the start – we're bound to have missed something.'

'But they won't keep her in custody for long, and it will piss her off. They'll get her first account, assuming she co-operates with an interview, and then she'll be out on bail.'

'Better than nothing.' He started back towards the door and I caught his arm to stop him.

'It bloody isn't. If we arrest her for insurance fraud and she turns out to be the key witness in a murder trial, we'll have shot ourselves in the foot. Any defence barrister would make use of it. That's the best way to discredit whatever she tells us.'

'Assuming she's around to tell us anything.' Derwent chewed his lip. 'If we don't lock her up, they'll say we went easy on her.'

'She knows something about Chloe's death. I know she does.'

'That's why you told her about Turner and the stepbrother. Looking for a reaction.'

'And I didn't get one.'

'We need to arrest her.'

'We can't.'

'Fuck this,' Derwent said loudly enough that Kate must have heard it.

'Shut up, for God's sake.' I took out my phone. 'Let's call Burt. Let her policy this.'

'That's not actually a bad idea for once, Kerrigan.'

'Thanks. It would be an even better idea if I had any reception,' I said, staring at the screen.

'Radio?'

That wasn't working either.

Derwent checked his own phone. 'I fucking hate the countryside. Is there a landline?'

There was an old-fashioned phone on a table by the stairs. I lifted the receiver and listened. 'Nothing.'

'Christ almighty. I'll have to drive back to civilisation.'

'Or find a payphone.'

'Did you see one on the way here?'

I tried to remember. 'I think so. On the way out of the village?'

'I won't be long.'

'No, wait. I think I should go.'

He glowered. 'Why?'

'Because I don't trust you to put both sides of the argument to Burt fairly.'

He pressed his hand against his chest, wounded. 'That hurts, Kerrigan.'

329

'Am I wrong?'

'Yes, you are. I can be fair.'

I folded my arms. 'OK then. Why don't you let me go on my own?'

'Absolutely not.'

'You don't trust me and I don't trust you.'

'But I outrank you.'

I raised one eyebrow and waited until he sighed. 'So what do you want to do? Leave Georgia here?'

'She can look after her,' I said. 'We won't be long.'

'All right. But let's not make a big deal of it. At the moment, legally, Kate could walk out at any second and there's nothing we could do to stop her. I don't want to give her the idea to give it a whirl.'

33

It took longer than I had anticipated to find a phone and to persuade Una Burt to make an actual decision. Much longer than I would have liked, considering I spent a lot of it jammed up against Derwent in a phone box that was fogged with condensation and smelled, regrettably, of piss.

To give Burt her due, she heard both sides of the argument and considered them with care. It wasn't entirely a surprise to me that she decided we should arrest Kate, but I was disappointed.

'I think we'll lose any chance of getting her to cooperate, boss. And it's going to cause us problems further down the line.'

'We'll have to deal with that when we get that far. At the moment we don't have anyone to put on trial so there's very little point in worrying about it.'

I disagreed, profoundly, but there was nothing I could do about it. At least it was no longer our decision. Now that I was more senior I was discovering that policing was at least as much about covering your arse as locking up bad guys.

This time we drove all the way up the winding drive and parked in front of the house. I beat Derwent to the door, running up the steps to get out of the rain that was heavier than ever.

'Did you leave the door open?' I pushed it without waiting for him to reply, and as I stepped into the hall I knew that something was wrong. I put a hand up to warn Derwent who checked his progress just a little too late, colliding with me.

'What's wrong?' he whispered.

I shook my head, trying to work it out. Silence, that was one thing. The door to the sitting room was open, a breeze stirring the curtains, but there was no sign of Kate and Georgia.

'Kitchen?'

'I'll have a look.'

He sidestepped me and slipped down towards the back of the house, not making a sound on the tiled floor. I stayed where I was, listening. A tiny noise broke the silence, a sound that could have been claws on wood or a soft fall of dust or the house settling. Probably a rat, I thought, or a mouse. The riverbank would be teeming with them. The gardens ran all the way down to the river, the letting agent had said. When it was cold, or they were hungry, the rodents would surely come to the house, to feast on threadbare carpets and faded curtains and old upholstery. I imagined them nesting in the innards of armchairs and mattresses and suppressed a shudder.

Derwent was back in a few seconds, shaking his head, the tension visible in the line of his mouth and the set of his shoulders. If she'd gone . . . And where the hell was Georgia? If something had happened to her . . .

I started up the stairs because I was closer, and because I knew Derwent wanted to go first. I would break him of his desire to protect me if it was the last thing I did, I thought, stepping as quietly as I could on the wooden treads. I hugged the wall, my eyes straining to make sense of the landing: a chair, an ornate chest of drawers, a door on the right that was slightly ajar. I turned back to check whether Derwent had seen it and he gave me a look: *Get on with it but be careful.* I didn't often regret that I wasn't allowed to carry a gun but the weight of it would have been a comfort. A torch and a metal baton weren't really all that reassuring when you came down to it. Nor was the hand in the small of my back, pushing me forward. Derwent, protective? Not today, apparently.

I pushed the door open gingerly and waited one . . . two . . . three. No attack. I pushed harder, letting it swing back against the wall with a hollow thud. No one standing behind the door, waiting for me. I stepped smartly through it and swung around, trying to take in every noteworthy detail of the room in a single sweep. A bay window, the curtains open on the gloomy weather outside. There was a lopsided dressing table in the window, with a three-part mirror on the top reflecting three tense versions of me. A chair. A wardrobe, the doors ajar to show it was empty apart from a couple of pairs of jeans and a jumper.

Kate's room.

If she'd gone, she'd gone without packing. I went back to the hallway, where Derwent was emerging from another bedroom shaking his head.

'Nothing.'

We checked the remaining rooms together, finding a dim bathroom and a single bedroom but no sign of Kate or Georgia. I had more or less ordered Georgia to take more risks. I had insisted on leaving her alone with Kate, who was prepared to be ruthless when she needed to be. What had I done?

As I came back down the stairs to the hall I heard the sound again and this time I had more luck in placing it: a door beside the stairs. I crossed over to it and listened, my own breathing filling my ears unhelpfully. Then I turned to Derwent and nodded. He tapped very gently on the door and there was a distinct sob from behind it.

'Georgia?' I hissed.

'Maeve? I thought – I wasn't sure it was you.' She sounded terrified, on the edge of hysteria.

'Where's Kate?'

'I don't know. She – she locked me in here.'

Derwent rattled the door. 'No key. Can you stand back a bit?'

'I'll try.' There was a shuffling sound. Derwent took a step back and kicked the door as hard as he could. The wood splintered. He kicked it again and the lock gave up. He pulled the door open and it swung back to show a tear-streaked, dusty face blinking at us from the depths of a cupboard that was full of old coats, deckchairs, a croquet set and cobwebs.

'Come on. Out you come.' Derwent took her by the arm and helped her out. 'What happened?'

'We were in the kitchen – I was making a cup of tea – and she put all the lights on. It must have tripped a fuse. The fuse box is in here. She asked me if I'd mind sorting it out because she was scared of spiders. The next thing I knew, she'd locked me in.' Georgia held out shaking hands: broken nails, skinned knuckles. 'I tried to open the door. I couldn't get any purchase on it. There was nothing to hold on to.'

'No, once you were in there you had no chance,' Derwent said. 'The trick is not getting locked up in the first place.'

'Has she done a runner? Is her car still there?' I asked.

'There's a silver Seat at the back of the house. I saw it from the kitchen window,' Derwent said. 'Hasn't moved.'

'Maybe she went on foot.' Georgia was shivering. 'My hands really hurt.'

'Did you hear her moving around, Georgia?'

'I couldn't hear anything. I heard the two of you moving around. I wasn't sure if I should call out or not. I didn't know what was going on. I didn't know it was you.'

'OK. No one's blaming you,' Derwent said, quite obviously blaming her. I was holding on to my temper with difficulty. 'Kate had a plan and you didn't spot it.'

'She was always going to run. Why hadn't she gone before, though? What was she waiting for?' I was trying to puzzle it out. 'As soon as she heard Chloe was gone she should have packed up and left.'

'Why don't we find her and ask her?' Derwent said, heading for the kitchen. 'If she went on foot, she can't have gone far.'

We scoured the outbuildings quickly and found nothing.

'Road or river?' I said as the three of us gathered in the small yard next to the house.

'She didn't know where we were going but she'd have known we were coming back by road. Let's go with river first,' Derwent decided.

If anything, the rain was heavier now, drumming on the parched earth. Weeks of drought had made the ground steel-hard and the water was sitting on top of it rather than sinking in. We hacked across the gravelled terrace behind the house and onto the sodden grass, our feet sending up a fine spray as we hurried towards the dense evergreen hedge at the end of the lawn. I was the first to reach the wrought-iron gate set into it. I stepped onto flagstones that were slippery-green with algae, and found myself in a walled garden. The beds were overplanted, the paths half-hidden under wildly flourishing plants that smelled sweet and fresh under my feet. There was a pergola at the centre, raised up a little, smothered in a mantle of some sort of creeper. I headed straight for it to orientate myself and decide where to go next.

That decision was made for me as soon as I got close enough to see the floor.

'Over here!' I yelled. 'Blood.'

There was a substantial amount of it – more than a scratch, I thought – and it was smeared in places, as if there had been a struggle. And in the middle of it all lay a battered kitchen knife, the handle smeared red, the blade snapped off at the tip. It was such an ordinary thing, domestic and familiar, the metal dulled with age.

'Fuck's sake,' Derwent snapped, looking over my shoulder. 'Not again.'

It was hard to see the blood that had splashed on the paving slabs: the rain had diluted it, turning it brown, and had washed it away almost everywhere. The trail seemed to lead to the left, where there was another gate out to the riverbank.

'You go that way,' Derwent said to Georgia, pointing right. 'In case this is another of her tricks.'

Georgia nodded and set off, huddled against the rain. I followed Derwent down the path to the left, noting a smudge on the wall and a drip of red on the outside of a planter, sheltered from the rain by its overhanging lip.

A wall of tall, whispering reeds confronted us on the river-bank. I could smell the water but I couldn't see it. A muddy path ran along the edge of the river, the ground rutted and uneven and hopeless for footprints. Trees lined the river, their branches forming a dense, dark canopy over our heads, and it was dark enough that I missed her the first time I looked. It was only when I was almost on top of her that I realised what I was seeing.

'*Shit.*'

She was curled up at the base of a tree, her head tipped back to lie on her shoulder. Her eyes were open, her mouth slack. One hand lay on the ground beside her, the fingers coated in red, the nails clotted with it. There was something in the way she lay that told me she was dead even before Derwent had pressed his fingers against her throat for a few seconds and looked up, his face grim.

'Not faking this time.'

Protocol said that we should start CPR, that we should work on her until paramedics came to confirm her life was over. I had no heart for it and neither, it seemed, did Derwent.

336

We were too late and all that we would achieve was the destruction of any evidence her killer had left behind.

I had spent so long thinking of Kate as a dead woman that it almost felt inevitable that she was lying at our feet, as if we'd been speaking to a ghost all along. The life in her had been like light shining from a dead star: finite and illusory.

I was putting on gloves. Gingerly, I lifted her jumper. It was starting to stick to the blood that coated her torso from at least two deep stab wounds. Plenty of force.

Plenty of anger.

'No way is that self-inflicted,' I said. Calm professional assessment was what was needed, not shock. 'She'd never have got the knife back out after the first injury. No shallow wounds. No practising.'

'If you were going to kill yourself with a knife you'd go for the throat or try to sever an artery. And Kate was a nurse so she would have known that.'

'How long ago, would you say?'

'She feels cold, but in this weather . . .' Derwent shook his head. 'No idea.'

I slipped my hand down the back of her neck, where the body heat was ebbing away more slowly than in her exposed hands and face. 'Half an hour, maybe? Less?'

'He could still be here.' Derwent said it casually, as if it wasn't a problem.

'That occurred to me.' I was shaking, angry. The trees seemed to press in around me. Was this what Kate had been waiting for? A blood sacrifice in memory of her beautiful daughter? Or was it an accomplice who'd decided she was too dangerous to leave alive? And under our noses, too, while we had argued about who was going to take the fall for a decision that was suddenly irrelevant. 'She knew he was coming, didn't she? That's what she was waiting for. That's why she told us we couldn't stay for long. I wondered why she looked at her watch.'

337

'Find Georgia,' Derwent said, taking charge. 'Send her to call for back-up. I want dog units and a boat, if they've got one. Tell her to get a scene log started and set up a cordon. We need to make sure the local CID know what's happening. They'll need to get their crime scene techs here.'

'What about me?'

'I need you to help me look for whoever did this.' He looked left and right, chewing his lip. 'I reckon he'll have gone downstream. That's what I'd do. If I go that way and you check the other, we've got the best chance of finding him.'

I nodded, not thinking about the danger or the cold or the fact that we were going to be in a world of trouble for letting Kate die, or even the fact that Kate had died. There was a job to do. Everything else could wait.

'Get going,' Derwent said, his face stern and I'd already turned to go when he added, 'And Maeve . . . be careful.'

34

I didn't waste time staring at Kate Emery's body when I got back to the riverbank. I could recall every detail of how she looked and what she had suffered.

Our fault.

My fault for insisting on going with Derwent, for fighting to be heard when really my voice didn't matter. If I had stayed instead of Georgia. If I had stayed *with* Georgia.

If I had done just about anything differently, Kate would still be alive, and the knowledge of it was pure bitterness in my mouth.

There was no sign of Derwent, or anyone else for that matter. He had gone left, following the river downstream. Left was towards Groves Edge, towards civilisation and people and main roads. Right was back along the river towards farmland, scattered houses, a whole lot of not very much. He had been certain that the killer would go that way, but I wasn't so sure. Colin Vale had said it: people always ran away from crowds. Instinct was a stronger imperative than common sense, and instinct insisted on bolting for the wilderness. I jogged along the path. The worn brickwork of the boundary wall for Crow Lane House was blank and solid on my right, while the reeds sighed on my left. I felt hemmed in, trapped.

What would I do if I had recently killed Kate Emery? Run, obviously. I wouldn't wait around for the police to find me. There was no need to worry. The killer, I told myself, was long gone.

At a bend in the river the reeds gave some ground so I could see out across the water for the first time. The river was wider than I had expected, swollen with rainwater and a lot of debris from further upstream. In the centre it flowed fast, the current dimpling the surface. The water looked cold and grey and wholly threatening. I swore as I tripped on an exposed root and almost fell.

Get a move on, Maeve.

I began to run again, scanning my surroundings as I went for anything human but no, a tree trunk, a bump in the path, a drift of leaves in a hollow, the rain striking down between the trees . . . Every shadow might have been the killer. Every gleam might have been the light catching on a blade, not a wet, glossy leaf.

He had left his knife behind, that was one thing. He probably wasn't armed any more. And I had my ASP.

Ahead of me the path took a sharp turn and I slowed, wary of what might lie beyond it. What I found as I rounded the bend made me stop in my tracks, but it wasn't the killer.

It was a car. Someone had driven it down a narrow track to the river; I could see the mud on the wheels and sprayed up the sides of the car, and the rain hadn't yet washed away the tyre-marks on the track itself. Someone had turned the car so it was ready to drive away again.

Someone.

I could give him a name, now, the man we were looking for – the man who had stabbed Kate Emery to death. The man, I guessed, who had killed Chloe, even though I knew he'd loved her.

340

Maybe he'd killed her *because* he loved her.

William Turner. I would have known his little blue Corsa anywhere.

Why did it surprise me? He was intimately familiar with stabbings, after all.

I took out my torch and shone it through the windows, checking that the car was empty. The doors were locked and a blanket lay rumpled on the back seat.

I had stuck up for him.

I had fallen for his charm, even if I hadn't wanted to admit it.

I had ignored the warning implicit in the fact that he had previously faced down the police and won.

I remembered his cold anger when he told me about Nolan molesting Chloe and it made me shiver.

I had been blind.

If Turner had made it back to his car, he would have driven it away. For whatever reason, he had run the other way – downstream. So if I wanted to find him, that was the way I needed to go.

On the way back I reached the house sooner than I had expected, covering what was now familiar territory more quickly. From the river it wasn't possible to see much of the house itself – it was almost as if Crow Lane House wanted to hide among its brooding trees. I hoped like hell the back-up would arrive soon and that Georgia would get on with sending them down to the river. Kate's body was still where we'd left it, stiffening into rigor mortis. I shied away from looking too closely at her face, at the accusation I thought I'd see in her eyes. *Why didn't you stop him? Why didn't you save us?*

The trees on this side were denser, the air cool and dark as I hurried along the path. How long had it been since Derwent started down the path? Ten minutes? Twenty? How far could he go in that time? He was a runner. He would be faster than me. He might even be faster than Turner, given the fact that Turner had his asthma to slow him down and had been limping the last time I saw him – although it occurred to me that Turner might have been faking it to look less of a threat. And the asthma – how bad was it really? I was questioning everything I had assumed I knew about Turner. How had he found Kate?

The answer came easily, as if I'd known it already. She had told him where she was. Colin Vale's voice again in my ear: *If anything happened to my kids . . . I'd want to kill whoever hurt them.* And his face, so calm but implacable.

She had invited him to her house. She had lured him there, hoping that when his guard was down she could get her revenge on him.

It hadn't worked out that way. Maybe she hadn't minded that either. Maybe it had come as a relief. So much of what she'd done had been for Chloe's sake as well as her own. What was the point of going on?

I had slowed my jog to a walk, cautious now. If Turner had somehow managed to overpower Derwent or dodge past him, he would be coming back this way. I didn't want to run straight into him. I was keeping to the edge of the path, under the trees, half-hiding, half-inclined to go back to Georgia and wait for men with dogs and searchlights and maybe even a helicopter to track Turner.

It was a stupid place to walk I realised a split second after someone caught hold of my elbow and hauled me backwards. I took a breath to fill my lungs and a cold hand came down over my mouth, hard enough to hurt. I elbowed him as viciously as I could in the stomach, just under the ribcage, and heard the air rush out of his lungs. It didn't begin to loosen his grip on me. He dragged me into the shelter of the trees, away from the path and hissed two words in my ear.

'It's me.'

I nodded fervently and Derwent slackened his grip on me enough to let me pull his hand away from my face and twist

342

around to look at him. His hair was plastered against his skull and he was shivering. His clothes were completely saturated.

'Why did you grab me?' I whispered, outraged.

'Any excuse. Why did you elbow me?' He was holding on to his stomach, wincing.

'I wasn't sure it was you. Any luck?'

'I saw someone but I lost him in the reeds. He was miles away,' Derwent added, defensive. 'I didn't have a chance.'

'Did you go in the river?' I was staring at his clothes, at the mud and grass stalks that clung to the material.

'A little bit.'

'You're lucky you're not a little bit dead.'

A grin. 'Don't tell me you wouldn't give me the kiss of life.'

'I wouldn't have had the chance. You'd be in the sea by now if it had gone wrong.'

He rubbed a drip off the end of his nose and pushed his hair back off his forehead, leaving a beautiful muddy streak that I thought he deserved. 'This fucking weather. I didn't get a good look at him.'

'It was William Turner.'

'*What?*' Derwent stared at me, obviously startled. It made me feel slightly better about having been taken in. 'How do you know?'

I told him about the car while the rain eased up, not that it mattered to either of us by then.

'Shit. He'll have wanted to get back to the car.' Derwent swore some more, peering up and down the path. 'Could he have got past both of us?'

'I don't think he can have gone by the river – you'd never be able to swim against the current even if it wasn't running high. Maybe he climbed the wall.'

Derwent hacked through the undergrowth to get to the wall. He clambered up it with a reasonable amount of skill and a frankly excessive amount of swearing. When he got to

343

the top he leaned over it for a minute or two, shining his torch along the wall in both directions.

'Anything?'

'Nope.' He slithered back down to the ground, and if the river hadn't done for his trousers, the wall finished the job. He examined the rip that exposed one knee as he trudged back to me. 'I mean, it's possible. But I think he went in the water.'

'He panicked,' I said.

'He saw I was after him, that's why.'

'If he'd known you were that old and slow he'd probably have taken his chances.'

Derwent glowered at me. 'Watch it, Kerrigan.'

We started to trudge back towards the house.

'I keep thinking about Kate,' I said. 'About the fact that we have to take some responsibility for what's happened.'

'Me too.'

'Really?' I was surprised. Guilt wasn't something that Derwent usually bothered to feel.

'The paperwork is going to be a fucker, for starters. Death during police contact?' He shook his head. 'I hope you like time off.'

'We weren't even there when she died.'

'Georgia was.'

'Well, she didn't do it.'

Derwent shrugged. 'Stand up for her if you like, but it's not worth you sacrificing your career for someone who wouldn't do the same for you.'

A shout from up ahead made me jump.

'That'll be the locals,' Derwent said, picking up his pace.

I could hear dogs barking and wished more than ever my radio was working so I could warn them that we were going towards them. Police dogs tended to bite first and ask questions later. But when we found them – or they found us – the dogs were on leashes.

344

'Lost someone, have you?' the sergeant said. His dog was dancing on hind legs, her tongue lolling crazily as she panted. There were three other police officers and one other dog, and all of them looked fiercely competent.

I gave them the description of Turner and told them about the car. The sergeant nodded.

'We'll split up. I'll get a couple of men on the water. If he's in the area, we'll track him down.'

They were true to their word. Before dusk had quite fallen, but after Kate Emery's body had been removed to the black private ambulance that would transport it to the morgue, they called me to the riverbank. It had stopped raining and the evening air was sweet. Georgia came too and the two of us traipsed along the path for a mile or so, in silence. There had been a lot of silence from Georgia since we had found Kate's body. She wasn't stupid; she knew she was going to be in trouble. We were all in trouble, if it came to that. I was too tired to mind, much. I could deal with it; I would have to. More important was doing my job while I still had the chance.

The first sign I had of what they'd found was a glimpse of an inflatable boat, lights mounted fore and aft, manoeuvring against the current. Then we came out from under the trees and I could see them: a small gang of police officers strung out along a narrow jetty that stretched into the river. One of them was manning a searchlight, angling it carefully into the water as two others grappled with something that the men in the boat were trying to pass to them. It was a black shape, formless, anonymous, and it landed on the jetty with a solid thump that made me wince even though I knew he was beyond feeling it.

Georgia let me go first and the two of us walked down to the end. Una Burt was there, square and unsmiling, which hardly seemed fair; she had wanted Kate Emery's body and we had found it, after all . . .

345

Derwent was crouching beside the corpse, inappropriately casual in borrowed jeans and a jumper. He checked the pockets deftly, coming up with a cigarette tin, an inhaler, a thin wallet with a saturated ten-pound note in it.

'Anything else?'

'Nope.'

'Keys?' I said. 'For the car?'

'Not so far.' He checked again. 'No.'

'They might have fallen in the water,' one of the other officers suggested. He was an inspector, I noted. 'The tide was pretty strong.'

Derwent looked up at me. 'They only found him because he was caught on a tree branch further downstream.'

I leaned across, bracing myself on Derwent's shoulder briefly to look more closely at the body.

'Problem?' Burt said.

'His face.' It was swollen, barely recognisable. His mouth was hanging open and I could see one of his teeth was missing. He hadn't had anything like that amount of damage the last time I'd seen him.

'Looks as if he did a few rounds in a boxing ring, doesn't it?' The uniformed inspector shrugged. 'That happens with drownings. Especially when the river is running high. Lots of debris in there, moving fast.'

I stepped back from the body. 'I want Dr Early to do the PM.'

'Our guy is good,' the inspector said.

I nodded. 'I'm sure he is. I just want to be sure.'

'You can have Dr Early if you want,' Derwent said, straightening up. 'But I'll tell you this for free. It's definitely Turner. And he's definitely dead.'

35

The next day, I went to the hospital. My first problem was getting through the security checks to gain access to the secure unit where Bethany was being treated. The second problem was sitting on a chair outside her room. Morgan Norris stood up when he saw me coming down the corridor towards him, and folded his arms.

'No way, sweetheart. I'm not letting you anywhere near her.'

'It's not really up to you,' I said, ignoring the way he'd spoken to me even though the word *sweetheart* was creeping up and down my spine on scuttling insect feet. 'I need to talk to her.'

'So you thought you'd sneak in to talk to her while everyone's back was turned. That's hardly ethical, Sergeant.'

As if you know anything about being ethical. I held it back behind my teeth and smiled. 'It's an important part of the investigation.'

And if I didn't get to do it now, I probably wouldn't. I was avoiding the office, avoiding Una Burt and the investigators who wanted to talk to me about Kate Emery's death. I was going to be on restricted duties – Burt had more or less told me so – and this was my last chance to interview Bethany Norris.

So I was absolutely not going to let Morgan get between us.

He was shaking his head. 'Can't do it. Sorry. If Eleanor and Ollie were here they'd say no.'

'Where are they?'

'No idea. They left me in charge.'

I wouldn't have done any such thing and it probably showed on my face because he looked offended.

'Do you have a problem with me?'

'Not personally.'

'What does that mean?'

It means I'd like to arrest you for raping Kate Emery and I'll never get the chance.

'My only interest is in solving the case,' I said.

'I thought it was all squared away. Turner is dead.'

'Yes, he is.' And in about half an hour he would be on Dr Early's slab, giving up whatever secrets his body held. I could imagine the sound of the saw, the tools snapping through his bones, the wet slither of organs detached to be weighed, measured, described and dropped back into the body. I'd proved my nerves still held by attending Chloe's post-mortem; I didn't need to endure William Turner's. 'I'm tidying up the loose ends.'

'Loose ends,' Morgan repeated.

'Like what exactly happened when Bethany and Chloe disappeared. I need to know how Turner found them and if he ever threatened either of them. When was the last time you saw Turner?'

'I have no idea.' His eyes were flat. He didn't care or he wouldn't tell me; either way I was getting nothing out of him.

'Where were you yesterday?'

'Here. All day.' He looked around vaguely. 'The nurses can tell you.'

'Why were you here?'

'Keeping an eye on Bethany.'

348

'And where was Eleanor?'

'She had to go. Ollie phoned her at lunchtime. He needed her to drive him somewhere.'

'Why couldn't he drive himself?'

'I don't know. Because Eleanor had the car here?' He said it as if I was stupid, which was fine by me. I wanted Morgan to think I was stupid if it meant he'd let me see Bethany. 'He needed her to pick him up. I don't know where he was, before you ask me, and I don't know when they came back. They were at home last night when I got there.'

'Did you see them?'

'I saw Ollie. Eleanor went to bed early.'

'What about today?'

'Eleanor was here. Not very communicative, as usual.'

'When did she leave?'

'An hour ago? Ollie rang her and she said she had to go.'

'Go where?'

'She didn't tell me.'

'Any ideas?'

'Home?' He shrugged. 'I really can't tell you. When Oliver calls, she goes. She's like his slave. Maybe that's why he married her. It definitely wasn't her looks or her sparkling conversation, was it?'

'I thought you saw her first, Morgan. I thought Oliver took her away from you.'

That hit home. 'It wasn't like that. I wasn't interested in her. I was messing around with her, that's all.'

'Did you mind when she chose him over you?'

'It wasn't like that,' he said again.

'Funny how it was just the same with Kate. She preferred your brother too. She actually wanted to sleep with him. He didn't have to force her.'

His face was slack. 'Did she – did she talk to you about it?'

'She did,' I said, for the pleasure of watching the fear sink

349

into his bones. I wasn't going to tell him that she hadn't said enough, that I hadn't pressed her hard enough, that he was going to get away with it after all . . .

I changed tack. 'Did you know that Kate was blackmailing Eleanor?'

'How did you— did she tell you that?' Too casual, the panic leaking through the very lack of interest he was evincing.

'There were plenty of clues. Plenty of evidence of lots of things.' I considered him for a long moment. 'Eleanor asked you to warn Kate off.'

'What?'

'You went around to scare her and you got carried away. You decided to teach her a lesson. Make her respect you. Take you seriously. You wanted her to realise that she'd picked the wrong brother even though – what was it you said? – you have no job prospects and no income, living in your dear brother's house, one step away from being on the streets.'

Morgan looked at me as if he wanted to kill me. 'Shut your mouth.'

'I'm only repeating what you said. There's no loathing like self-loathing, is there, Morgan? I bet you'd do almost anything to prove that you're still a real man.'

'God, I'd like to show you—' He cut himself off, shaking his head. 'You're good, aren't you.'

'So they say.'

'Things got a little crazy. With Kate.' He shrugged. 'If she'd been that bothered, she would have called the cops.'

'But she couldn't, could she? Not when you'd have told us she was blackmailing Eleanor.'

'Eleanor wouldn't have let me do that.'

'But Kate didn't know that. She couldn't take the risk.'

'That was her problem. Her choice.' Morgan smiled, in control of himself once again. 'You know, I *like* women. I even like them when they're doing their best to piss me off.'

To make absolutely sure I knew he meant me, he winked. I fought the urge to peel his eyelids off his face.

'I'm just doing my job.'

'Why do you have to go on harassing us? What's in it for you?'

'The truth. That's all I want.'

'And you think Bethany can help you?'

'I know she can. I know she saw William Turner yesterday. I need to know what she told him. There'll be an inquest, you know. It's not me being curious for the sake of it. I need to know what sent Turner down to Hampshire, so whatever Bethany said to him is relevant. If I can talk to her now, it might save her from having to give evidence in front of the coroner.'

He thought about it for longer than I would have liked, weighing it up. 'I don't know what Ollie would say. I should call him.'

'OK. Call him if you don't trust your own judgement. And find out where he is, would you? He's next on my list.'

'It's not that I don't trust my own judgement,' Morgan snapped.

'Right.' I leaned against the wall and took out my phone, idly skimming through the messages. 'Let me know when he's told you what to do. I mean, he left you in charge, but we both know that doesn't mean he trusts you.'

Morgan leaned in, dropping his voice so only I could hear him. 'Did they teach you how to be a manipulative bitch during your training or does it come naturally?'

'A bit of both.' I glanced up at him. 'So? Yes or no?'

36

Bethany was staring out of the window at the jumble of rooftops outside that was pure London, grey and featureless with the occasional surprising flash of green leaves. She must have heard me come in but she didn't look around straight away. When she did, and saw me, she flinched.

'Hi.' I stayed at the end of the bed. 'You look better.'

'Thanks.' It was a whisper.

'How's the food?'

She shrugged. In fact, she didn't look as if she'd been eating much of it. I put a paper bag on the blanket near her feet.

'I brought you some snacks. In case.'

A nod.

'Are they looking after you?'

'Yeah.'

'They told me you haven't said much about why you're here.'

She went back to looking out of the window. She looked older, all of a sudden, in part because she was thinner. The childishness had gone from her face, now that her cheeks were hollow and blue shadows streaked the skin under her eyes. I wanted to give her a hug and I had to keep my distance.

'You almost died, Bethany. I was there. I know you were determined to go through with it, and I want to know why.'

She shook her head.

'Was it because of Chloe?'

Nothing. No response.

'You asked me if I knew the bible. I looked it up – the things you said to me on the railway embankment. "For I know my transgressions and my sin is ever before me." Psalm fifty-one. It's about forgiveness for a broken and contrite heart. "For you will not delight in sacrifice or I would give it." There's no bigger sacrifice than killing yourself though, is there?'

A tiny shrug.

'Isn't it a sin, to think of it?'

The corners of her mouth turned down, holding back tears.

'You said I didn't know what you were,' I said.

'You don't.'

'What are you? Tell me.'

'Behold, I was brought forth in iniquity and in sin did my mother conceive me.' The bitterness in her voice made me wince, and I knew immediately what she meant, and what she'd meant on the embankment. *Blood guilt.*

'Oh, Bethany. It's not your fault.'

'I'm a child of sin. My mother—' she broke off, screwing her eyes shut.

'Your mother loves you. And so does your father.'

'He's not my father.'

'He is in every way that matters,' I said. 'He's always loved you.'

'Only because he thinks I'm a miracle.' She shook her head. 'How could she lie to him? To me?'

'How did you find out? Did your mother tell you?'

'No. She has no idea I know, even.' Panic flared in her eyes. 'Don't tell her.'

'I won't. But I think you should talk to her about it. Give her a chance to explain.'

353

'Explain what? That I was born because of a sinful act? That my whole life has been a lie?'

'I'm sure that's not how she sees it. And it's not how I see it either.' I waited a beat. 'So your mum didn't tell you, and your dad doesn't know. Who else knew? Who told you?'

She looked down at her hands, not answering.

'Was it Kate?'

Absolute shock. 'How did you know?'

'Lucky guess.' I was surprised by how angry I felt with Kate. She must have known it would shatter Bethany's world and she hadn't cared. Selfish, entitled, vindictive woman . . .

Bethany saw the look on my face. 'She didn't mean to tell me. It just came out.'

'That's a hell of a thing to say by accident.'

'She was angry with me. I was shouting at her and she shouted back.'

'Why did you shout at her?'

'We were in the house on Constantine Avenue a couple of weeks ago – me, Chloe, William. Hanging out. Drinking a bit, smoking. You know. They were kissing, on the bed and I was by the window. They didn't mind me being there but I felt a bit awkward about it. You know how it is.'

I nodded.

'I was looking through the window to distract myself from what Chloe and William were doing.' She swallowed. 'If I hadn't been there, I'd never have known.'

'What did you see?'

'Dad was in the kitchen. Talking to Kate.' She was staring into the middle distance, seeing it again. 'He pushed her up against a cupboard and he had his hands on her neck. I didn't know what he was going to do – I couldn't really see properly. But he looked angry. Really angry. I thought he was going to kill her.'

I remembered Oliver Norris in interview, calmly describing

354

how Kate had wanted to end their relationship and how it had been a relief.

Not the truth. Not even a little bit.

'Then what happened?'

'She talked to him. She was smiling at him, stroking his shoulders. She got down on her knees. He was sort of hidden behind a cupboard but I could see her head moving and – and I know what she was doing to him. It was *disgusting*.'

It was survival, I thought. Kate had calmed him down. She had made a careful calculation of what she could bear to offer to buy her safety, and offered it, and it had been accepted.

'And you watched?'

'No! Not once I knew what they were doing.' She was pale, sweating. 'I ran out of the house. I didn't know where to go or what to do. I went for a walk by the river. Just . . . walked. I was trying to get it straight in my head. What I'd seen, what it meant. I ended up back at my house and I could see Dad was watching TV in the front room, as if nothing had happened. It made me *sick*. He's supposed to be a good husband. The head of the family. He's supposed to be in charge. How could I trust him when he was such a hypocrite?'

'Did you talk to him?'

'No. I was too scared to confront him. I went to Kate. I thought it had to be her fault that he'd broken his vows. I wanted to hear her say that he'd tried to stop himself from cheating on Mum, that it was a one-off thing.'

'But she didn't.'

'No. She didn't.' Bethany looked up, her eyes swimming. 'I told her she was an evil woman, a harlot, and she would go to hell. She said it was his idea. She said he wouldn't leave her alone. And then she told me that if she was going to hell, she'd have my mother for company. She said Mum was much worse because she'd given birth to another man's child and pretended it was her husband's.'

Ouch. 'Did she tell you how she knew that?'

355

'Something to do with the clinic where Mum and Dad went when they were trying to conceive. She worked there, I think.' Bethany looked exhausted. 'I didn't really understand.'

'It makes sense to me.'

'Does it?' Her face puckered. 'Do you know what it's like to *be* a sin?'

'It's not your sin,' I said gently.

'Sin is the whole reason for my existence. Every time my mother looks at me, she sees her own weakness. And my father sees a lie. My whole life is a lie.' Bethany rubbed her eyes. 'That's why nothing works out for me. Everything I touch is defiled. Everyone I love comes to harm. Chloe and William are dead and it's my fault.'

'It's not your fault.' I gripped the rail at the end of the bed. 'People like William Turner are manipulative and dangerous. There was nothing you could have done to stop him.'

'He loved her.'

'That wasn't love,' I said. 'It was obsession. He wanted to own her. To control her.'

'No, you're wrong. He loved her. No one has ever looked at me the way he looked at her, and no one ever will.'

'You're lucky, then.'

She shook her head and I could tell it would be hard to convince her Turner had been anything other than a hero.

'You know, he was very handsome,' I said. 'He was very charming. I liked him. It's only natural that you liked him too.'

She blushed, her eyelashes sweeping down over her cheeks.

'Were you in love with him?'

'He loved Chloe.'

'But he didn't mind you hanging around. He liked the extra attention.'

'He liked talking to me.' She whispered it. 'We were friends.'

'Friends . . . but you didn't tell him where you were hiding when you and Chloe ran away.'

'I thought it was safer.'

'Because you were scared of what he might do?'

'No. No, I was never scared of him.'

'Was Chloe?'

'She knew he loved her. He looked after her.'

'Was he angry about her running away?'

'I don't know.'

'He came to see you yesterday, didn't he?'

She shut her eyes, frowning.

'I know he was here, Bethany. I talked to the nurses. He was here. So what did you talk about?'

'Nothing.'

'That surprises me. He told me he wanted to talk to you about Chloe.'

Her face crumpled. I moved a step or two closer, still careful not to crowd her.

'Did you hear what happened to him, Bethany?'

'He drowned.'

'That's right. He drowned. Just like Chloe, although William's death was an accident.' Another step. 'So he can't hurt you any more, Bethany. You can tell me what happened to Chloe now.'

'Hurt me?' Her eyes flew open. 'William would never hurt me. Or Chloe. He *loved* Chloe. That was why I didn't want to tell him—'

'Tell him what?' I leaned in. 'Bethany, please.'

'I didn't want to tell him what happened to her.'

Frustration burned in my veins. 'You have to be honest with me, Bethany. What happened to Chloe? Were you with her when she died?'

'No. No, definitely not. I didn't even see her. We came back and she took her away.'

'Who did?'

'My mother.' She looked at me as if it was obvious, as if I should have known. 'Mum took her.'

37

There was no one home in Valerian Road. That would have been too easy, I thought, calling the local police station to ask them to send officers around later (known as a 'please allow' in police jargon, as in 'please allow an officer to call'). Did I think Eleanor Norris had done a runner, I was asked politely, and I said no, because I didn't. She had no reason to run away, as far as she knew. No one was looking for her. It was all over. Kate was dead, Chloe was dead, William Turner was dead. The circle was closed.

Except, of course, that it wasn't.

Because it was Eleanor who had taken Chloe away, a lamb to the slaughter. Bethany hadn't told me why – and maybe she didn't know, or maybe it was that she was shocked to have said as much as she had. Bethany had been scared and she had run away with Chloe because she thought her friend was in danger. But they had had nowhere to go. It was cold, she said, at night, even though it was summer. It wasn't safe, sleeping on the street, and then she had started to feel ill. She'd been shivering, running a temperature. They had to go home.

And then her mother had taken Chloe away and she'd never seen her alive again.

I was fairly sure I wouldn't be allowed to interview Eleanor when she eventually turned up, given the investigation into Kate Emery's death. All the more reason to have a drive around the area myself to see if I could spot her or the family car. I had set up a locate/trace marker on the police national computer so if the registration triggered the number plate recognition in a patrol car, they'd get pulled over. I also left Derwent and Una Burt a message each, telling them what Bethany had told me. There was no mobile phone reception in the morgue, something that I didn't really mind when I was there.

I was getting back into my car when I saw a thin figure moving up the road towards me: William Turner's mother. Her face was vacant, her eyes staring at nothing. For a moment, I thought she was sleepwalking, but then her head turned and she saw me watching her. I crossed the road.

'Mrs Turner, I don't know if you remember . . . I met you last week.'

No flicker of recognition. A thin string of drool hung between her upper and lower lip. Her hair hadn't been brushed. I reached out tentatively and took her arm. Her skin was papery under my fingers, her bones sharp.

'Mrs Turner, I'm so sorry about William. Can I take you home? Or wherever you were planning to go?'

'William,' she said. 'William.'

'I know, Mrs Turner. I'm very sorry for your loss.'

'He never did anything wrong.' It was as if she was starting to wake up, her eyes focusing on me. 'Give a dog a bad name and hang him. That's what they say, isn't it. You never gave him a chance.'

I suspected she meant the police rather than me personally. 'We did want to speak to him, knowing that he'd come to police attention before, but he was just one line of enquiry, Mrs Turner. We had to investigate whether he was involved. He and Chloe were close.'

'They barely knew each other.'

I didn't want to argue with her – what was the point? I nodded. 'We spoke to William a few times and we took a sample of his DNA, but I believed he was telling me the truth.'

'He always did. He was a good boy.'

I wondered for a fleeting second if Ben Christie's mother would agree with that. Mrs Turner had gone back to staring into space.

'He was a good boy. A bright boy. He had everything going for him except his health.' Abruptly she started to cry, horrible rasping sobs. 'I kept him alive. I was there in the middle of the night when he was scared. I took him to hospital when he couldn't breathe, and I promised him – I *promised* him – I wouldn't let him die.' She looked back at me. 'Do you think he was scared? Do you think he called out for me?'

'Mrs Turner,' I began, and stopped. What could I say that would give her comfort? What could anyone say? 'I'm so sorry.'

She blinked. 'He was everything to me. He was everything, and now I have nothing.'

The traffic was heavy. It was a flat, grey day, oppressively warm and humid, and even though the sun wasn't shining there was a glare off the tarmac that made me squint behind my sunglasses. I cruised around the streets, scanning pedestrians and parked cars, coming up with nothing more than a headache. Where did they go, the Norrises? The supermarket, the gym, their church. Oliver had called Eleanor and she had gone to him. He was probably at work.

Swearing under my breath, I inched towards the big, dingy building that housed the Church of the Modern Apostles. The car park was empty. They weren't there. I drove in anyway to turn the car around, frustrated.

Why weren't they there? It was a working day. How had

they slipped away at the very moment I needed to talk to them?

I parked the car and walked around to the back of the building, past the side door and the bins, and there it was: their car, parked where it couldn't be seen from the road.

Hidden.

Why was it hidden?

I went back to the door and let myself in as quietly as I could. The corridor was cool and dark and completely silent. I went right, towards the office, and found it was deserted. The computers were off, the desks tidy and neat. No sign of Gareth or the secretary. No sign of Oliver Norris.

No sign of his wife.

Maybe she had been jealous of Chloe – pretty Chloe, with her uncomplicated, naive enjoyment of male attention. What had it been like for Oliver Norris to have his lover's daughter living in his house? She was old enough to fantasise about, I thought, with her long legs and pretty face, and if she wasn't clever that made her more accessible, not less. Eleanor devoted a lot of time to being obedient but I didn't think it came naturally to her. Chloe was sweetly biddable, docile. Uninhibited, when Eleanor was hemmed in by doubt, shame, suppressed emotion, secrets.

There was no one in the kitchen. I went on down the corridor and found there was only one way out from there: through the door that led to the main hall. I leaned against the heavy soundproof door and it opened a millimetre or two – not enough to draw any attention to me, I hoped, but enough so that I could see what was going on inside the hall.

I needn't have worried about being noticed. The two people in the hall were fully occupied with what they were doing.

All the lights were on, blazing down on the velvety red carpet as if it was a stage. Oliver Norris stood in the centre of the platform, his shirt soaked with sweat down his back and under his arms. His attention was focused on the woman who lay in front of him with her hands on his feet, a supplicant.

'Tell me.'

'Oliver, please.' Her voice was barely audible, her face pressed against the carpet.

'I need to know who. You owe me that much, Eleanor.'

'Please forgive me. Please.'

'There'll be a time for forgiveness but you have to earn it, Eleanor. You have to purge yourself of your sin first.' He was as matter-of-fact as if they'd been talking about what to have for lunch.

'I'm sorry . . . I should never have done it. I should never have lied.'

'An excellent wife is the crown of her husband, but she who brings shame is like rottenness in his bones.' Oliver leaned forward. 'On your knees, Eleanor.'

Slowly, painfully, she pushed herself back on to her hands and knees. He waited. It seemed to take a long time for her to sit back on her heels and turn her face up towards him, and when she did I felt the shock run through me like a current. Her face was bloated with bruising. I'd seen what Oliver was capable of before, but the violence he'd shown to Turner was nothing compared to what he'd done to his own wife.

'Now, I'm going to ask you again. Who was it?'

She shook her head, very slightly, and opened her mouth to answer him and didn't even get the chance. He backhanded her viciously so she pitched to one side, almost losing her balance.

'Don't shake your head at me, you bitch. Tell me. *Tell me*. You told me she was mine. You told me she was a gift from God.'

'That's how I think of her. That's what she is.' She turned her head a bit. 'Please, Ollie. Please. She's always been *our* child. No one else's.'

'The devil was in you.'

'No.'

'You know what that means, Eleanor. You need to go into the water.'

'No. Please, no.'

'You need to be washed clean. Whiter than snow.' It was what Bethany had said to me on the phone when she was waiting for a chance to kill herself, it came back to me with a flash of insight. *Wash me and I shall be whiter than snow.*

'Please no, Ollie. Please.'

The cover was off the baptismal pool.

Wash me.

Whiter than snow.

Chloe, lying on the grass.

They had put her in the water and held her down. Gareth's special ceremony, to persuade her demons to leave her. Everything Kate had feared, with the outcome she had dreaded.

And now Oliver was planning to teach his wife a lesson the same way.

'Even Satan disguises himself as an angel of light,' Oliver said. 'St Paul said that.'

'Bethany isn't Satan. Please, you can't blame her for something I did.'

'I can do what I want. I am your husband and you owe me respect.' He brought his leg back and kicked her with stunning force, and I realised one thing: if I didn't intervene, Oliver Norris was going to kill his wife right there, in front of me and his God.

'You didn't think about being her husband when you were sleeping with Kate Emery.' I stepped through the door and let it swing shut behind me. 'You're being a little bit hypocritical, if you don't mind me saying so.'

'What are you doing here?' Oliver spun around to face me, his hands balling to fists. 'How did you know where I was?'

'I was looking for Eleanor. Can you step away from her, please?'

He didn't move; I hadn't really expected him to. She was lying at his feet, moaning softly.

'Are you on your own?'

'You know better than that,' I said, smiling. If only he knew the truth. 'But go back a bit. Why would I be looking for you, Mr Norris?'

'I assumed.'

'Because you're feeling guilty. Not about this. And not about having an affair with your neighbour.'

Eleanor made a tiny noise and Oliver glanced down at her swiftly before returning to me.

'It's none of your business.'

'It's entirely my business. But as I said, that's not why you feel guilty.'

'Why, then?'

'Because you killed Chloe Emery. And you killed William Turner. And you killed Kate Emery.'

'That's ridiculous,' Norris spat. 'An invention.'

'The last time I came here, before Chloe died, you mentioned a special ceremony that was going to take place here. You thought Gareth had been rehearsing for it, remember? And then you and he covered it up and changed the subject. That ceremony was for Chloe, wasn't it? It was what you'd always wanted Kate to let you try. You've been trying to establish the church in this area, working on growing the congregation, trying to ingratiate yourself with the community by donating food to the poor. A miracle would be a big help for publicity. There's nothing as desperate as the parents of sick children. And there was Chloe, who was perfect because she wasn't as ill as her mother claimed, was she? Kate had worked to get her diagnosed with all of these worrying ailments and really she wasn't so badly off. You saw the potential in her. The hope you could sell. A beautiful girl saved by the grace of God and the prayers of the Church of the Modern Apostles.'

'You're talking about things you don't understand.'

'I understand perfectly well that preying on credulous people is a good way to get rich. But it went wrong, didn't it? You misjudged it. Bethany and Chloe came home when they thought it was safe but Eleanor brought Chloe to the church, like a lamb to the slaughter. And Chloe drowned.'

He wavered. 'It wasn't like that.'

'How was it?'

'Oliver,' Eleanor said from the floor. 'Be careful.'

He glanced down at her but he was distracted, thinking about what had happened. 'It wasn't my fault. It was Gareth. He – he got carried away.' He shook his head, baffled. 'It was so quick. If she'd been holding her breath . . .'

'But she wasn't. She was too scared. She breathed in water instead.'

'We tried to revive her. I tried.'

It explained the broken ribs. A memory floated up from training: an instructor shouting at us. *If you're not breaking ribs you're doing it wrong* . . . 'You didn't call an ambulance.'

'She was gone. Dead. It was too late.'

'Who dumped the body?'

'I did. Gareth told me to. I – I felt awful. I felt terrible. You can't understand how distressing it was for all of us. It was an accident, nothing more.'

'And William Turner?'

He looked shifty. 'What about him?'

'Did you know Kate was still alive when he came to see you? Was it all planned or did you have to think it through on the spur of the moment?'

He shook his head. 'You've lost me.'

'I know Bethany told William what had happened here – what happened to Chloe. I think he came to talk to you about it. Maybe he threatened you. You beat him to a pulp and then you dumped him in the river when you went down to see Kate. It was your bad luck that we were there already, but actually it couldn't have worked out better, could it? Because we saw Turner's car and found his body and it looked as if he'd been the killer, as if he'd gone into the river and drowned, and that was supposed to be an end to it.' I laughed. 'It's no wonder you thought God was on your side.'

'I didn't. I didn't do any of that.'

'When I spoke to Kate, she asked me one thing about Chloe's death. It was something a lot of people want to know when their loved ones are murdered, but the way she asked it was strange, when I thought about it afterwards. She said "Did *they* hurt her?" not "Did *he* hurt her?" I thought maybe she wasn't sure if it was a male killer or a female one, but she meant "they". She knew what you'd done, you and Gareth. She couldn't get at Gareth but she could get you to come to her, and that's exactly what she did.'

He shook his head, but without conviction.

'You went rushing down to see her. You couldn't believe that she was alive, when you'd been grieving for her in secret. You probably thought she'd forgive you for Chloe – after all, you'd meant well when you forced her into the water.' I could see from the look on his face that I was right. 'You never had any common sense when it came to Kate, did you?'

'She took everything from me. *Everything.* She made me break my vows. She made me betray everything that mattered to me.' Oliver Norris's chest heaved as he fought back tears. 'I destroyed everything I cared about. That woman made me. She tempted me and I fell.'

'Oh please,' I said. 'You fancied her and you fucked her.'

'I was a loyal husband and a good father and that – that *whore* took everything from me.'

I understood it at last. 'So that was what Kate did. That was her revenge. You took her daughter and she took yours.

An eye for an eye. She told you Bethany wasn't your daughter and you stabbed her.'

'She attacked me with the knife. It was self-defence.'

'Oliver, you weigh twice what Kate did. You took the knife away from her and then you stabbed her, repeatedly. You murdered her because she made you realise you weren't any of the things you thought you were. Not a good husband. Not a principled servant of the Church. Not a father at all. You're right. She left you with nothing – because you'd left her with nothing.'

'She didn't deserve to live.' He started to walk towards me.

I took a step back, and then another, wary. He was bigger than me. Stronger. Not as fast, possibly, if I ran for the door. But if I ran I'd leave Eleanor alone with him.

'You are on your own, aren't you?' Oliver bit his lip. 'You blundered in here alone.'

'No, my colleagues know where I am.'

'You're bluffing.' I could smell the tension in his sweat as he got closer; it was rolling off him in an acrid cloud. 'I can tell.'

Eleanor had tried placating him. I went for defiance. 'So what? What are you going to do – beat me into silence? That's not going to work.' He slapped me, which I hadn't been expecting. I put the back of my hand to my face, considering whether shutting up might actually be a good idea. It was too late for that. 'You might as well hand yourself in. It's over, Oliver. This church, your job, your family – it's all finished.'

'Not yet,' he said. 'Not quite.'

Then his hands were on my neck, squeezing hard, and black flowers bloomed in front of my eyes. I stumbled backwards, colliding with a wall, the edges of my vision flashing with white light. I kicked, knowing it was too late, that I didn't have the coordination or the strength to free myself, and all I could see was Oliver's face, contorted with effort, glazed in sweat. There was no doubt in his eyes, only the determination

367

that comes from believing you have a God-given right to behave as you like. I was nothing to him but an inconvenience, and that was how I would die. It wasn't heroic or worthwhile.

It was, I found myself thinking, such a waste.

And then the world fell away from me.

38

I opened my eyes and stared dully at the carpet. It was a shade of red so bright that it actually hurt to look at it.

Or maybe that was just because everything hurt. *God, my throat.*

I closed my eyes again.

Scuffling sounds nearby.

'You . . . you *bastard.*'

Choking. That sounded unpleasant, I thought. I should find out what was happening.

'You were sleeping with her. *Fucking* her. How could you? How could you do that to me? To our family?'

Slowly, infinitely slowly, I put a face to the voice. Eleanor Norris. Which meant she was talking to her husband.

And the last time I'd seen him, he was killing me.

That was worth a look, I thought, knowing that I wasn't thinking completely clearly. I could only deal with one thought at a time. Well, that would have to do. I leaned on my left elbow and pushed myself up with the other arm.

Eleanor Norris was kneeling on her husband's back, hauling his head towards her with as much force as she could muster. A loop of black electrical cable from the sound system was pressing into the flesh of his neck, cutting off his air supply very effectively.

'It was always me, wasn't it? *I* was the problem. *I* was the one who needed to be taught lessons.' She jerked on the cord and he choked again. 'I wasn't allowed to ask questions. Of course you knew better than me. You were my husband, the head of the family. You *bastard*. If only I'd known. I was *never* the problem. *You* were infertile, not me. *You* were weak, not me. *You* were unfaithful, not me. You made me feel as if I should be grateful to you for staying with me when I should have left you *years* ago.' She punctuated every sentence with another tug on the cord and Oliver was in serious trouble now, his face purple, his lips turning blue. His eyes were bulging out of his head.

'Eleanor,' I said, or tried to. 'Stop.'

'Were you ever going to tell me the truth?' She released the pressure for a second, waiting for an answer. Oliver took a couple of shuddering breaths before the cord tightened again. 'You were going to torture me into telling you about our daughter, but you've been lying to me all along.'

'Eleanor,' I said again. 'You have to stop. You'll kill him.'

'Were you in love with her? Were you? I don't know if it's worse if you were in love or not. If it was just sex, you're pathetic. You're pathetic anyway. *Pathetic*.'

I had managed to sit up but I was weak, trembling all over. 'Eleanor. Think of Bethany. This isn't what she'd want.'

'Oh God, Bethany.' She let the cord slacken again, her eyes screwed tight. 'My poor little Bethany. What can I tell her? At least you're not her real father, I suppose. That's something. I've always felt guilty about sleeping with Morgan, but he's twice the man you are.' He jerked, almost dislodging her and she hauled on the cord again. 'That's right. Your brother. I let Morgan fuck me and Bethany is his child.' She hesitated for a second, then added, 'And he was better in bed than you.'

Oliver groaned; I couldn't tell if it was anger or pain. I was still struggling to come to terms with what Eleanor had said. *Morgan.* His own brother.

It almost made me feel sorry for him.

'I've waited years for this,' Eleanor said. 'Years for you to see what it's like to be on the receiving end. This is what it's like, Ollie. This is justice at long last.'

'Not like this,' I said. 'Eleanor, not this. This is what he would do. You're better than that – you said so yourself.'

'This is what he deserves.'

'This will get you put in prison for years and Bethany needs you. More than ever, she needs you.'

'She *hates* me.'

'You can explain it to her. You can make her understand that you did everything for the best. I'll talk to her too. It'll be all right, Eleanor, I promise.' *Unless you kill your husband in front of me, in which case everything will be a lot more complicated.*

'I love him,' Eleanor Norris said to me as her husband choked under her. 'I love him so much.'

'I know.' And I did.

It was as if anger was all that had been sustaining her. As it ebbed away, Eleanor crumpled. She let go of the cord and slipped off Oliver's back to sit on the floor beside him. He rolled onto his back and stared up at the ceiling, his stomach heaving as he gasped for air.

I crawled over and put my arm around Eleanor's shoulders. She turned and hid her battered face against my neck, weeping as if her heart was broken. When she could speak again, it was to say: 'At least Morgan acted like he'd enjoyed having sex with me.'

The door opened with a noise like an intake of breath and Derwent came through it like an avenging angel. He stopped dead when he saw us, as Pettifer crashed in after him and Una Burt appeared in the doorway behind them.

'What the fuck happened?' Derwent demanded.

'Long story,' I croaked, wondering what exactly I looked like, given the way he was staring at me. 'But you could arrest him.'

'For?'

'Murder.'

'And being a bastard,' Eleanor said. 'A complete bastard.'

Derwent's face lit up with amusement for an instant. 'Not illegal, luckily for me.'

I started laughing, aware that at least some of it was shock, knowing that it could just as easily have been tears.

I sobered up enough at last to explain what Oliver Norris had done, and why, and how, while he sat in handcuffs on the edge of the platform. All the fight seemed to have gone out of him, not that we were taking any chances. Pettifer, who was not a small man, was sitting beside him and Derwent stood in front of him, his head lowered, daring him to try and escape. I had seen him angry before but I'd never seen him look at anyone the way he was glowering at Oliver Norris.

'And why did his wife attack him?' Una Burt asked when I got to the end of what Oliver had told me.

'Because she's quite angry that he was sleeping with Kate. And,' I added, being fair, 'he was strangling me at the time. So I'm glad she did.'

'You need to get that looked at,' Burt said, unemotional as ever.

'I will when the paramedics have finished with Eleanor.' My neck ached. I didn't really want to think about it.

'Do you think she'll give evidence against him?'

'I don't think you'll be able to stop her,' I said. 'But we need to get a statement from her before she calms down. And we'll have to arrest her for her part in Chloe's death. According to Bethany, she was the one who took Chloe from the house to the church. She might not have known what they were planning to do to her, but she was involved.'

372

'And so was Gareth Selhurst. I've got people out looking for him.'

'I would really like to talk to him,' I said quietly. 'They can try and argue Chloe's death was an accident but she had bruises on her shoulders. They held her under the water. It should be a murder charge. And the same goes for Eleanor, even if she didn't do the restraining. It's joint enterprise. She brought her to the church. She was involved in Chloe's death. We'll have to see what she says in interview, but if she says she knew what they intended to do here – and it's hard to see how she wouldn't have known what they were planning – she's not going to get a slap on the wrist for it.'

'Have you cautioned her?'

'Not yet.'

'I'll do it when the paramedics are finished with her.' Una looked across at them and sighed. 'Poor Bethany.'

'Because her parents are going to prison? I can't help thinking it's a good thing for her to have a break from them. A break from all this.' I gestured at the church. 'Maybe she can learn to live normally while they're inside. Work out what she wants out of life. Shed some of the guilt she doesn't deserve.'

'Get to know her real father better?' Una suggested and I shuddered.

'Not that, no.'

The paramedics – two nice, brisk women – decided that I was fine, if bruised, but that Oliver Norris and his wife needed to go to hospital to be checked out. Deprived of the chance to interview Norris 'like it was Judgement Day', Derwent sulked. I found him sitting outside the church on a bench, watching two uniformed officers pack Norris into a van for transport.

'Cheer up,' I said, sitting down beside him. 'He's still having a worse day than you.'

'Being arrested for murder?'

'Finding out his own brother fathered his daughter.'

'Morgan?' Derwent whistled. 'Nothing like keeping it in the family, is there?'

'It means you don't have to explain away any awkward resemblance to the milkman. I think Eleanor was very clever about it, actually. She knew Morgan and Oliver were competitive with one another. She'd been involved with Morgan before she met Oliver, so she knew he was attracted to her – and she knew he'd do anything to get one over on his brother. I don't think Morgan has much of a conscience at the best of times. She can't have found it too hard to coax him into bed. She was unfinished business.'

'I made a mistake. You were the one I preferred all along and now it's too late,' Derwent said.

'Exactly that. And it explains why Eleanor was able to persuade Morgan to warn Kate off sixteen years later when it all came back to bite her in the arse. She must have thought there was no chance of anyone finding out and then Kate turned up, armed with evidence that Oliver was infertile. Kate didn't know the whole truth, but she knew Eleanor wanted to keep it quiet. And Morgan wanted the same, or he'd have been out on the streets. He must have known how Oliver would react and he was depending on him for a roof over his head. Eleanor might have been being blackmailed but she has a good line in manipulating people herself.'

'The thing is, it's bullshit,' Derwent said. 'Norris is going on about how he's not her father any more, but he *is* her dad. He's the one who's brought her up. He's the one she loves.'

'Like you and Thomas,' I said, knowing it was dangerous territory.

'Yeah. Like that.' Derwent's face was unreadable behind his dark glasses. 'He's mine now, whatever happens. There aren't many people in the world I care about, but he's on the list.'

'Who else is on the list?'

Derwent snorted. 'Well, not you. You're on the other list.'

374

'What's the other list?'

'People who don't listen to me. People who act like twats despite my advice.'

'I didn't have time to call for back-up,' I said. 'He was going to kill her.'

'And he almost killed you.' He reached out and lifted my chin, examining my neck.

I jerked my head away. 'You'd have done the same.'

'I keep telling you that's not a good thing.'

I stood up. 'Come on. Let's get to the hospital. With any luck they'll be able to tell us when the Norrises will be fit to be interviewed. The clock's ticking.'

39

The clock was ticking in more ways than one. Before I had taken more than three steps Una Burt emerged from the church to inform us that justice, in the shape of the department of professional standards, had finally caught up with us.

'You're on restricted duties until further notice. I'll contact you when the DPS are finished investigating what happened to Kate Emery.'

'We know what happened to her. She ran off and got herself killed,' Derwent said. 'She was determined to see Oliver Norris. There was nothing we could have done.'

'Then I'm sure the DPS will sign off on how you handled it.' Her face softened. 'Strictly between you and me, I think Georgia is the one who's going to end up taking responsibility for it.'

'That's not fair,' I protested. 'She was the most junior officer there. I shouldn't have left her on her own.'

'Kerrigan.' There was a world of warning in Derwent's voice but I ignored it.

'I should have stayed.'

'You thought Georgia was capable of looking after Kate in your absence. And she should have been,' Una said.

'Kate gave us the runaround from the very start of this

376

investigation. She fooled all of us at different times,' I pointed out. 'And it was Georgia who found the reference to her previous employment that started us off on the right track. We'd never have known about the blackmail if it wasn't for Georgia.'

'She's a talented officer in some ways but she has a lot to learn.' Una sniffed. 'I feel it wouldn't be too much of a hardship for her if she learned it elsewhere.'

'We all make mistakes,' I said stubbornly. 'We've all made mistakes during this investigation. She'll learn.'

'We'll see what the investigators say.' She checked the time. 'In the meantime, I'm waiting for Chris and Pete to get here to handle the interview.'

'What about Gareth Selhurst? Someone's got to track him down,' Derwent said.

'Already done.' Una Burt smiled a slow, catlike smirk. 'They just picked him up at Luton Airport, on his way to Spain. He booked the flights yesterday. Strange how he felt called to preach there all of a sudden.'

'God moves in mysterious ways,' I murmured. 'Did he say anything?'

'He said it was an accident. He swore they tried to save her.'

'What about the fact that she was too out of it to know what was happening to her?' Derwent asked.

'Nothing to do with them, he said. They didn't notice until it was too late. He said no one gave her anything to eat or drink, and if she was drugged it was before she came to the church.'

'How convenient,' I said.

'We'll see what he says in a proper interview,' Una Burt said. 'I think your main problem will be getting him to shut up. I've never met anyone who liked the sound of his own voice more.'

'Well, we can deal with him while we're waiting for Oliver

and Eleanor Norris to be discharged from hospital,' Una Burt said briskly. 'Which means you two are free to go.'

There was no point in arguing. I walked ahead of Derwent, more conscious of my neck hurting now that I had nothing else to think about.

He caught up with me in the car park. 'What was all that about?'

'What?

'Georgia. Why are you sticking up for her? You don't even like her.' A patronising smile spread across his face. 'That's it, isn't it? It's *because* you don't like her.'

'That doesn't make any sense.'

'You feel guilty about not liking her so you'll end your career rather than let her take responsibility for what happened.'

'This is not a career-ending incident,' I said.

'Let's hope not.' He held out his hand. 'Car keys.'

'Why?'

'Because you shouldn't be driving. I'll take you home.'

'I don't want to go home. I want to go to the office.'

He rolled his eyes. 'Jesus, Maeve, take the rest of the day off. You've earned it.'

'I've got things to do.'

'And plenty of time to do them. Restricted duties, remember? You're going to be bored shitless by the time the DPS get back to us. You might as well save up the paperwork.'

'It's not paperwork.'

'What, then?'

'I want to call Brian Emery. I think – I think it might help him to know what happened to Chloe. And I think it will definitely help if he knows the people responsible are in custody.'

Derwent wanted to argue with me, I could tell, but he was a good police officer and a fair one, and he could see my point. 'All right. But then I'm taking you home.'

*

By the time Brian Emery picked up the phone I was regretting my devotion to duty. I had shut myself in Una Burt's office so I had some privacy for what was going to be a difficult conversation, and once I was alone I found my hands were shaking. Don't think about Oliver Norris, I told myself, and dialled Brian's number firmly. But my throat ached and when I closed my eyes I saw Norris's reddening face glistening with sweat as he tried to choke the life out of me.

It didn't take long to explain to Brian Emery what had happened that morning, but it took a long time to work through the details of the investigation. Once he had stopped crying he started asking questions, showing the steely mind and focus that he usually disguised behind his pleasant demeanour. I told him about Kate's difficulties and her efforts to protect Chloe as well as her illegal activities and he sighed.

'She was a brilliant mother, Kate. She loved Chloe more than anything. Far more than she loved me, obviously. I wish she'd told me the truth about her financial situation. We could have worked something out.'

'You were very generous to her,' I said. 'This isn't your fault.'

'No, but I could have done something to stop it, don't you see? If she'd had money, she wouldn't have needed to embark on this course of action and neither of them would be dead.'

'You weren't in possession of all the facts and you couldn't have known how things would play out. Even Kate didn't anticipate what happened to Chloe, and she thought of almost everything.'

'She didn't know about Nolan.'

'No. No one knew except Chloe, and she didn't tell the right people.'

'She told Belinda.' There was a world of sorrow and anger in those three words.

'Mr Emery . . . I wanted to ask about Nolan and Nathan.'

'What about them?'

'I'm concerned about them. More specifically, I'm concerned about Nolan.'

'He's not a good kid,' he said heavily. 'Takes after his father.'

'He needs help, Mr Emery.' Or locking up. 'He's going to hurt someone if he carries on the way he has been behaving. If he's lucky, he'll only hurt himself.'

'I just wonder,' Brian Emery said evenly, 'if it's worth even trying.'

'It's always worth trying.'

'What if he's gone too far to be helped?'

'Then at least you know you tried.' I squeezed the bridge of my nose. I was thinking about Morgan and Oliver Norris, two brothers whose competitiveness had led them to behaviour that was literally lethal. 'I don't want anyone else to be harmed, Mr Emery – you, or your stepson, or your wife, or whoever Nolan comes across next.'

'I'll think about it,' he said eventually.

When my phone call ended I dragged myself out of Una Burt's office. I missed being in at the kill. It would be interesting to know what Eleanor was saying in interview. It was funny how she had capitulated as soon as I accused her of being involved. *Oliver,* she had said, *be careful.* And then she had admitted it all. But it had to be a relief to her to tell the truth. Dishonesty came hard to her, blooming all over her skin. The strain of keeping secrets from her husband must have been intolerable.

Well, it wouldn't be my job to untangle the whole story, I thought, knowing that I would need to do it anyway, that I would have to chase down every niggle and every doubt until I was sure we had understood what had happened, and how, and why. I would do it even if it was on my own time. I would do it because I had to, because I needed to know the truth.

What else did I have to do?

What else was I, if I didn't have that?

380

Suddenly going home seemed like the best idea anyone had ever had and I looked for Derwent to see if his offer still stood. He was on the other side of the room, his head close to Liv's as the two of them peered at something on her computer screen. I strolled across, stretching as I went.

'What are you looking at?'

I wasn't expecting the reaction I got. Derwent jumped up in a hurry, knocking his chair so it rolled back in my direction. I caught it without looking, my attention on the screen. It was a Facebook page, I registered, before Liv turned her monitor off.

'What's going on?' I looked from Liv to Derwent and back again. She was red-faced. They were both silent, and it was the kind of silence that falls after something has been broken irretrievably. 'What is it? Just tell me.'

'Nothing,' Liv said.

'It's not nothing.'

'Don't worry about it.' Derwent had recovered himself. He dropped an arm around my shoulders and started drawing me towards the door. 'Ready to go?'

'No, I'm not, actually.' I pushed his arm away and turned back to Liv. 'What was that on your screen?'

A look passed between Liv and Derwent – *She saw too much/there's nothing we can do* – and then Liv reached out, very slowly, and switched her monitor back on.

'I was just checking Facebook and this popped up.' She swallowed. 'You know how if you're friends with someone you see pictures and posts that they're tagged in.'

I nodded.

'I've got a friend who I used to work with when I first started in the job. She moved back to Manchester a few years ago and now she works on a murder investigation team there.'

'And?'

'She was out yesterday . . . to celebrate two of her colleagues on the team . . . um, getting engaged.' Liv's voice faltered and faded away to silence. She scrolled down and pointed at the screen, and I stepped closer to look.

It was a photograph of a couple. The man was looking at the camera, while the woman was staring up at him adoringly. He was dark-haired, with blue eyes and a heavy beard. The beard was new but I recognised him all the same; I'd have known him anywhere. His smile lit up the photograph. The woman was petite, fair-haired, pretty – and nothing like me. She had one hand on her fiancé's arm, showing off the large ring that glinted on the third finger of her left hand.

The other hand was draped across the top of her small but noticeable bump: four months along, if I had to guess.

My ex-boyfriend, Rob, who had disappeared without so much as a backward glance, and found a new job, a new girlfriend and a new life in short order.

'Wow. Well, of course he would marry her,' I said. 'He'd do the right thing. Glad to see he looks so happy about it.'

'Maeve,' Liv said, her face stricken. 'Maeve, I didn't know.'

'How could you know?' I tried to smile, and knew it was a failure. 'It's fine. It's a long time since he left.'

They both knew it had been a long time and they both knew I'd been waiting, like the fool I was, for him to come back.

'You're better off.' Derwent's voice was rough.

I could do this. I could hold it together. I could cope.

I turned around and stepped blindly in Derwent's direction, and felt his arms go around me.

He held on to me so tightly it was as if he was trying to stop my heart from breaking by holding it together.

The shock was so huge, the damage so absolute, that I didn't manage to speak again until Derwent had driven most of the way to my flat.

'I never thought I was good enough for him.' I stared out

of the window, not seeing anything we passed. 'I didn't know he wanted children. I didn't know anything.'

'You don't know it was what he wanted. Accidents happen.'

'He looked happy.'

'Anyone can look happy in one photograph.'

I looked at Derwent, curious. 'Do you think I want him to be miserable?'

'I don't know. I, personally, wouldn't mind if he was crying himself to sleep at night.'

'She looks nothing like me.' I felt as if I was disintegrating very slowly, losing tiny traces of myself with every movement, until eventually there would be nothing left at all. 'Maybe I was never his type. Maybe we would never have gone the distance anyway, even if things hadn't gone wrong.'

'Don't try to take the blame for this. He cheated on you and he ran away. He found someone else, knocked her up and he's getting married and you haven't had as much as a word from him to say sorry, let alone to let you know he's moved on.'

'Maybe he thought it would upset me,' I said.

'Maybe he was too scared. If only he'd known you'd find an excuse for him, whatever he did.' Derwent frowned at me. 'Where's the fight, Maeve? Where's the anger?'

'I don't know.' I felt so tired, weary in body and soul. 'I hate myself for thinking it would all work out some day. I really believed it, too.'

'That's how you are. You want to make everything right. You want to believe in happy endings.'

'There's no such thing,' I said softly. 'There's just life.'

He shook his head but he didn't say whatever he was thinking, and I was glad, on the whole.

'I'll be all right,' I said.

'You'll be fine.' But when he looked at me, his eyes were doubtful.

'It was safe – waiting for Rob to come back. It was the

easy option. Now that I know he's not coming back, I can move on. I'm free.'

'Of course you are.'

'You could at least try to sound like you mean it.'

'Sorry. I'm doing my best here.' Another glance. 'I haven't even said I told you so yet.'

'Keep that up,' I said. 'Keep not saying that.'

'You deserve better than him anyway.'

He stopped the car near my flat, on some convenient double-yellow lines. 'Do you want me to come in?'

'No. Why would I want that?'

'If you wanted some company? A friend, I mean?' He was floundering, I was touched to see. This didn't come naturally to him and I appreciated the effort he was making.

'No. It's OK. I need to be on my own for a bit.' I looked up at the building and then back at him. 'There is one thing you could do for me. But it's a big favour.'

'What?' The wariness was turned up to eleven.

'I was wondering if you'd rented your flat out yet.'

He closed his eyes briefly. 'Not yet.'

'I know someone who's looking. She's very reliable. Responsible job, good references, highly organised. Clean. Tidy.'

'Doesn't sound like anyone I know.'

'I can't stay in Rob's flat,' I said. 'Not now. I – I can't bear to stay. I'll pack up my things and move out as soon as I can. I have to find somewhere else and I don't know how long it will take.'

'London's full of places to live.'

'It could take weeks to find the right place.' I bit my lip. 'Please?'

'I'll think about it,' Derwent said.

The look on his face was as good as a yes.

40

It was a beautiful day, the trees turning red and gold in the bright October sunshine. The zoo was busy with families and tourists taking pictures of the animals and each other, leaning over barriers, pointing, fighting, laughing: normal life.

Bethany sat on a bench, her knees drawn up to her chest, *other* from the top of her head to the folds of her long black skirt. Not part of a family. Not interested in the antics of the penguins who were waddling around their enclosure adorably. Not normal, not like the people who strolled past her, sharing food, joking around, complaining about their sore feet or the cost of ice creams.

Normal life. That was what she had heard her aunt saying: *Paul, we've got to look after her. We need to give her a normal life for a change.*

Normal life seemed to amount to buying her a lot of stuff: a phone, new clothes, make-up, shower gel and shampoo and conditioner and detangler and micellar water and liquid eyeliner and a rainbow of nail varnish and anything else she showed the slightest interest in possessing. It was driving Lia insane.

Mum, why does she get everything she wants? It's not fair.

Because, her aunt hadn't said, she has nothing. Because her parents are on remand and they're going to go to prison and they weren't doing a very good job of being parents anyway. Because she's not normal and we have to try to make her seem normal, so the least we can do is to make her look right.

Lia. She ate too much, wheedling biscuits and sweets and Coke out of her parents, swelling out of her clothes, self-loathing rising in her body like yeast. She sat in her room watching make-up tutorials on the internet, emerging with alarming eye make-up, brown streaks on her cheeks, over-drawn lips.

Normal.

'You're a freak,' Lia had said to her, the second week they were at school. 'Everyone thinks you're weird.'

Bethany had given her *the look*: heavy-lidded disdain.

'Do you know what the boys call you?' Lia couldn't wait to tell her. 'The nun.'

Bethany rolled her eyes. 'Original.'

'Have you ever even kissed a boy?'

'Have you?'

Lia faltered. 'That's not the point.'

'I bet I know more about fucking than you do, Lia,' Bethany had said.

Lia had blushed, and muttered something, and abandoned her to the lunch she wasn't eating. Bethany sat on her own, staring into space, remembering William's smile and the way he would look at her over Chloe's head and how she'd been sure – so sure – that he liked her more than Chloe. It was just that she was young, that was all. *Jailbait*, he'd said, when she had been alone with him in the empty house and she had run her hands around his neck and pressed herself against him. Chloe was late, and they were alone, and she'd touched her lips to his. It had sort of been a kiss: she'd meant it as a kiss.

But, really, he hadn't kissed her back. He'd jerked his head away.

'What are you doing?'

Barely able to speak or stand, her heart full of love. 'I want you. I want you to be the first.'

'Come on, Bethany.' And he'd pushed her away.

'Please.'

'I thought Chloe was your friend.'

'She is.'

He had smiled, uneasy, flattered, running a finger down her cheek. 'Bethany. I couldn't do it. You're too young. They call girls like you jailbait.'

'I'm old enough to know what I want.'

'Maybe,' he said slowly. 'Look, it'll be your turn one day. Probably not with me, though. You have more sense, don't you?'

No, Bethany had thought, helpless. *I really don't.*

'I can't do this,' he'd said. 'I just can't.'

Footsteps on the stairs: Chloe, her lovely face full of innocent joy. Full of love for them both. No suspicion, no doubt.

And Bethany's heart had withered inside her, turning black, decaying to something utterly poisonous that was death to everything it touched.

'There you are. Clever of you to find a bench.' Brian Emery sat down beside Bethany, leaving a decent space between them. He handed her an ice cream cone. She took it carefully, avoiding any contact with his fingers.

'Thanks.'

'I hope it's OK.' He frowned, his whole forehead creasing. 'I thought – it's such a nice day.'

'It's good.' She concentrated on sculpting the ice cream with her tongue and the silence lengthened.

'The penguins are cute.'

'I suppose so.'

Brian sighed. 'Maybe this wasn't such a good idea for an outing. You're probably too old for the zoo. Chloe loved it here.'

'It's nice,' Bethany said. It was the fourth time they'd had this conversation and she was getting tired of reassuring him. 'I'm glad we're here.'

'Me too.' He turned to her, too quick, too sincere. 'It's good to be with someone who loved Chloe too.'

Bethany ate the chocolate flake before she answered. 'I was glad when you called my aunt.'

'Well.' He looked down at the remains of his cone. 'I knew you were on your own. And I'm on my own too, now. I moved out last month. I'm going to get a divorce.'

'Oh.'

'It wasn't going to work.' His forehead wrinkled again and for an awful moment Bethany thought he was going to cry. 'I can't blame my wife for putting her sons first. That's what parents do. That's what they should do. But I can't bear to be around them. I can't help blaming them for what happened. And I blame myself – of course I do. If I'd known what was going on . . .' He looked blindly at the penguins, gnawing his lower lip while he got his emotions under control.

'You shouldn't blame yourself,' Bethany said. 'There's plenty of other people to blame. Like my parents.'

'They said it was an accident.'

'They drugged her,' Bethany said, her voice hard. 'She was so out of it on tranquillisers that she couldn't walk in a straight line. She didn't even know where she was, let alone what was happening to her. They held her under the water until she died. That makes it murder.'

Brian flinched. 'I suppose. I can't imagine what it's like for you – knowing that.'

'Really hard,' Bethany said. She let her voice quiver. 'I know they're my parents, but I don't think I can ever forgive them. I don't know how they can make it right.'

Because it was true, wasn't it? The betrayal of her birth was so huge that there was no sacrifice her mother could make to make up for it, no penance great enough.

Not even agreeing that she had brought Chloe to the church, when it had been Bethany who had dragged her there, promising that it was all going to be all right.

Not even admitting that the diazepam was Eleanor's own supply (which was true).

Not even accepting that she had crushed them up and spiked Chloe's drink with them (which was *not* true. Bethany had done that herself).

Not even assenting to the suggestion that she'd known Chloe was too heavily drugged to react when she started to drown. (Only Bethany had known, and had said nothing.)

Not even going to prison.

It was what any parent would do for their child, if they loved them, Bethany thought. It was what her mother *should* do.

'Nothing works out the way you think it will, does it?' Brian sighed and dropped the remainder of his cone in the bin. 'People let you down. You think you fall in love and it will last forever and then it doesn't.'

William and the way he had looked at her in the hospital, when she'd told him they could be together now, now that Chloe was gone forever.

His horror.

Her heart.

Her black heart.

'You have to pick yourself up and go on.'

Sending him to confront her father about Chloe. Calling her father from her hospital bed to say William had touched her, that he had forced her to do disgusting, depraved things. Sobbing down the phone, sounding heartbroken because she *was* heartbroken; William Turner had broken what was left of her heart, so that all that was left was dust and ash.

But no one would ever know, now. No one would ever guess.

No one saw her as anything but a victim.

'You have to make the best of it and keep going,' Brian Emery said bleakly. 'Or else what's the point?'

Bethany edged along the bench, moving closer to him. He

wasn't her father and she wasn't his daughter, but she leaned her head against his shoulder and it was some comfort to both of them.

'That's funny,' Brian said, his voice rumbling through Bethany's body so she felt the words rather than heard them. 'What's she doing here?'

'Who?' Bethany sat up straight, trying to see.

'I was just thinking about her.' Brian Emery was waving. 'DS Kerrigan!'

It still took Bethany a second to pick her out, tall and slim in her usual dark trouser suit as she made her way towards them. Behind her sunglasses she looked paler, thinner, more tired than she had been in the summer, but her focus was unwavering. The scowling detective inspector was beside her, making a path for them through the crowd. Bethany looked around, suddenly noticing the people who were standing around in twos and threes, watching her rather than the animals: faces she recognised and faces she didn't. Faces that all said the same thing: the lies she had woven into proof of her innocence had come undone. Someone, somewhere, had thought about what she'd said and decided to see if the evidence backed it up, and Bethany had a feeling she knew who that might have been. DS Kerrigan, with her warm smile and her clear eyes and her trick of understanding more than she should.

'I wonder what she wants,' Brian Emery said, and Bethany, who could have told him, said nothing.

Acknowledgements

This book would have remained nothing more than an idea without the help and encouragement of the following people:

Everyone at HarperCollins, particularly Julia Wisdom who edited *Let the Dead Speak* with patience, kindness and, best of all, rigour. I feel very lucky to have her! I'm also very grateful to Lucy Dauman, Finn Cotton and Fliss Denham for their hard work. Special thanks to the team at HarperCollins Ireland for their enthusiasm and support, and my foreign publishers for their commitment to the series.

The team at United Agents, the best support any author could wish for. I'd particularly like to thank Ariella Feiner, to whom this book is dedicated. She makes it her business to make my dreams come true and she has impeccable judgement in all things.

My fellow crime writers, especially the Killer Women and the CS gang. The crime-writing world is small and close-knit, full of encouragement and fellow feeling when it's needed, and I am very lucky to be a part of it. I'd like to thank Sinéad Crowley, Liz Nugent, Alex Barclay and the rest of the Irish crime writers for their friendship and solidarity.

The librarians who work so hard to provide an essential and underrated service to the community. Properly staffed and funded libraries give so much to their users and to authors. They are a precious resource. I would not have been able to write this book without the facilities in my local library: huge thanks to the librarians and staff of Earlsfield Library.

The bloggers, reviewers and book club admins who give their time and attention so generously, for love of reading. Special thanks to the indefatigable Liz Barnsley who is a true champion of good writing and Tracy Fenton of TBC who has a genius for promoting authors and making reading fun.

My lovely readers, who keep asking me for a happy ending. (Possibly this should be an apology.)

My friends and family, who waited patiently while I tackled this book and learned not to ask how it was going. Nothing would get done without my husband James, who is always willing to talk police procedure or sort out domestic chaos while working on terrifyingly complex cases in his day job. He makes it look easy, and I know it's not.

Finally, my thanks to Edward and Patrick for being the best distraction there could be, and Fred, who burns the midnight oil with me and only walks on the keyboard now and then.